"Stasi does an amazing job of mixing science with religious paranoia in this compelling thriller. . . . Dan Brown and Steve Berry fans have another controversial novel in which to lose themselves."        —*Booklist*

"A riveting, fast-paced tale that had my heart pounding on more than one occasion."
                                    —*The Washington Times*

"A roller-coaster ride from start to finish. So hugely entertaining, I couldn't put it down."
                                    —Aphrodite Jones,
                        *New York Times* bestselling author of
                                    *Cruel Sacrifice*

"If you liked Steve Berry's *The Templar Legacy* and Heather Graham's *Phantom Evil,* you'll love Stasi's provocative, pulse-pounding thriller."
                                    —Douglas Preston,
                *New York Times* bestselling author of *Impact*

"A fascinating story that combines religious history with suspense and intrigue. . . I find that it makes me wonder, if Jesus walked the earth today, how would the public respond?"        —Monsignor Jim Lisante,
                                    TV and radio personality

"A fabulous journey into a world one rarely uncovers. This book is fabulous! I love it!"
                                    —James Van Praagh,
        bestselling author, producer of *The Ghost Whisperer,*
                            and world-renowned psychic

# The Sixth Station

## LINDA STASI

FORGE®

A TOM DOHERTY ASSOCIATES BOOK
NEW YORK

This is a work of fiction. All of the characters, organizations, and events portrayed in this novel are either products of the author's imagination or are used fictitiously.

THE SIXTH STATION

Copyright © 2013 by Linda Stasi

A Forge Book
Published by Tom Doherty Associates, LLC
175 Fifth Avenue
New York, NY 10010

www.tor-forge.com

Forge® is a registered trademark of Tom Doherty Associates, LLC.

ISBN 978-0-7653-6982-6

Forge books may be purchased for educational, business, or promotional use. For information on bulk purchases, please contact Macmillan Corporate and Premium Sales Department at 1-800-221-7945, extension 5442, or write specialmarkets@macmillan.com.

First Edition: January 2013
First Mass Market Edition: January 2014

Printed in the United States of America

0  9  8  7  6  5  4  3  2  1

For Jessica Stasi Rovello who conceived it,
Sid Davidoff who encouraged and enforced it,
and Dona Heywood who *literally* passed through the
boundaries of time and space to make it happen

# ACKNOWLEDGMENTS

With all my heart I wish to thank:

Liza Fleissig and her partner, Ginger Harris-Dontzin, of the Liza Royce Literary Agency for their total commitment to me and to this project—and thank you, Liza, too, for your constant love and unstinting support.

Bob Gleason, my editor at Tor Books, for seeing right off what others couldn't—and also for "getting" *me* right away. You had me at hierophant!

Tom Doherty, publisher and the founder of Tor Books, for taking on such a controversial book *and* believing in it—and me.

The late, great Father Peter Jacobs, negotiator, priest, and Vatican exorcist, who gave unselfishly of his wild access to Vatican secrets, who drove with me—at age eighty—to Manoppello to view "The Veil" in person, serve as my interpreter, and acknowledge the miracle even though it did cause him to faint on the altar. I thank him, too, for making his last wish that I travel to Rome, swipe his locked-with-a-key laptop full of Vatican secrets from his apartment, and then smuggle it back to the States. You were my co-conspirator!

Antonia Katrandjiva for her love, tireless support, incredible insights, and brilliant (endless) translations of—how many languages was it again?

Karim Babay for all the help with Arabic and French translations.

Reporter and author Paul Badde, the foremost scholar and researcher of "The Volto Santo," for his wisdom and his unselfish help.

Jack Boland, whose words changed my life.

Kate Davis and Brenda Walsh for their meticulous copy editing.

Sister Blandina Paschalis Schlomer for allowing me into her hermetic life and sharing with me her research, artwork, and the microscopic evidence she has amassed during her investigation in pursuit of the truth about "*il Volto Santo di Manoppello*" (aka "The Veil of Veronica").

Father Carmine Cucinelli, rector of the Shrine of Manoppello, and all the other monks there who treated Father Jacobs and me like family, fed us, drank with us, and helped me find the truth.

Damien Miano, who read and reread all the way giving me concrete and solid advice—and then finding my agent, Liza Fleissig, for me when I thought no one would accept this controversial book.

Dr. Michael A. Bonilla, a self-taught archaeologist, whom I do not know, but who called me at the *New York Post* one day out of the blue to tell me about his theories on genetics and Jesus.

Author S. J. Rozan, with whom I studied at Art Workshop, Assisi, Italy, for helping me to structure this novel and develop my narrative.

The Newswomen's Club of NYC for allowing me to form a writers' group and use their glorious space once a week.

To the great writers in that group, Jillian Jacobs, Mary

Reinholz, and most especially to Jessica Seigel, who came up with the idea of starting this book with a trial.

Kenny, Marco, Dean, and Reed Rosenblatt for forcing me to get away from it all for whole weekends at a time at the beach and get back to real life—as in cooking, chasing kids, total chaos.

Michael Volpatt of Larkin Volpatt for jumping in feetfirst to put us on the map.

Every single friend and family member who read the manuscript along the way and gave me invaluable advice.

Whitney Ross, Kelly Quinn, Patty Garcia, and Linda Quinton for all their behind-the-scenes hard work.

Lea and Yehuda Kaploun for all their help with Aramaic interpretations as well as their help with Talmudic text.

Jim Krugman for interpreting the Tel Dan discoveries.

Lisa Sharkey, who gave freely of her time and ideas.

Hulya Terzioglu, scholar and guide in Ephesus, who first brought me to the House of the Virgin Mary and helped me map out the trail.

Thank you, Mustafa Cesur of the Troy Rug Store, Arasta Bazaar, Istanbul, for lending his name to a great character.

And Leo.

**Fact:** The most important relic in Christendom is hiding in plain sight in a monastery church of the Capuchin friars outside the small village of Manoppello, Italy.

**Fact:** The House of the Virgin Mary—where evidence suggests that Jesus' mother lived out her final years—is located in a Muslim country.

**Fact:** The Virgin Mary, venerated by most Muslims, is the only woman mentioned by name in the Koran, is only one of eight people to have a chapter named for them in the Koran, and is mentioned more often in the Koran than in the Bible.

**Fact:** In 1209, Pope Innocent III initiated the Albigensian Crusade—and with it the Papal Inquisition—to wipe out the Cathar faith, the fastest-growing "heretical" Christian sect in Europe. Although estimates vary widely, the death toll from that Crusade is estimated to be 200,000–1,000,000.

# The Sixth Station

# PROLOGUE

They laid her down and told her to be still, not to push until they said she could. All she wanted was to be rid of the pain, rid of the thing inside her that felt like it was ripping her tiny body to shreds.

Why did they have to choose her? Why couldn't she have a life like other children?

When the Girl's screams turned to howling, unbearable and animal-like, the older man, a priest, dropped to his knees, lifted his hands to God, and began praying.

*"Shlom lekh bthoolto Mariam. Maliath taibootho moran a'ammekh mbarakhto at bneshey,"* he chanted in Aramaic, tears spilling onto the small sheet that still covered her.

The Girl howled again.

The other man, a soldier, who would soon be the Girl's husband, looked to the woman in the burqa for approval, then finally laid his hand on her swollen belly and told her, *"Now,* push! Push!"

The promised relief of pushing was almost as unbearable to her not fully formed body as the holding back had been. Would they let her go home when it was finally over?

Then the baby stopped its kicking. It was still, but the pain was worse. Then it—the boy inside her—moved, propelling itself toward the light.

His head was beginning to crown, so the woman, wearing gloves, carefully and with trembling hands, took surgical scissors and snipped the stretching skin downward to enlarge the vaginal opening.

They had told her that was how it would happen, when she first became pregnant.

There was no other way she could have known these things unless they had explained them to her beforehand.

She was thirteen. And she was still a virgin.

# 1

**New York City, N.Y., USA**
**Thirty-three Years Later**

It wasn't my beat, it wasn't my assignment, and it wasn't my intention to alter reality that morning when my cell phone rang at 7:15 after a night highlighted by too many martinis with Donald, the ex.

Oh, God. Why didn't we stay away from each other? Again.

We had no future and the past was a decade-old fantasy.

**Baghdad, October 5, 2005**

Kick-ass war correspondent and bad-boy photojournalist married by army chaplain amidst horrors of war in the lounge of the Palestine Hotel. Many drunken colleagues in attendance.

Or something like that.

Two days after the terribly romantic nuptials and drunken party that followed, the retreating Iraqis gave Donald and me an unforgettable wedding present: A bomb hidden inside a cement-mixer truck was detonated outside the hotel, taking out the lobby. Gucci bags and Fendi fur coats from the high-end lobby shops were blown out of the stores and lay among broken glass and giant hunks of falling plaster.

When the blast hit (we were in bed, of course), Donald jumped up, threw on jeans, and grabbed his cameras. He wasn't worried about our (my) safety; he was worried about missing the action, i.e., the photos.

Instead of thinking he was a big horse's ass, I jumped into a tracksuit and we both took the partially collapsed stairs four steps at a time. I too was probably more terrified of missing the action (i.e., the story) than I was about the danger. I should have realized it was a defining moment.

We weren't allowed back into our hotel to collect our things, so we bunked down with three other journos in the apartment of a friend of a friend.

Donald left early one morning—he was imbedding with the Second Battalion of the Fourth Infantry Regiment. He gave me a perfunctory kiss, but I grabbed him tight and pulled him close. "Be careful," I said.

He put his big hands around my face and kissed me as though we were alone. "I'm too mean to get hurt," he said.

About two hours later Donald was riding shotgun in a jeep when another roadside bomb exploded, throwing him thirty feet, breaking his femur and a few ribs.

When I finally got to him in the makeshift army hospital, I kissed his head and said, "Time to get outta Dodge, baby," trying for sardonic and missing completely.

I made arrangements for us to get back to NYC, where I nursed his cranky self back to health and got my first and only Pulitzer nomination from the *New York Post,* who'd employed me at the time.

Our crazy wartime marriage was hot and dangerous.

We couldn't get enough of each other—and even though he was a giant pain in the ass when he was busted up, the broken-femur sex was sensational. Who knew?

I—we—were very happy, happy enough, in fact, for me to start thinking about maybe having a baby. Yikes.

Donald said he didn't think a baby was a great idea, because a family would keep me tied at home when he knew I'd be desperate to get to the next war/murder/scandal/whatever. I pouted for three months straight.

Finally, one night when he was well enough to hit the road again—he was off to cover the wildfires in Texas—he turned to me with a dopey grin and said, "Okay, whatever you want."

"You're acting like I want to get a dog," I said.

"Not a bad idea—maybe test-drive the mother thing with a nice German shepherd for a few years first?" he teased, and we fell onto the bed laughing.

Somehow, though, *it*—a pregnancy—never happened. Great sex doesn't always lead to greater things.

Two years later we ended as abruptly as we had started, although not as dramatically.

It was a fast and clean break to a messy marriage, which involved much sex and even more fighting. Kiss-and-make-up is only fun in the movies.

One Monday morning Donald and I were off to cover different assignments—he back to Iraq, me to cover the presidential campaigns.

As I got out of the cab at JFK, he kissed me hard and simply said, "Time to get outta Dodge, baby." I knew he wasn't talking about leaving the country. He was talking about leaving the marriage.

And that was that.

I knew he was right. He liked gambling on sports, staying up all night, and hanging out in strip clubs in disease-riddled cities with names that weren't composed of letters in the English alphabet. He was a horrible dancer who made duck lips when he was really feeling it.

I like sports that I play myself, getting into bed early with a good book or, better yet, a bad boy, and going dancing with my gay men friends who never make duck lips no matter how much they're feeling the music.

Donald and I had nothing in common other than that we were both agnostics, preferred fast stick shifts to fancy SUVs, and would risk everything for a story.

He was resentful that I'd been nominated for a Pulitzer for covering the same war at the same time, while his newsweekly, *U.S. News,* hadn't nominated him. And he'd taken one for the Gipper, while I'd come home in one piece.

Me? I was jealous that I never got sent back to a war zone again. Weird? Sure.

But I took his leaving me like a bullet to my heart anyway. I cried for a month straight, drank too much with my friend Dona and my hairdresser pals, hardened my heart, and threw myself into my work.

A decade after we'd said "I do," however, we still couldn't say "I won't."

And so I found myself—all those years later—faced with a ringing phone. Since it is for reporters a genetic impossibility to ignore a ringing phone, I reached for it.

I sincerely wished he wouldn't call the morning after the night before. (Big lie.) Better yet, I wished we wouldn't ever have a night before again. (Truth.)

Be careful what you wish for.

I picked it up without bothering to look at the caller ID. "Go away, Donald," I said.

"Alessandra?" I heard a copy kid at the other end say. Oops.

"It's the City Desk. Can you hold for Dickie Smalls?" As if holding for Dickie Smalls were an option. I knew it would take about fourteen seconds for the whole newsroom to know I'd slept with Donald. Damn!

Mildly surprised, I held on, of course, knowing that it was usually not good when a call came through from Dickie early in the morning: It always meant something unexpected—an assignment that would send me to the Bronx or Queens or, worse, complaints about a story I'd filed the night before.

Bleary and hung over, I nonetheless held on for Managing Editor Dickie Smalls, a man who devoted his life to overcoming his name. His job was second only to that of editor in chief—the only one to whom Smalls ever spoke with any respect.

"Russo? Dickie," Dickie yelled into my headache. Dickie, who usually didn't have his first drink until at least 11:00 A.M, was probably still sober, I realized.

"You got the TV on? Put on New York One," he continued yelling without expecting an answer.

I obliged by reaching for the remote on the nightstand, and flicked to NY1. They were showing a helicopter view of my neighborhood, the United Nations area of Manhattan, while the voice of Simon Franks, one of their top reporters, clearly trying to keep his voice controlled, was announcing, "I'm looking down on this massive sea of humanity, the likes of which I certainly have never seen! The crowd, the mob—whatever you can call such a thing—stretches along the Dag Hammarskjöld Plaza park over onto Forty-seventh Street and First Avenue, up and down First Avenue from Forty-second Street to Fifty-seventh Street, and the cross streets from Forty-fourth through Forty-seventh as far west as Madison Avenue!

"Seriously folks, this city has never experienced a sight like this before!"

And he was right about that. Today was the start of

the terror trial—tribunal, actually—of terrorist Demiel ben Yusef.

While a tribunal like this one would normally have been held at The Hague, the World Court building had sustained huge damage in a terrorist bombing several months earlier and was still uninhabitable. The perpetrators had never been caught. So, no, while most New Yorkers were not happy to have this mess of a security risk in our town, we reporters were thrilled.

You could hear it in Franks's voice:

"And I venture to say," he continued, not missing a beat, "that every person down there is desperate to catch even the tiniest glimpse of Demiel ben Yusef, who goes on trial today—perhaps as soon as a couple of hours from now!"

I am a jaded reporter. I have reported on everything from 9/11 to war to Hurricanes Katrina and Sandy, the earthquake in Haiti, and many of the increasingly now-commonplace natural disasters of incalculable suffering around the planet.

This was different. Something, indeed something I didn't really understand—maybe it was blind faith or deep hatred—had driven hundreds of thousands of folks out of their homes, jobs, and schools. They'd wheeled, walked, and traveled from their apartments, condos, houses, hospitals, nursing homes, churches, synagogues, mosques, banks, and government offices to protest, to ogle, to see in person the most vicious criminal of our time.

Even I was shocked by the size of the crowds.

"You watching? You understand what's going on here?" Dickie said.

"Of course I do," I said, trying not to let my excitement show.

My heart started pounding. What did Dickie really want?

*Please let this be the break I need. I swear this time I'll do it their way. Please tell me something good. Tell me I'm gonna cover . . .*

All Dickie would give me, though, was, "Un-freakin'-believable!"

The man all these people had come to see was Demiel ben Yusef, a known terrorist who was believed by most of the reasonable people on the planet, as well as a worldwide coalition of governments who'd hunted him and finally captured him, to be the one responsible for terrorist bombings around the world. These terrorist acts had left death and mayhem from capital cities to historic and religious sites—with thousands of people dead or maimed not just from the bombings themselves but from the violence and turmoil that too often followed.

Today would mark the opening day of the trial of the millennium, the ben Yusef terrorist tribunal.

On the other side of the law (and not necessarily the world any longer, since his believers were multiplying) were those who had been burning up the Internet with bullshit about how ben Yusef was actually a great prophet, a man they believed was—yes—the second Son of God.

Or maybe even the Second Coming of Jesus Christ himself. The U.S. government, the CIA, MI5, the Russian FSB, Mossad, the UN, the Vatican, Iran, Iraq, North Korea, the oil companies, al-Qaeda—you name it and they were the ones who had *really* committed the atrocities.

Everyone *but* Demiel ben Yusef was responsible for the massive death and destruction. Sure.

Conspiracy-theory Web sites posted daily warnings and updates. None of them, however, ever explained how all of these governments and all of these people—who hadn't gotten along for thousands of years—were suddenly all allied for the sole purpose of destroying one ragtag prophet / alleged terrorist.

The conspiracy theorists postulated that all the terrorist attacks were carefully planned (pick any of the above) simply to generate hatred of Demiel ben Yusef.

Yes, they said that this international cabal backed by the United Nations was actually responsible for blowing up buildings, marketplaces, houses of worship, nightclubs, passenger planes, and even cruise ships filled with innocent people—simply to make one man look bad.

Thousands of videos and postings portrayed ben Yusef as a prince of peace. They'd show him preaching to the masses, very Jesus-like. If you watched the videos as carefully as I had, and as many times as I had, you could, of course, begin to have your doubts.

Yes, he was a very compelling speaker, and no, he never preached violence. His voice was at once soothing and fiery, if that makes sense. His accent was universal—not American, not European, not Middle Eastern.

"Everyone is the Son of God," he famously said in his "Perfect Order" sermon given on a hill to thousands of followers somewhere in Israel two years earlier. All that was missing were some loaves and fishes.

> The universe is in perfect order. Everything, everyone, is simply a part of God's whole. The moon directs the tides; the earthworms in the Amazon aerate the ground so that we all have oxygen. Every creature is as important as every other to that perfect order. The only time the order is disrupted, upended, thrown into chaos is when human beings—the only creatures on earth with free will—step in. Other creatures do not kill just for the bloodlust love of killing.
>
> But every religion that preaches that they are

the only ones who know the true words of God, demands just this of their followers: "Kill in His name," they say. I say, "Do not kill in God's name. Or my name. Or anyone's name. Defy those leaders who urge you to kill to preserve what *you* have." What they mean is "Kill to preserve what *I* have." They are false prophets, false leaders.

Ben Yusef was, if you watched often enough, incredibly charismatic—for an unattractive, skinny guy, that is; for someone who preached peace and practiced terrorism, that is.

Ben Yusef had become the rock star of terrorists.

Second Coming, my ass.

"This is some mess," Dickie yelled, pulling me out of my reverie. Without waiting for my response he blared, "You got credentialed in case—right?"

I, along with half the staff at *The New York Standard,* had indeed been "credentialed" by the United Nations Press Office earlier in the week, by submitting birth certificates, passports, and NYPD press credentials in person. We were fingerprinted and interviewed. No electronic applications were accepted because of the volatility of the situation.

"Yeah, a week ago," I answered. I had already been assigned backup in case the first string—the macho male columnists who were treated like gods by guys like little Dickie Smalls—couldn't for some reason (which never happened) show up. I knew, or believed at any rate, that there would be no screwups today, because, after all, this was nothing less than the most important trial of the millennium. The current millennium, that is.

"Good," he screeched. "Frankie, that putz, is stuck in traffic on the Brooklyn Bridge. It's at a standstill." So the impossible had happened after all.

"Get your ass outta bed, Russo. . . ."

"I'm not in bed," I lied, my heart racing like I'd been shot up with adrenaline. I was back in the game!

"Whatever. Get your ass outta bed, and get over to the UN. It's right outside your door, so make it fast. You caught the winning lotto number."

You mean the one dropped by Frankie, that putz, I wanted to say, but didn't. Frankie was golden, and I was still—what?—tarnished. At forty-two, I was, yes, a known front-page-breaking reporter, but one who had a real talent for running afoul of the powers-that-be wherever I worked. Rebel or maybe just too bullheaded to play the boys' game, I always bucked whenever they wanted to saddle me, tame me, and teach me to behave.

I'd been given a second chance at *The Standard* when they hired me following nine long months of unemployment. I'd been "laid off" at my last job—a political Web site—after uncovering the fact that the editor's best pal, a supermarket mogul slash movie producer, had a penchant for Filipino midget hookers. The mogul, in addition to supping once a month at Rao's with the publisher, had also been, up to that point, the Web site's biggest advertiser. Oops.

Editorial differences, they called it.

Bottom line: I wouldn't protect the editor's friends when it came to voicing my opinion, and they didn't protect me when I stood my ground.

So when I was offered the gig at *The Standard,* I grabbed it in hopes of one day getting a column again. I was back to general assignment reporting, and I'd been behaving.

"The kid whazzizname is already at the UN Press Office making the switch," Dickie continued. "We want you to file throughout the day and final copy half hour after the close. Got it? Good."

"Do I get to column on it?" I asked.

"Depends on what you get," he said, and with that he hung up—and I found myself out of bed and under a hot shower in less than sixty seconds.

A column possibility on the biggest story of the decade? Oh, baby! I said a quick prayer to whatever god might be listening at that moment that I'd somehow score an exclusive "get" despite being a pool reporter heading into a venue that was as tightly orchestrated as any in recorded history.

I had been out of work two years earlier when taxi-cab bombs had detonated simultaneously outside St. Pat's, the Abyssinian Baptist Church in Harlem, the Synagogue Adath Israel in Riverdale, the Light of God Tabernacle on Staten Island, and the Imam Al-Khoei Islamic Center Benevolent Foundation in Jamaica, Queens. The terrorist attacks, dubbed the "Unholy Day Bombings," killed almost two hundred innocent people. I started a blog, but it was just one of thousands, perhaps millions of blogs out there. It wasn't the same; it was too crowded. Cyberspace had evolved into a worldwide public-announcement system for ill-informed windbags with too little knowledge and too much time on their hands.

And now? If I had believed in God I would have prayed for a break like this—a chance to not just cover but possibly voice my opinion on the ben Yusef tribunal for a mainstream news outlet. Yes, I was unprepared, bleary-eyed, and retaining water. But still . . .

I hadn't done serious prep work, because I'd been told earlier in the week that I was to cover "color" only—getting reactions from local parish priests, imams, and rabbis.

But I was never better than when I was under pressure.

I picked up the same white T-shirt that had looked so

good when it was still clean the night before. I sniffed it. Clean enough. I pulled on a pair of black jeans, my beat-up brown leather jacket, and Frye boots. Then I looked down. Damn! Dead center on the T was a moderate-to-terrible chicken-scarpiello stain from the night before. With no time to change, I grabbed the white gauze Gap scarf hanging on my doorknob, looped it long around my neck, and—voilà—instant stain repair. Good enough.

I hauled my red leather satchel that held my iPad holographic tablet, cell phone, four reporter's pads (I still take notes the old-fashioned way), pens, wallet, keys, lipstick, and under-eye concealer, which I buy by the kilo, onto my shoulder and started out of my apartment.

A quick look in the mirror revealed that my formerly chic bob had frizzed and I now looked like I'd stolen Eleanor Roosevelt's head.

Whatever.

I hung my press credentials—three plastic cards with my photo—on a cheap hardware-store drain chain around my neck and checked that my passport was in the zipper compartment of my bag for backup ID just in case. Then I took the elevator down the twenty-four flights and walked out of my apartment building into the gorgeous spring day and into the end of my life as I knew it.

## 2

Outside I became part of a sea of people filling Forty-eighth Street, busting out from the police barricades erected to keep them in. Parking was suspended and traffic banned on the avenues, with the exception of single lanes for emergency vehicles between Twenty-third and Fifty-seventh Streets, to discourage the protestors from coming in.

Right, good luck with that.

And of course there were countless protestors even on my street, which is several blocks from the United Nations. It looked like pickpocket paradise—more crowded than Times Square on New Year's Eve, suffocating even on this crisp day.

The NYPD had recruited cops from all over as well as whatever U.S. soldiers could be spared from fighting on the fronts in the endless wars on terrorism. They were manning the metal detectors set up all over the city.

The plan had been to keep demonstrators at the west side docks (ben Yusef's supporters up toward the Intrepid Museum, and his detractors downtown at Chelsea Piers) and, failing that, on Tenth and Eleventh Avenues—twelve full blocks away from the UN. When the crowd projection swelled to millions, that plan went out the window and U.S. President Lydia Wallingford-Hudson decided that the best course of action was for the cops, soldiers, and security forces to take a Gandhian approach of passive resistance—unless and until the paid troublemakers and rabble-rousers acted up.

That didn't stop the crowds from pushing, yelling, and smelling, however. It just stopped the uniforms from pushing back. The cops and soldiers were so polite, I noticed that they were saying things like, "Excuse me sir, but I would appreciate it if you'd put your backpack on this screening device, please." What city was I in?

Not known for my patience, I didn't even attempt to get into the passive resistance groove. In fact, I felt trapped inside the rudeness, the pushing, the incessant pressing against my body, the constant shoving of my bag against my side; the arms, the legs that were everywhere, refusing to allow for any kind of personal space. I could smell the onions on the fat lady's breath next to me. Somewhere cigar breath; elsewhere the unavoidable body odors from a thousand different cultures—curry seeping from the pores of some, garlic oozing out of others, and everyone was sweating despite the sixty-eight-degree temperature.

With an unbelievable effort, I pushed and shoved like all the other people who had to be there that day for whatever reasons, and managed to skirt over to the outer edge of the street on the south side.

Being on that side, albeit shoved up against the barricades, gave me a good view of the sidewalk, where the vendors were hawking everything from T-shirts with ben Yusef's picture emblazoned on the front baring slogans like "King of the Terrorists" and "King of the News," to the obscene, "He Made a Killing in New York!" Others were selling flags, balloons, and other totally inappropriate items for an occasion that was supposed to be so solemn.

It seemed like foods from every nation were being sold from carts whose smells assaulted and invigorated my senses: Thai satay, peppers-sausage-onions, steaming hot dogs, and toasted soft pretzels that could always bring me back to my first autumn in New York as cub reporter, when I'd left the comfort of my parents' Hicksville, Long Island row house to make it "on my own" all of thirty-five miles away.

Despite being 1960s hippies who were still true believers in peace, love, and granola, they acted like overly protective suburbanites when it came to my brother and me, as they went about saving the world—my dad as head of a NYC homeless organization, and my mom as a pediatrician in a clinic.

When I moved out of the first apartment I'd had with roommates in the city and took a studio in the Village on my own, they worried I'd be lonely and alone at best, and murdered by an intruder at worst.

Despite their terror, I had not been murdered by a crazed serial killer/intruder, nor had "alone" ever been my problem. Except for when I was out of work, I always felt, if anything, that my life was *too* crowded. There was always another story, never a shortage of interesting friends and interested men. No one like Donald, of course, but I suspected that he was my excuse for not getting involved with anyone who might actually be available. I wanted my freedom to rush to a story wherever there was one.

Now I was in it again full force—in a massive mess of humanity. And I loved it.

But even more overwhelming than the smell and sight and push of the crowd was the din. The Super Bowl, the

World Series, *and* the World Cup at the same time. It seemed that the very air had turned solid with sound—filled with deafening chants, curses, and complaints.

Over all of that was the ever-present blast of police-car sirens, ear-shattering blasts when they were near you. I made a mental note to never have a drink again as long as I lived.

"SOS. Save our Savior!" "Kill the pig! Kill him dead!" "Kid killer!" the protestors screamed, trying to out-decibel each other.

*Crazy,* I thought, *that there hasn't yet been an incident.* Incredible, actually. But that day there weren't any—unless you count the personally earth-shattering incident that awaited me not half an hour later.

The angry people, I understood—but it was the others, the terrorist's so-called "followers" and "believers," that I didn't understand—or want to.

*Crazy conspiracy-theorist morons,* I thought. I wished the damned Internet had never been invented. It alone had made the mass-murdering "prophet," whom we'd all nonetheless come to see that day, possible.

To millions he was the Savior; to others, Hitler reincarnated—and they were all out here yelling.

It had taken only four years for ben Yusef to rise, via cyberspace, from just another tweeting YouTube ranter to a man known throughout the world.

By the time the mainstream media paid attention, it was almost too late. They filled their editorial pages with fire and filled their airspaces with TV talking heads gas-bagging about how such a terrorist monster was loved and slavishly followed by the loonies, the lonely, the desperate, "the fringers"—in other words, people for whom life hadn't been good.

For everyone else—including me—for whom life had been good, he was a terrorist.

As I continued to try to make my way, I thought about the first time I'd ever heard of Demiel ben Yusef—maybe three or four years earlier. He was first identified as part of a terrorist cell based somewhere in or around Ankara, Turkey, which had allegedly planted a bomb in a marketplace full of citizens and tourists in the resort town of Bodrum.

Almost immediately after that bombing, credit had been taken by a renegade cell (is there any other kind?) of al-Qaeda, a cell that no one had ever heard of, called Al Okhowa Al Hamima, roughly translated to mean "Beloved Brotherhood."

Nobody thought much about him or the group. I mean, how much more harm could a young, uneducated dirty desert rat (granted, a very angry rat) hiding out with other filthy desert rats do on the lam? It would be, they thought, a matter of days before they were caught. They were wrong.

To deny that group's involvement in the marketplace carnage, the group's spokesperson, a woman who called herself *il Vettore* (Italian for "the Vector"), appeared in podcasts from places even the most sophisticated spy satellites couldn't recognize. Their beloved leader, Demiel ben Yusef, il Vettore proclaimed in perfect English, French, Spanish, and Arabic, was not a man of violence but a man of peace, the embodiment of the Living Christ. Right. Christ with a car bomb.

As I was remembering all of this, I felt someone grab my shoulder from behind and heard a familiar voice scream, "Ali! Hey, Russo!"

I turned, as much as I could in that sea of humans, and saw that it was my friend Dona Grimm, whom I'd known forever. "Going to Holy Family to interview a priest?" she asked, squeezing up alongside me. Since I stand all of five feet four, I normally had to double-step to keep up with all six feet of her, but today it was so crowded we were moving like slugs, and it only got worse when we hit the sidewalk skirting the outer edges of Dag Hammarskjöld Plaza.

"Frankie-the-genius Donahue, who is too good for public transportation, is stuck on the bridge. So I got the gig."

"This sucks," Dona said, referring to the crowd, and we both simultaneously held our UN credentials, newspaper credentials, and all-access NYPD "Permitted to Cross Police Barricades" press passes aloft, as she started pushing and calling, "Press coming through. . . . Excuse us. . . . Let us in and see yourself on TV tonight," she yelled.

Dona and I were pals, despite the fact that aside from being reporters we basically had little in common. We'd often worked side by side over the years, and it had led to a friendship.

I had seven years on her, and she had eight inches on me. I was working at one of only three remaining NYC print dailies left in the digital world, and despite evidence to the contrary, I was a believer who, God help me, continued to believe in print almighty. I followed the journalistic rules as closely as I could, while Dona, the video blogger who had to fill up dead air, did precisely as she pleased, going to air with rumor, innuendo, and often a brilliant breaking story.

We both look exactly like who we are on and off the job.

I'm smallish, constantly worried about being fat, and tend to be lazy about the whole makeup routine, so I've always let my Italian complexion do the heavy lifting for me. It's my best feature. I try to keep my thick black hair always well cut. I have dark brown eyes and wide lips, and never scrimp on the reddest lipstick I can find, which I have convinced myself takes the place of bothering with a whole makeup routine. All in all an OK package, but I would never stop traffic.

Grimm, on the other hand, is a British-born, deep-cocoa-skinned beauty, roughly six-one in her heels (and she always wears heels), with this fantastic head of totally unruly shoulder-length hennaed curls. Earrings that could have been pressed into service as rolling pins offset the red cashmere sweater coat she was sporting that day.

She could, and did, stop traffic.

Dona pulled me into the Korean deli on the corner. "Can't meet him with ripped panty hose, can I," she said.

"What? Are you insane? We're late." I tried reasoning against reason. But it was go with the giant or try to push through the crowds alone again.

"Panty hose! Who the hell even wears panty hose anymore?"

"Plenty of people, darling," she retorted. "Obviously. Or they wouldn't be selling them in the delicatessen."

"You want to be fashion forward to impress the mass-murdering terrorist baby killer? That makes a lot of sense."

"Excuse me?" she said, stopping to give me a withering stare. "We should at least try some objectivity here. Have you decided it's 'guilty until proven innocent'?"

As though she hadn't just smacked me down, and rightfully so, she picked up a pair of panty hose, paid the guy, and said, "Block me, will you?" as she pulled on the only ones they had in stock, in size "gigantic."

"Those panty hose must be older than me. They're in a plastic egg, for chrissakes! And they're blue," I chided her as we ran out, leaving the shocked deli owner shaking his head.

"No need to take the name of the Lord in vain. Press coming through!" she yelled.

We tried pushing through the mass of humanity, all of

whom wanted to be exactly where we had to be—at the gates of the United Nations building, still half a block away.

"I can't believe we're going to be shut out!"

"We're not going to be shut out, and I'm going to meet him, too," Dona said.

"You drive me nuts."

"O ye of little faith!"

"You mean ye of *no* faith," I corrected her.

"Press coming through!" we both then called out.

"If I miss this trial . . . Damn—why did I stop with you?" I moaned as I elbowed a man who turned around and pulled back his arm, ready to let one fly right at my eye. "Just try it, you bastard!" I said, which caught the attention of one of the riot-gear-suited cops, who came barreling through.

"Hey, you! Put down that fist," he called to the man, grabbing his arm and pulling it behind him in one motion so swift I hadn't realized at first what was happening.

The cop, still holding the man with one arm, started talking into his shoulder two-way when he stopped, surprised, and said, "Wait a second—aren't you, whazzername—the reporter?"

"Well, yes, I am," Dona said, always assuming that all men were talking to her at all times. "And you, gorgeous man, are . . ."

"Holy crap," the cop answered instead, realizing who she was too. "On Fox, right? And you're in the paper, right? *The Standard*—Russo—right?" he asked.

"Yup," I said.

I looked at the cop desperately. "We're gonna be locked out if we don't get through. . . ."

The cop waved over two other cops, who elbowed their way through the crowd. "Let's get these ladies inside there," the first cop said, pointing to the UN drive-way, and within seconds the seas began to part before us and our armed escorts.

Dona looked smug as she was pressed through the throng. I felt besieged.

The cops brought us to the barricades skirting First Avenue, signaled for one of the patrolmen to unlock a link on one barricade, and we walked through as the crowd grew increasingly unruly behind us—all demand-ing to know why we got preferential treatment.

"Hope I see you tomorrow . . . ," the cute cop said.

"Do you think he'll call me?" Dona asked, never even thinking he might have been addressing me, as we trot-ted across First Avenue. "I mean he knows how to find me—at Fox, right?"

Ignoring her, I turned my head toward downtown. Coming toward us at a good clip was a caravan of fifty-something armored vehicles.

"Hurry up. They're almost here!" I screeched, and we rushed the UN gates. They'd already started closing.

"Please, please, sir, please let us pass," I cried to the guard, who looked right through us and continued the slow slide of the automatic gates.

"No, wait!" Dona said to him, holding her press pass aloft. "I'd love to get your comments on camera—Dona Grimm, Fox News," she said, reaching in with her video cam.

"This one is for history," Dona added. The offer proved too much for the officer, and he said in clipped English, "Okay, but hurry up," smiling into the camera. "Ser-geant Mohammed Fahreed—that's spelled F-a-h-r-e-e-d," he said as he checked and rechecked our credentials and we slipped all the way inside the gate.

I could feel my stomach relax a bit for the first time all morning. At least we were inside the gates. After a perfunctory interview with Fahreed, which would never see air, we rushed to the press area outside the entrance to the building. Hundreds of reporters from all over the world were jockeying for position.

Settling for spots in the back of the horde, which was three reporters deep, I said, "You should carry me on your shoulders for what you've put me through today."

The pack of hungry reporters suddenly all moved as one as the gates swung open again. "Tell me what's going on! Please," I begged, because I could see nothing but a lot of backs.

"The gates, they're opening. Wow . . . two tanks, five vans, you name it," Dona reported.

As the caravan started to make its way around the pavement in front of the General Assembly Building, the reporters went wild, rushing the vehicles. The cops, in turn, rushed the reporters. It couldn't have been more than thirty seconds before a scuffle broke out between three cops and four reporters who'd tried to climb the lead van, hoping to shoot from its roof.

Suddenly, the entire bunch rushed from the sidewalk, giving Dona and me the chance to move directly to the curbside. Better to have a front-row view of "him" than report on a bunch of squabbling reporters.

When two dozen cops in riot gear moved in, the pack of reporters angrily but obediently moved back to the curbside. Two of them even tried to unseat us from our new curbside positions. Good luck.

"Step two checked and completed," Dona said. "Now it's just a matter of seconds before I meet 'him' personally and deliver into my producer's grubby little hands the interview of the century."

"Right," I answered, looking skyward. "And I'm going to have his baby."

I whipped out my notebook, and she set up her Minicam on a tripod and started shooting footage of the police commissioner, who got out of the lead vehicle behind his own bodyguards and walked up to a mic on the police podium that had been erected on the lawn to address the reporters.

"Now listen up, you guys," he said. "That scene that just transpired? On *my* watch? If I have to ban the whole damned lotta you, I will. And don't think I'm some candy ass who won't." The reporters, unbowed, jeered as he signaled for the circus to begin.

The vehicles began slowly moving again around the section where we were standing.

"This doesn't feel good," I said. "Do you think they're scamming us and bringing him in a whole other way?"

"Probably not. I wouldn't be able to meet him if that happened, would I?"

"Will you stop with that? Anyway . . . something isn't right. . . ." I felt my stomach flip. Dona peered over the cops' heads in front of us to watch the circus train and its clown cars full of freaks, Feds, and fanatics move forward.

The twentieth vehicle, an armored van, pulled up and around the driveway, and then it stopped—directly in front of us. Would what happened next have happened if it had stopped in front of different reporters? That I can never say, can never know.

What I do know is that the doors slid open and six Secret Service agents simultaneously jumped out of the van, assault rifles at the ready, wearing body armor and helmets, followed by two other "plainclothes," who stood on either side of the open door. The terrorist Demiel ben Yusef appeared in the opening. He stepped out of the van, an agent in front and in back, his head down. He was shackled hand and foot with heavy chains that were just long enough to allow him to walk. A bulletproof vest bulged beneath his jacket.

Although we'd seen video of him a million times, he was much smaller than I'd expected—maybe five-nine, with no heft to him at all—even thinner than he normally was, since he'd been fasting for the past month. But his scruffy long beard, waist-length dreads trailing out from under his NYPD riot helmet, dark, swarthy complexion, and calm face were nonetheless unmistakable. He was, after all, the most famous man in the world.

His attorneys had dressed him for the occasion in a second-rate dark blue suit, white shirt, blue-striped tie, and fake leather loafers that smacked of cheap when they hit the ground.

"Dear God! I could lift him with one hand," Dona said, directing her sexiest smile his way.

The troops began rushing him inside as the roar of the reporters grew deafening. "Over here! Demiel! Over here!"

Demiel, suspected terrorist leader and mass murderer, whom many called "Savior," simply shook his head so slightly that eyewitnesses—of which there would be thousands more than were ever *there* that day—would later say it was more of a thought than an actual motion. While that motion would remain forever in dispute, what I can never dispute is that after that shake, thought, or whatever it was, everything grew quiet—for me, at least.

In fact, for me it had all become so still that the deafening din on the packed streets, which moments before had sounded like the roar of ten oceans, went so quiet I could hear a single birdsong in the park. I think it was a robin.

It even seemed that the federal agents who were supposed to be perp-walking Demiel—parading him in shackles for the benefit of the media—slowed down and walked calmly, neither rushing him nor pushing him.

It felt as though a mass fugue had suddenly affected nearly everyone who had come to see the sight. It wasn't until later that I learned that I was the only one who was suddenly so calm and distant.

I could hear Dona's remote Minicam running next to me. I was holding on to my reporter's notebook, but I was no longer all that interested in writing anything down. It wasn't that I couldn't; it was just that I didn't want to.

All I could really focus on was Demiel slowly moving forward, the sound of his shoes slapping the pavement growing louder as he came nearer to me. And then that sound seemed to die away, too. When the shackled suspected terrorist was right in front of us, he stopped and looked directly at me. I could see the pores in his face, the small irritation where his starched collar had scraped his neck, and even smelled his freshly laundered shirt.

Reflexively, without knowing why, I returned his stare.

He leaned into me, and I could hear the hundreds of reporters, in unison, letting out a muffled "Ohhhh," as I stood there, unmoving.

Then he kissed me on the lips.

## 3

It took a quarter of a second for the federal agents to realize what had just transpired on their watch. It took another quarter of a second for ben Yusef's two "handlers" to spring back to action in unison, shove him hard, and hustle him inside the building.

Immediately the world around the UN came back to life for me—the din, the frenzy—as though it had never stopped. The realization that something very, very strange had happened finally hit the crowd as ben Yusef was being hustled inside.

When I personally could no longer see him, I became conscious that my fingers were on my lips. I'd done it blindly, unaware that anyone was watching, when in fact the whole world was watching.

I could feel the wetness of his kiss on my lips and closed my eyes as though savoring the kiss of a lover who had just walked out the door. It was similar to the feeling I'd had when I'd kissed Donald good-bye that last time—when I knew he was going for good. All of that seemed to happen in the nanosecond before I instinctively wiped his saliva off my mouth and cheek with my scarf. But regardless, I could still feel his wiry moustache and the bristles of his beard on my face against the background of whizzing, clicking, buzzing cameras. I put my fingers to my lips again.

Dona smacked my hand away protectively and whispered, "Stop it . . . just stop it."

It was pretty much all they had, the images of me touching my lips, in place of the big photo—the one of the kiss—that every reporter had gotten from some obscure angle, but none had gotten up close and personal the way Dona had. She had both shots from *thisclose* in 20-megapixel still, and video versions.

I heard her saying somewhere in the background, "*Damn,* girl! And *I'm* the one who bought new panty hose!"

Inexplicably near tears, I croaked, "Why me?" The answer I would later learn was more complex, more dangerous, and more horrible than any poison gas or weapon of mass destruction that humans in their infinite wisdom had yet to devise.

Within an hour those pictures of me touching my mouth were posted on the front page of every media and gossip site in the free and unfree world, blasted to millions of e-mails, Tweeted, Facebooked, forwarded, YouTubed, Instagrammed, and you name it on millions of monitors and phones, shown on JumboTrons, and on loops on every 24/7 news channel.

Dona knew, though, that she alone was holding the best video of the kiss, and with that she could become a very wealthy woman. Because Fox News had relegated her to "permanent freelancer," Dona's film did not belong to them.

" 'God works in mysterious ways,' my mother always told me," Dona said as we began to make our way inside.

Before I could focus, we were shoved so hard that Dona almost lost her cameras. "What the hell . . ." she snapped, turning around to see what looked like the entire media descending upon us.

The frenzy snapped me out of my confused state. *Oh, my God.* I realized I was no longer part of the pack covering the story; I was now a part of the story. No longer one of them, I was one of *them*—the people that people like me chased down the street.

What was I supposed to do? Give interviews? How weird would that have been? But there was no time to think, because in seconds the crowd was pushing us both, surrounding us, suffocating us.

"Hey Russo—you know ben Yusef personally?" "Ali— over here! Over here!" Microphones were shoved in our faces, and for the first time in my life, I knew how terrifying it was to be on the other side of all that need, that want—that terrible insatiable hunger of the 24/7 news machine. I, Alessandra Russo, was dinner.

We then both did what we hate for news "victims" to do: We hid our faces and tried to run like indicted Mafia capos—from our own colleagues.

The police commissioner finally gave the OK for a few cops to go in and grab us. The commissioner was proving a point: show the taxpayers that the "mainstream media" were self-serving lefties who'd eat their own young for a story.

Two plainclothes cops grabbed Dona, while a bruiser of a woman and her slightly smaller male colleague grabbed either side of me, wires clearly poking from their suit jackets into their ears. "C'mon ladies, let's get you inside," the bruiser said calmly.

"Stand back!" the commissioner bellowed over the electronic megaphone. "Everybody back!"

Then he said under his breath, "Bunch of animals. Real

goddamned animals." The statement was nonetheless picked up by the hundreds of mics in the hands of the hundreds of reporters, which caused a near riot. Police officers in equal number to the reporters immediately put up their riot shields and began moving on the pack. We were hustled toward the entrance.

"I wish we were covering us," I cracked, trying to bring some sense to what had just become a completely surreal experience. We were led to the glass doors of the UN, frisked, scanned, and then rubbed our index fingers on the fingerprint scanners for approval, before being escorted inside into the General Assembly, where the proceedings would take place.

We could see the Secret Service agents conferring and watched as they changed all the assigned press seats around. We were seated in the front of the press row.

"Nice," Dona noted, raising her eyebrows in approval.

"You're hot to*day* thanks to *moi,* my friend," I replied, settling into my newly assigned seat and breaking out my tablet.

"I stand in your reflection, baby girl. You are not just hot today," Dona said, "you are on fire! Do you realize what just happened back there?" She turned on her cameras to get her first look at both the still photos and taped footage she had managed to shoot.

"Will you look at this? Jee-sus! Excuse me, Lord!" she said, practically jumping out of her seat with joy. Dona was a die-hard New Age born-again Baptist, despite the fact that she had the body of a stripper and the hair of a supermodel.

I, just as anxious, leaned over and was shocked at the kiss image.

"I have my eyes closed like I'm being kissed by a man, I mean a lover—oh, hell, I don't know what I mean," I said, stunned. "What the . . . ? I mean the guy's a dis-gusting, mass-murdering terrorist! I can't have done that," I snapped. "Can I?"

"You can and you did. Yikes."

Dona and I had been put on the very end of the row—I assumed in case we'd have to be whisked out quickly. We looked up as the doors opened, and we saw—and heard—the reporters straining like dogs against choke collars, waiting to get in.

"Here we come," I said, wincing, as into my "elite" row came bow-tied, bald Alex Peyton of PBS, who was seated next to Dona. He nodded his head toward us, almost a bow actually, as though we were in a nineteenth-century courtroom drama. Normally we would have dined out on that bit of foppery for a month, but not this time. I grew a sudden new respect for journos with re-straint.

The remainder of the row was then seated, and the rest of the press was led to their seats.

TV and film crews had set up their equipment earlier (all of it had been searched and gone over with bomb-sniffing dogs and every explosive-detection device known to the modern world) and were now escorted one by one to their equipment by federal agents.

Each form of media was given one "pool" photogra-pher and one video and live-feed camera crew. It still added up to dozens of shooters in their flak jackets, pock-ets filled with assorted lenses and meters.

"It could take the rest of our lives to get these guys settled," Dona whined. "I mean, I don't have all day!"

"Yeah. You do. It'll give you time to call your agent to start negotiating fees for *my* photos. Lucky you."

"Lucky you too," Dona sniffed. "I'm not stiffing you, so don't be so bitchy."

"I'm having a bad day."

"No, my sweet. You are having the best day of your life. You're the woman with the story—and your big news is going to make us big money. And win you a Pulitzer, of course."

"*Et* tu, *Brute?!* And seriously, keep your voice down. You want the entire reporter pool to hear you?"

"Oh, sorry," Dona snapped back. "Like they don't know . . ."

"What *I* don't know," I whispered back, "is how everything stopped. I mean, it seemed like everyone was suddenly paralyzed as he approached me before the kiss."

"What the hell are you talking about?" she asked, pulling back in her seat to give me a hard stare. "I never saw our so-called friends and colleagues going so wild. I mean, there was rioting!"

"What?"

I just looked at her. This would have to be a discussion for another time. Clearly, something had happened to me beyond being kissed by a killer.

It took nearly an hour to seat the press in the designated area. The UN ambassadors and foreign-service types, then the "distinguished guests," who were seated in the front VIP assembly viewing areas, followed us in. Packed to capacity—over eighteen hundred people would be admitted that day—the room buzzed with the excitement from the chosen few who were invited to witness history.

The two lead prosecutors (and an international team of twenty) plus two lawyers for the defense (period) milled around the front of the chamber, where huge desks had been set up for both sides.

In the front, a massive golden-hued wall that rose to the ceiling framed a specially built massive marble desk on a raised platform, four steps above the throng.

We all waited anxiously to see who would become the

seat's temporary occupants—the four justices and one presiding justice from around the globe who had been chosen by the 203 member countries of the United Nations for ben Yusef's terror tribunal, a tribunal that had not just international political ramifications for all concerned, but would have ramifications for every established religion on earth.

The wrong verdict—not guilty—could, would, rock the world order of things (Demiel had famously referred to it as "the man-made *dis*order of things"). Scholars and TV "talking heads" had speculated for months that a decision favoring the terrorist—which was as likely as a second virgin birth—could destroy humanity's very notion of God.

The world leaders who were to occupy the second row came next. For the opening day, the vice president of the United States, Lester Wallace, the Speaker of Israel's Knesset, and top governmental ministers of countries such as Russia, Great Britain, Iran, North and South Korea, and China were seated. In all, 314 leaders from 203 countries were present to witness this historic event.

To the shock of even the jaded press, the clerics were seated next.

"And you didn't think this was about religion," I whispered to Dona. The religious leaders were actually being seated after the heads of state—the place in line, so to speak, reserved for the most important.

"Well, of course they'd be here; it was their houses of worship that were blown up, their followers killed." There's no doubt but that we were all taken aback not just by the magnitude, but more specifically by the choices of the clerics who'd been invited—and who had actually shown up.

Since, for security reasons, the guest list, so to speak, had been kept so secret, a court officer began passing out the press materials at this point, identifying the clerics present.

First came the secretary to the pope, who was followed by John Cardinal Benning of the Archdiocese of New York, then the high rebbes from both the NYC and Jerusalem Hasidic communities, followed by four of Iraq's five Shia Grand Ayatollahs, as well as two Sunni leaders. Next came the "lesser" Catholic, Anglican, and British archbishops, as well as the president of the American National Association of Evangelicals, the prophet and president of the Mormon church, Lane B. Gardener, as well representatives for the Bahá'í, Jainist, Shinto, Cao Dai, and Zoroastrian faiths. Representatives of the Quakers and the Unitarians, both large faiths in the United States, declined to take part in what they called a predetermined lynching.

Next to last came the secretary to the Dalai Lama, and finally, like the star of the show, the Reverend Bill Teddy Smythe, celebrity preacher, founder and former head of the chain of American megachurches, the Light of God Tabernacle, wheeled in, thick silver hair shining atop his massive head like a halo.

The whole show, so far, essentially verified the Internet rumor about a secret conclave earlier in the month, in which every cleric present this day had supposedly participated.

Indeed, as I later found out, it *had* actually taken place. It was unprecedented but it had been *necessary*, apparently, if they were to keep their followers from joining forces against them. Paranoid? Sure. But in light of what later happened, perhaps not.

The goal of the powerful, or so it went in the blogosphere, was the destruction of the man the "mainstream media" called "raggedy false prophet-cum-terrorist," but who actually was the true Son of God; this, they claimed, had been "proven" by the fact that he had amassed millions of followers in a very short period of time. So had Hitler, Stalin, Saddam Hussein, Idi Amin, and Fidel Castro, to name just a few, but the bloggers forgot to mention any of them.

The governments and the world's great religious leaders, even those with thousands of years of bad blood between them, had allied this one time in order to capture Demiel and bring him to justice. He must, they in turn proclaimed united, be made to pay for his unprecedented acts of terrorism and be exposed for the fraud they knew him to be. There were not just the preposterous claims of cures and "miracles" he'd supposedly performed, but, most important, the heinous and very dangerous claim his followers perpetrated about just who he was supposed to *be*.

And so here we all were together, along with presidents, prime ministers, and dictators—all to see a thirty-three-year-old skinny, badly dressed man of dubious origins attempt to defend himself against all the power in the world.

How had it come to this? That was the question on everyone's mind.

And it was the question that was still burning on my lips as the court officer appeared in front of the door through which the magistrates would enter.

## 4

**New York, United Nations General Assembly,**
**War Crimes Tribunal of Suspected Terrorist Leader**
**Demiel ben Yusef**

"All rise," the officer announced, and in a scene worthy of a TV courtroom drama, introduced the until-then secret ad hoc panel of international judges—their anonymity deemed a necessary safety precaution.

Even though the function of the World Court (officially the International Court of Justice) is to resolve disputes between sovereign states, this case of international terrorism involved so many of the member countries that it was declared a matter for the World Court, albeit with a specially appointed panel of judges. Although the United States withdrew from the court in 1984, we still keep a standing, permanent judge on the panel. I know, it makes no sense.

The first judge entered. He was the chairman of the Supreme Court of Sweden, dressed in a black robe with a red stole that went around the neck, falling onto the chest.

"Appropriate," I whispered to Dona, noting the duds. "Inquisitionists! They should be dressed like monks!"

Dona shot me a surprised glance, whispering, "Hello? I thought you were ready to see the bastard fry—no?"

"Yes, of course. I'm just saying . . ." I muttered, embarrassed.

"Man, one kiss and you're acting like a fat girl without a date for the prom."

The rest followed: chairwoman of the Corte constituzionale della Repubblica Italiana, the chief justice of the Saikō Saibansho of Japan, and the newest appointment to the U.S. Supreme Court, fifty-four-year-old scholar and right-wing-leaning Harvard Law School grad Alberto Sant'Angelo.

"You knew they'd choose that charmer," I whispered sarcastically.

Finally, amid much flourish, the chair of the tribunal entered—this would be the person presiding, the one who would have the final say if there was a tie vote—the one everyone had been speculating about for months.

"Oh, my God! I can't believe it," Dona exclaimed under her breath as the officer announced, "The Honorable Judge Fatoumata Bagayoko, president of the United Nations' Special International Criminal Court, presiding."

The chief judge entered sporting what looked like a crown of braids atop her head. She carried herself with the haughtiness of a star—which she was within the international judicial system. This was going to be the tribunal that would make her name live forever. It was the most important public tribunal since the Nuremberg Trials.

"I told you it would be her," I whispered back.

Bagayoko was the most public jurist in the world, a woman who was such a media hound she would probably have gone on *Dancing with the Stars* if she thought it would help her gain more exposure. Still, her reputation was so stellar she instilled fear in everyone around her.

When she was seated, the officer called out, "The Tribunal of Demiel ben Yusef for Crimes against Humanity is now in session."

To the consternation of the sitting judges, without warning or provocation the Reverend Bill Teddy unsteadily rose from his wheelchair and began an invocation.

Bagayoko's angered face said it all. But who in her right mind was going to stop an eighty-nine-year-old legend who had managed in his supposedly frail state to organize all the world's religious leaders and have them here sitting side by side like fraternity brothers?

"May God bless this assembly," Bill Teddy began in a clear, strong voice.

"Frail, my ass. The God fraud strikes again," I mumbled.

"May You, dear Lord, help us to find the truth," he continued, "and bring justice to those who have been martyred—be they Christian, Jew, Muslim, or Hindu— for their beliefs! God bless the United Nations and God bless America, the land upon which this proud institution stands!" The shocked assemblage broke out into spontaneous applause.

"Order! I will have order in this courtroom," Bagayoko declared as all the lenses in the world trained back on her.

"Was he supposed to stand up and do the God thing?" I asked Dona. "How inappropriate was that?"

"Or maybe how appropriate," she answered.

Next, four United Nations security officers led in a handcuffed and shackled Demiel ben Yusef. They unlocked the handcuffs, but the leg shackles remained in place as he was seated between his attorneys at the front of the room facing the judges. His back was to the press area but sideways to the dignitaries.

Bagayoko, clearly annoyed that the reverend had tried to steal her moment, plowed on as though he didn't exist.

She stood to address the courtroom, resplendent in her black robes, and began in her strong, slightly accented English:

"The privilege of presiding over this trial is a responsibility so grave that it weighs heavily upon all the justices seated here today.

"The crimes for which the defendant has been accused are global in nature, crimes against the peace of the world, if you will.

"But be assured that we are not here to find a quick and easy way to apply a salve on the terror that's been perpetrated against the world these past few years. Yet we will not allow even the most august of legal minds to automatically lay at the feet of one man responsibility for the terrorist bombings that have taken place around the globe—unless these crimes are proven to have been perpetrated and planned by the defendant, Mr. Demiel ben Yusef, beyond a reasonable doubt. We cannot and must not rush to judgment seeking vengeance, not truth, satisfaction in place of proof. We must keep these things in mind despite the fact that our hearts are heavy with the pain of loss of human life and limb that has become the by-product of terrorism in the name of God.

"Let us then be guided to find the truth so that justice, not the mindless will of the mob, will prevail."

She then looked directly at the accused. "This tribunal will now arraign the defendant, Demiel ben Yusef. Mr. ben Yusef, are you represented by counsel before this tribunal?"

Ben Yusef neither answered nor looked up, which prompted Bagayoko to ask again, "Mr. ben Yusef, are you represented by counsel?"

When again he did not acknowledge her or the court, she asked rhetorically, "Perhaps you need an interpreter, Mr. ben Yusef?"

One of the attorneys assigned by the International Criminal Court to represent ben Yusef, Randall Mohammed of Amnesty International, stood. "Your Honor, if I may speak for my client, Mr. Demiel ben Yusef? My name is Randall Mohammed, and I, along with my co-counsel, Ms. Johanna Edmonds, am representing Mr. ben Yusef."

He was dressed to the nines in a bespoke suit, with a red-striped tie and foppish matching pocket handkerchief.

"Mr. Mohammed," snapped the judge, her Mali accent beginning to surface, "does Mr. ben Yusef need an interpreter? And if he can't answer for himself, then I will assume that he does not speak English." She knew full well, as we all did, that the defendant was in fact fluent in English and perhaps as many as eight other languages.

"Well, ah, no, Your Honor, the defendant can in fact speak English—" Mohammed said, before the chief judge again cut him off.

"Perhaps *you* need an interpreter then, Mr. Mohammed, because if he understands, then your client, *not* you, is instructed to answer the question." She bored her eyes directly into the defendant sitting calmly in his cheap suit, not displaying pride, shame, or even any indication that he was present in mind or spirit.

"Mr. ben Yusef, once more I'll ask you: Do you need an interpreter?"

Again, ben Yusef neither acknowledged the judge nor his counselors, who were beginning to look distressed even though the tribunal had yet to get under way. Johanna Edmonds, second-chair attorney from South Africa, a slim Caucasian woman, hair pulled back in a conservative bun, wearing an understated blue suit, stood.

"On behalf of our client, we state to the court that

there is no authority in this tribunal to pass judgment on our client."

"Noted," Bagayoko answered. "Regardless of what you or your client thinks, this tribunal will proceed as scheduled."

Edmonds then sat back down and whispered in her client's ear. Ben Yusef picked up the pad and pen in front of him and wrote something down, which he handed to her.

She stood again.

Edmonds asked, "May I approach the bench, Your Honor?"

"Yes, you may, counselor."

"A plea? This early?" Dona suggested.

Edmonds walked across the platform and handed the judge a piece of paper, which she looked at briefly, clearly confused. "What is this?" Bagayoko asked, holding the paper in her hand like she'd been handed a used tissue.

"It's a note given to me by my client, Your Honor," Edmonds answered.

On the note, which was later reprinted and released to the media, was written: ܐܡܝܢ ܐܒܐ ܕܒܫܡܝܐ .

"I can see where this is headed. . . ." Judge Bagayoko said sotto voce, turning the note upside down and around, clearly annoyed that the terrorist had already gotten one up on her. She put on reading glasses and then said, exasperated, "What language is this exactly?"

Edmonds answered, "I believe it is Aramaic, Judge."

"Oh, I see. Is there a United Nations translator of Aramaic present in the courtroom?" When no one stood, she then asked, "Is there any spectator present that can interpret Aramaic?" A man in a white galabia (robe) and red-and-white-checked keffiyeh draped around his head stood up while everyone in the entire room craned their necks, shocked.

Bagayoko stared at him a second before saying, "What is your name, sir?"

"Mahmoud Haniyah, Your Honor." The senior representative of Hamas! "I speak all forms of Aramaic."

"Then please step forward, Mr. Haniyah." The courtroom was abuzz. A terrorist using a terrorist as an interpreter? Fantastic!

A court officer took the paper from the chief judge and handed it to the representative of Hamas, who looked at it and then said loud enough for most of us to hear, "Your Honor, it is Aramaic; I believe it is Herodian, as used in the time of Jesus Christ. It says: ᵓagēb lᵓabī belḥōd. This means, 'I answer only to my father,' or it can be interpreted as 'He answered to my father,' or both."

"Both?" Bagayoko asked, removing her glasses.

"Your Honor, it is much the same way that the English word *read* can be both present or past depending on the context."

The courtroom was absolutely silent. Everyone was thinking the same racist thing: a terrorist who speaks ancient Aramaic and modern English? How many of us can do that?

"Thank you, sir. I appreciate that. You may return to your seat," which the Palestinian did with a pleased expression on his face.

Then the chief judge addressed ben Yusef directly. "Your father, according to FBI documents, was named—" At this she keyed something into the built-in tablet in her bench and continued. "Yes, one Yusef Pantera, who was listed as a soldier of fortune. Killed in a plane crash in 1982."

With controlled anger in her tone, she added, "Mister ben Yusef. It is your right not to answer, but that is the last time you will interrupt these proceedings with your manipulations."

She asked him to stand, and when he refused, his lawyers on either side of him took hold of his elbows and gently persuaded him up, and then the chief judge began to read the Crimes against Humanity charges for which he stood accused.

They included twenty counts of conspiracy to commit murder, fifty counts of terrorism, one thousand counts of murder in violation of the law of war, attacking civilians and civilian objects, intentionally causing serious bodily injury, destruction of property in violation of the law of war, and providing material support for terrorism. The death count she estimated at "tens of thousands."

"How do you plead, Mr. ben Yusef?" Silence.

Randall Mohammed stood. "Once more, Your Honor, on behalf of our client, we state to the court that there is no authority in this tribunal to pass judgment on our client."

"Then let us proceed with or without your client's consent," and she called on the prosecution to give their opening statement.

The prosecution was represented by an international band of attorneys under the ICC banner but newly appointed for this tribunal.

"It's the dream team of media whores," I whispered to Dona, taking in the group who would have practically skinned themselves alive for a chance at this much exposure.

The lead prosecutor, Lawrence Finegold from Great Britain, gave as expected a rousing opening statement, which was capped by him holding up photos of each bombing for which ben Yusef stood accused.

"Ladies and gentlemen, the monster before you, Mr. Demiel ben Yusef," he thundered as he held up photo after photo of carnage and heartache, "isn't a man of the cloth. He is nothing but a psychopathic killer who claims"—he sneered in disgust at the defendant, who still hadn't moved a muscle or shown any emotion whatsoever—"*claims* to be, yes, a man of *God*!

"A devil claiming to be a man of God, or maybe God Himself." He laughed disgustedly. "Caligula claimed to be a god; Hitler thought he was a god, too. Shall I go on?

"Demiel ben Yusef is no god, nor even a man of God, despite his claims to some sort of dubious connection to early Christianity! This is enough to make any God-fearing Christian sick with disgust!

"Yet this mass murderer, who is responsible for every death, dismemberment, and ruined life you see before you, claims he's doing"—again he paused and then pointed his finger directly at ben Yusef—"God's work. God's work?

"He of the shadowy life, who seems to have no history before he suddenly appeared a few years ago, on Web sites and, yes, YouTube. YouTube! If Jesus, Moses, Mohammed walked among us today, I promise you they wouldn't be making videos on *YouTube*!"

The audience broke out in inappropriate chuckles as Dona and I exchanged knowing glances. "Damn, he's playing us like a bunch of cheap fiddles," she whispered.

Finegold waited until the snickers stopped before continuing as though he'd never heard the snickering. "Now his latest ploy is to say he answers only to his *father*? Who *is* the father of Satan, or for that matter, the mother? We have some loose information that Mr. ben Yusef *once* had a father who died in a plane crash. And there is *no mother of record*. Astonishing, really, in this day and age when it is impossible to keep anything hidden. Yet this, this man just appeared and *has no history*?

"How is that possible? I'll tell you how: Demiel ben Yusef has no history of record because intelligence leads us to believe that his birth, his schooling, his very life have never been recorded because he was born and reared to become an enigma—a way to make the deluded *believe* he somehow miraculously just appeared out of nowhere to save us all!

"Well, the truth is he is a thirty-three-year-old man reared by parents, or perhaps by others who took him in, inside a terrorist camp, somewhere, probably Afghanistan. Nothing glorious or mysterious about that, is there?

"So who could have even birthed such a soulless creature? We don't know; that's how terrorists operate, in back corners and filthy desert hovels. But I *can* tell you this: Whoever his parents are or were, they weren't people of God. The devil, perhaps, but not God!"

At that the Reverend Bill Teddy Smythe pounded his fist and declared, "Amen, brother! Amen!" He did this knowing it would create a commotion and knowing that the judge would admonish him. But the good preacher didn't get to where he was by missing his moment. Ever.

Bagayoko rapped her gavel, while Bill Teddy smugly looked unfazed and even quite righteous—or quite self-righteous, at any rate.

Finegold let the furor die down and continued as though he'd not been interrupted. "Again, no one seems to know precisely the who, what, where, and, for the love of God, *why*.

"What we know is that Demiel ben Yusef suddenly appeared out of the desert four years ago, with dubious claims and clichéd sermons about how we should all love one another, while masterminding terrorist attacks around the world. We know this, and we will prove this beyond any doubt—to this august body.

"Nonetheless, via cyberspace he has, as you've seen

outside this hallowed assembly hall this very day, amassed a worldwide following of deluded believers.

"Why, you may ask, could, *would* anyone follow a man who preaches 'love of every living thing' and yet carries out a personal jihad against the innocent whom he thinks deserve death because they are not 'true believers'?

"Believers of what? Of the endless suffering and death of the innocents? Are the thousands of children and adults who have been killed and maimed merely the detritus of war? What war? Demiel ben Yusef's personal holy war?

"Why indeed would anyone call this monster a man of God?" He finished and held aloft a horrifying photo of a mother and dead child lying on the once-grand steps outside the Matriz Church in Manaus, Brazil, a city at the tip of the Amazon.

The photo showed the woman covered in the blood of her child, screaming while holding her dead five-year-old, whose legs had been blown off. They lay amid the rubble of the bombed-out steps, after an explosion that took the lives of 350 churchgoers that Sunday morning, including 120 Sunday-school kids.

He then turned to the judges and addressed them.

"Judge Bagayoko, assembled justices, if I may, I would like to bring in some of the children who will be called before this assembly."

Since everyone in or near the courtroom had been cleared well ahead of time, the gesture was a mere courtesy. The dramatic move had most likely been approved beforehand by Bagayoko, who quickly consented and gestured for the chamber doors to open.

None of us, even the most hardened, was prepared for what came next. A line of ten parents entered, wheeling children with every manner of horrific injury. Some were burned, some scarred without mouths, some blind, some quadriplegic, some clearly horribly brain damaged. "These children, once whole, now destroyed, are the handiwork of one man, a monster who in a few short years callously killed, callously destroyed at his whim. Why? Only God knows, but clearly the so-called man of God," he mocked, "knows no God."

Leaving the packed room totally silent, save for the sobs that could be heard coming from dignitaries and press alike, Finegold rested.

Even Bagayoko was holding back tears. "Please, Mr. Finegold, take the children to the private dining room and make sure they have a good, hearty United Nations feast." She then called for a one-hour lunch break.

As the crowd started to file out, I stayed seated, knowing that I'd be swarmed by media, but also feeling that I really needed some time to take in what had happened to me—and that it was all caused by the man who had committed the horrific acts against those children.

"Pee for me," I said to Dona, trying to sound as tough as I like to think I am, when she got up and made her way out of the chamber. The second she opened the door, I saw the media rush her, yelling, "Dona! Over here! Did he say anything . . . ?"

Grateful when the guards closed the doors and locked them, I found myself alone for the first time that day. I stood up and walked around the grand room. I was spent. I mean, sure, we'd all been prepared for the monstrous experience of seeing ben Yusef's alleged crimes displayed in living color. But I personally somehow wasn't prepared to see those children. The suffering of those little kids simply overwhelmed me, and I started to sob. I sat in that big room and tried to comprehend what I'd seen and what had happened that day.

In an hour the court doors opened again, but it took another two whole hours for press and spectators to get scanned and file back in.

When everyone was finally seated and the dignitaries had finished giving their boilerplate statements to the media, Bagayoko called for opening statements from the defense.

Edmonds got up and walked to the front of the chamber.

"If I may, Your Honors," she began, "on behalf of our client, we state once more to the court that there is no authority in this tribunal to pass judgment on our client."

"Noted," said the chief justice and glared at her, expecting something further, which was not just forthcoming but about to rock the room.

Edmonds thanked the judge and then continued, saying, "That being said, I want to explain that we took on this case not because other attorneys would not represent this man who has been labeled 'terrorist,' 'monster,' and 'mass murderer,' but because Mr. Demiel ben Yusef is completely innocent of every heinous crime of which he has been unjustly accused.

"Demiel ben Yusef is an innocent man. He is a man of God—yes—but also a man who opposes what organized religion has done in the *name* of God. And because his writings, sermons, and philosophy have turned people away from the bonds of organized religions, he has amassed millions of followers. Not thousands, but millions worldwide. Is every one of these followers wrong to believe he is a man of peace who wants to set them free from the fear of God and replace that fear with the love of God?

"Mr. ben Yusef has never killed, maimed, nor committed acts of terrorism and violence in the name of God nor of any organization, for that matter.

"What he has done is heal hundreds of fatally ill people—and we will prove that. He has fed thousands of starving people, and we will prove that.

"We will also prove that in those cases—such as feeding the anti–Wall Street demonstrators in New York City and Oakland, California, in 2011—he *did* perform a modern-day miracle, the miracle of getting past bureaucracy to get food to the demonstrators.

"And he did it again when he got relief supplies to thousands of starving survivors of last year's devastating earthquakes in the Middle East.

"His miracle was that he found a way to avoid red tape and get donated food into the mouths of the stranded and starving. And we will prove that.

"Further"—and at this she smiled—"Demiel ben Yusef was not, unlike conspiracy theorists claim, hatched, spontaneously generated, or created as a clone from some mysterious donor's DNA. We can't prove that—but really, how do you prove conception?

"Even in this day and age of spying eyes and built-in cameras, luckily we are still allowed to *procreate* in private. And surveillance cameras were certainly not even a question in 1982." She paused, looked at each judge in turn, and then said sardonically, "So, no, we cannot prove that Mr. ben Yusef is human or was conceived by humans!"

As Demiel sat without moving a muscle or blinking his eyes, even the most distinguished of visitors began to giggle, causing Bagayoko to slam her gavel for quiet, with the admonition that she would clear the courtroom if any further disruptions occurred.

Edmonds, unfazed, continued. "But then again, how would I show *anyone's* moment of conception in this entire courtroom? The very idea is so absurd I am left helpless to even comment further, other than to ask whether this is 2015 or the twelfth century.

"What next? Magic spells, witches, and devils?

"Yes, Mr. ben Yusef had actual flesh-and-blood parents—dead now. His father, Yusef Pantera, as Her Honor mentioned, died in a plane crash; his beloved mother, Meryemana Pantera, as has not been reported, was, we believe, killed last year in the Mumbai terrorist attack. Yes—the very one that ironically enough was credited to"—she paused here for dramatic effect—"the Al Okhowa Al Hamima terrorist organization, which Mr. ben Yusef has been accused of *heading*."

The courtroom once again broke out in murmurs of shock.

Edmonds continued through the murmuring. "And the names of the real killers will shake the very foundations of this United Nations! And we will prove this as well."

At that moment, Demiel ben Yusef, as though he were the judge, raised his hand slightly. Immediately the courtroom became as silent as a tomb, while Bagayoko raised her eyebrows in surprise.

Edmonds walked to the defense table, leaned in as ben Yusef whispered something to her, turned back toward the judge, and simply said, "On instructions from my client, Your Honors, I have concluded my opening statement."

"You have the right to cut short or not even give an opening statement," Bagayoko scolded, leaning forward in her chair, "but you will be expected—required—to mount a defense for your client in lieu of a plea, whether he wants one or not. Is that understood?" Then, turning toward ben Yusef, who again sat as though in a trance: "Mr. ben Yusef, do you understand?"

When he didn't answer or even acknowledge her, she

again slammed down her gavel and said, exasperated, "Under the circumstances, the chamber determines that the best course is to adjourn the proceedings until nine tomorrow morning. I will confer with my esteemed colleagues on how we will proceed tomorrow." She glared at the defendant. "I will not have this courtroom turned into a circus—media or otherwise. I will order the gates closed—no exceptions—by seven forty-five. Court dismissed. Mr. Mohammed, Ms. Edmonds, please meet me in the justice's chambers in one hour."

Her gavel slammed. "All rise," commanded the court officer, as Chief Justice Bagayoko stood and exited, trailed by the other world-famous jurists, who followed her out like ducklings after their mother.

"Early to bed," Dona said as we began gathering up our equipment.

"At least it gives me a whole hour to file my column," I answered, happy for the luxury of what I thought foolishly would be sixty uninterrupted minutes to write before the bosses started calling me, screaming. For reasons that still escape me, I hadn't filed one word about the kiss. I guess that had been my fugue time.

What *was* I thinking?

"This is going to be the column of your life, honey," Dona reminded me, "so you deserve the hour. But then, you know I get your exclusive interview. . . ."

"Interview?" I asked.

Dona looked up. "Du-uhhh! The Chosen One—remember?"

Meantime, the assembled heads of states—many of whom had simply come for opening day just to have history record the fact that they were there, were probably ready to be important elsewhere.

As the General Assembly emptied of dignitaries, the security teams made sure everyone else was kept back, making it impossible for any press to get to any of the world leaders.

Finally the agents assigned to Demiel spoke briefly to his attorneys and led him out, followed by his lawyers and the prosecutors. As Dona and I watched and recorded his movements, Demiel ben Yusef abruptly stopped in front of us again and again moved in closer than he should have been allowed to. He carefully mouthed, inches from my face, what sounded like *"Ani oneh rak le-Elohi,"* then, "Go forth for I am six," before he was roughly shoved away by one of the security men.

"What? What did you say?" I called out.

"Oh, shit . . ." Dona said, turning around at the sound of rushing feet behind us. The press horde was descending like a crazed beast. Security rushed to meet them up the rows, guns drawn.

So much for passive resistance inside the United Nations, home of peace.

I, however, still in a kind of semishock, looked at my friend, trying to figure out not just what *"Ani oneh rak le-Elohi,"* and "Go forth for I am six," could mean, but also what "Oh, shit!" meant.

"Honey, we gotta blow this joint," Dona said, grabbing up her stuff and my leather satchel too.

"What?" I asked.

"C'mon, Ali, snap out of it! We've got to get out of here. They're coming for us. Or for you, at any rate!"

I looked back and saw people I'd known all my professional life, folks I thought of as friends and colleagues, scuffling with UN security to get to me, like vigilantes after a child molester.

The agents who'd led us inside were headed our way again. "Here comes Brunhilda," Dona said. "Thank God!"

They grabbed onto our arms and, with the assistance of four more of their uniformed colleagues, surrounded us and walked us to the front doors, out the cleared driveway, and to the gates, where the crowds seemed to have grown since we'd entered earlier in the day.

"Kid killer," the crowds closest to the gates yelled, behind police barricades manned by cops standing in front, heels to the curb.

"Save our Savior!" screamed an overweight middle-aged woman whom we could see was being dragged away to one of at least fifty NYPD prisoner vans lined up on the street in front of us. "Save Him! Save Him, Jesus!"

"She wants Jesus to save the terrorist!" I screeched mockingly over the din to Dona.

"I guess we won't be filing back in the UN office," Dona cracked.

"Let's get to my place and file from there," I said. We looked at our captors for permission. The bruiser said, "Ladies, it's not safe out here for you. We'll escort you wherever you need to go."

We made our way, full contingent intact, out the gates and along the outside of Dag Hammarskjöld Plaza, hugging the curb, where more barricades had been erected.

As we approached the Japan Society, a crazed TV reporter who'd been monitoring the events from his mobile unit, attempted to reach us, microphone out, cameraman shadowing.

"Ali! Ali," he cried, using the name that was not on my byline but the one used by my friends.

"Do you know him?" the bruiser asked.

"No, she doesn't," answered Dona. "The nerve." Protecting her turf, I knew.

The crowd noticed the commotion, and it moved toward us.

"Oh, shit," I moaned, more scared than I'd ever been in my life.

As we approached the Church of the Holy Family,

almost at a run, the steel gate of Mary's Garden swung open and a young priest, holding a key, looking as frantic as we felt, said, "Hurry up, get inside!"

We all ducked inside quickly. As Bruiser and company watched our backs, the young priest said to Dona and me, "Man has much more to fear from the passions of his fellow creatures than from the convulsions of the elements."

"Is that from scripture?" I asked, shaking his hand to thank him.

"Edward Gibbon, eighteenth-century historian," he answered. Then, "I'm Gene. Eugene Sadowski, Father Sadowski, Father Eugene, whatever. Come on in and take a load off. . . ."

"You have Internet access?" I asked. I didn't know if this was one of those old-fashioned churches that talked directly to God or needed outside assistance.

"High-speed, wireless, holograph—you name it."

"Is this heaven?" Dona asked.

"No. Forty-seventh Street," one of the cops answered. Then into his two-way: "We got a situation. Church of the Holy Family."

Father Eugene led us into the rectory kitchen, and it smelled—I swear!—like fresh-baked bread and wine.

A woman and what I assumed was her adolescent son stuck their heads in the kitchen's swinging door. The kid was holding a dry-cleaning bag with his altar-boy black-and-white robes. "Need anything before we take off, Father?" she asked.

"We're good, Laurie, thanks."

In half a second the bruiser was all over the pair like a bad smell. "ID, please, ma'am."

The thirty-something-year-old mother in her too-tight jeans and too-blond hair looked at Sadowski.

"Mrs. Braunthauler works for me," the priest said to the cops. "It's all right. I can vouch for her."

*That's a church lady?*

"ID, ma'am," the second cop repeated, as though Sadowski had said nothing.

Mrs. Braunthauler reached into her purse and pulled out her wallet and showed her driver's license. "Take it out, please," the bruiser said.

Mrs. Braunthauler complied, and the cop wrote down the information.

"Is that necessary?" I asked, putting my two cents in where they didn't belong.

"Yes," was all Bruiser said, and I swear she sounded pissed off. "In case you don't understand, you are in danger, Ms. Russo."

"Right."

*This whole bullshit is because of me! Everything I know is changing at the speed of light.*

If only I'd known then that my world had already changed. Thing is, everyone knew that but me. And that was only my first big failing. If I'd only understood. . . .

## 5

The second sign that I was no longer just plain old (and feeling very old at the moment, actually) Alessandra Russo was that Dona started bugging me about the interview. I mean, I couldn't even imagine interviewing her. We already knew everything about each other. But I knew that if I didn't give in, she'd keep it up until I did it.

Feeling all banged up from the day's bizarre events, I managed to compose myself as Dona turned her camera on me. No, I'd never met Demiel ben Yusef; yes, I was shocked that he kissed me; no, I didn't feel compromised nor did I feel assaulted or shamed. I intended to continue working as though nothing extraordinary had happened, and I could only assume it was because I was in the right place at the wrong time. Or something.

God knows what she got me to say, because I was in such a rush to get my column done that I wasn't paying all that much attention.

I'd also forgotten to turn my cell phone back on after I'd left the UN because, hey, these things can happen when you're being chased by a mad crowd into the sanctuary of a Catholic church (OK, a garden of a Catholic church), an institution you hadn't stepped into for at least ten years.

When I turned my cell back on, I saw that I had forty messages and that my mailbox was full. I assumed thirty-nine of them were from Dickie Smalls, so without playing any of them back, I called the desk.

"What the hell have you been doing?" Dickie screamed into the phone without once pausing to hear what I had to say. "Do you not know this is the biggest story of the frigging year? Have you written your column? We want forty inches—more if you want. What was it like? The kiss? Wet? What? Why you? Direct from Bob, put in how disgusted you were by the whole thing and that you want the world to know that this baby killer should die."

"But Dickie—" I tried to say.

To which he responded, "Get it done in fifteen minutes. We're putting out a special because of this, and we're going big and going early."

"Am I columning on it?"

"You bet." And with that he again hung up.

Father handed me coffee and a big cognac, while I feverishly wrote and then filed a column exactly twenty-three minutes later using the present tense. (Newspaper reporters always write for the next day, but if you're filing online, you write in the present tense.)

*Kiss of Death*
*By Alessandra Russo*
   *Nothing would, could, should have, in my life, ever prepared me for what happened to me today.*
   *Not kissed by a lover nor a friend but by someone I thought of as a mass murderer. And after nearly being mobbed by reporters because the man I thought of as a mass murderer had kissed me, that man once again sought me out.*

*At the end of today's proceedings he came up to me and whispered words that I still can't decipher or comprehend.*

*I can see by the instant blogs and rush-to-air / should-know-better newscasts that I am now considered a "friend" of ben Yusef's, someone who's known him secretly or, as one idiot blogger maintains, "for longer than she will admit."*

*Admit? Admit to what?*

*No, I'd never met this man before in my life. No, he's not my Facebook "friend," and no, we aren't secret lovers who plan to overthrow the world.*

*I don't know why I was singled out. I still can't figure it out—and I would love to say that I don't want to figure it out either and be done with it, but I do of course want to figure it out.*

*Why me? What does he want with me?*

*I'd like to think that it's because I'm so important, so irresistible, and so well read, but, hey, that's just not true.*

*So, really, here's how it went down, and this is all I know myself:*

*As the reporters scuffled in front of the UN today, my pal, video blogger and Fox 5 reporter Dona Grimm, and I managed to steal some space at the curb. We expected to get a good look at the suspect from that angle. We got the shock of our lives instead.*

*For reasons I still can't explain, except for maybe dumb luck or bad luck, the van holding the suspect, Demiel ben Yusef, stopped right in front of us. As you know by now, as he exited the van, shackled hand and foot, we saw him (and this I can positively attest to) nod his head so slightly that it was almost more of a thought than an action.*

*At that moment, everything stopped for me. The roar*

*of the crowd, the insanity of the mob, the aggression of the reporters, and even the movement of the federal agents turned into slow motion, or maybe* sluggish *is a better term.*

*Then I found that even I, intrepid, note-taking reporter, lowered my pad as ben Yusef ambled toward me. He stared at me—and I was shocked to see a depth of feeling in those eyes (and I can't for sure explain what the feeling was), and then without warning, he leaned into me and kissed me on the mouth!*

*So what does it feel like to be kissed by an alleged terrorist? I'd like to say that it's no different from any kiss I've ever received, but that would be a lie.*

*It was, in fact, not like any kiss I've ever received. For one thing, the world has never stopped when I was kissed before. I always thought that was just an expression! But in fact, the world did stop; everything seemed so calm and serene in the midst of the madness.*

*Yes, his mouth was like the mouth of any other man, but then again, not like the mouth of any other man.*

*And a second later he was gone—pulled away by the federal and UN agents, and suddenly the world around us became filled once more with movement and sound. I don't know what happened. I don't know why it happened. And for sure I don't know why it happened to me.*

*Later, when the tribunal wrapped for the day and the suspect was being escorted back out of the grand hall of the UN General Assembly, Demiel ben Yusef again leaned into me and whispered what sounded like "Annie one rakes lehi." I have no idea what this means. It sounds like a sports headline for a high school girls' basketball team. Then he whispered, "Go forth for I am six."*

*I'm sure the experts will figure it out. Again, Grimm and every camera crew there recorded it all.*

*I was, of course, once more stunned. Why me? What does he want? Where is this going? Already, the bloggers are calling for my head, as though I am his co-conspirator. That is probably as unsettling and as awful as everything else that has happened to me today.*

*You know, today I made some remark to Grimm about "mass murderer" and she brought me up short, saying that I must ascribe to a philosophy of "innocent until proven guilty."*

*She was right, and you, bloggers and rumormongers out there in cyberspace, couldn't be more wrong about me, either. But it made me realize that in the same way that you are rushing to judgment about me, I have rushed to judgment about him.*

*As Judge Bagayoko wisely warned today, no matter how it looks from the outset and the outside (and that's you in the blogosphere and all the TV talking heads who don't know what the heck you're talking about), "Let us then be guided to find the truth so that justice, not the mindless will of the mob, will prevail."*

*Edward Gibbon, the eighteenth-century historian, once said about mob mentality, "Man has much more to fear from the passions of his fellow creatures than from the convulsions of the elements."*

*I heard that from a priest today—as I was being chased by a crazed mob.*

*Again: Why me? What does Demiel ben Yusef want from me? Where is this going? Stay tuned.*

## 6

Father Sadowski offered us more coffee and then ordered in Chinese takeout.

"Can I get another cognac?" I asked. Not that I knew one from the next, but the label, "Courvoisier L'Esprit," sounded calming—and expensive.

Sadowski poured me a generous snifter full, and I downed it like a frat boy chugs a carton of wine cooler, just as the garden-gate bell rang. He checked the video surveillance monitor, and we could all see it was thankfully the delivery guy from Mee takeout.

As we were divvying up the moo shu chicken and fried rice, we were astonished to see our delivery man already on TV, and every other outlet, standing terrified outside the gates of Mary's Garden, saying to hundreds of crazed reporters, "Nobody! I have paper! Legal! Nobody inside. Priest! Fathah! That all!"

"Oh, God," I moaned. "How the hell are we ever going to get out of here?"

"There's a tunnel," Sadowski said calmly.

"A what?" Brunhilda, whom I'd found out was named Sergeant Carol Clements, said. "Why in hell, excuse me,

Father, for my language, but why is there a tunnel, and where does it go?"

"I think it led to a bunch of old storehouses for the riverboats that delivered along the river."

We knew he was lying. Why he'd lie about such a thing, I couldn't say—then—but I knew why we thought he was lying. We were all New Yorkers and, worse, reporters and cops, so we naturally assumed most people were lying about most things most of the time. After all, in our businesses we generally only asked questions of people who had something to hide.

"Or whatever," Sadowski continued. "Anyway, there is a tunnel that comes out in back of the Family School next door, and into the back of Forty-eighth Street."

It was oddly quiet.

"Where do you live?" he asked me. Why did I have the feeling he somehow already knew?

"Right on the corner there—that white building."

Carol née Brunhilda informed us, "That's why it's closed off to pedestrians except for those with ID who actually live on the street and need to get home."

I was astonished. Clearly they knew where I lived and so had closed off my street.

"Look! Here we are," Dona broke in, glued to Sadowski's giant flat screen, excited to see her interview with me not just on Fox 5 but on Fox News.

"I look fat," I said. Nobody answered.

"Good, then," Carol said. "When you're ready we'll get you home. We'll have some officers outside your building and outside your door tonight—"

"Oh, that's not necessary, really—"

"Yeah. It is," was all she said.

Concerned that I hadn't heard back from Dickie or anyone since I'd filed my story, I made one last call to the newsroom before we packed up our stuff.

"News desk," one of the copy kids answered.

"Hey, it's Russo. Is Smalls around?"

He put me on hold, then came back on the line. "Dickie said you're good to go." *That's it?* I thought at least I'd hear "Good job" or "Rewrite" or something. "Good to go?" That could mean "it's edited and in"—or that they were spiking the story.

"So I'm okay?"

"I guess," answered the kid.

I hung up uneasily. Sadowski stood and walked us across the well-appointed rectory, through a door, and down a flight of stairs to the basement, which held what looked like a wine cellar worthy of the Franciscan brothers in Assisi. "Come back on a less-crazy day and we'll talk about God and mobs over wine," the good father quipped.

A door at the back of the wine cellar led to a tunnel—or more like a passageway—which was illuminated with fluorescents when Sadowski flicked the wall switch.

"It's straight," he joked. "Can't get lost."

We—that would be Dona, four cops, and me—walked the hundred feet or so and came to another stairwell. Ten steps up to another door, and sure enough we were in the back of the adjacent school. It was literally just a stone's throw through a new construction site to Forty-eighth Street.

Meantime, the crazed mob, trying to get a "get" with Dona or me, was on Forty-seventh, completely surrounding the church and Mary's Garden.

Forty-eighth between First and Second Avenues was fairly quiet—mostly just sanitation trucks and crews noisily running overtime trying to clean up the masses of flyers, candy and gum wrappers, napkins, half-eaten hot dogs, pieces of bready NYC-style pretzels, cans, and debris that the protestors had heedlessly left behind.

Crossing the cordoned-off avenue with a bunch of cops was a breeze, and within a minute I was back at my building and Dona was in a patrol car on her way— home? Who knew with her.

George, the doorman, usually the one with a joke, a bit of gossip, and an inappropriate question, was on duty. He was uncomfortably quiet as I passed through the lobby with just a head nod his way as three cops led me to the elevator and to my apartment door.

I walked in, flicked on the lights. The cops did a cursory search to make sure no one was lurking, ready to spring out from behind the curtains for an ambush interview.

"Me or one of my officers will be right outside your door all night. Here's the cell number," Carol said, handing me her card. "Just in case you hear, see, or smell something and don't want to open the door."

"Not necessary, but thanks," I said.

"It's our job."

With that she and her minions stepped outside before I could even offer them a Coke or a cookie.

My answering machine was flashing. That meant that my voice mail had automatically gone to the machine.

I hit the "play" button. There were ten messages from various media who needed/wanted/had to have an interview. My number wasn't exactly secret: They had mine and I had theirs from years of working side by side.

Then, "Ali? It's Donald." (He *never* called the day after, before this.) "I'm around."

*Now that I'm famous, or is that genuine concern?*

I was too exhausted to call him back.

I took a very hot shower, didn't bother to remove my makeup, brushed my teeth until they bled, and turned on my tablet, saw the story hadn't yet been put up (very odd), and called the desk again. Dickie had gone out for a smoke, and his next in line told the copy kid who had answered the phone to tell me my story had caused the site to crash from the number of hits, so they had to pull it but were working it out.

Satisfied, and even excited, I nonetheless fell into a coma of a deep sleep.

## 7

I woke up at 5:30 the next morning, desperate to see how *The Standard* had played the column.

I turned on my iPad and saw this:

*EXCLUSIVE TO* THE NEW YORK STANDARD

*Kiss of Death From the Lips of the Terrorist*
*By Alessandra Russo*

*I was violated, pure and simple.*

*Nothing would, could, should have, in my life, ever prepared me for what happened yesterday.*

*And by now you know what happened to me yesterday:*

*I was kissed against my will as Demiel ben Yusef, head of the Al Okhowa Al Hamima terrorist organization, responsible for the deaths of thousands of innocent people around the world, was "perp-walked" after exiting the armored van driven by our own American heroes—the Federal Bureau of Investigation agents—to the doors of the UN. . . .*

I shut off the tablet without finishing "my" column. I knew the rest of it would be even worse than the lead. What had they done to possibly the most significant news story and column of my lifetime?

Within thirty seconds I was on the phone to the City Desk. A sleepy kid answered. *"New York Standard."*

"It's Russo. Gimme Dickie."

"What?" the kid said, mystified. I then realized he thought it was a dirty call.

"Dickie Smalls. Gimme Dickie Smalls!"

"Oh. Mr. Smalls doesn't come in until nine A.M., Miss Russo," the kid said, finally figuring it out. "It's like five thirty."

"Then gimme his cell number."

"I don't know if I'm allowed to do that. . . ."

"Allowed? Who is this?"

"Smalls's cell is 917-221-9864," the anonymous copy kid spat out, terrified.

On the fourth ring, a half-asleep Dickie answered. "Yeah?"

"Worm! Traitor! What happened?" I yelled. "Who rewrote—no, let me rephrase that. Who wrote my goddamned column? This crap is the opposite of what I wrote."

Dickie was never one to back down. "Russo, it's five friggin' thirty. I was up all night with that goddamned column of yours. Don't like it? Take it up with the editor. Yeah. Bob himself rewrote. Said it was a piece of terrorist propaganda and when he saw you, he was going to kill you."

By 6:30 A.M. I was putting my iPad back into my red bag, and by 6:45 I whipped open my door and stopped dead at the sight of my captors standing there. I'd forgotten all about them in my fury—but on the upside, they did offer to drive me to work. I'd be on my own from then on, they said. Too much going on in the city for them to be concerned with one reporter. Good.

By 7:15 I was sitting outside Bob Brandt's office looking, but most definitely not feeling, like a kid outside the principal's office. I felt more like the kid who wants to blow up the school and is waiting to take the principal hostage.

Bob's secretary wasn't at her desk, but the morning editors were just starting to trickle in.

"Nice work on the Yusef column, Ali," Carly McNally, an editor, said as she passed by.

"Be sure to commend Bob," I said, the sneer rising to a level I didn't know I was capable of.

She turned back knowingly. Then out of conscience, I guess, she came back, put her hand on my shoulder, and said, "C'mon, honey. We're too old for this. Think before you go off the deep end. There aren't a whole lotta jobs out there anymore."

"None, actually," I answered, "but . . ." I didn't finish and just let the sentence hang in the air, because gossip is to a newsroom what Big Macs are to gluttons. We are reporters, so that's what we do—report. Even about one another. I could feel in my bones that I was about to do it again—really piss off another editor and end up on my ass. I couldn't stop, though. What they'd done was so wrong on so many levels.

At 8:20, Bob came slouching in carrying his coffee and cursing because he'd spilled it all over his new tie. I knew this was the worst possible time to confront him, but the destruction of my column—the turning it into a right-wing rant against fairness and justice—had to be addressed.

"Russo, Russo, Russo," Bob said wearily, spotting me clutching my iPad. "Well, you may as well come in and get it over with."

OK—that wasn't good. We went in and he sat behind his desk and put his feet up, leaving me to sit in the "bad student" chair in front. No matter, I still felt like the mad bomber despite the power-seating trick.

Bob went immediately on the attack. "I'd like to say 'nice job' but you should be down on your hands and knees thanking me for saving your sorry ass—and the good name of this paper! What you turned in was a lefty, amateur job that belonged in the NYU student newspaper.

"If I would have let it run as it was, we'd have picket lines around the block, and I'd be out there with them. What in hell were you thinking?"

"Wait a minute, here," I growled out, sounding possessed, fear and loathing rising in equal measure. "I should be the one asking that question! I mean, for whatever reason Demiel picked me—*me*—out of the crowd—"

He cut me off. "Demiel? So you do know him personally?"

"Are you crazy? Of course not. I never laid eyes on him except in photos and videos, as you well know!"

"After that column, I know nothing about you."

"Puleeze. Anyway, can I finish? As I was trying to say before you cut me off: Dammit, Bob, the world has the right to know exactly what I saw, how I saw it, what I felt, and how I was affected!"

He slammed his feet back onto the floor and slammed his fist onto the desk. "What are you—Patty Hearst? No. No more bullshit like that—and I don't give a rat's ass if the asshole confesses to you personally. We are not apologists for mass murderers who want to overthrow the U.S. and our right to worship as we please!"

He was up out of his seat, so red in the face he looked like he was on his tenth straight-up scotch at Langan's.

"Are you telling me," I screamed back, now standing

up facing him too, "that I'm not supposed to write the truth?"

"Not if the truth is a lie," he said implausibly, angrier than I'd ever seen him.

"I don't even know what the hell that means," I shot back.

He came around the desk and menacingly put his finger in my face and said low and dangerously, "It means *our* truth."

"I can't do *our* truth."

Bob turned his back. "Then you can't write for this paper."

Again. But this time it was probably finished, the end. Yesterday I had the "get" of gets, and today I was out with yesterday's paper.

As I was turning to go, he said, from behind his desk again, "You blew the biggest opportunity of your life, Russo. Maybe you never were as good as I thought you were."

"May I say the same about you?" I snapped, and then: "Can I get my stuff?"

"You can get whatever you can carry in your bag."

I went back through the newsroom to my desk, intending to pick up what few things I could carry, grateful that most of the staff wasn't in yet. Why I was embarrassed for being canned for doing the right thing, I don't know.

Not knowing what to pick up first, I hit the button for my voice mail, before the dreaded HR ladies cut that off and I wouldn't be able to access what was already there. Maybe somebody was offering me a job, what with my new notoriety and all.

"You have sixteen messages," the recorded voice informed me. "Your mailbox is full; please delete any unnecessary messages."

"Hey, Ali, Tony Boxer, CBS, here . . ." "Hey, Alessandra, Morgan Stiffe, BBC America . . ." "Miss Russo, I'm a reader, and I just want to say you are so coura—" "Alison Rizzo? Hold on for Pierce James . . ."

Then: "Ms. Russo? This is Maureen Wright-Lewis. . . ." I hit the rewind button. I wanted to hear that message again, make sure it was real. Wasn't that the name of a famous double agent who was involved—was it the Iran-Contra thing?—way back in the Reagan administration? I was a kid when it happened, but I remember either reading about it or seeing a PBS documentary about it. Wasn't she dead?

The message replayed. "Ms. Russo? This is Maureen Wright-Lewis. I'd very much like to speak with you. I have some information about the terrorist ben Yusef. I know who he actually is. Or I should say I know who he is not.

"You'll see that there is no identifying number on this phone. You can contact me at 012-292-766-8588. I think you need to hear what I have to say. And, Ms. Russo? Take care. You don't know what you're dealing with."

Huh? Either she'd started whispering at the end or the connection had turned bad. I couldn't be sure. *I don't know what I'm dealing with? I think I already figured that out, lady.*

I wrote down what I thought the number was on a scrap of paper, but when I tried to rewind, I heard, "This extension is no longer valid."

The dreaded HR machine had cut me off already. I had no job, but I did have a lead: Maureen Wright-Lewis. *Maybe I could get a magazine to assign me the story—if I had the right number.*

I Googled "Maureen Wright-Lewis" into the browser on my cell. Bingo! Big-time traitor—never caught. Double agent for the United States, who was accused of selling secrets to the Soviets. Traced as far as the netherworld of the backstreets of Luxor, Egypt. Alleged spottings over the decades in Baghdad, Jerusalem, and Tibet. The latest Wikipedia entries had her both dead and currently living in Fallujah. Right.

*She gets around pretty good for a—what?—dead sixty-whatever-year-old.*

## 8

Intrigued, however, and not wanting to read it on the small screen of my phone, I hit the power key on my desktop, and typed in my username and password.

"Invalid" popped up. Oh.

I guess Brandt was worried that I would, God forbid, steal my own e-mails. I'd become a non-person—one that Peg, the office manager, would "clean up," by packing up my things as though I'd never been here.

Was there really anything I couldn't live without on top of or inside that desk? Not anymore.

I rushed out through the newsroom past the dozen or so reporters who still, unaware of what had happened, either gave me half waves or "Hey, nice job" comments before turning back to their screens.

I walked as quickly as I could without raising suspicions and then bounded out the glass double doors and to the elevator bank, before HR had a chance to yank my press credentials. I knew the NYPD press pass and my standard ID door pass would be invalidated, but if I was successful in finding Wright-Lewis she'd never know they had been invalidated. But then again, she used to be a spy. . . .

I slowly made my way back to my apartment through the crowds that had re-formed while I was getting shit-canned, holding my press credentials high over my head. The police and agents along the way let me pass in the cordoned-off security lanes, but I wondered how much longer I could get away with it and whether I was committing some kind of crime in this terrorist-paranoid atmosphere.

I made it up to my apartment, opened the door, and walked in. The first thing I spotted was the overturned bookcase: Hundreds of books lay scattered; the coffee table, leg broken, was overturned and off to the side; clothes that had been in the front coat closet were thrown everywhere. Even the refrigerator was opened, with fresh produce and frozen food lying in piles on the floor, along with boxes of cereal, sugar, and you name it tossed from the cabinets.

I'd been to enough crime scenes to know that this was a professional trashing. Someone or *someones* wanted to scare me—let me know they'd been in and had violated my living space.

*Trust no one.*

I ran out, slamming the door behind me, and decided the monitored elevator was a better bet than the stairs, in case someone was lying in wait for me.

When the elevator door opened at "1," I called out, "Larry!" to the day doorman, who hadn't been on duty when I'd left earlier that morning. "My apartment's been broken into! Who came into the building?"

"No one, I swear, Miss Russo, no one," he said, rushing over and leaving the door unmanned. But we'd been notified that during the trial, the lobby entrance doors would be locked to keep protestors out. I could see the crowds outside pushing against the barricades.

I reached into my bag and rooted around until I found Sergeant Clements's card, grabbed my cell phone, and dialed her number. Nothing. Right. My cell phone was company-issue, and it too had been turned off.

I asked Larry for his phone and dialed her up. It went directly to voice mail. I walked outside in the crowd, holding up my press credentials, and flagged down the first cop I saw.

"Alessandra Russo, *The Standard*," I said, grabbing onto her uniform shirtsleeve to keep from getting shoved. "My apartment's been broken into," I screamed over the din of the crowd, who had picked up the chanting where they'd left off the day before.

"I'm sorry, ma'am, but . . ." she said, gesturing to the crowd. "The precinct is just—"

"I know where the precinct is!"

"I'm sorry . . ." she said, and turned back to the crowd.

I spotted a man watching me. Short sandy-to-gray hair, fifties, well-cut suit. Not good. Was he the guy who'd trashed my place?

I pushed my way through the crowd more aggressively, heading for the Seventeenth Precinct on East Fifty-first Street, but the crowd was going in the opposite direction, heading right toward the UN, and it would have been like pushing back a wave.

The man was as far from me as he had been before—about ten feet. What the hell? No one looked like that except—what?—German garmentos or maybe the kind of slick assassins you see only in the movies. I had to get out of his line of vision. Chances were good he wasn't following me so he could knock off line-for-line copies of my old leather jacket for the Düsseldorf runway shows.

Holding my press creds up, I let the crowd pull me

onto Second, and pushed my way onto Forty-seventh Street. As I neared Mary's Garden, I could see Father Eugene inside the gates, waving frantically at me. How did he know I was coming?

I could see the "German" reaching into his jacket. Je-*sus*!

Eugene reached his arms outside the gate and grabbed onto my jacket sleeve to pull me up to it. He opened the gate a hair—just enough for me to get leverage to squeeze inside, the gate locking behind us.

"My savior!" I exclaimed.

"Hardly! There are only two of them. I'm just a priest," he laughed.

I wouldn't think about that remark until later.

## 9

I shook myself off like a wet dog and tried to get my equilibrium back as we headed to the rectory living room. I collapsed into the fat couch, and Sadowski handed me a cup of coffee. "Light, one Sweet'N Low, right?"

"Too bad you're a priest," I cracked, feeling embarrassed that I'd let my jaded-reporter persona creep back in with someone who'd been so kind to me.

He laughed. "Good thing I never thought that."

"Father—" I started to say, when he stopped me.

"Eugene."

"Okay. So Eugene," I blurted out, trying like hell to not cry, "my apartment was broken into."

"What? When?"

"While I was off getting canned this morning," I said, feeling suddenly overwhelmed.

He came around and put his arm around me.

"Well, that stinks," he said, oddly unsurprised. I guessed he'd heard everything as a priest. "What did they get?"

"Just my identity," I answered; a bad attempt at sardonic humor.

"Holy crap," he said, slapping his forehead. "Your license, passport, credit cards?"

"No, no. I have them all with me," I said, tapping my bag. "Even my passport. I stuck it in the bag yesterday in case I'd need extra ID at the UN. I meant my job. I kind of identify myself, you know, with the job. . . ."

"Yes. Of course. We all do. But you're more than a job, Alessandra," Sadowski said. "You, dear girl, are very special."

"Was. *Was* very special . . ."

"Are you kidding? You, not your friend—*you*—were picked out of all the millions of people yesterday by ben Yusef himself."

"Yeah, well tell that to my boss. My ex-boss, I mean. I was picked by a mass murderer as his—what?—girlfriend? My luck—it's the first time a man ever picked me over Dona. That special pick cost me plenty."

"Not as much as you'll gain from it."

"Huh? No disrespect, Father, but I don't get you. The guy's a damned terrorist killer and, just for starters? He particularly hates your religion. That doesn't bother you? And don't tell me 'Turn the other cheek.' "

"No? Why not? Isn't that what my religion is based upon?"

"May I remind you of the Crusades?"

"Yes. Terrible. Many fought back. Kept relics out of the hands of the infidels. . . ."

I continued as though I hadn't heard him: "I certainly don't want to tell you your business, but Jesus was an itinerate preacher whose death went unmarked at first. No? Do you honestly think somebody chopped that one cross to make souvenirs? I'm sure they crucified fifty more guys on it before it got used for firewood."

Sadowski grinned. "O ye of little faith . . ."

"That's the second time I've heard that in two days."

"Maybe third time's the charm?"

"No," I chided back, before the conversation turned serious again. "I don't try to get you to play for my side, do I?"

"Okay, okay, you're right. But no matter what your religion, you will admit that Jesus died for all of us. For all of our sins."

"Maybe He died for yours," I said, getting annoyed now. "But I wasn't born thousands of years ago, so you can't peg that on me. And maybe He died for His own sins. Ever think of that?"

Sadowski looked genuinely pained by my sarcasm. He stiffened and just said, "Let me ask you another hypothetical. What if this man, this ben Yusef, actually did turn out to be a new Jesus. Would you believe it then?"

I stared at him. "I think you need to seek professional help. You sound nuts."

He smiled. "Okay, but remember, Jesus was a seditionist set up by the powers-that-be back then. The Jewish priests and their Roman rulers."

"You can't be serious. You're buying into the conspiracy theorists' nonsense? You?"

"No, but you have to wonder. Okay, back to reality. Your job and now your apartment. Are you sure they didn't get anything?"

"Not sure. I ran outta there like my backside was on fire. I mean, it was terrifying. And the cops? Way too busy with a few million lunatics to investigate. I couldn't even get to the precinct to make a report.

"The goons who broke in made a huge mess—trashed the place. It was like they wanted me to know that they'd been in there, whoever 'they' are." Then I remembered the Wright-Lewis call and, switching gears, asked, "Can I use your phone? Mine is company-issue and I'm temporarily without visible means of communication."

He answered by saying instead, "You really should find out if they got anything. . . ."

"I don't really care right now." The man was a real one-track-mind kind of guy, I thought, so I reached into my bag and pulled out my iPad. "All I care about is right here."

He let out a breath and visibly relaxed. "Well, that's a damned relief."

"Right," I said, trying to get him focused on my life crisis, of which the apartment break-in was only one part.

"And you're still wearing that same scarf from yesterday, right? Nobody gave you a new one or anything, right?"

"What are you—the check-in guy at the airport?"

"It's just that, I mean, as a reporter and all, you have to keep your stuff private. And maybe you can use that scarf someday for DNA evidence."

I looked at him, puzzled. "It's Father Hercule Poirot. Who knew?"

"Sorry, I guess I am playing private eye, but you never know about these things."

"How about concerning yourself with this one instead: ben Yusef's words to me were 'Go forth for I am six.' Do you know of any theological meaning to 'I am six'?"

"Hmmm. As a priest, no. As a spiritualist, yes."

I looked at him, cocked my head, and smirked. "Are you pulling one over on me?"

"No. I'm not so one-sided as my calm, handsome demeanor would indicate," he joshed.

Then: "Well, six six six is the 'number of the beast,' or the Anti-christ, as you know. But the number six alone has a totally different meaning. Six is the number that is supposed to help a person unfold solutions to mysteries in a calm, rational way. It also means 'enlightenment,' or a light on the path to solving a spiritual dilemma. Like whether a lapsed Catholic should come back to Christ, perhaps?"

"'Oy,' as they say in Latin," I joked back. "Forget I asked."

He had another thought. "When you spoke of the Crusades—ever hear of the Albigensian Crusade against the Cathars?"

"Who?"

"A Gnostic Christian sect that flourished in the Middle Ages. Historians divide the Albigensian crusade into six phases—if that means anything . . ."

"Talk about obscure. No, I don't think so," I said, my sarcasm dripping, even though he certainly didn't deserve it.

*Damn! Stop it—he's a nice guy.*

I dropped my attitude, pulled out the note I'd made with Wright-Lewis's prepaid phone number, and looked at it instead.

"You ever hear of an area code like this?" I asked him as I handed him the paper.

"No, where is it?"

"Don't know. But if I got it right, it's the number of a woman named Maureen Wright-Lewis."

"The spy?" he asked, visibly astonished.

"Yes, and how do you know that, and why do you look so shocked?"

"Do I look shocked," he said, not as a question. "I'm a history buff."

*Right.*

I looked at him, more confused than certain of what this guy was all about, and punched in the number, sure I'd written it down incorrectly anyway.

It picked up after one ring. Sadowski had moved to the edge of his seat in the chair directly across from me. He was trying to listen in, I was certain of it.

"Hello, Ms. Russo," came the voice on the other end of the phone.

Jackpot! I had gotten the number right after all. "Ms. Wright-Lewis?" I wasn't sure if it was her secretary or the woman herself.

"Yes, I'm here."

"If I may ask where 'here' is?"

"Rhinebeck, New York."

"I thought you—"

She cut me off. "Do you know Rhinebeck?"

"Yes, I do. About ninety miles north of the city up on the Taconic . . ."

It may as well have been in Europe if it meant getting out of this insanely cordoned-off city. How the hell was she in the USA?

"I'm in Rhinecliff, actually. Tiny little village next to Rhinebeck. You need to drive up to see me," she commanded.

"Well, I'm in Midtown Manhattan right now," I explained. "It's like a city under siege. It *is* a city under siege actually. . . ."

"Yes. I know that," she said quietly, her voice urgent. "Still, I need to see you. Today. It's about ben Yusef. He's not who you think he is, and he's not the one who should be on trial. When can you be here?"

She left the reporter part of me no choice.

"I'll try my best, Ms. Wright-Lewis. But besides the city being cordoned off, you know, ever since what happened to me yesterday, I'm kind of under siege myself. I can't go anywhere without being mobbed or followed. But if it's that important . . ."

"Yes, it is that important." A pause. "Here's the address. Have you a pen?"

"Hold on a sec," I said, reaching for my pen. "What's the address please?"

"It's Twenty Grinnell Street, Rhinecliff, New York," she answered. "When may I expect you, Ms. Russo?"

"Well, like I said, Midtown is cordoned off, and I can't get to my car, which is parked in the garage under my apartment building, because my street is closed to traffic. . . ."

"I'm sure you'll find a way," she said.

*Man!* "I will certainly do my best," I answered. "But I think I might be like a hippie trying to get to Woodstock back in the day."

I don't know if she heard that or not, because I realized that she was no longer on the line. Nonetheless I said, "Hello? Ms. Wright-Lewis? Hello?" Nothing.

"That's odd," I said to Father Sadowski. "She wants to see me and she wants me to drive to Rhinecliff. How in hell am I supposed to do that? I couldn't get my car out of my building garage if I were Jesus Himself."

"I have a car," he offered, "but it's parked in Harlem. Cheaper there."

I thought about it a minute and said, "I guess I could take the subway to Harlem . . . but I'm sure the goons are waiting for me, though. . . ."

His eyes twinkled. "They aren't waiting for a couple of priests walking on Forty-eighth and Lexington," he said. "Sit tight a minute."

Sadowski left me sitting there and went out the rectory door, which led, I presumed, into the Church of the Holy Family proper. He returned about a half hour later dressed in his blacks with starched clerical collar and requisite big black priest shoes.

He was holding a dry-cleaning bag in one hand and a beat-up shopping bag in the other.

"I figured the priest thing was too corny," he offered, handing me the bag. "So I lifted one of the nun's habits. Some of the young nuns like to dress up. Makes them feel more . . . I don't know. Anyway, you can slip the whole habit over your regular clothes."

"Me as a nun? The church might collapse," I said.

"We should get a move on," he urged, ignoring my quip.

I slipped the nun's garment over my head and stepped into the bathroom, where I scrubbed my face clean, slipped on the black stacked heels, which were somehow exactly my size, then some black sheer panty hose (*Isn't panty hose how I got into this mess?* I thought) and a pair of horrible no-prescription lens granny sunglasses, and slipped my jeans back on. The last item I attempted was the starched wimple. I tried keeping the hard white vinyl headband in place on my forehead while I pulled on the veil, but then realized the veil came first. I tucked in all my hair and was happy to see Velcro tabs at the back that would keep the damned thing from falling off.

"Voilà!" I said, happily emerging from the bathroom with a curtsy.

"Dear God," Sadowski said. "Put on your rosary, Sister!"

When I looked totally stumped as to how one would do such a thing, he stepped in and draped it for me. "Thanks, I almost hung myself trying to get this veil on."

"Let's go," he said, handing me my red satchel. I put my Fryes and leather jacket into the shopping bag and then put a newspaper on top.

He looked me over and shook his head. "Hmmm. Not very nun-like, but too late to do anything about that." We began to head toward the door that led to the stairs that led to the tunnel that led to Forty-eighth Street.

"Sadowski," I said, pausing midstep, "why are you doing this? What do you care if I get an interview with someone who nobody's heard about in decades who lives God-knows-where doing God-knows-what?"

"I'm living vicariously?"

"Right. Not to look a gift horse, and it's a big gift—but, I mean, why have you rescued me from mad crowds both times I was in trouble, and now this? And the car and all."

"I'm a priest. I help people," he said, his hand on the knob of the door.

"Pardon my Latin, but bullshit."

He opened the cellar door and flicked on the wall switch. "Guess the light's broken," he said, as I followed him through the door and down the pitch-black stairwell, beginning to think that maybe this wasn't a great idea.

He must have picked up my concern, because he called back, "Don't worry, God is on your side."

Oh. "Next time he chooses up sides, you think I can be spared from His team?" I said, waiting for an answer that didn't come.

"Eugene? Father Sadowski?" I heard him mount the stairs and open the door. Then I heard it slam shut.

## 10

I tried to feel my way along the wall. It was damp and felt cool-going-to-cold. Like a tomb. *Like the tomb of Jesus Himself,* I thought for no reason, and I suddenly had an overwhelming need to get out of there.

I felt my way along the damp walls and reached the stairs. I mounted a few steps, forgetting that I was wearing the damned habit, and caught a stacked heel on the hem. I fell backward probably six or so steps and hit my head against the rear stone wall. *OK, I really, really need to get outta here,* I thought, frantically rubbing the back of my head over the veil. Was I bleeding? I didn't feel anything wet, so I stood back up carefully and felt for the stairs again.

I made my way back up and reached for the doorknob. Locked.

Panic hit in a way that I hadn't experienced since I let go of my mom's hand at the Macy's Thanksgiving Day Parade when I was seven. The difference was on Thanksgiving my mom had reached through the crowd and grabbed me up in about ten seconds. There was no one to grab me now—although I feared that right outside that locked door there may well, in fact, be two people: one in Armani and one in a clerical collar. Was I simply having an anxiety attack, or were my reporter instincts taking over?

*Be rational.*

I moved back down the stairs and felt my way through the tunnel and up the opposite stairs to the rectory door. Locked again. Why would Eugene lock me in?

Just then I heard the other door opening on its old hinges. Sadowski called out, "Alessandra? Where are you? It's safe. Come on, we don't have time."

In full anxiety attack mode now, I heard him climbing down the stairs.

"Oh, boy," I heard him mutter. Then, "Alessandra! Dammit. Where are you? Alessandra!"

I was barely breathing, or trying my hardest not to, my heart pounding so hard I was sure it was echoing around the tunnel.

"Alessandra!" *Ms. Russo, you don't know what you're dealing with.*

He called out, "I had to check to see if there was anybody out there."

At that, the lights came blazing back on, and there he was standing right at the bottom of the steps below me. Holding a gun.

I let out a cry, and he looked down and said, "Oh. This."

I tried to make myself as small as possible as he started up the stairs. "I went back into the rectory to get it," he said. "In case—"

"In case of what?" I whispered, my voice almost leaving me completely.

"In case the goons who trashed your place were out there." He was three steps from me now.

"It's all clear," he said, holding out his free hand.

"No!" I said.

He seemed surprised. "I told you, there's nobody out in the school or the yard. It's okay. Really."

"What do you want? Why are you doing this? You have a gun and you locked me in."

"No," he said, dragging out the word. "I locked *them out,* in case there *was* a them, that is. But there isn't. Come on now . . . just step down toward me. . . ."

"No."

"What choice do you have? You can trust me, or you can stay there until you get older than the wine."

"Not funny."

"But I think you have more important things to do."

"What?"

"Alessandra, Alessandra, Alessandra," he said more like a frustrated dad than a frustrated father. "Haven't you started to figure anything out yet? Me? I think you're the one who gets to tell the story. . . ."

"I don't know what you mean!" I looked at him, one hand held out like a lifeline, while in the other he held a gun that could end my life.

When I didn't move, he raised the hand with the gun, as I let out a groan. "Oh, God . . ."

"Here," he said. "Take it."

Was he going to fire the instant I grabbed the gun? Self-defense and all that? With no choice, I took the gun from him. Just like that.

He took my free hand. "Come on now, we don't have much time."

I had no idea what he was talking about. Time? As of that morning, I either had too much time or none at all. I slipped the gun into my red bag and held on to his hand. Crazy? Definitely.

We walked through the church's tunnel once more, came up the opposite stairs, and emerged into the same area we'd walked through the night before. School was not in session. The crowds made it too dangerous.

Sadowski and I walked through the play area, filled with the overflow crowd avoiding the construction site, onto Forty-eighth Street.

How can life go on normally when everything in yours is in upheaval?

For now we were just two clerics walking through. There was a full contingent of guards at the Libya House across the street where Gadhafi used to stay when he gave his rants at the United Nations.

If I'd thought that a press pass helped in parting the crowds, it was nothing compared to a nun's habit. Nobody messed with the sisters. The sea of humans parted like the Red Sea before Moses. Sadowski chuckled at my reaction. I was starting to trust him again.

"There are some advantages to a life of celibacy," he yelled above the noise of the protesters.

We managed to turn onto Second Avenue, push through the walls of people, and finally make it to Grand Central. There were police posted at every entrance. I boldly pushed forward and stood on the line to get in.

"Ah, you can't pass through the metal detectors," Sadowski reminded me. "The gun?"

"Oh. What now?"

I felt him reach into my bag and slip the gun out and under his cassock.

"How will you get on the subway with the gun?" I asked.

"Clearly, I won't. You're on your own. The parking garage is West 125th Street between Adam Clayton and Malcolm X. You can't miss it. Well, you could, but most people wouldn't." He handed me a keyless remote thing and said, "It's spot number G156—self-park."

When I was near the front of the line, the priest handed

me his iPhone. "Good luck. And remember, God is on your side!" In a second he was swallowed up by the crowd—just another cleric in a city full of them. I climbed down into the belly of the station until I got to the "7" train's dirty platform, where I peered down the tracks for an oncoming train, and then back around the platform for—what?—I didn't really know. The "German"?

The train finally roared into the station, and hundreds of passengers rushed out as an equal number rushed back in. It was beyond "SRO," so I planted my fat stacked heels on the floor, grabbed a pole, and held on, making sure not to curse un-nun-like at anyone who would have dared to push me. But no one did. It was the habit. In fact, two people got up to offer me their seats. I took one, I'm ashamed to say.

I switched to the "D" train at the Bryant Park station. I was a nun—not a reporter. *Don't call attention to yourself,* I kept repeating like a mantra.

Again several people who'd probably gone to Catholic school offered up their seats. The fear of nuns runs deep.

I exited at 125th Street, Harlem's busiest, where fast-food chain restaurants thrive along with the local fried-chicken joints, coffee shops, and mom-and-pop clothing stores blaring old-school funk out of their exterior speakers.

I almost cried at the real life out there that had nothing to do with the unreality that my life had become.

I walked a couple of blocks in my nun's habit noticing how people nodded and smiled and showed the kind of respect that New Yorkers just don't give to people wearing normal clothes.

In the middle of the block, I saw the big illuminated plastic UPARKIT.COM sign mounted sideways to the building. A low-rent joint if ever I'd seen one. It would be safer to park on an abandoned street. Didn't Sadowski ever watch TV? Everyone who walks into a parking garage on TV gets beaten, killed, and/or raped.

Luckily the G in G156 stood for "ground," so at least I didn't have to climb any stairwells.

*Who'd rape a nun? Oh, right, Riverside, California, Chicago, and here in Harlem, when they left that nun carved up with twenty-seven crosses decades ago—case study Journalism 101. Don't think about that now. . . .*

A big brand-new shiny black Cadillac SUV—like the kind the mayor drove around in—was in the space.

This had to be wrong. It was like renting a Smart car and getting a Rolls by mistake.

I clicked the key-lock button for the hell of it and heard the door unlock. I jumped in as quickly as possible, heard it lock, and removed the habit, keeping on the wimple. The GPS lit up, and I punched in "Grinnell St., Rhinecliff, NY." "No address found" was the answer.

Hoping I'd figure out all the electronics as I drove, I pulled out into the bright light of day, turned east onto 125th Street and from there over the Willis Avenue Bridge, onto the Deegan, past Yankee Stadium, and onto the Taconic Parkway.

Checking my rearview mirror, expecting a tail—the "German" maybe—I saw nothing. But, hey, I'd been on enough surveillances myself to know that meant nothing. A tail was never detectable unless an amateur was at the wheel or the professional driver wanted the tail to be seen.

Twenty minutes into the drive north I finally relaxed, fairly sure I was OK. I removed the wimple, hit "cruise control," and let go and let God, as Sadowski might have said.

I hit the satellite button for Fox all-news radio to catch up on the morning's events at the tribunal.

Whose voice did I hear but Dona's! *Radio?* She was reporting live from the UN. Her firsthand, eyewitness reports yesterday on the tribunal must have made her "sourced" enough to take the lead for all of the Fox outlets. *At least something good came out of this fiasco,* I thought. I also felt a twinge of jealousy. *She gets to lead and I get led out the door. And I'm the one he "chose"?*

Her first words snapped me back to reality. "It's been a wild, wild day so far at the trial of suspected terror mastermind Demiel ben Yusef. As of now, we do not have an answer as to why ben Yusef spoke as though his biological father were still alive. According to his lawyers, Demiel ben Yusef was either an orphan or raised by a single mother, who also is now dead. If you recall, in court yesterday ben Yusef had handed his attorney a slip of paper, written in Aramaic, which stated that he would only answer to his father.

"When court resumed this morning, Chief Judge Fatoumata Bagayoko addressed that by informing the defendant and his attorneys that since the man on trial has, on record, no living relatives, and we know that his father is dead these past thirty-three years, he must have been talking about the 'Master of the Universe' or 'God.' In that case, she went on, and I quote, 'That means Mr. ben Yusef, that you will have to answer to this court, because that is the closest you are going to get to God. In this lifetime, at any rate.' The remark caused even the assembled heads of state to snicker.

"However, not everyone was amused. A reporter from Aljazeera, Abdul-Basit Hassan, yelled out, 'And not in the next lifetime, either, traitor of Allah!' Again, for the second day, near rioting broke out as Hassan was grabbed kicking and screaming by UN security forces and escorted out to a loud chorus of boos by reporters in the press area.

"It is unclear at this time if the words written in Aramaic correspond to or are connected to those that he whispered to *New York Standard* reporter Alessandra Russo at the opening of yesterday's tribunal, since she was only able to repeat them phonetically, which was how she wrote them in her column. If so, the implications are great, because, according to at least one linguistic expert at the United Nations with whom I spoke, it is possible that he was trying to give her some sort of coded message. Reporting live from the United Nations, this is Dona Grimm."

*Message, my ass. The whole brouhaha was over a clichéd phrase like that? Jesus! Holy crap!*

Comfortable now with the fancy car, I clicked on the priest's iPod icon on the dashboard, figuring I'd get Gregorian chants. I hit "favorites," and Sadowski's voice filled the car.

"Hello, Alessandra," the recording began. "By now you know this is more than blind good luck. . . ."

## 11

"Good luck?" I shouted to the invisible Sadowski. "Bastard! You set me up, didn't you?" as though this were a two-way.

*What's he up to? He was probably responsible for the effing break-in!*

Sadowski's voice continued; clearly the recording hadn't heard me.

"Well, despite what you are thinking right at this moment, Alessandra, the fact that you are sitting in this car means that your luck is not just good, but so extraordinary that it took thousands of years for you to be right here, right now. Can you believe that?"

*No!*

"In fact," he continued, "we don't even know why you're in this car or where you are supposed to be headed. We just had a car standing by in case. Frankly, until yesterday, we thought it was meant to be your buddy, Dona. You weren't even on our radar. But it's a wonderful, wonderful surprise, by the way," and then he cackled. Cackled!

"Wonderful? Maniac," I called out, hoping that

somehow he could hear me. I was sure there was a camera somewhere and I was being watched.

*And I was worried about the damned "German"? He'd probably sent the "German" just to scare me into this whole situation. Maybe even the Maureen Wright-Lewis call was part of the setup. What a schmuck.*

"Wherever this car is taking you, we wish you Godspeed," he went on in his best sermonizer voice. "Oh, and that phone I gave you? It's a satellite phone with a secure line. There's a charger in the glove box. Please take it out and put it in that red bag of yours. Remember to do that, will you?

"Anyway, my number's programmed in, as well as others you may need on your journey. God! I hate saying things like that. I sound like the secret love child of Dr. Phil and Oprah." Another giggle. *A regular laugh riot, Father Lying Bastard!*

Then: "If you need money, there's an ATM card in the dash." *Why would I need your money?*

Then the message went dead. I tried flicking on the "playlists" button, but I nearly hit a deer, so I figured I'd look for more when I got wherever I was going. I hit the dashboard phone icon and then "contacts," and it lit up with about ten names and numbers. I hit "Eugene" and it immediately began to ring although a number didn't show on the screen.

"Hello, Alessandra," his voice mail chirped from the speaker. "I can't imagine, frankly, that I'm not sitting here waiting for your call. But clearly I'm not. Maybe I'm serving mass; it could be the only reason I'm not answering the phone. I will call you back in a second if I'm not at the altar, and depending on the service, anywhere from a half hour to an hour, if I am. Got to keep up appearances, you know." *Beeeeeep.*

"No. I don't know!" I screamed. "You call me, and you call me immediately."

*Immediately must be different in the priest realm,* I thought, when forty miles became ninety miles without a return call, and I soon saw the exit that would lead to Rhinebeck.

I turned off and found myself on one of those long stretches of road that must not have changed since the 1960s. Neither did the people at the roadside stands selling organic and hydroponic vegetables in their tie-dyed shirts.

I followed the signs to Rhinecliff, and at the next sign, made a sharp turn up a one-lane road, but that seemed to simply go back down again to loop around a sad little park. After two attempts, I stopped at the Rhinecliff Bar & Grill, an old wooden place that looked like it was about to collapse. Three guys who looked like they drank for a living were belly up to the rail, under signs reading 110% AMERICAN and WE DON'T SERVE FOREIGN BEER AND WE DON'T SERVE FOREIGNERS! Another guy, shooting pool by himself, eyed me like fresh meat.

"Can you tell me where Grinnell Street is?" I asked loudly.

"Nope," said one guy, revealing a mouth that had fewer teeth than a newborn. The others looked at each other like I'd asked where one could buy a Democratic campaign button. "Never heard of it," said another.

The bartender, a chubby woman who should have been jolly but wasn't, said, "I know where that is."

"Great," I said, then realizing the directions weren't free, continued: "And I'd sure love a cold beer. Got a Miller Lite draught?"

"Yup," she answered without affect, pouring the beer

and pointing up. "Just hook a right. You musta hooked a left. Then go straight up. Can't miss it."

"Thanks," I said, gulping down the beer, which tasted better than any beer I'd ever had in my life. Either I didn't realize how parched I was or they put something in the beer that made people never want to leave the bar, even when their teeth fell out.

I asked for another, finished it, left a generous tip, and walked out feeling like I'd just been on the set of *Barfly* minus Mickey Rourke.

Back in the Caddy, I "hooked a right," or what I assumed was "hooking," since it seemed more like bearing, and the road turned suddenly steep. *I hope the formerly dead lady spy has a driver.*

When I got to the top, there was a road with houses on one side, and a grassy area on the other that ended in a cliff that looked like it fell straight down to the Hudson River. There weren't many houses, and they didn't have numbers for the most part, so I drove as slowly as I could with my head out the window.

I saw an old metal number "20" on the doorjamb of a house on the right, although the sun was beginning to set, so it was hard to know for sure.

I drove the car up its steep driveway, set the emergency brake, got out, and walked across the lawn to a little cedar-shingle cottage with a vine-covered trellis over the dark green wooden door. I lifted the old brass knocker and knocked.

In a few seconds, the door opened and a quite tall, thin African-American woman, still gorgeous in her (my guess) mid-to-late sixties, stood before me. Not the bent old lady I was expecting. She was barefoot, wearing a beautifully cut navy blue pantsuit and starched, expensive-looking white man-tailored blouse, her salt-and-pepper hair pulled back severely in a ponytail.

"Miss Russo?" she asked, opening the door wider after inspecting my face. "I'm Maureen Wright-Lewis. Won't you please come in?"

I followed her into what felt like another age. Her spotless living room was filled with American antiques, authentic-looking Hudson Valley paintings. A black lacquer Steinway upright piano had an enormous jewel-encrusted cross on an elaborate stand placed on top, the way Liberace had kept that giant candelabrum on his grand piano.

Without asking, she left and came back carrying a small tea tray and a plate of cookies. She poured out two cups of tea and actually asked, "One cube or two?" as she wielded a beautiful antique set of silver sugar tongs. "It's apple tea, so you may want to taste it first."

*Must be from one of those organic granola-cruncher farms up here.*

"It's not made here," she offered, seeming to read my mind.

"It doesn't need sugar," I politely answered, refraining from asking about its origin. Secrecy and intimidation were clearly still part of the old dame's game.

She offered the plate of cookies. "Very good, by the way."

I took one, and suppressed my reporter's urge to ask her to skip the small talk and tell me what I was doing nearly one hundred miles from the city. Or, more important, what she was doing here—a spy convicted in absentia.

She put down her teacup and looked at me. I reached into my bag and pulled out my reporter's notebook, knowing she was about to spill whatever beans she had, and hoping she wouldn't tell me to put the notebook away.

Instead, she said, "Fine, but no recording. Do you mind?"

By that she meant, "Do you mind if I frisk you?" which she did, indicating that I stand. After the pat down, she searched my red satchel.

When she was satisfied that I wasn't carrying, recording, or whatever-ing, she looked me in the eye and began. "Ms. Russo, when Demiel ben Yusef kissed you yesterday? It was the sign that many in the world have been waiting for—the one he'd choose."

"What do you—" I started to say, but she cut me off quickly.

"Excuse me, I'm not finished. Thirty-three years ago, President Reagan was in office and I was at the agency."

"Yes, I know. . . ."

Ignoring me, she went on, "We did something that I still haven't come to grips with. . . ."

"I assume—"

Again she cut me off. *Slow down, let her talk.*

And she did: "No, it's not what you assume at all. At any rate, at first I knew—*knew*—this ben Yusef person couldn't be who—*what*—he says he is."

"Sorry, but I don't understand. You mean that business about how he's the Second Coming? Like the communion host, he represents the flesh and blood of Jesus?"

"No, not represents, Ms. Russo. He, or someone, was actually born from the blood of Jesus." I tried not to let what she'd just said knock me over. Had this woman of the steel-trap mind gone senile?

"Real blood? You mean like that kid in India who has the stigmata, or that girl in Florida who cries blood?"

"I'm trying to be clear here, so I'd appreciate it if you would knock off the mocking tone," she sniped.

She got up, walked to the wooden wall cabinet, found a bottle of Scotch, and poured herself half a tumbler, then said matter-of-factly, "You see, Ms. Russo, I was in charge of the elimination."

"Elimination?"

"Don't act dense. The assassinations."

"Plural? Who were you in charge of killing?"

"Jesus and His family."

## 12

"What?" was all I could croak out.

"I said, I was charged with killing Jesus and His kin. By order of the director of the CIA, with, I always assumed, the tacit knowledge of the president. Of course, I had no direct knowledge of that."

"Ahh, just to be clear here, Miss Wright-Lewis? You're telling me that you think that Jesus walked the earth thirty-three years ago?"

"No. Not walked. He was just an infant when He—or some male infant that was supposed to be Him—was slated to be eliminated," she said, as though she had been speaking of any of the hundreds of average orders issued at the agency on any single day.

*10:34 A.M., install bugs in the Soviet embassy; 11:15, kill Baby Jesus; 3:15 P.M., arrest international gunrunner . . .*

Ignoring my upraised eyebrows, she continued, her voice getting more vehement, as though letting go of this loopy secret was somehow a relief.

"Do you remember that there had been a blackout thirty-three years ago that affected parts of Europe and the Mideast? Oh, probably not. You were just a baby yourself."

"I was nine, actually, but no, I didn't know about it."

"Well, that was the day we got confirmation. . . ." She poured herself another large one. "I assume you're driving, so I won't offer you any," she said. And didn't.

"Confirmation . . . about . . . ?"

She knocked the Scotch back straight, sat down, and continued. ". . . That a baby had been born. Not a human baby—no, in fact, it was the first human clone. Illegal, of course."

"A clone," I said, suddenly fascinated. "I've heard there have been experiments but none had actually been successful."

"Well, it did happen. In Turkey. And this baby? It was supposedly born from the blood of Jesus Christ."

I stopped writing and just looked at her. *Oh, crap. What a bunch of crap.*

She read my mind, or probably my smirk.

"I just, I'm—"

"I know what you are. Frankly, I never trusted the press, never will. . . ."

"You aren't the first person who's said that to me. I mean about being chosen. And you certainly aren't the first person who told me she hates the press."

"And I won't be the last," she said calmly. "Look, I don't know why he, they, whomever, chose you. Maybe they figure you'll be able to dig out the truth. Maybe they want to use you."

"I beg your pardon?"

"Oh, please. These days everyone from terrorists to disgraced politicians plays the media like a video game— and for the most part even the most desperate fringe bloggers and conspiracy theorists have worldwide access and get attention. Maybe the gods play you, too," she added, teasing me. Well, I thought she was teasing me at least.

"So it makes sense he or they picked a reporter—one that supposedly has that oxymoron, 'journalistic integrity.'"

I actually laughed. *Our truth.*

"I know what you're thinking about me," she went on to say. "Let's just say I took one for the team. After that, they naturally wanted me out of the way. I'd done my job thirty-three years ago, but then they doubted me—thought I might be, well, it doesn't matter. Yes, I was the one responsible for setting up the kill for this Jesus thing. I mean, cloning the Son of God? The implications seemed horrifying." More horrifying than infanticide, I wanted to add, but didn't.

"I'd been tracking a report on the birth of a baby supposedly cloned from the DNA of Jesus, when a blackout hit the Middle East and elsewhere. And it had happened at almost the same moment that a new star became visible. Religious fanatics in Turkey were already saying it signaled the end of the world. Little did they know . . ." She paused, remembering.

"I was already in Turkey trying to track down the cloning lab—and that's where the birth occurred. Officials you've never heard of—or most people had never heard of—from the Soviet Union, China, most of Europe, Israel, and even an operative from the PLO—all met together, in a secret location in Istanbul. The pope had sent his Vatican agent, Cardinal Riccardo Renzi. We were actually meeting around gas lanterns—not for the intrigue but because that area was blacked out—and somehow they kept this part contained—not even batteries were working.

"The cardinal announced that he believed that the

birth of what he called a 'devil spawn'—the clone of Jesus Himself—had been born."

*She didn't really say that, did she?* "Devil spawn" and "Jesus clone"?

I leaned even more forward in my chair. I needed, wanted, to catch every syllable, as I wrote furiously in my notebook.

"But what about the president of the United States? What was his position?"

"It was not within my purview to ask such a question, nor would I have asked even if it were. Suffice to say he was a member of the nonradical arm of the Fellowship. Or at least he attended their prayer breakfasts."

"The Fellowship?"

"The White House Prayer Breakfasts are probably what you've heard about."

"With all due respect, ma'am," I continued, "how could a prayer group who prays for breakfast even have a radical arm?"

"*Arm* is probably the wrong term. *Fringe element* is more like it. They call themselves Face of God Fellowship. Their detractors just call them the 'Black Robes.'"

I looked at her inquisitively.

"There were a lot of judges allegedly involved."

My mind immediately shot to the judicial panel as they walked in yesterday, resplendent in their black robes, and to my odd, out-of-nowhere comments to Dona about how they looked like Inquisitionists.

I refocused. I was there to do an interview, not to muse on life.

"All right, then. I can understand, if such an event did really happen, how there would be some, ah, sign that religious crazies around the world would interpret as evil or something but . . . but why would the United States get involved?"

"For one thing," she answered rapidly, "the Girl whom they'd impregnated was American."

*You people killed an American's baby?* I couldn't control the look of disgust on my face.

She ignored me. "And let us not forget what happened to you yesterday, Ms. Russo—and you are as typically American as they come. Third generation?"

"Fourth."

"Sorry. I digressed. Anyway, somehow 'it' had been born, and the cardinal told us that their intent had been to eliminate it in utero—but they failed. He said that the pope himself believed that such a creature would have been a being without a *soul,* someone who could grow up, the pope feared, to destroy the world!"

"So abortion was condoned by the Vatican? That's almost more incomprehensible than the cloning of Jesus," I said, unable to control the snarkiness in my voice.

"Don't be condescending, Ms. Russo," she shot back, staring me in the eye.

"Anyway, once our sources confirmed the pregnancy—we didn't know where exactly yet—so many of the world's security agencies were ordered to combine forces and find this thing. That's how significant we all believed this event to be. And, yes, for a few brief hours all the conflicts were put aside; this was just a few months before Israel invaded Lebanon, remember. The representatives of several enemy nations were able this one time to make a pact together. It was unanimously agreed that the baby and its mother had to be eliminated before this thing could wreak havoc."

*OK, that's two Americans so far.*

"My immediate boss, whose name is not relevant, was quite confident that he had a personal relationship with Jesus—and not the new one, either," she actually joked.

"He, my boss that is, *was* born-again. The Reverend

Bill Teddy Smythe, of the Light of God Tabernacle in Plano, Texas, became his pastor."

"Excuse me for interrupting, Ms. Wright-Lewis, but where did this blood come from for the cloning?" Wright-Lewis got up and walked to the window. She peered out, took a brief check, and came back and turned on a table lamp, then stared at me so hard and so long that I started squirming.

"Anything wrong?" I asked her. "Is my Freudian slip showing?" She didn't think it—or I—was funny.

"Just trying to figure out what he saw in you, that's all."

"Hey, you're not the first person who's said that to me, either!"

That softened her up a bit. "As I started to say, they were all advised about what we believed had transpired. As far as my intelligence had reported before the blackout, the birth occurred near Ephesus sometime after three A.M. Eastern European time.

"The cardinal simply said without hesitation to the assembled group, 'This threat must be eliminated before "it," or we, see another day.' "

Wright-Lewis got up and poured herself another generous shot of Scotch—I saw it was Johnnie Walker Blue, no less—while I tried to calm down. Was I in the home of a crazy woman, or was I hearing something so extraordinary it defied belief?

"The Mossad representative informed us that they'd had a bead on the whereabouts of this thing, this child," she said, sipping her Blue, "to within a hundred-mile radius.

"My boss, who was on a satellite conference call, yelled 'What the bloody hell good is a radius of one hundred damned miles in a country that no longer has electricity?'

"The cardinal actually raised his arms to God. 'We need to find them and do the right thing. That devil spawn and its Satan-fornicating mother and the whole damned band of Satanists she's with must be eliminated, before the next sunrise.' He said he believed that the lights would not come back on until the thing was disappeared. He declared that it was 'sucking the energy right out of the world!' And he was right. I said, 'Cardinal Renzi, I assure you we'll find this child. . . .'

"That put him into orbit. 'It is not a child,' he roared. 'Because it is not a human!'

"I've thought about that these thirty-three years—after what we did. Anyway, I said to him, 'Excuse me, Your Eminence, but really we don't know what it is until they examine it.'

"That drove him crazier. 'Examined? You mean autopsied!'

"Our orders were clear. It was to be destroyed, and so were the people behind the cloning, because this must never happen again."

"Do you mean cloning a human, or do you mean cloning Jesus?" I asked.

She pierced me with her gaze. "Frankly, both. The Vatican as well as top Jewish leaders, four Shia Grand Ayatollahs, and several Sunni leaders had, we were told, condoned the decision of the president and other world leaders on this issue. They wanted whoever was responsible to know that cloning was not going to be allowed and that killing cloned babies was not infanticide; it was the right thing to do. They all agreed that it was not just bad science, it would create a race of godless monsters."

"Well, maybe the baby was the Prince of Peace, after all," I injected sardonically—I hoped. "Who else could get all those enemies to agree on anything?"

Instead, a sadness passed over her face, which was totally unexpected. "You have no idea how much that has weighed on—" And then she changed the point abruptly, bringing herself back upright and stone-faced.

"At any rate, using the blood, the actual DNA, or whatever to reproduce Jesus? Do you think that the pope or any leader of any Christian country in the world could allow scientists to decide when the Second Coming would take place? And it wasn't just the Christians. Every religion's power base would be vulnerable to a new Messiah.

"I tried to tell them that even if we killed 'the thing,' it was just as important to find out where the blood had come from. Or it could happen again. I never doubted that whatever the source, it still existed and still held the DNA."

Bursting with curiosity, I asked, "What kind of vessel held the DNA or blood that this mysterious laboratory supposedly possessed?"

"Don't know. It may have been something that a few godless knights—*perfecti* is the proper term—of the heretic Cathar cult carried down Montségur Mountain in France in the thirteenth century; supposedly some kind of treasure. But logic tells us that one can't rappel down the backside of a mountain in the middle of the night carrying a treasure chest. Legend has it that one or perhaps two of them were women."

*Not that again. Another true cross meets the Holy Grail.*

But then I remembered, even in my exhausted state, that Sadowski had said something about that same cult earlier.

*He called them Gnostic Christians, though, not godless heretics. Hmmm.*

"Can you spell that for me—*catheters*," I joked.

She laughed—finally. "Well, I suppose DNA would

have been left on a catheter if they had such a thing in the thirteenth century. But it's C-A-T-H-A-R, a Gnostic heretic Christian sect."

"Oh, I see," I said, not seeing at all.

Then she made a joke. Another actual joke. "Speaking of catheters, you probably need a bathroom break."

"Thank you, Jesus. No pun intended," I said.

## 13

She showed me to the bathroom, where I reached into my pocket, retrieved Sadowski's phone, and tried him again. Again I got the recording.

"Where the hell are you? I'm up here with that woman, and I've got your car. Call me back or I'm sending your Caddy and the witch over the cliff. Got it? Good."

I peed and walked back in.

"The real problem," she continued, as though we hadn't been interrupted, "was that the people who were in possession of the baby might actually escape, what with all the tracking devices in that area of the world down while we were sitting around a damned campfire!

"And it then got worse. There we were in this super-secret setting at the edge of Asia and Europe, and suddenly the door swings open and in walks the Reverend Dr. Bill Teddy Smythe, dusting off his Stetson on his jeans like it was just an ordinary day. How he got there, I will never know. How he knew where to find us, I would never say, but it was pretty clear."

"Right. Your boss. Yesterday I couldn't believe it when

Smythe made that fake-spontaneous speech at ben Yusef's tribunal."

"Yes, that would be one and the same."

I had to smile at her candor.

"He walked over to Cardinal Renzi, kissed his ring, stood up, and said, 'Cardinal Renzi, my friend. It's a great day for a hanging—eh?' Then he knelt down and declared, 'The devil has come to feed among us in the form of our Lord Jesus!' Yes. He knew everything."

The reporter in me couldn't take it one more second, and I jumped up. "Wait a minute! If it was the clone of Jesus, how in hell could they also say it was Satan?"

"According to Smythe and Renzi—and they made a good argument—humans are created with one soul each," she answered. "And that would apply even to God's own son. That meant they—whoever 'they' were, and we didn't know at that point—had created a soulless being. Got it?"

"No, not really," I said, getting up and walking to the window to see if it was dark out yet. That road and grassy thing next to it didn't look safe during the daylight, let alone the dark.

"I mean, wouldn't God make an exception in the case of His Son, Ms. Wright-Lewis?" I asked simply as a throwaway question. Her answer floored me.

"That, Ms. Russo," she said without hesitation, "is a question people have been asking since the First Coming."

"The First? You mean you think there was more than one?" I responded, spinning around to face her.

Ignoring my question, she simply said, "Anyway, they all wanted it eliminated. And we believed that we had destroyed it, and the rest of them, too," she said, tears of triumph or maybe regret forming in the corners of her eyes. "Yes, dead before the boy was twenty-four hours on this earth! Or so we thought for sure—until this ben Yusef showed up."

I walked back to the couch and sat down, my legs feeling rubbery. "Well, whoever ben Yusef is, we know he *is* a killer and he is without a soul," I said.

"Is that how you felt when he kissed you?" she said, to my surprise. "That you were kissing a man without a soul? One who may be a sociopathic killer?"

The last thing I wanted to do was share the crazy feelings that that kiss had stirred up in me. My words about that kiss had already cost me my job and, I was beginning to fear, my sanity.

"*Maybe* he's a killer? I mean, is there any doubt?" I asked instead.

"There's always doubt about everything, except what you know about power. When joined, world powers and organized religion can move mountains when they set their collective minds to it. That has only happened once before in history—and now once again. Both times over this man."

I felt very claustrophobic in that dark house suddenly—and dirty. This was an ugly world she'd inhabited, or still did in her mind, anyway.

"So, you're saying that the people in power killed innocent folks and caused worldwide panic to defeat an enemy they're afraid could grow more powerful than all of them?"

She leaned forward. "What do you think?"

My mind was reeling, so I went back to the easier question: "Okay, so even if that were true, how did you manage to find it—that baby—that day?"

She answered coolly, "Our operatives had found that the birth had taken place at the House of the Virgin Mary—supposedly where the Blessed Mother had lived out Her last days on earth—Selçuk, near Ephesus, Turkey. Clever, don't you think?" she added rhetorically.

"And why exactly would Jesus' Mother be in Turkey, of all places? Long way for Her to travel, no?"

Wright-Lewis ignored my sarcasm. "She'd been taken there by John the Apostle."

"So you're saying the Blessed Mother took up with a disciple of Her Son's?"

"You really don't know your Bible at all, do you?" And so she quoted it for me: "'Jesus said to his mother: "Woman, behold your son." Then he said to the disciple, "Behold your mother."' Gospel of John nineteen, verses twenty-six to twenty-seven."

"So the disciple John was another son?"

"No. *Like* a son. Not her son."

I sat back confused. "I'm not getting it. . . ."

"The argument that some fundamentalist Christians use to show that Mary did *not* have other children is that Jesus said this to John as He was dying on the cross."

"But why Turkey? Isn't that a Muslim country?"

She looked exasperated at my ignorance. "Organized Christianity as we know it was practically born in Turkey, Ms. Russo! In fact, John established seven churches there. Have you never read Revelation?"

Embarrassed by my lack of biblical knowledge, I answered her with a question instead: "So you believe John took that old woman all that way? How would She have survived the trip?"

"The Blessed Mother? She was only forty-six or so when Her Son was crucified."

"What? I don't know all that much about the New Testament," I admitted, "but I do know that Jesus died when He was thirty-three. Right?"

"Right. The same age as Demiel ben Yusef is now."

*Holy good God! How had I not thought of that before? This is getting even weirder.*

Maureen leaned back, pleased with my reaction. "The Blessed Mother was probably twelve or thirteen years old when She became impregnated. She had already been betrothed to Joseph, an older man, before that. Remember, in those days a girl was promised in marriage between the ages of eleven and fourteen at the latest."

"Thirteen! So the Mother of Infant Jesus wasn't a thirty-year-old blue-eyed white woman in a light blue burqa?"

"Hardly. And after Her Son, the seditionist—what we might call a terrorist today—was crucified, Her life was no longer safe in Jerusalem. Thus Mary's house in Selçuk. It stands to this day."

I must have looked surprised, so she said, "Why, Ms. Russo, with that good Italian Catholic last name, I'm frankly surprised that you don't know your Catholic history."

I countered: "Do you always judge a book by its writer? The Russos are proud agnostics, well, deists more specifically. I was brought up to never trust a religion that requires big gold hats and massive golden cathedrals in order to worship God."

She looked disgusted.

"My parents were hippies back in the day."

She dropped her point.

"As I was saying, we found that a group was escaping with the infant boy and its thirteen-year-old mother—yes, she was the same age as the Virgin Mary. A girl named Theotokos Bienheureux, who had been hemorrhaging very badly. We were told she probably would have died anyway—"

I cut her off. "Who exactly was this girl? Where did she come from?"

"America. New York City, actually. She went to the Friends Seminary school there, and then suddenly she wasn't there anymore. Her parents skipped town when the school came looking. The cops thought they'd murdered her. We learned differently. They'd simply pimped her out to these freaks."

I swallowed hard.

"As I was saying," she continued, "she was traveling with three of the most evil humans that ever lived: a renegade, defrocked Catholic nun named Grethe—no last name we knew of, and a Vatican priest named Paulo Jacoby, plus a twenty-something-year-old soldier of fortune named, yes, Yusef Pantera. The same man who was named by the chief magistrate this morning. I assume you've been listening to the news?"

I didn't dignify the question with a response, but said, "You know ben Yusef said to me, 'Go forth for I am six,' but if I'm counting correctly, you're telling me there were five of them, including the baby."

"Yes, there were five of them. And there was no question that they and the baby had to be 'disappeared.'"

*American-ordered infanticide of Christ, for Christ's sake?*

"Disappeared as in 'shot'?" I asked, trying to look unaffected.

"No, as in blowing their plane out of the sky," she said sarcastically. "Two hours after our meeting had begun, the electricity was restored and they began tracking all ports, sea, rail, air. We found that they had boarded a private aircraft during the blackout.

"We never figured out where all their resources came from. But trust me, theirs was the only aircraft that was able to take off, as opposed to just land, that day. That's one reason we—all the operatives—knew it was their plane. It was also the one thing that proved that in fact this infant was no ordinary child.

"It was clear—at least to us and our higher-ups, from whom we were taking our orders on a minute-by-minute basis as things changed, and they were changing rapidly— that this child or whoever was in charge of this child seemed to be able to harness and block energy! Could it be true that the baby was some kind of superbeing? Or a clone of Jesus? Who else could harness power? It was an earthshaking concept, to say the very least!

"An international fleet of fighters was launched. They surrounded it and, just like that," she said, snapping her fingers, "blew their aircraft out of the sky! Or a plane we *believed* was their aircraft."

She carefully drained her glass and wiped her mouth as if she'd just had a cup of tea instead of half a tumbler of Scotch and had told me about capturing a spy instead of describing the assassination of a thirteen-year-old girl, a newborn baby, a nun, a priest, and their—what?— bodyguard/father/child molester?

"Interestingly," she added, "no one noticed, because at that same exact moment the plane was exploding, that new star that had risen a few days earlier just happened to explode as well. I know for a fact that at least one of them—Father Paulo Jacoby—survived. He's shown up in the newspapers. Always in the background of some important event. So either he wasn't on the plane or"— she got up and poured another Scotch—"none of them were."

"Oh, I see. But let me digress here a second," I said, wishing like hell she'd offer me a drink. "You mentioned it earlier, and I meant to ask you: What new star? I never read about a new star in my astronomy classes."

"That's because it was called a comet. And it was only

visible over a small part of the sky, over Ephesus in Turkey. Anyway, it exploded in spectacular fashion. The plane, the star—one big bright mess! The scientists explained that it was the comet's unexplained emergence that had literally drained energy in the areas it passed over, causing the blackout."

"Didn't the astronomers know it was a lie?"

"It was before the real Internet, so rumors didn't spread at the speed of light . . . and those that knew, well, let's just say they either forgot immediately or unfortunately would have met with tragic accidents."

"So you're telling me the U.S. or whomever killed astronomers—passive professor types?"

"No."

"But . . ."

"No," she said again, without affect.

A standoff.

"Let me continue," she said, clearly not willing to go there. "The UN put their professional spokespeople on TV to explain that the explosion of the comet returned things back to seminormal."

"Semi?"

"That was the year of the wild El Niño winds. They were the strongest and most devastating in centuries. The trade winds unaccountably reversed direction in 1982. It caused disasters on almost every continent. Australia, Africa, and Indonesia suffered droughts, dust storms, and brush fires. Peru's coastal water temperatures rose by over seven degrees.

"The story of the cause of the international energy drain and subsequent climatic changes was a great cover. And maybe it was true—or maybe it had been caused by a man-made attempt at the 'Second Coming.'" Wright-Lewis winked conspiratorially.

Oh, please! She was too good a Mata Hari to suddenly forget herself and show her poker face and her hand at the same time.

"Even though the crisis had passed," she continued, "they wanted proof that we'd done our job. Of course, there was nothing left: The plane had exploded over the ocean. 'Was the new Jesus on that plane?' was all they wanted to know."

"Was He? On the plane I mean?"

She walked to the cabinet again, but instead of looking for more booze, she took out a folder and handed it to me. It was an old CIA dossier, marked "classified."

I opened it and read: *Demiel ben Yusef, approximate age: 11–13, parents unknown/Tel Dan, (aka Tell el-Kadi, Tel el-Kady, Tel/Tell el-Qadi, Antiochia, . . . Dan): The Biblical City (Israel), July 1993–1994.*

"You—ah, they," I corrected myself, "knew about this guy as far back as 1994?"

"Yes and no," she said, not quite answering. "Demiel ben Yusef became a person of interest for the first time in 1994, true. But not for the reason you might suspect. In the early nineties, they—government agencies in the U.S. and Israel—did put the child on their radar. Not because the boy was a danger but because anything out of the ordinary in Israel or in any of its enemy states was immediately made record of—no matter how seemingly unimportant."

"Why?" I asked, trying to see what any of this had to do with the man on trial. "Were they looking for any signs that this supposed clone baby was alive?"

"Hardly. After the Cold War ended, everyone was scrambling, frankly, to find ways to stay employed and to keep their agencies relevant. This boy made a scene that caused local media attention."

"But you weren't with the company any longer, and yet . . ."

She ignored me completely, continuing, "The boy had showed up at a construction site being prepared for tourists in Tel Dan, in the northern Golan, near the Jordan River. He was bothering the workers and telling them they should dig in different areas. A man, seemingly his father, would come and fetch him away but everyday he'd show back up.

"Then one day, when they were excavating—right where the child had told them to dig—they came across what might be one of the greatest archaeological discoveries in Jewish history."

"What was it?"

"A fragment from a large monumental inscription. It was a piece of a stele and it mentions King David's dynasty. Then in June they uncovered two other fragments in separate locations, locations that the boy had also pointed out."

"Why is that so significant? There must be millions of fragments of all kinds of things in that area—no?"

"Not like this," she said, actually raising her voice for the first time. "Ms. Russo, it was nothing less than proof *positive* of the dynasty of King David!

"Stranger still, before it could even be deciphered by the archaeologists, the boy reappeared and started arguing with the rabbis in a town nearby. The argument went on for days and yet his parents were nowhere to be found.

"The boy insisted that the stele was made by an enemy of the Jews, and that it was a memorial boasting about their exploits in conquering the descendants of the house of David. The boy called the discovery a 'boastful document' that had then been smashed by a Jew of royal blood, perhaps Jehoash, who reigned from BCE 798–782.

"His frantic parents—unnamed—finally found him at

a temple, but a media crowd had already gathered when they heard about the argument. A man, presumably his father, swept him away, saying he'd been lost."

"So there was footage and photos of the boy at that time?"

"No. That's when I knew, you see."

"Knew?"

"That he was the clone baby. Every bit of film taken by every reporter was blank. The boy was twelve, the same age as Jesus when He'd been found questioning the rabbis. It wasn't a coincidence. I *knew* it was history repeating. . . ."

"How did you know it was *that* boy, though?"

"He *told* the rabbis, that's how. He said, 'My name is Demiel ben Yusef and I come at the behest of my father.' "

"And you believe he was the clone baby from Ephesus?"

"I am as sure as I can be without definitive proof."

She got up from her chair. I'd seen this move dozens of times. It meant the interview was over.

"Think about this instead, Ms. Russo. What if the man on trial, who seems so particularly fond of you, is the real child born from the blood of Jesus? For whatever reason, you were the one ben Yusef chose to kiss. Let's hope it wasn't a Judas kiss."

"I guess it depends on who I give up. . . ."

She walked to the door and opened it. "It's not a joke. There are powerful people who will want you to find out the truth, and equally powerful and more dangerous people who will keep you from ever finding it out—or even living beyond tonight, I assume," she said, as though she were giving me directions to the bar down the hill.

*That's what you say to someone as you're escorting her out of your house?*

"Where do you suggest I start looking?" I asked her, trying not to show fear.

"You're the investigative journalist—you'll figure it out. I can only tell you that you've come this far, so surely you'll be able to connect the dots—or in this case, the drops. And yes, I do believe that other droplets of blood still exist somewhere.

"But of course, you'll have to do what every agent assigned has been unable to do for the past thirty-three years—find the rest of that blood. I believe it's contained in some kind of vessel. If you find it, and if the DNA matches ben Yusef's—well, you may be able to stop the second Crucifixion of Christ."

"What? I'm just one person. . . ."

"Again, it's finding whatever it is that holds the droplets first. It is simply the most important relic in Christendom, and would make the most important story any reporter has ever written, and you, dear, have clearly been invited to participate in the hunt."

*"The hunt"? Jesus!—no pun intended.*

I stood up, too, and started gathering up my stuff. She said, "You were Chosen, remember that. So just trust your instincts."

"How in the hell do I know I can even trust *you*?"

She just said, "What I did is something I can never forgive. Prove that I failed. They can't be allowed to kill Jesus one more time."

"So you want me to prove you wrong, find the relic, and somehow manage to steal it and get the DNA off it? You can't really think . . ."

What in my life had ever equipped me to parse out the unbelievable story she just told me? But, other than this, possibly the biggest (and the second greatest) story ever told, I had nothing to go on. *Can I do this? Am I capable of forgetting it and not even trying? Is the pope a Muslim?*

With that last question hanging, she cut me off cold. "Thank you for your time, Ms. Russo. I hope you're as good an investigative reporter as they, whoever 'they' are, think you are. And, if you can keep it in mind—a little respect for authority can go a long way," she chastised me, while ushering me out.

"No disrespect, ma'am," I retorted, "but you had nothing but respect for authority and look what happened to you. You've spent the last thirty-something years in hiding!"

"In plain sight . . ." she said.

"You don't really live here, do you?"

Silence. Oh, right. Respect.

"Okay then. How about 'How can I find you if I need to?'"

"I'll find you when I need to," she said, closing the door. "Have a safe journey, Ms. Russo." Then, almost as an afterthought: "The world depends on it."

It was dark by then and cold. Fog was settling in, too. Great.

I heard the dead bolt lock behind me as I made my way back to the car, wondering about that house and trying to feel my way in the dark. For sure it wasn't her house. I mean, she was still wanted by the Feds. But still, Wright-Lewis clearly knew a lot more about me than I knew about her. Just who was the investigative reporter here? She even knew my favorite brand of Scotch.

Just for the record? It's Johnnie Blue. Not that she offered me any.

## 14

I didn't know where to go.

I got into Sadowski's Caddy, turned it on, and then punched in Dona's number on his satellite phone. "Hey, it's me," I said, when her cheery voice mail picked up. "Sadowski gave me his cell to use, but I don't know what the number is. It's a secure line, though, so I don't think the number will pop up on your end. I was wondering if I could bunk with you tonight? Call me. Well, call me if you can. And tell Sadowski to call me the hell back, too! He can give you this number, which I'd like to have myself, thank you very much."

I sounded much more flippant and upbeat than I felt.

My apartment had been broken into, so I wasn't about to go there—at least until I could get the cops to pay attention. And I was being watched. But by whom?

Damn. I didn't even have my fallback home—the newsroom—to return to any longer.

I sure couldn't ask for room and board with Sadowski, because for one thing, the SOB, my supposed friend, had stopped answering my calls.

Sitting there in the dark, without caring that Wright-

Lewis was probably peeking out her window at me, I then turned on the radio. I was desperate to know what had transpired at the tribunal that day.

I tuned to 1010 WINS and caught them midstory—something about a murder.

On the second day of the trial, they bother with a routine murder at the top of the hour?

Then I got it. "The body had been found bound and naked and shot through the temple," the female reporter was saying. "The priest, a favorite in the Turtle Bay / United Nations area, had last been seen opening the gate to the rectory of the Church of the Holy Family to allow former *New York Standard* reporter Alessandra Russo to enter."

The next voice was that of Ron Pearl, the NYPD spokesman whom I'd known for twenty years. "Alessandra Russo has been on our radar since the incident with the terrorist, ah, alleged terrorist, ben Yusef at the UN yesterday," he said as though he weren't an old friend. "As of four P.M. this afternoon Ms. Russo remains the prime suspect in the murder of Father Eugene Sadowski. . . ."

Then it went back to the beat reporter. "According to one police source, who spoke to me on the condition of anonymity, Alessandra Russo's fingerprints were found on the murder weapon. This is Juliet Papa reporting."

I banged my head on the steering wheel. Dead? The guy I'd just cursed out to Dona? I was overcome with grief—until I began to process the reality of what I'd just heard: "Alessandra Russo's fingerprints were found on the murder weapon. . . ."

Of course! I'd handled the gun and I'd recently been fingerprinted for clearance for the tribunal. I had been set up! And somehow this nightmare I'd entered was connected to the man on trial, the one his nutty followers claimed to be the new Jesus.

So what now? Return to the city and give myself up to face murder charges? Run for my life? Or find out if the United States had killed Baby Jesus thirty-three years ago by high-tech missile?

I tried Donald. He picked up after half a ring.

"It's me," I said. "Don't ask any questions but just let me know if you know why I'm being set up."

"Honey," he said. Damn. He never called me "honey." He was scared for me. "Run like your ass is on fire. They're probably tracking my calls."

"I'm on an untraceable satellite phone."

"Why do you have an untraceable satellite phone?"

"I said no questions."

"Right. So, listen. It's time to get outta Dodge, babe. As in get the hell out. As in right now. Got it?"

"Got it. And Donald? Next time, call the morning after."

He didn't laugh. I hung up. I typed "Toronto International Airport" into the Caddy's GPS, made a very careful U-turn, and headed due north.

*Damn!* Shining like a beacon in my rearview mirror were the headlights of a car higher up the street making the same U-turn I'd made. Then those headlights went out. I could still hear the engine hum as the car came closer and closer. It was like "Christine"! Even though I couldn't see anything on that dark street, I knew it was too close to me and I was too close to the cliff. If I slipped on the wet road, the car could careen onto the grassy part and fly over the cliff.

Nonetheless, I hit the accelerator and said the second prayer I'd said in less than two days to a god I didn't believe in, in the first place.

My tires screeched as I navigated the road. I could see the end of the street up ahead. Before I reached it, I tried to shut off the car lights, but the Caddy's damned safety feature would not allow it. Talk about stupidity! So I made a sharp right and a then quick left, passing an inn and onto a flat, straight road again, with my car lights like a beacon to the pursuers.

I couldn't see it in my rearview mirror, but I could still hear it, and it sounded like it was right on my ass.

The safest bet I figured was to drive into the town of Rhinebeck and onto the main drag, where, hopefully, stores and restaurants would still be open and where whoever it was in that lightless car following me would be exposed to the lights of the town. Of course, I would be exposed as well, and now that I'd somehow turned into a wanted fugitive, it wasn't a great choice, but it was better than leaving myself open to whatever/whoever it was that was following me.

I could see streetlights up ahead. Thank God. The town was indeed alive—in fact, throngs were gathered on the sidewalks and spilling out onto the street. What the hell? Equinox festival or something equally insane that brought out the neo-hippies?

It was so packed that I had to slow way down so that I didn't plow down any pedestrians—or more accurately, spectators—since I saw they were all standing still and staring off in one direction. I checked my rearview mirror and saw—nothing. Where the hell had the car gone? Two seconds before the damned thing had sounded like it was practically attached to my bumper, and now—gone.

I very slowly navigated my way down the street. Everyone was standing mesmerized in front of a tavern with a sign that read BILLY'S LOCAL, SPORTS BAR AND CAFÉ. These people in the street and on the sidewalk were just the overflow crowd; the place was jammed inside. But oddly I didn't hear any of the loud noise, or *woo-woo*ing that is the language of sports bars. In fact, it was way too quiet.

As I slowly drove past, and the people moved aside, I glimpsed what it was that had had them all so fascinated: On every one of Billy Local's giant 3-D flat screens was the face of Demiel ben Yusef. Filmed earlier in the day, the footage showed a close-up of ben Yusef's calm demeanor and slight smile as he was being walked out of the tribunal, shackled, wearing the same clothes he'd worn the day before, his Rasta braids reaching down to his waist in the back.

People had gathered to see the spectacle together. Remarkable. In an age when everyone had become so insular, each of us so comfortable staring alone at our own computer screens at night and communicating virtually—even virtually having sex—the folks of Rhinebeck had joined together as a community to watch this remarkable event.

Instead of the shouting, fist-waving threats, and arguments that had become commonplace wherever and whenever ben Yusef showed up, everyone in this town seemed to be taking it all in calmly.

The reporter in me was of course desperate to jump out of the car and start interviewing people, but I'd somehow ducked that car following me, so I wasn't taking any chances.

Instead, the fugitive I'd just become kept moving ahead at only 10 or 15 mph with my eyes trained alternately on the parting crowds and the rearview mirror. I felt like I'd entered *The Twilight Zone*.

A middle-aged, plump woman with out-of-control gray hair, wearing a tie-dyed schmata, approached the car. She walked in front and stood there, causing me to slam on the brakes.

She walked to the driver's side and smiled at me through the closed window, demanding I look at her, which I finally did. Her eyes seemed glazed over.

*Jeez, just what I need—a town full of stoned lunatics.*

She lifted her left hand, which caused me to flinch, but instead she crossed herself twice—the first one in the traditional manner and the second one starting at the chest!

*Have another toke, lady, before your high wears off.*

She pulled back a bit, blew on the glass, and lifted a single finger. In the fogged area she drew a double cross with these sorts of *v* shapes at the four ends. I acknowledged it with a nod of my head, as though I were one of them, when in fact I had no damned idea—then—what the hell she meant, but it seemed to satisfy her. She moved away from the car and waved me on like a demented traffic cop.

Had the whole world gone insane in my one-day absence?

*And where the hell was the car without the lights?*

## 15

I wouldn't find the answer to that question until the next day. Meantime, the GPS was barking orders: "Make a slight left, make a slight right, obey the local traffic ordinances." If I weren't afraid of being completely lost (or more than I already felt), I would have shut the damned thing off. "Christine" was not following me—or so it seemed—which should have given me more than enough food for thought.

When you think you're not being tailed, then for sure you are.

With the satellite radio tuned to Fox, I listened for any updates on the story, watching in the rearview mirror for the tail.

I exited off the turnpike in Albany. It was a big enough city that for sure there had to be a twenty-four-hour drugstore. It was a little after 9:25.

At a strip mall, I found a CVS and went quickly as possible through the aisles, picking up a small Crest, a hairbrush, a travel hair dryer with an international currency switch, disposable razors, a thick cloth headband with an elastic closure at the back, six cotton gramma panties—all white—in a bag, and a good pair of surgical-looking scissors.

I browsed the hair-color aisle. Blondes have more fun, but I wasn't looking for a good time, so I was thinking redhead.

I picked up a box of L'Oréal Féria with a seductive-looking model on the front with bright red hair. It was a color called "R76 Spicy Red." *Punk red. Too old for that one—perfect!* The directions seemed pretty easy, but since I had no ability to do anything but comb my hair, I knew I could end up bald or worse—with clown hair. But the price was right: $9.95 including everything. Since the kit had shampoo and conditioner already in it, I didn't have to buy those.

I turned the cart and headed to the checkout, which had no line, thank God, at this hour. My immediate impulse was to pull out my AmEx card, but for the first time it consciously hit me that since I was suddenly on the lam (I always wanted to say that—or so I thought until I actually was on the lam), I could no longer use a credit card—nor even get money from the ATM.

I reached into my red bag, knowing that surveillance cameras were watching me—and everyone else.

*Do not look in any way like you're trying to boost even a hairpin.*

I rooted around until I found my wallet and counted up the cash I had on me—$176.46. I quickly added up what was in my cart and realized that I didn't need a $50 hairdryer. I put it on the side. The damned scissors were $22, but that wasn't something I could skimp on—even though I suspected that I'd have to leave them behind. Damn! I estimated the total at less than $45.

As I was checking out, my bag started vibrating and then ringing with an old-fashioned bell-ringer sound—the phone. Afraid to pick it up, I smiled weakly at the sneering kid, who didn't notice since he was staring at my breasts.

"Ya phone's ringin,'" he said without looking up.

*Do not call attention to yourself.*

"Yes, I know," I answered, handing him $45. His sneer turned into a leer.

"Boyfriend?"

I grunted, which he interpreted as an answer, and nodded his head conspiratorially.

*Moron!*

I waited for my change, which he counted out in my hand: three quarters. "The penny's on me."

"Thanks." *Sport.*

I rushed back to the car, which was one of three or so in the entire parking lot, hit the "unlock" remote key, and hopped in quickly, happy to hear the automatic lock click behind me.

*Duck your head; surveillance cameras must be everywhere.*

I reached into my bag and dug out the phone. "Unknown voice mail."

I immediately hit the voice-mail arrow and heard Dona's lovely voice. "What the hell?" was how she started. Then: "Call me back. I'm at a phone booth. Or filthy phone kiosk, anyway. In case the number doesn't come up," which it didn't, "call me back at, let me see here, what the heck does it say on the phone thingy? Oh, it says nothing. You can't call me back.

"Try to hit 'call back' or something. It's getting cold, but I'll hang around another half hour or so. I'm wearing a skirt so short my ass is out. I'm fairly sure I'm not being watched. I figure I'm okay because, well, remember that cute cop? I looked him up. We just had a, hmmm, I guess you'd call it a date. He's got my back."

*What a woman.*

When I hit the "call back" button on Sadowski's magic phone, it automatically brought up a Google map, and I saw the exact place she had been standing when she made the call: Thirty-eighth and Tenth—near the entrance to the Lincoln Tunnel.

*Good girl.* This was serious hooker territory. And here I thought she'd worn that skirt for the cute cop. I had always teased her that she had the legs to be a hooker while all I had were the shoes. Anyway, nobody would find it suspicious for a woman to be near a pay phone in that location. That's why the Russian mobsters who ran the girls there put in these phones under some legitimate guise. I knew (everybody did, actually) that these were the only busy pay phones left in the city. Hookers got calls from their Russkie pimps there, because when the heat was on, the cops couldn't trace their "dates." *Brilliant!*

I hit "call back" again, and after a few seconds, I could hear it ringing. *Please, please, please be there.*

"You all right?" was what she said when she picked up, and I had to fight back tears.

"No."

"Where are you?"

"Not a good question." I knew she wouldn't have been able to map my location anyway because she was at a pay phone and I was on a secure line.

"Right." I could hear the wind whistling behind her and car horns of impatient drivers desperate to get into the tunnel. *All so far away and normal.*

She took the phone away from her ear, and I could hear her telling some tunnel-bound husband looking for a quickie on the way home to his wife, "Sorry, honey— I'm booked tonight."

Then back to me: "Sorry. So Donald managed to do something or other to get your number. You heard about Sadowski, I assume?"

"Yes. I'm just sick about it."

"Me too." And then as though she weren't dropping a big bomb, added, "They're saying you killed him in a jealous lover's rage."

"Who's saying that?" I demanded, feeling the fury rise in my throat.

"The cute cop told me that's the word. They're going to announce tomorrow that a person familiar with the case says you caught him with a young boy and went nuts."

"What the—?"

"They even say they know who the child is, which of course will never be revealed under the Protection of Minors Act."

"Oh, my God. Who?"

"I don't know. But my money's on that cheap blonde in the jeans at the church."

"No!"

"Makes sense, right?"

I had to admit that, yes, it made a whole hell of a lot of sense.

"Is there nothing they won't stoop to?"

"Who?"

"If I knew that, I wouldn't be in this jam."

Time was limited and this wasn't a gossip call, so I cut it short.

"Listen, I really need you to do something for me. I'm not comfortable getting online much while I'm still on American soil."

"Shoot."

"Go to the Fox archives, or better yet, the *Post* morgue. . . ." A "morgue" is where newspapers and media keep the old clippings, tapes, and papers.

"I know it well. Basement at 1211 Sixth—right? I'm tight with the librarian; she'll bring me down."

"Great. See what you can find related to a comet in the year 1982."

"A comet?"

"A comet. And a blackout in parts of Europe and elsewhere."

"Okay . . . but—"

"Also, see if, earlier that year or the year before that, there is anything on a missing girl from Manhattan named—what is it again?" I reached into my bag for my reporter's notebook and rifled the pages. "Here—first name, Theotokos, with a *k*. Last name, wait a sec—last name, B-i-e-n-h-e-u-r-e-u-x.

"Blessed one?"

"No, I said, 'B-i—"

Dona cut me off. "Bienheureux—it means 'blessed one' in French."

"You're kidding me. Seriously?"

"Is this the time for jokes?"

"Not really. No."

"What else?"

"Also see if there's anything on a Catholic priest—or maybe not Catholic, but a cleric by the name of Father Paulo—that's P-a-u-l-o Jacoby; I think it's J-a-c-o-b-y. Please, whatever you can dig up would keep me indebted to you forever."

"You already are."

"Damn! You're right. Anyway, if you call me from a pay phone tomorrow morning, I'll tell you where to fax it."

"Fax? Who faxes anymore?"

"Nobody. That's why I'm going old-school all the way. Go to a Staples and get it faxed. No e-mail, no nothing. Fax."

"You got it. Anything else?"

"Yeah. Two things. I need for you and Donald to both

buy prepaid phones. And two: If you make any money on the street tonight, send it to me," I joked.

"You need money?"

"Was Jesus a Jew? Yeah, I need money."

"Let me figure out how to get you some."

"Bless you. But I can't generate any trail, so I don't know if it's possible."

"Right."

"Now listen up. More than money, I need Donald to get somebody trustworthy who's not connected to me in any way to book me an e-ticket for tomorrow. Not that anyone he knows *is* trustworthy, but at least they're all so untrustworthy that they'd never turn. Tell him to make sure that whoever he picks isn't using a damned stolen credit card or something."

"What did you ever see in him again?"

"I like bad boys. You like cute cops. Okay?"

"Destination?"

"Ephesus."

"Turkey?"

"I think you have to fly into Istanbul."

"But they'll be looking to track you. You can't get past immigration anywhere."

"Maybe. I'm counting on some old foolishness of mine to buy me a few days. See, in some bizarre, desperate bid at saving my marriage, I had renewed my passport in my married name of Zaluckyj."

"You didn't!"

"Is this the time to give me a lecture on independence?"

"No," she said, and I could hear the sadness in her voice. It was all different now. "From where?"

"Toronto. There's a shot they won't be looking for that name. Oh, and my first name's really Alexandra with an *x*—I changed it when I got my first byline at twenty-one because I thought it sounded much more sophisticated. So the passport is in the name Alexandra Zaluckyj."

"Oy. Anything else I don't know about you?"

"Sure. Anyway, I'll set up a Hotmail account, and you both need to do the same. Donald is to just e-mail me the ticket number and confirmation code to the account of . . . Got a pen?"

"I've got my iPhone."

"No. A pen. Then tear up the paper. Old-school, remember?"

"Gotcha." I could hear her digging through her bag while juggling the receiver on the pay phone.

"Shoot."

"C-A-T-H-A-R-A-Z at Hotmail dot com. Got it?"

She repeated it verbatim. "What is he supposed to pay his connection with for the ticket? I'm sure the Feds and Interpol and everyone else will be looking at his credit card and ATM records."

"Tell him to go play poker or some goddamned thing. He knows how to get cash better than anybody."

"Got it."

"Dona? Thanks."

"Don't mention it."

"Be careful. Don't get yourself in trouble because of me."

"Too late for that, pal. What about your folks?"

"Oh, God. Please tell them nothing. If they know nothing, they can't inadvertently give away anything. Do me a favor, though. Make sure they get plenty of media exposure. They'll want to defend me all over the place. The more they're on camera, the safer they'll be 'cause the cops will surveil them twenty-four/seven."

"That should make your pinko parents happy," she said in her jaded, loving way. "You sure I can't hint to them that you're okay? So far?"

"Dona? No. Noth-ing! They'll know. At Columbia they helped draft dodgers escape to Canada during the Vietnam War. They know they didn't raise a sissy." We both let the Canada irony go by without mention.

I really didn't want to put them in any danger. And my corporate lawyer brother in LA? Definitely not. The twins were only six years old. God—I didn't want them tainted with *this* filthy brush.

With that we hung up and I put the car into "drive," and started to pull out.

I could see "Leering Boy" at the store's glass front door staring out at me. He was wagging his tongue lasciviously.

Instead of shooting him the bird as I would normally have done, I waved politely and drove slowly out of the parking lot and back onto the Thruway.

*You can never find a good hit man when you need one.*

## 16

The GPS informed me that it was still 380 miles to Toronto with a driving time of six hours and thirty minutes. With no "Christine" in sight, I headed north. If I could get halfway—drive another three hours and get some rest—I figured I'd be safe enough.

Weary but determined, I drove another 143 miles to Syracuse, exited, and found a Best Rate Motel. I took the satellite phone charger, the registration, and, yes, Sadowski's ATM card with me; I didn't want to leave anything in the car.

One look at what passed for a lobby and I knew that for sure no one would remember me here, because, for one thing, no one was around. I actually rang the desk bell (OK, to be fair, it was after midnight), and a sleepy Indian lady came shuffling out in her bedroom slippers and sari.

The deluxe single room with continental breakfast came to fifty-four dollars. I complained, and the woman lowered it to fifty. I signed in as "Rochelle Cherry." Don't ask.

*It sounds like a whiny stripper.*

She handed me the room card and didn't ask if I had luggage, just pointed to the door and told me to drive around to the back, where I could park my car right near the stairs to my room.

Room 204, which reeked of cigarette smoke, had one sad, sagging double bed, with a crumpled-up tissue still left on the spread.

It partially covered the large cigarette burn in the middle of the horrid orange-and-red quilted bedspread. The whole room looked as beat up as I felt. No need to worry about bedbugs. Even they wouldn't stay there. I pulled the rubber blackout curtains together and then the white-ish sheer drapes over them, turned on the heat, which sounded like a tambourine band, and headed toward the bathroom-*ish*.

The 1970s pink tiles and matching toilet had seen better days. Or maybe not. Regardless, I unwrapped the miniscule bar of Cashmere Bouquet soap in the dish and scrubbed my face with the rough washcloth so hard I nearly bled.

I ran the shower until it approximated something like hot water, peeled off my clothes, and jumped in. I washed my underwear under the shower with the Cashmere Bouquet and prayed I wouldn't develop a giant perfume rash on my southern regions. I remember Donald telling me once that all men who cheat in cheap motels get caught because they come home smelling of Cashmere Bouquet. If a man smells of it, he's cheating. Period.

I put my wet undies on the heating unit to dry and, naked, I crawled into the bed and immediately rolled into the middle sag. I plugged Sadowski's phone in next to the bed, set it to wake me at 6:00, and fell into a fitful sleep.

*I was alone in an ancient city in front of a great wall. Everyone was passing by, but only I could see that there was a code written on the wall. Why couldn't anyone else see it, and, more important, why couldn't I interpret it?*

*I tried to climb up to the top of the wall but fell back and landed hard on my head. I started bleeding profusely onto the road, where I lay helpless.*

*No one came to my aid, and I could feel the life draining out of me.*

*If I could only read the code, I could save myself.*

*Then someone, a woman, standing over me, unwilling to help, said, "You can't save the world. You are not the Chosen One." And she began laughing so hard that tears—which were made of blood—were pouring down her face.*

I woke up sweating like a lady in the middle of menopause and sat straight up. My heart was beating so fast I thought it would explode.

Totally disoriented in the blackness of the room, I felt around and felt the creepy polyester quilted bedspread and knew immediately I was in a motel.

I flicked on the light, still disoriented but grateful that I'd been dreaming—until I remembered that the truth was far worse than bleeding on a street in a foreign country unable to read a code.

The reality was that I was being hunted by the police for murder in my own country—and followed by God knows who from God knows where—and my real prospects for getting away with murder, or even getting away alive, were, well, slim, none, and you're kidding me, right?

I slammed my head back down on the skinny thing that passed for a pillow and tried to get back to sleep. Right then the only thing I had going for me was my brain, and when it was sleep deprived it was a nasty, unworkable thing.

Somehow, I felt like I had been tossing and turning until dawn, but in truth I must have fallen deep asleep, because the next thing I knew I was startled awake by the alarm: Sam Cooke's version of "You Send Me" on Sadowski's phone. It was 6:00 A.M. I switched on the light and crawled out of bed.

I made the little cup of coffee in the machine they provided, loaded it up with sugar and white powder nondairy "creamer," and gulped it down. I still wasn't functioning, so I pulled on my clothes (underwear was still damp, so I went commando—forgetting I'd bought some nice old lady underpants at the drug store) and headed down to the lobby for the free continental breakfast. I don't know which continent it is exactly that serves frozen cheese Danish in a bag for breakfast, but there must be one. Somewhere.

Anyway I gulped down three cups of joe and popped two cheese Danishes into the microwave. They tasted better than anything I can ever remember eating, so I popped in another. Then, like my grandmother, I stuffed another three in my bag, while the Indian lady's husband, who was in charge of restocking the continental goodies, glared at me like I was the last beggar in Mumbai.

*Like you never ate six cheese Danishes, Raj?*

Instead of being ashamed of myself, I poured another cup of coffee and took it to my room.

By 6:35 I was wired out of my mind on caffeine and sugar. I turned on the iPad and immediately made sure that the global tracking device was set to "off." Not that I ever had it working. The idea that a company (and now the authorities) had the ability to track a person wherever and whenever was always something I wanted to avoid—unless I was trapped on a mountain with no way down or something equally as ridiculous.

The free Wi-Fi in the room required a guest name and

password. I tried to remember what the hell name I'd registered under. Marie? Roxanne? Then I remembered the improbable Rochelle Cherry and opened a Hotmail account under the name "CATHARAZ."

I went into the bathroom and took out the scissors. Oh God. I started with my bangs. I'd had bangs since I was two. Snip, chop, slice. And then the bob. Snip, snip, slice, chop, chop. My hair was sticking up all over, and the sink and floor were covered in my lost hair.

*Do not leave one single strand. DNA and all that. But what was my crime here? Bad hair?*

I opened the box of Féria "R76 Spicy Red" and, following the directions, applied it to my hair, didn't wait the appropriate time, then washed it out and conditioned it with my head under the shower, the color running in rivulets into the tub. It looked like the aftermath of a brutal slaying.

That was somehow appropriate, because when I stood back up and looked at myself in the mirror, what I'd done to myself was akin to murder. My formerly brunette bob was a red one-inch mess. I looked like one of those aging rocker chicks that can't get over the fact that she's no longer a groupie. I looked like my name *should* be Rochelle Cherry.

I dried it, which left a lot of red on the white towel, so I stashed it in my purse, planning to throw it out somewhere far away. I'd covered enough crimes to know that it's best not to leave anything suspicious behind. I ran the shower until the red dissipated somewhat. *What a mess.*

I went back to the tablet and—bingo!—there was a message. It was from Leftyoneeye@hotmail.com. Lefty One Eye was the name of our dog, the one I took in when I came home one night and found the poor guy shivering on the steps of the brownstone. When I couldn't get pregnant, Lefty was like my consolation gift from the heavens.

We once had a throw pillow on the couch that read, "We're staying together for the sake of the dog," which turned out to be true.

When Lefty died after eating three Costco-sized boxes of frozen burgers we'd bought for a BBQ, he killed off the last part of us as well.

I could feel myself welling up again. If only Donald could see me now. . . . Oh, shit, who cared anyway? I ate another cheese Danish. Unthawed this time.

I opened the e-mail, and there it was—God bless him—a confirmation number, bar code, and all, for a Delta flight from the Pearson International Airport in Toronto at 7:05 P.M. that night, arriving Istanbul, 2:15 P.M. the following day with an hour-and-a-half stopover at Paris Charles de Gaulle Airport.

I couldn't tell by his e-mail if I had a direct with a layover or a switch of aircraft. If it was a plane change and the first plane was late or the gates far apart— which they always are at de Gaulle and which inevitably involves a shuttle bus—I was screwed. I'd play it by ear.

*Hey—if I even get that far without being apprehended or shot, I'll be happy.*

I still hadn't gotten a call from Dona, so I took a chance and hit "return" and typed in the fax number with the annotation "Bates Motel f#." I hit "send" and figured it would get me nailed, totally confuse Donald, or somehow he'd know it was for Dona.

In rapid order two more messages arrived. The first was from "Hot Sexy Viagra Male" (how do they find you two minutes after you open an account?), and another one from Edward.Gibbonsays@libero.it. *Dona! Only she would manage to get an Italian Internet account.*

I opened it.

It was also written in Italian: "*La prenotazione prepagata è stata fatta in nome di Alexandra Zaluckyj in Europacar all'aeroporto di Istanbul.*" "A reservation—prepaid—has been made in the name of Alexandra Zaluckyj at Europacar at the Istanbul Airport."

Why would she write in Italian? Did Dona even know Italian?

I took a chance and hit "return," and typed in the fax number again.

With no time to waste and scared that I could be tracked by my tablet even with the tracking shut off, I shut down, put on my almost-dry underwear, slipped on my jeans, T-shirt, scarf, boots, and leather jacket, and went back over the room to make sure I'd left nothing behind as evidence.

*Of what—a bad dye job?*

I called the front desk and asked if by some miracle a fax had come for me, but Mrs. Wife said, "No, no fax."

I waited another fifteen minutes, called again and again. She said, "No, no fax."

"I will call you from my next location and perhaps you can fax it to me there?"

"How will you pay me for this fax?"

"I will leave you five dollars. How's that?"

"Okay."

"I'll leave it in an envelope in my room."

I hopped into the Caddy without saying good-bye to my hosts. Mr. Husband was still glaring at me for the six Danish I had glommed, two of which were squished in my red satchel at the moment. Yes, I had eaten four Danish, something I had never done in my life. My limit had always been half of one.

As I was pulling out of the drive, Mr. Husband came running out, frantically waving at me. I stopped the car short and he said, "You owe fifteen more dollars!"

"For what—the Danish?"

"You have the faxes. It costs fifteen dollars."

"For a fax?"

"It's five pages, that's fifteen dollars."

"Fifteen dollars? I left five dollars in the room." A fortune. And the choice was?

"Three dollars a page," he said, and I knew he was making it up as he went along.

I grudgingly handed over the ten dollars and tucked the envelope with the pages into my red satchel.

I set a course for the Toronto airport—it was nearly 8:40 A.M., which gave me around ten hours before take-off, but I had much to accomplish and a long way to go.

I drove a few hours and pulled into a travel plaza. I parked close to the entrance in case I had to make a quick getaway. I also had to figure out what the hell I was going to do about gas. My funds were dangerously low, and I was desperate for some salty Roy Rogers fried chicken, but on my limited means, I settled for a Diet Coke and, yes, another cheese Danish.

Needless to say, I was excited that the Roy Rogers lady just handed me an empty cup, which I was supposed to fill myself.

*Too bad I can't fill it with gasoline.*

I went back to the font three times, until I was as blown up as a balloon over Macy's.

The travel plaza offered emergency everything, and I bought a sports bra in a tube (ten dollars), two I LOVE NY T-shirts in black (fifteen dollars), and a plastic pretend Louis Vuitton large carry-on bag (twenty-one dollars), with the initials LU instead of LV.

The TVs around the rest stop were reporting on the manhunt for Alessandra Russo, who was wanted for the murder of Father Eugene Sadowski, in what was now being described as a crime of passion. My press photo was on the screen and so were pictures of me in Iraq with my foot up on a pile of bombed-out bricks, like some crazed hunter. There was no way anyone would recognize that person in my present state. I hoped.

The bigger news, of course, was that the United Nations area around the ben Yusef trial, which had already begun for the morning, was more unruly than ever, with protestors from both sides jamming up the streets. Demiel's face, as he was perp-walked in front of the press that day, looked surprisingly serene.

Maybe I could learn something from him.

I looked anything but serene, and I felt scared and frantic. I filled up the cup again and plopped down in a booth like a bag lady.

*I'm trying to escape to Istanbul looking for—what, I don't know—with roughly seventy dollars to my name. If I don't get nailed, I may in fact starve to death. How long can I last on one more Danish-in-a-bag? Of course, I've eaten enough this morning to hold me for the entire month. I wonder if they still serve food on Delta. . . . Do I dare try to cash a check? That could take a few days to trace. No.*

Feeling sorry for myself wasn't going to get me anywhere. Clearly. So I got up and headed back out to the Caddy.

As I approached the big glass doors, I saw Sadowski's car, and it appeared that someone was in it.

*Shit.*

Yes. Someone was in my car! I peered around the side of the door, keeping away from the front. The driver's side door opened slightly, and in a flash I saw the intruder. It was the German! He exited, shut the door, and quickly walked away and toward the doors to the pavilion.

The Düsseldorf assassin/garmento had done something

to my car, of that I was certain. But how the hell had he found me again? How? Impossible! I had been very, very careful.

Before the man spotted me, I hurried back to the women's bathroom to think a minute. Not the most comfortable of places—they are built to get travelers in and out as quickly as possible—but I settled into a stall, figuring I had maybe ten minutes before the restroom attendant / cleaning lady would knock on the door to see if I was dead or shooting up.

How the hell had he found me? I had been so damned careful.

Then it hit me, and I slapped my forehead so hard the other ladies must have thought I fell off the bowl.

The GPS! How could I have been so freaking stupid? It was like a built-in tracking device. *Are the cops barricading the place right now?*

I was sweating and had to control myself from shaking.

*Do not bring attention to yourself.*

After eight minutes I walked out—sauntered actually, or attempted to—and scanned the building. There was only one cop—a highway patrol officer—and he didn't seem to be in the mood to catch a killer. He was adjusting his fly as he walked out of the men's room and headed, I swear, to the Dunkin' Donuts counter.

I had to get out, and the car was no longer an option.

At a kiosk, a woman in a fake Canadian Mounties uniform was selling bus tickets to the Niagara Falls area. Why they would have a bus operator in a travel stop for cars, I didn't know. Then I realized that there was a casino up in the Niagara Falls area. I seemed to recall from a news story I'd once done that this casino was operated by the Seneca tribe (or as they were called in the newsroom, "casino-owning Americans"). Seniors probably drove here, parked their cars, and then mustered up for day trips spent squandering their Social Security checks on the slots.

The good: There was a way out.

The better: I had my satchel with my computer, my passport, and the phone with me. I had just bought some essentials. *This could work*.

The bad: Oh, money. Right. *Damn*.

"How much are the tickets?" I asked the Mountie ticket lady.

"New York or Canadian?" the woman asked perkily.

"Huh?"

"New York or Canadian side of the Falls," she then said.

"Oh, Canadian. For sure."

"Do you have proof?"

"I need to show you proof to buy the ticket?"

"Not for me, dear, but you're crossing borders. The officers at the border sure need proof! You don't want them to think you're a fugitive from justice, do you?" She giggled as though this were the first time she'd made that joke.

"Oh, yes, of course. I mean, no. And how much are they?"

"Seventy round-trip—or twenty if you buy twenty-five in casino chips. The bus stops at the casino on the way in and the way out."

Fifty bucks would wipe me out!

"Oh, great . . . but I need to get some cash first," I said, knowing for sure I'd get traced with Sadowski's ATM, but I had six hours and maybe I could dodge the Feds, or whoever the hell was on my tail, and the German for that long. I said my fourth prayer in two days.

I stuck the card in the ATM and a request for my password popped up, of course. *Shit. Shit. Shit.*

The fake Mountie was watching me.

*What? You never saw a woman with clown hair who was down to her last Danish?* I smiled and waved like an idiot.

I pulled the card out and noticed it wasn't even in Sadowski's name. It was in the name of "Alazais Roussel." *What the hell?*

I flipped it over and saw that written on a piece of Scotch tape on the back were the numbers 42 15 0 13 45 0.

It was worth a shot. I put the card in again, pulled it out, and punched in the numbers. Immediately, the machine responded with the words "cash withdrawal?"

You bet your ass.

I punched in $300, an amount I thought was safe, and those green beauties came flying out. It was like hitting lotto. What the hell! I did it again and got another $200.

I went back to the Mountie's kiosk and bought a round-trip casino special—no sense in calling attention to myself with a one-way ticket.

"The next bus is in twenty minutes. In front," she grinned.

Since I couldn't go outside and risk being spotted by the German, I walked around and bought a horrifying pink hoodie with rhinestones in the shape of a horse, some equally terrible fake Indian moccasins, and some knock-off Ray Bans, which will be in style until the next coming—maybe even the one after the next coming. I went back into the bathroom, put on the sweatshirt, the moccasins, and the glasses, and put my leather jacket, T-shirts, and toiletries into the carry-on.

Ten minutes until I could blow that joint. I paced and studied wall maps and uninteresting local history lessons printed up in big plastic reproductions of 1790s-era documents—anything to keep my face to the wall.

Something, a hunch, a feeling, a whatever, made me glance over my shoulder just as the German walked toward me.

*Son of a bitch!*

But he didn't make me, and instead glanced all over, looking past the seriously unattractive tourist with the aging rocker-chick hair, pink hoodie, and mock mocs. He turned and walked to an area that faced the women's bathroom, and watched every woman who came out.

The guy was good. Normally an act like that would get him pinched as a pervert, but he was totally unobtrusive.

I took my shot at the same time and walked outside with my head down and headed for the bus pickup area. *Five minutes, four.*

The seniors were already lined up outside in front of a sign that said CASINO DAY TOURS. I didn't exactly blend in as I'd hoped I would have, although some of those dames were as done up as I was in pastel rhinestone tracksuits. I kept looking around nervously until one old gent asked me if I was waiting for my husband.

"Don't worry, honey. We guys never miss the Wednesday bus."

"Oh."

"Texas Hold'em tourney day."

I nodded knowingly and looked around again. I was sweating.

The big tourist bus with a smiling Seneca Indian holding a hatchet finally pulled up. Happy Trails was the bus operator. Right.

I wanted to knock those seniors down and rush aboard, but I couldn't and I was at the end of the line. Slowly, ever more slowly, they boarded. Without warning, the bus driver suddenly shut the door before I and a few other stragglers could even board. He walked to the back and lowered the electric ramp to allow a parade of walker- and wheelchair-bound senior gamblers to wheel onto the bus.

*Damn it! I'm standing out here and the freaking German is going to come out and blow us all away.*

Why the driver had to shut the door and keep the rest of us outside as he let the invalids board I couldn't even begin to understand. Like we were going to try to steal a ride when we were all trapped on the same damned bus!

I headed to the back ramp, where a morbidly obese man with an oxygen thing attached to his wheelchair and a tube up his nose tossed his cigarette on the ground and wheeled onto the drop-down ramp.

"Excuse me, sir?" I called to the driver, who was moving different levers as the asthmatic smoker grunted his way inside.

The driver looked annoyed. "I'm helping people board here, ma'am."

"Yes, I know, but I, um . . . need to use the restroom. Right away," I said, pointing to my stomach. "It's serious."

Even more annoyed that I was going to stink up the restroom before we even left the curb, he nonetheless had no choice but to let me step on the wheelchair ramp, cutting in front of a lady waiting to wheel on.

"Come on," he said. "But I could get in trouble for this."

I handed him my ticket and raced aboard and straight into the lav. When I heard the bus doors finally close and the hissing sound of the hydraulics signaling we were set to take off, I came out, put my carry-on bag up on the rack, and plopped down hard in an empty row in the back.

I was watching out the window, scanning the area for

the German bastard. As the bus began to pull away, I saw him, cigarette dangling out of his mouth, standing, scanning the cars, right on the curb. So close.

As the bus passed him, he instinctively looked up and saw me. For the briefest moment, our eyes met. I turned around to stare out the window, trying to follow my tormentor's progress or lack thereof. He started heading at a swift pace back toward the parking lot.

As the bus pulled around and passed the row where the Caddy was parked, the German stopped dead in his tracks, close to the car. He saw me again through the glass. Our eyes locked. I pressed my lips against one of the back windows and planted a kiss obscenely on the glass and then waved at him, like a forlorn lover, with a tiny wiggle of my fingers. He was standing there alone— I hoped—at least as far as I could tell with the limited sight range I had out the window.

As the bus swept past him, I reached frantically into my red bag, pulled out the Caddy's keyless remote, pointed it out the window, and hit "unlock."

The explosion from Sadowski's car shook the ground and rocked the bus. Flames shot ten feet in the air. *Damn!* It was nearly as terrific an explosion as the one that had blown out the lobby of my honeymoon hotel.

*Auf Wiedersehen, Fritz.*

## 17

The seniors all screamed and ducked as best as they were able to when the Caddy blew. The driver, who had seen it all (or thought he had), didn't stop the bus to look back. He just immediately sped his bus safely out of harm's way and then came on the PA to assure the passengers that everything was OK.

"Car fire, folks. Lucky we were far enough away from it."

The "incident" gave the passengers a full hour to repeat the same things over and over to each other. It was the most exciting event in years.

"If we'd been a few feet closer . . ." "Did you see those flames? Thirty feet at least!" The morbidly obese guy, however, was still complaining. "Driver! Crank up the air conditioning. I'm dying back here. So damned hot. I need a smoke. My nerves . . ."

I sat back smugly until the truth sank in. Dear God, had I just killed someone? Technically, I assumed that, yes, I had killed someone, even though it wasn't really my doing.

*Yes. It was. You knew he wired that car the second*

*you saw him inside of it. It's not murder. It is so. Oh, my
God. I just killed a human being. Now I really am a
guilty fugitive on the run.*

I kept my eyes glued to the TV screen at my seat and
tuned it to a local TV station, WKBW. Within minutes,
they had a reporter on the scene of the "tremendous car
fire and subsequent explosion." The Caddy was still burning like crazy, and ambulances and fire engines were surrounding the whole area of the parking lot.

"The service area has been closed," the excited young
man was reporting. "No word on when it may reopen.
Eyewitnesses in the parking lot tell News Seven that sheets
of metal flew as far as twenty feet!"

Then a second, more terrible thought hit me: What if
flying sheets of metal had also killed or wounded innocent people? The reporter had no word on deaths or injuries yet.

Then, courtesy of Happy Trails, the TV abruptly went
black and the preprogrammed selection of movies began. For the next several hours I would be in a news
blackout.

I checked Sadowski's secure phone for messages from
Dona or Donald. There was one. It was from Edward
.Gibbonsays@libero.it. Dona.

"Good work" was the entire message.

How in hell did she know that an obscure car fire in
an Upstate rest area had been my work? Of course she
didn't, she was talking about something else. But what?

I didn't know whether to answer or not. I chose cau-
tion and shut the phone down.

When we passed a highway sign indicating that it was
seventy miles to the Canadian border and Niagara Falls,
my heart started pounding again. This spiky-haired redhead looked nothing like perky brunette Alexandra
Zaluckyj on my passport, but I was still nervous.

I had only one ID with that name on it. My credit cards were all in the name of Alessandra Russo, and so was my license.

I pulled down my carry-on from the rack and went into the bus lavatory. I pulled out my expensive scissors and cut up my cards. I stuffed the non-name parts of the cards into the built-in garbage thing on the wall. I opened the window at my seat a bit, and every mile or so discreetly threw out another piece of plastic credit card.

The bus exited onto I-190N and the Robert Moses Parkway and then followed the CITY TRAFFIC sign to Rainbow Boulevard. It made a right at Fourth Street and into the casino parking lot. The megalopolis that is the Seneca Niagara Casino was so overwhelmingly large, it could give the MGM Grand in Vegas a run for its money.

Most of the seniors exited the bus, but roughly a quarter of the passengers stayed on while others boarded.

A woman in her eighties sat down next to me.

"Going to the Falls? I try to ride the *Maid of the Mist* at least twice a year," she said. "I love the slots too and come as often as I can. And you? Vacation?"

"I'm meeting my husband at the Falls," I lied for no reason whatsoever. "We honeymooned there."

*What? Who are you? Marilyn Monroe in* Niagara?

"Yes, the honeymoon capital of the world—when my mother was a bride," she quipped, as the bus pulled away from Upstate's gambling mecca. Was she eyeing me suspiciously?

"We thought it would be romantic. I mean, anyone can go to Bali, right?"

*Oy. Shut up.*

The lady—her name was Lexi—then went on and on about her three marriages and how each one was more thrilling than the next. Husband number two was a sex addict.

"How can you not love that?" she said.

I was beginning to like her a lot, when about five miles out from the Canadian border the fat guy, who surprisingly had not gotten off at the casino, started complaining out loud that he needed a cigarette—despite the fact that he was attached to an oxygen supply!

"I don't know why he didn't smoke up when we stopped at the casino," I complained to my new best friend, Lexi.

As I feared, the guy pulled out a cigarette and lit it.

A frightened elderly lady in the seat across the aisle jumped up. "Put that out," she screamed. "You're gonna kill us all."

He just snarled, "Mind your fucking business, you old bat," and blew smoke in her face.

*Don't, don't, don't, don't, don't, don't, don't, don't, don't, don't, don't, don't, don't get mixed up in this.*

Lexi jumped out of her seat and rushed him and knocked the cigarette right out of his hands and stamped it out.

This sent him into a rage and he spewed out, "You stupid bitch!"

*Don't, don't, don't, don't, don't, don't, don't, don't, don't, don't, don't, don't, don't get mixed up in this.*

I got up from my seat and walked over to Lexi's side. Not that she needed me.

Just then the driver came on the PA to announce, "Everyone back to their seats immediately! The police have been notified."

*Oh, damn. Just what I need.*

"Lexi, this isn't a fight you need to make," I said to her as she shrugged me off with her elbows, nearly poking my eyes out. She was much taller than me.

"Stupid fat bastard!" she snarled as I wrangled her back to her seat.

At the Canadian border crossing, the driver pulled into the bus checkpoint area and was immediately pointed into the customs office.

Several U.S. Customs officers and an equal number of Royal Canadian Mounted Police boarded the bus, spoke briefly with the driver, and announced that we were to take our luggage and exit the bus. Tubby started yelling again.

"I'm a citizen of the United States of America, and I protest this treatment. What is this? Iran?"

The officers immediately stood beside him and asked who else had been involved, while the rest of the passengers tried in their disabled ways to exit the bus.

Although the bus check-stop at the border crossing normally takes about a half hour, this would, I realized, be considerably longer and would involve more intense scrutiny.

"These two," he said, pointing to Lexi and me as we were trying to exit.

*Goddammit!*

"Not true," said the lady who started all the trouble with the smoker. "This lady," she said, pointing to me, "tried to break it up. He's just pissed that she had diarrhea and ran on the bus ahead of him." Great.

The cop asked for my identification, and I handed him the Alexandra Zaluckyj passport. I cringed as he inspected it, took off his glasses, looked at me more closely.

Which country isn't a breeding ground for terrorists?

"It's Polish," I said, as though he cared. Then, worse, "My family was in the Holocaust."

*What?* I made a face like my stomach was about to erupt again.

As the driver lowered the back ramp, the cop looked at me like I was just another crazy lady with the runs, and he dismissed me with a wave.

To make myself look even more innocent, I ran back to the lavatory, came out with a satisfied look on my face, and began unfolding wheelchairs and walkers and helping whatever passengers we could to get out of the bus, while making idiotic small talk with them. My heart was about to explode.

We had to put our bags and luggage on the ground outside the bus, and the customs agents pointed out several bags to go through, mine of course being one. Forty-two-year-old women with rooster hair are the most likely drug couriers.

As I presented my bag and passport again, the fat guy was being lowered from the bus's handicapped ramp. How it didn't crash to the ground, I still can't fathom. He was still cursing and screaming.

The customs agent was so intent on not missing the action that he briefly glanced at my passport and asked only, "Business or pleasure?"

"Pleasure. I hope," I joked. "Second honeymoon at the Falls. My husband was on business in Rochester, so we decided to meet up there."

I could have said I was carrying a nuke for all he cared. The fat guy's rage escalated when his wheelchair touched the ground. He then also lit up again and started yelling curses at the officers.

*Thank you, Jesus.* Or whoever.

The big guy was taken into custody along with Lexi, and the rest of us were allowed to board once more, and just like that the bus cruised across the border right into Canada.

"Stupid bastard," I heard Lexi yelling just before we pulled out.

The Niagara Falls bus depot looked exactly as I'd expected it would and featured, in addition to other depressing attractions, a TGI Friday's.

I paid cash for a Greyhound bus ticket (forty dollars) to the Toronto airport—which would involve another hour-and-forty-minute ride, according to the schedule, which left me a little more than five hours until departure. Figuring on at least two hours of travel time—without traffic—would put me at the gate three hours ahead of the flight, which left me roughly an hour to clear check-in.

*If only.*

Traffic was especially heavy—highway construction—and I arrived at the Delta terminal with only two hours and fifteen minutes to spare. I went to a kiosk, punched in the confirmation number of the prepaid ticket, said a thank-you to Donald somewhere in the world, and watched gratefully as the ticket slid out.

I went to the check-in line, which was very long, and after fifteen minutes, I started to sweat. The security line was as long as at an outlet mall on Black Friday.

I showed my ticket to a Delta agent on the floor, and she further distressed me by saying, "You're on the wrong line."

*No! How did you screw this one up?*

"Oh, my God, I need to go through immigration and everything and I won't make the plane in time," I said to her.

"No," she laughed—laughed! "You should be on the BusinessElite line."

"The what?"

"Your ticket—it's for business class."

"It is?"

"You booked it and you don't know?" she then said, eyeing me.

*Terrorist / wanted killer / baby snatcher trying to board!*

"Oh, the band—they booked it for me."

"The what?"

"My husband, he's in a rock band. The, um, The Pan. Have you heard of them?"

*You are such a fool! The Pan Band? You should be arrested just for that.*

The agent looked at me blankly. "No, I don't think I have. It's the line right over there," she said, handing me back my ticket.

*First class? Why Donald, I didn't think you cared!*

The line was short—that's how the rich do it—and the woman at the counter quickly checked me in, surprised that I had no luggage to check. All I had was the terrible fake Vuitton carry-on and my red bag.

"My husband's in a rock band. They forwarded my stuff to Istanbul."

"Really? Wow! Do I know them?"

"Pan," I replied—*again!*—which caused her also to immediately lose interest in my exotic life as the wife of a rock star.

"Just go to the Elite security check-in on the far left."

That line was nearly empty, and I sailed through immigration in no time, thanks to the help of one of Delta's Elite agents. Yes, when you've got a big-ticket ticket, you are treated like a rock star. Even if your husband is in the Pan Band.

I even had time to sit in the first-class lounge for a few minutes. It kept me out of sight of the cops patrolling the airport terminal.

I walked in, showed my ticket, ordered a big glass of Chianti, plopped down at an Internet carrel, and logged in as CATHARAZ@hotmail.com.

Nothing.

Within fifteen minutes, they announced that the flight was boarding, and I proceeded to the gate, showed my ticket and passport, boarded without incident, settled into a big, luxurious seat, and took the glass of champagne the flight attendant offered. Bliss: No one was seated next to me and I was drinking champagne. Too bad my new friend had been brutally murdered and I was wanted for Murder One.

It wasn't until the plane's door had closed and the Jetway was beginning to roll back that I finally relaxed. Good luck with that. Abruptly the Jetway began rolling back into place and the airplane door in front of the Elite cabin opened. Six police officers and four men in suits boarded and immediately conferred with the captain.

*Oh, God.*

The captain's voice came on the PA: "No problem folks." *Right.* "Just a quick random check by these fine officers to make sure everyone's passports are up to snuff. Can't be too careful in these times."

*Horse crap!*

The officers began looking up and down the rows, checking random (my ass) passports. When they approached my row, I voluntarily offered up my passport. They looked at the photo, looked at me, looked back at the photo.

"Miss, Za-lucky-Jay?"

"Yes," I said, automatically touching my hair. "It's terrible, right?" I asked, trying for some humor. Or something.

The officer didn't acknowledge my remark at all and instead waved over a colleague who was busy checking the IDs of what looked like an honest-to-God rock-star couple two rows up: ugly guy with bad teeth, spectacular girlfriend.

The agent handed his colleague my passport when she arrived at my seat.

"Miss Zalucky-Jay?" she inquired.

"Yes," I said again, touching my red spiked hair.

"May I ask why you've traveled to several countries

in the Mideast?" *Oh, no. Tell the truth that you're a reporter, and you're dead; lie and you're dead.*

I went for the lie. "Well, not for a looong time. My husband's in a rock band. Played for the troops. I was the publicist. The Pan—ever heard of them?"

"Yes, I have," she answered inexplicably. Then she conferred with the male officer. As they were doing that, the rock couple started complaining. Loudly. In rock-star Cockney.

"Bloody hell," the man said, "I have to make a connection to Istanbul. This is bullshit!"

His companion, a platinum-blond, hard-body, rocker chick, started laughing. Very loudly.

The officer automatically handed me back my passport and went over to them. When the agents inquired about something or other, the rocker got furious.

"Do you know who I am?" he said menacingly.

*Maybe he's also in the Pan Band.*

When they asked again for his passport, he said, "Bugger off," and went back to his drink. Within seconds a scuffle ensued, and the couple was hustled off the plane kicking and screaming.

This was getting weird—two checkpoints and two violent passengers—both had been there just in time to take the heat off of me. First the fat smoker and now a skinny rocker.

*Naaah.*

By 8:00 the flight attendants had offered more drinks (yes), blanket and pillow, choice of entrées for dinner (yes, yes, and some of that), and after-dinner drinks (yes).

I reclined my seat to the full, yes, full sleeping position, which almost worked wonderfully, but then I tossed, turned, and tried to make myself comfortable enough to sleep. As I was drifting off, I remembered. *The envelope!*

I put the seat back up, turned on my reading light,

and dug into my red bag and pulled out the faxes from Dona.

The large Best Rate Motel envelope did indeed hold five pages. And each one was so explosive, I could have been arrested as a mad bomber.

The first was a photocopy of an old clipping from the *New York Post* that was probably half a tabloid page in its original size, including the photo of a somber, freckle-faced girl with medium-length, medium-colored hair, wearing a dark crewneck sweater over a light shirt. It was clearly her school picture, but the child wasn't smiling.

"Theotokos Bienheureux in happier times," the caption read. That was her "happier times" face? The story was a shocker—for me at least.

*New York Post*
*April 14, 1981*

*Honors Student Goes Missing: Cops Seek to Question*
  *Parents*
*By Marsha Kranes*
  *A twelve-year-old brown-haired, freckle-faced seventh grader, Theotokos Meryemana Bienheureux, a student at the Friends Seminary Quaker school on Seventeenth Street, has been missing since Thursday.*
  *When the girl, known affectionately by classmates as "Theo," did not show up for school either on Friday or Monday, her teacher, Ms. Debbie Chasen, became concerned and called the child's parents, Leah and William Bienheureux, at home.*
  *Chasen's concern turned to worry when messages left on the family's answering machine were not returned. Two days ago, she tried reaching personnel at the Catari Relief Services Worldwide offices, located in*

Rockefeller Center, where the Bienheureux couple works.

The CRSW is a philanthropic organization that sends missionaries, teachers, emergency relief workers, and supplies to third-world countries around the globe.

Chasen told the Post, "When I still hadn't heard back from Mr. and Mrs. Bienheureux, I called the CRSW office. Theo has never missed class. Ever. She's a top student who has a perfect attendance record.

"I spoke to a receptionist, who said the Bienheureuxs were out of the country, but that someone would return my call," Chasen added. "But I never heard back. I tried again and was put through to Mr. Bienheureux's answering machine, which indicated that they were no longer working at the New York City offices and have been reassigned to Indonesia. I know that they move around a lot, and right now Indonesia is suffering through a terrible drought. We at Friends are working with relief organizations there as well. But still, the Bienheureuxs never signed Theotokos out of school.

"I've asked Quaker relief workers in Indonesia if there is any way they can find out more for us."

Lt. Det. Richard Marino, of the NYPD Missing Child task force, told the Post that the bureau is investigating the strange disappearance of the girl.

"The child has not been seen for over a week. The parents, however, were going about their normal activities until three days ago, even though the messages on their answering machines had been placed probably six days earlier," he told the Post exclusively.

"This sends up a red flag for us, because in that period of time—from the last time Theo was seen leaving Friends Seminary on Thursday until today—nothing. It's like she disappeared off the face of the earth."

*Since her parents were French nationals, he said, the disappearance took on all sorts of international complications, if they chose to go that route.*

*That being said, immigration has no record of Leah, William, or Theotokos Bienheureux leaving this country. They did not, as far as we can determine, ever enter Indonesia, either.*

*The question then, is "Where is Theotokos Bienheureux?"*

The story went on to describe the parents' prestigious Fifth Avenue apartment building, where, it was stated, they occupied—get this—a ten-room spread.

Why would missionaries live in that kind of Wall Street hedge-fund luxury? It made no sense.

Also quoted were the comments by neighbors who spoke about the "strange" Bienheureux family, who seemed to have only late-night visitors and who often took in children from other countries for short periods of time.

The story finished with this quote from one of the building's doormen, Frank Wilson, thirty: "Theo? She was a good kid, never in trouble, always behaving," he said. "I thought she had come home from school that day, but I can't be positive. But I know I never saw her after that day. That I know for positively sure. I'm scared for her. I hope she knows she can call the building if she's in trouble. I'll personally go get her and bring her home."

When questioned about the parents, Wilson would only say, "I don't know anything about them. Quiet. You have to ask my supervisor."

I wondered if this Wilson guy was still alive—if I could find him, or better yet, if Dona or Donald could find him—he might be a source of untapped info.

I reluctantly put the faxed document down and picked up the next one.

On the top of the story—though very badly distorted by time and the old faxing method—were three head-shots of young men in various religious garb.

### March 27, 1982
*Special to the* International Herald Tribune

*Blackout Blamed on Explosion of Comet*

*A comet, visible only in the skies over Turkey, which had unexpectedly emerged, then brightened and ex-ploded in record time, was the cause of the blackout that affected most of Turkey and parts of Europe, it was reported by the International Astronomical Union.*

*Three astrophysicists who are credited with being the first to discover the astral phenomenon late last week—Professor Gaspar Bar-Cohen, director of as-tronomy at the Wise Observatory in Tel Aviv, Israel; Dr. Mikaeel Hussein, astrophysicist-in-residence, Uni-versity of Cairo, Egypt; and Dr. Balaaditya Pawar, head of the Mount Abu Observatory, Rajasthan, India—admit that the massive size of the comet led them to believe at first that they were witnessing the emergence of a new star.*

*"We regret this error and apologize for having mis-led our colleagues with premature announcements we inadvertently passed along to the IAU," they wrote. "The comet's collapse resulted in its 'coma'—a cloud of gas and dust illuminated by the sun—to grow big-ger even than the planet Jupiter. Furthermore, unlike most comets, VCH1244 [self-named by the three as-trophysicists] lacked the tail usually associated with such celestial bodies. This resulted in our mistakenly jumping to an inaccurate conclusion."*

As for the blackout, the Gazette Journal of the Astronomical Union explained, "Because there are sink-holes in the nucleus of VCH1244, which gives it a honeycomb-like structure, and because this comet had grown to such astounding proportions, it created a brief energy vacuum."

In a conference call to the three scientists yesterday, the International Herald Tribune also learned, "This energy drain occurred as VCH1244 collapsed, which then exposed the comet's ice to the sun, which in turn transformed the ice into gas," Professor Bar-Cohen explained.

On March 23, the comet, which had been visible in the night sky over certain parts of Turkey, suddenly erupted and expanded as it lit up the skies over all of Turkey.

Added Professor Hussein, "What comets do when they pass near the sun is very unpredictable. We expected to see a 'coma cloud' and a tail, but this was more like an explosion, and we saw the bubble of gas and dust as it expanded away from the center of the blast."

Experts estimated that the comet's show and the ensuing energy drain it created would last for several weeks and perhaps as long as several months.

However, the dire predictions proved to be completely, if inexplicably, wrong. In fact, the comet self-destructed within hours of exploding, and by late last night all power had been restored throughout Turkey and the affected areas of Europe.

Dr. Pawar concluded, "This was a once-in-a-lifetime event to witness, similar, I expect, to what observers must have experienced in the night sky during the birth of Christ."

I was astounded that a far-fetched explanation, the ridiculous story, and its accompanying apology—by three astrophysicists who actually said that they mistook a comet for a star—was published without question. And that was back in the day when investigative reporters actually were allowed the time to investigate a story.

But even more interesting than the cock-and-bull that those three distinguished star-men had carefully scripted for whatever reason, was Pawar's one unguarded comment. You could almost feel his companions kicking him under the table.

He had actually compared the star or comet or whatever the heck it was to the Star of Bethlehem at the time of the birth of Jesus.

Why? And why would they embarrass themselves by admitting that they'd been so stupid as to not know the difference between a star and a comet?

Fear? Intimidation? All of the above?

I hoped to God (or whomever) that those astrophysicists were still alive and that I could find them. The story didn't give their ages, so they could be sixty, ninety, or dead and buried.

A sidebar to the piece, which I almost didn't read because I thought it was unrelated, actually detailed some of the reactions—and predictions—to the comet's appearance. In addition to all the Regular Joe "loonies" who predicted it presaged the Second Coming were these bulleted items:

• *Canadian prophet Doug Clark called the comet a "star" and said that it signaled that Jesus was to return and lure Christians away from the Tribulation by April 1982. His basis was something called "The Jupiter Effect," a theory put forth in a best-selling book by John Gribbin and Stephen Plagemann. The book claimed that on March 10, 1982, an alignment of the planets was supposed to trigger earthquakes and fires that would kill millions.*

• *On March 22, psychic Benjamin Torre took an ad in the* Los Angeles Times *proclaiming, "The Christ is now here."*

• *Rev. Pat Robertson took to the airways to declare on his* 700 Club TV *show, "I guarantee you by the end of 1982 there is going to be a judgment on the world."*

My first thought was: freaky, rapture-obsessed loonies. My second thought was even crazier: These freaky, rapture-obsessed loonies were all only off by a few decades!

I started thinking, and couldn't stop, and turned on the screen on the pop-out computer terminal attached to the seat. No log-in was required for searching, and I keyed in "disasters of the new millennium."

*Christ!—no pun intended. It reads like the end of the world, for real!*

There are too many to cite here, but it was the new millennium that had kick-started the chain of natural and unnatural disasters, right off the bat with devastating floods in 2000 in Southeastern Africa, which killed nearly 1,000 people. This was followed in 2001 by the World Trade Center attack, which in turn triggered the Iraq and Afghanistan wars, followed by constant war and unrest around the world—particularly in the Mideast—which have killed millions.

On Boxing Day 2004, there was the giant tsunami along the coasts of landmasses bordering the Indian Ocean, killing something like 230,000 people in I-don't-know-how-many countries and destroying thousands of acres of land.

In 2005 there was Hurricane Katrina, which killed

nearly 2,000, displaced millions, and ruined forever thousands of acres of land in the South.

In 2010–2011, the devastating floods in Australia, the 2011 earthquake, tsunami, and subsequent nuclear plant disaster in Japan . . .

As the info was flowing, it all started blurring together in my tired brain: earthquakes, volcanoes, tsunamis, plagues, pestilence, floods, forest and city fires, which had killed millions. No country was immune.

In fact, world-changing disasters had become so common that we had begun, I realized, to lose our collective memory about what "normal" was supposed to be.

Tabloids hardly even put giant disasters on the front pages anymore, unless they killed at least 500.

*Maybe we do need a Second Coming. Shut up; you sound like a moron!*

That was the last thought I had before I nearly jumped out of my seat when the cabin lights came on and the flight attendants started passing out hot towels, as dawn was beginning to break.

## 18

Yes, for the first time in recent memory I had actually fallen dead asleep on an overseas flight. My mouth was hanging open, and I could feel drool down the side of my chin. The Best Rate Motel folder was on the seat next to me, but all the news clippings were scattered under the footrest on the floor.

I felt like those people that you pray are never seated next to you on a flight, let alone an overnighter. I opened the shade and could see that the sun was starting to rise and the sky was turning orange.

The captain informed us that it was currently 6:00 A.M. local time and that it was a glorious day in Paris. That announcement would have gladdened my heart and excited my senses at any other time in my life. Now, it just gave me anxiety.

I made my way to the lavatory and used everything in the bag of goodies they still offered in the expensive seats: mini sizes of toothpaste, hand sanitizer, a tiny oxygen spray, and a comb that no one who wasn't sporting a St. Anthony haircut could possibly get through their hair.

We landed on time, and as I figured, I had to shuttle it to another terminal, but thank God Turkey had just entered the EU finally, and I didn't have to go through French customs, just passport control, which was a breeze.

I actually made the next flight, although it required begging my way through security so that I arrived just as they were closing down the gate and taking the last passengers aboard. I was able to board quickly after a brief check of my passport and e-ticket by the gate agents.

Same business-class deal for the three-and-a-half-hour flight—more coffee and a basket of croissants, which I planned not to eat, but did.

*No one will ever recognize me after these last two days: I must have gained forty pounds!*

The hours spent flying gave me a false sense of security—as though I were just that same old reporter being sent somewhere terrific to cover something horrific. But no news organization had my back any longer. In fact, no one had my back any longer.

*Not true. Dona and Donald . . .*

I read and then re-read all the news clippings in the envelope. Two were follow-ups on the missing child, Theo Bienheureux.

One detailed the police investigation, in which an elderly neighbor who'd been walking her two Yorkies at dawn on the Saturday in question swore that she saw a sleepy child with a blanket around her being taken into a car, along with a man, a woman, and a priest!

She said the priest even tipped his fedora hat to her. It looked a little odd, but since the chauffeur carried and then loaded several suitcases into the car, she assumed it was just another nouveau riche family off to meet their private plane to take them somewhere "fabulously sacred," the woman acidly stated. Her disgusted sniff practically jumped off the page.

The dawn episode, I knew, was a good cover, but it seemed like really bad news for the child.

Someone—and it sounded like the trio that Wright-Lewis had described to me—had abducted the girl from her apartment. But what about her damned parents?

The next clip was supposed to have explained it all:

People *magazine*
April 27, 1981

*Exclusive*
*"Missing" Theo Isn't Missing After All!*
*By Harry Francescani*
   *Little Theotokos Bienheureux, who had been re-ported missing by her teacher at the prestigious Friends Seminary school in NYC, has been found alive and well, and as it turns out, was not missing at all!*
   *The twelve-year-old, who hasn't been seen since she disappeared from school in March, had simply moved to a remote region of the Amazon with her parents, Leah and William Bienheureux, who are missionaries with the Catari Relief Services Worldwide.*
   *According to Leah, thirty-five, in a letter to People magazine, which was forwarded to our offices from the CRSW Brazilian office:*
   *"We wish to thank all our New York friends and neighbors for their concern about the whereabouts of our beloved daughter, Theo, who is safe and sound with us in our new missionary post.*
   *"Our organization, you see, was the first to be in-formed by the Brazilian government last month that two lost tribes consisting of just twenty and twelve*

*people, respectively, had been discovered deep in the Amazon rain forest by two engineers working on a dam project in the area.*

*"The Brazilian relief organization Indigenous Peoples Relief and Rescue contacted our group, the CRSW, who then negotiated with the Brazilian government to secure for these indigenous peoples a protected area consisting of twenty square miles, deep within the Amazon.*

*"Our hope is that they can form a new clan together and begin to rebuild their families.*

*"As you can see from the attached photos, Theotokos is thriving in our new jungle home. Although she is only twelve, she is the official 'teacher' of the group and is working with the five children who are clan members.*

*"We have much work to do and we will remain here as long as needed. When Theo comes of college age, she can choose to attend a university or remain here doing what we think of as 'God's work.' "*

The rest of the article was an apology from the mother, who said both she and her husband were distressed that they had caused concern, but because they were (supposedly) not American-born, they therefore didn't understand our customs.

Like pulling a kid out of school without formal paperwork or even an explanation? Right. They knew how to enroll her in school, but they didn't know how to terminate that enrollment.

The story was accompanied by grainy photos of the family in their new home, which looked like a bunch of thatched-roof, open-sided huts amidst giant vegetation. The child in the pictures looked like Theo Bienheureux, but black-and-white photos of a twelve-year-old with her hair all frizzy from the Amazon air and wearing native dress could make any differences between the real deal and an imposter hard to decipher. And since the story had been reduced to fit the 8½ × 11-inch fax paper, the photos were very small.

At any rate, other pictures showed Theo "teaching" in an open hut while five little kids sat on a long bench alongside an indigenous bare-breasted woman who was nursing an infant. Across the photo in a young girl's foolishly fancy script was scrawled in what looked like crayon, "I love it here!"

And finally, I pulled out the last clipping, which, if possible, was the strangest of the lot. It was a full-page story with photos from my own newspaper.

*Special to* The New York Standard
*By Joe Michael Dogherty*
*October 3, 1979*

*The Sermon on the Mound*
   *Yesterday Pope John Paul II greeted the masses at Yankee Stadium and succeeded in doing what the Bombers have failed to do this year: come up number one!*
   *To a packed house, the pope delivered a stirring message of hope, peace, and tolerance. . . .*

The rest of the long-winded article was a gushing report about a New York event assigned to a reporter who was clearly a Catholic overwhelmed by seeing His Holiness in person.

But, what the hell? What did this have to do with anything I'd asked Dona to find for me?

I read the whole thing and found nothing of interest.

Then I studied the photos, of which there were two. The faxed copy had again been reduced to fit $8\frac{1}{2} \times 11$-inch paper, so again, the pictures were very tough to see.

I could barely even make out the caption, but then I saw something that would have made my hair stand up on end if it weren't already doing so on its own.

Standing next to the pope, as he touched the crowds on a receiving line, was an ordinary priest. Odd, because every other cleric around the pontiff was a cardinal. The caption listed two cardinals—one from Boston and one from India, and then, "Father Paulo Jacobi, Istanbul, Turkey." Could it be one and the same? I had assumed the name was spelled with a *y* but that had been just a guess.

This Father Jacobi looked to be in his forties, very thin. Most odd was his body language. While the cardinals and everyone around Pope John Paul II in the photos displayed submissive, adoring postures while gazing in awe at the pope, this Jacobi guy—a mere priest—stood next to him as an equal. Or a close friend.

*Blessed is she who comes in the name of the news. Dona—you are one helluva reporter!*

I had to laugh thinking of how she wrangled this. God knows what librarian she'd suckered into going into the basement at midnight to dig up and search through all those old files.

Just then, the plane touched down with a tough thump, bringing me back to my senses, and within seconds all the rushing passengers were hopping out of their seats before we were supposed to and grabbing their bags from the overhead compartments. Since I wasn't sure where the hell I was supposed to go other than to try to get through immigration and, if I managed that feat, to head to the Europacar counter, I took my sweet time.

Customs was fairly easy—especially since *again* there was a problem that took the attention away from me. I had nothing to declare, and no one asked to look in my carry-ons, which saved me not just from myself but also from the possibility that I would again start in with the Pan Band insanity that had beset me earlier.

I was starting to think that God or someone even more powerful, someone who could play with immigration, which was even beyond God's control in this day and age of paranoia, was watching out for me. Yes, I said "God."

First thing I did in the airport was to go to a currency exchange—or in plain English, "money changer"—to convert my dollars into euros. The place charged so much interest it probably qualified as a sin. I kept one hundred dollars in American and converted the rest to euros at the terrible rate of exchange. No wonder Jesus wanted to beat the crap out of their predecessors at the temple.

The next thing I did was to look for the Europacar counter. I hurried along the corridors filled with high-end shops bustling with tourists fat with cash, and stopped at an Internet kiosk, sat down, and logged in to find I had three messages.

Two were from my new Internet best friend, "Hot-SexyViagraMale," and one was from Edward.Gibbon says@libero.it.

Again in Italian. What was with Dona and/or Donald anyway? Whichever one it was sure was digging the cloak and dagger, but meantime, I was in no mood for idiotic games. This was anything *but* a game.

It said: "*Informazione importante dentro l'automobile manuale.*" My Italian wasn't that good. What a pain in the ass this was. The best I could come up with at that hour was: "Information on how to drive a manual car is"—something or other.

Like I didn't know how to drive stick? Had to be Dona. Donald knew this about me. I had driven everything ever invented.

Europacar had my reservation, but I knew there'd be a hitch—or worse—when I handed them my license, which was under the name "Russo," even though my passport was under "Zaluckyj."

"I'm divorced," I told the clerk, who happened to be dressed in a full burqa with EUROPACAR emblazoned on the head scarf and on the front of her "uniform," while the other women at the counter were dressed in a modern miniskirted uniform. *My luck.*

Burqa clerk studied my face and grimaced. I couldn't tell if she thought I was full of it or was just disgusted by my marital state. She called over one of the other clerks, and both compared my license to my passport.

"Ah, like I said, 'divorced.'"

Eventually she handed me a set of keys and the paperwork with the parking-spot location of my car and said, in impeccable English, "Thank you, Miss Zaluckyj," she said, pronouncing it correctly. "We have the credit card on record already. There is a GPS in the car. Drive safely." She immediately leaned over and whispered something to one of the other women, who all stared at my hair and started giggling—but hardly discreetly.

*Whose credit card was on record?*

I forgave Dona or Donald for the ridiculous Italian messages and was amazed anyone could have gotten some bogus credit card numbers preapproved.

If it was Dona, perhaps she used her own credit card to secure the car. Or better yet, a family member back in merry olde England. *Angel.*

I found the car in no time—*nice, an Alfa Romeo!*—and hopped in. But the car was automatic. Not a stick shift after all.

I was desperate to get out of there (where I was headed, I had no idea), but the message had been so adamant, so surely it was for a good reason. Was it a warning that if the car was anything other than a stick shift that someone had played around with it?

I went over the message in my mind again. Or tried to. When I couldn't retrieve it in my brain, I knew there was no choice but to open Sadowski's phone and get up an Italian translation site.

I typed in "*Informazioni importanti dentro l'automobile manuale*" and it translated not to "Information on how to drive a manual car," but "Important information inside the car manual."

*Of course!*

I opened the glove box, took out the manual, and took out the thick envelope tucked inside. Holy good God!

A French passport in the name of Alazais Roussel, but with *my* photo—albeit with a long blond curly 'do that made me look like I belonged on an old Fleetwood Mac album cover.

*How in hell had she done that? Or was it Donald's work? It had to be Donald. He was the one who knew how to pay off anyone anywhere anytime.*

No time to worry about it. I'd simply ask them when I was somewhere safe enough to use the Internet again. Anyway, unsure of where to go next, I realized that Sadowski's phone must be filled with contacts. If I turned off the 4G and simply scoured his contacts list, perhaps I could scare up some names.

The people the "simple" parish priest had (supposedly) known was astounding. There were phone numbers for everyone from movie stars to the pope. *Sadowski has the private numbers of Pope Francis, Prince Charles, Justin Bieber—and are you kidding me?—Maureen Wright-Lewis?*

He had never indicated to me that he knew her. What there wasn't, however, was a contact for the only person I *wanted* to find in Turkey, Father Paulo Jacobi.

*Maybe you should call Maureen and ask why Father Sadowski had her phone number. It's an old one, though. It's a 212 exchange. What the hell?*

There were too many names and numbers to study at that point, and I was nervous about any kind of satellite trace, even though he'd said it was untraceable, so I turned it off, tucked it into my bag, and started up the car—no explosion—and set the GPS to English.

I hit the display for "lodging" and booked a room at the Arena Hotel near the Blue Mosque. I plugged in the address and headed toward the signs that read IS-TANBUL.

If you've never been to Istanbul, or worse, driven through it, just know there are more one-way streets there than there are in Manhattan, and more crazy drivers than on Queens Boulevard (aka Boulevard of Death!).

I checked in under the name of Alazais Roussel, went up to my sparkling clean room, and stood under the hot shower until I thought my skin would peel off. Unfortunately, I seemed to not have done the dye job all that well and red color was still running off and lining the tiny shower stall.

I got out, dried myself off with a genuine Turkish towel, plopped down on the comfy single bed, turned on the TV, and flipped to CNN International. Marietta Tomasina was in front of the United Nations doing her stand-up. The din of the crazed crowd nearly drowned out her report, which had been filmed earlier in the day.

"The fourth day of the trial of Demiel ben Yusef has been nothing short of shocking, with the prosecution presenting survivors of the so-called 'Unholy Day bombings,'" she said.

"The Reverend Bill Teddy Smythe riveted the entire courtroom when he testified. Because this is a tribunal and not a trial per se, he was allowed to be both a spectator *and* a witness for the prosecution.

"The Reverend Smythe testified that he had been visiting his NYC branch of the megachurches he founded, the Light of God Tabernacle on Staten Island, that day. He left not five minutes before the church was bombed. He rushed back to find the tabernacle in ruins and many parishioners who volunteer there badly wounded. Two people, a visiting pastor from Texas and a young woman, died in the explosions, and Reverend Smythe brought the chamber to tears describing how he ministered to the sick and particularly to the two who had died that fateful day."

*There's something more than just being a media hound about that phony bastard. . . .*

The rest of the report went on to describe the day's proceedings and ben Yusef's refusal to acknowledge the judge or even his attorneys.

"Newly released sermons that were apparently secretly recorded of Demiel ben Yusef lecturing to a small band of followers have recently surfaced on the Internet and are available and unedited at CNN dot com slash benyusef."

There were additional links listed, and I turned on my tablet, which I had plugged in the night before.

*Thank you, Hotel Arena, for supplying the free converter plugs.*

I opened up a search engine with the intention of getting up the old bastard's testimony, but instead I was riveted by the name of tomorrow's witness. His name? Dr. Mikaeel Hussein.

## 19

I reached into my bag and switched on the phone to "contacts." Nothing under the name Mikaeel Hussein. It wasn't under "M," "H," or "Dr." although—*damn!*—if under the "Dr." section he didn't list every famous TV medical expert you ever heard of including, I swear, Dr. Phil *and* Dr. Oz.

Why the guy had acted all wide-eyed and naive I couldn't imagine. Or had he? Maybe since he was young-ish and sweet-faced, I'd simply assumed he was naive and wide-eyed.

*Idiot. The guy was priest to the stars or some crap like that, and you're thinking he was impressed to meet a couple of reporters. He probably hung out at Gramercy Tavern and played poker with rappers. He's probably got "Russo" under "N" for naive. Damn!*

And what about this Jacobi guy? Could these two bizarre priests have known one another? I tried, "Father," "Jacobi," and even "Paulo"—nothing. Then I tried "P. J." and got a number with 90+212+335+6941. *What the hell?* I tried it. A voice-mail message picked up and said in Italian, "*Ciao. Non sono qui in questo momento, ma se lasci i tuoi dati ti richiamo.*" I figured it meant the usual, "Hello. I'm not here right now, but I'll call you back if you leave your blah, blah, blah." No name.

The chances I'd gotten it right were slim and none, and I'd probably called Italy or maybe even *Little* Italy, but I took a shot. I spoke in English because the guy had been in the United States and seemed like a mover and shaker so chances were great that he spoke English better than I did. "Hello, Father Jacobi? I am a friend of Father Sadowski. Or was. I'd very much like to speak with you. Please return my call. I don't have the number, but hopefully it will come up on your phone. If you have Father Sadowski's cell phone number, you can call me back on that number."

I decided that the best thing I could do for myself now was to get one of those famous Turkish steam baths to clear my head. *The Things to See in Istanbul* booklet in my room recommended the Cağaloğlu Hamam (bathhouse), built in 1741, because it was "the last hamam to be built after a long period during the Ottoman Empire." It was also located within walking distance of the hotel, so I had the front desk call and book a bath for me, although when I arrived at the ancient building and walked inside, I realized that I may have been the first person since Sultan Mahmut to make a reservation.

It was bizarrely empty, and the stone walls and floors echoed with every footstep. It was also magnificent, although you'd never know it by walking in the front door. There was a little window where you picked what services you wanted and then were directed to an upstairs changing area.

I entered a tiny wooden common changing room with a door where I stripped, placed the thick towel around myself, locked my stuff in a foot locker with the key (yeah, good luck with that move), and walked out into the giant steam room with its gorgeous domed ceiling and marble slabs.

I was holding on to Sadowski's phone like an eighty-year-old man holds on to his Viagra when he's got a hot date. The steam was so dense it was like standing inside a hot geyser—albeit one with a vaulted ceiling, gorgeous stonework, tiled floors, and risers upon which I was supposed to—what?—lie down?

Within thirty seconds a big, fat, topless woman, wearing just bikini bottoms, appeared or seemed to in the thick fog and indicated for me to lie down on the towel on the slab. I did, and she then threw a giant bucket of hot water on top of me and left. *What?* I just stayed there all wet and miserable on my soaking-wet towel. Other women on the round, raised marble slab didn't act like anything was amiss so I just stayed there pretending I wasn't weirded out.

Fatty Topless came back about ten minutes later, and proceeded to beat the hell out of me. Okay, it was with wet leaves, and buckets of hot soapy water, but still. Then she began scrubbing me down—hard. My God. Yes, it hurt like hell, but it was just what I needed, or so I was thinking, when the phone blasted me back to reality.

The massage lady was not pleased and quickly indicated that phones were *izin verilmez,* which sounds like "definitely not allowed" in any language. Trying to excuse myself while attempting, at the same time, to wrap back up in the soaking wet towel, I ran for the exit, hoping it wasn't the exit to the street.

It wasn't, but it was worse—it was the men's changing room. But I didn't care. It's not like I haven't seen one before.

But in reality it wasn't anything like anything I had ever seen before. Not exactly.

The two startled men in there were in unusual states

of undress, and they were galabia-wearers, so it looked like they were in the middle of removing long lady-dresses. In America I would have thought I'd wandered into a gay bathhouse. Their protests about my sudden appearance fell on deaf ears, while I tried to get them to shut up by making gestures with my free hand about the importance of my phone call.

"American insolence," I heard one clearly mutter.

The caller was male—no particular accent I could discern other than, say, international mash-up.

"Miss Roussel? It is my understanding that you are requesting a meeting with Father Jacobi."

I couldn't believe my luck. I would have been thrilled with a phone call, but I was getting a full-on meeting! My luck must be changing!

"Yes, yes, that's correct," I answered, trying to hide my excitement.

"As it turns out, the good father is in Istanbul, and he will see you in one hour." He told me to jot down an address and phone number. I wasn't exactly prepared with a pen, so I told him to hold on while I tried to key the info into Sadowski's contact list under the "P. J."

"I want to read this back to you, ah, sir. I'm sorry I didn't get your name. . . ."

"It's Mr. Cesur," he replied.

"Thank you, Mr. Cesur." I read it back to him.

"Yes. Any cab can take you."

Making my apologies to the half-naked men, and tipping the masseuse generously for the half massage, I got dressed and was out of the hamami as quickly as I could. My terrible red hair was stuck to my head, making me look like I'd been scalped while getting steamed. Worse, the topless lady had washed it with god knows what in that bucket.

I handed the woman at the front desk the cell phone

with the address, and in perfect English she told me it wasn't far. In fact it was very close, but I wasn't about to try to navigate the streets and possibly miss the appointment. So she offered to have one of the workers there walk with me. We walked for no more than ten minutes along the lively streets. I was glad to have an escort, because we were assaulted by salesmen selling everything—but mostly carpets—literally every two feet.

That world quickly slipped away when he led me into the Grand Bazaar, however. "The address has to be just a few doors in," he said. I tipped him and he walked away. "It's right inside. No problem." Right.

If you've been to New York and you've seen how the world literally changes from block to block, it's nothing compared to the way the world changes inside a souk in Turkey. And it's no wonder that it does. After all, this is a country bordered by both Europe and Asia.

The bazaar smelled of spices and leather and animals and humanity. I didn't see any spices, but I did see hundreds and hundreds of store stalls selling more beautiful jewelry than I ever saw on Forty-seventh Street in the jewelry district.

The smells alone immediately slammed me back in time to that day in Dag Hammarskjöld Plaza when I was heading innocently enough to the tribunal of ben Yusef. Had it really only just been, what—four days earlier?

The Grand Bazaar is so massive it's hard to comprehend. It takes up sixty-one covered streets with over 3,000 shops. I was lucky to be somewhat near the entrance in the twisting and turning cavernous place. There were hawkers, thieves, and people hawking me to buy everything I could ever imagine for any price I could afford to pay.

Ignoring them as only a New Yorker can do, I instead found a reasonable-looking woman, dressed unreasonably in what had to be the best knockoff Chanel I'd ever seen, manning a knockoff-purse stall. I asked where I might find the address of Mr. Cesur. Forget three stalls in, it was actually past leather and over in carpets.

She directed me "two aisles down on the left." The address was not what I had expected, but what I should have anticipated: Istanbul Carpets II by Mustafah Cesur.

*Oh, crap. It's a carpet shop! I've seen* Midnight Express—*how could I have been* that *naive?*

I paused outside the shop. The call had been a come-on, I realized.

*The SOB wants to sell me a freaking rug. Sadowski's "contact" is a damned rug shop! I knew this was too good to be true.*

A thin, wiry man opened the glass door to the shop while I was still trying to figure out what to do. "May I ask you to step inside and enjoy a glass of tea, madam?"

"Thank you, but the last thing I want or need right now is a rug."

I could feel we were being watched, as everyone watches everyone in that market.

"Ah, but I only offer tea. I don't expect you to purchase anything."

"Right."

"Perhaps you care to see Istanbul's only *real* magic carpet?"

"Perhaps not," I snapped. "And *perhaps* I have no time and no money for a rug. And perhaps I don't appreciate that you tricked me into coming here," I continued, clearly forgetting that I was in Turkey and not New York, where I could get away with that kind of smart-ass lip.

"Father Jacobi isn't in there, is he?"

"Yes, of course he is."

"What's he doing? Sitting on the magic carpet?"

I turned on my heel, indignant, as though I had somewhere to go and as though I didn't have a price on my head. My short fuse had gotten the better of me again, and although I knew I was standing inside an ancient souk full of men who I thought looked like they'd sell their sisters for a good price, I still couldn't help mouthing off.

*Shut up! You're a skanky-looking redhead with a price on her head who is now probably worth her weight in gold. And after all the baked goods you consumed over the last few days—your worth must be escalating faster than the gold market in 2011.*

The mild-mannered rug salesman grabbed me by the arm from the back and jerked me hard, against my will, into the dark interior of the shop. Rugs were rolled and folded in giant piles, and he expertly pushed me through a small pathway down the middle of them all. I could feel them and smell them more than I could actually see them—it was that dark.

With my arm held tightly behind my back, I was shoved down onto a small wooden chair, and the rug man released his grip. As I groped the wooden table in front of me, a hand grabbed mine from the opposite side and held it tight. A black shadowy figure in a hooded cloak leaned in close. "Oh shit," I heard myself say. *The grim reaper.*

I couldn't see much as my eyes tried adjusting to the dimness inside. It got even darker when Cesur pulled the curtains shut around the display window in the front of the shop. He then pulled down the louvered metal gates and it became pitch black inside.

*Locked in!*

Cesur lit a candle and then walked around the shop pulling ceiling-lamp chains down to lower glass lamps, lighting the candles inside, giving the room the appearance of a deliberately set scene. One in which I was the heroine who needed rescuing.

"Goddammit, let me out, you freak!"

"Somehow one would expect the Chosen One to be a bit more refined," the dark figure said, his voice old and with an affected international air to it, as he put his cold hand on top of mine. His bony fingers tightened around my right hand in what felt like a death grip. "But, ahh, Headquarters never fails to surprise, do they, *Miss Russo?*"

## 20

"Who?" I rasped.

"Headquarters," the man repeated as he leaned in closer. I got a look at him, and he at me. Cesur, or the man I assumed was Mr. Cesur, pulled down the last chain on a candle lamp hanging over the table and lit it. He then set down what appeared to be a silver tray upon which sat a silver teapot and two glasses. The smell of boiled apples filled the already spicy-fragrant air of the carpet shop.

I could almost make out the man across the table from me now, who still had the death grip on my hand. He finally released it, leaned in, and said, "May I offer you some apple tea, Miss Russo? It's quite good." He poured us each a small glass.

*That again!*

"Excuse me, but you know who *I* am, but I'm afraid I don't have the privilege of knowing the name of the person offering me tea after nearly having my arm broken. And you sir, are . . . ?"

"I am Father Paulo Jacobi," he said.

Under the hood I could discern a man, perhaps eighty; thin, with heavy-lidded, rheumy blue eyes. He wore a black cassock, similar in style although not in color to the kind worn by monks. A large gold and jewel-encrusted cross of a type I'd never seen glittered dramatically on a heavy gold chain on his chest. All four posts of the cross had *v*-shaped wings that curved outward.

"Aha. Father Jacobi. So I see," I said, my meaning both literal and figurative.

"I'm afraid you seem to 'see' as well as a blind man," he replied.

"Okaaaay." I pushed the glass of hot tea away from me, and it spilled on the table.

"Miss Russo, may I remind you that you are no longer in New York. Manners count for much here, and yours seem to be sorely lacking."

"Excuse me? You are the one who had me dragged into this place kicking and screaming. In what country—or perhaps what time period—is *that* considered mannerly behavior, Father?"

*Did you sell that little girl to some sex ring way back in the eighties, you freak?*

This old bastard was really beginning to tick me off, my fear turning back to good old-fashioned New Yorker intolerance. No wonder Maureen had sort of warned me about him.

My crack about *his* having bad manners seemed to bring him back to reality—or civility at least—and he turned cordial on a dime.

*Slime bag.*

"Please. Let us begin once more then," he said, reaching for my hand.

"No, not that maneuver again! I prefer to keep my typing fingers intact, thank you very much."

He won.

*Fast for an old creep.*

This time he held it gently and turned my hand over

several times the way a palm reader might, studying it. He then did something incredibly creepy: He lifted it and, yes, *kissed it!*

When I snatched my hand back from him and looked at it, I could see a red trickle coming down the center of my palm. *Damn!* It had started to bleed. But strangely there was no cut, puncture mark, or scratch that I could see.

"What the hell?"

"No, not hell, Miss Russo. Anything *but*." With that Father Paulo got down on his knees before me. "You are indeed the Chosen One!" he cried, in a sort of ecstatic state. Mr. Cesur bent his head, made a double sign of the cross, and got down on his knees as well.

In, I assumed, devil-worshipper tongue (which turned out only to be Turkish), they began chanting, something like, *"Tan ree I yidder, Tan ree buy'd a car, tan ree eclipse the sun,"* over and over again.

I later learned—via Google Translate—that it was probably: *"Tanrı iyidir. Tanri büyüktür, Tanrı elçisidir korur!"* "God is good. God is great. God bless the messenger!" That would be me apparently.

He—they—were insane. Clearly.

"The Chosen One needs a Band-Aid," I said. "I cut my hand somehow. You didn't bite it, did you?"

*I'm thinking AIDS, I'm thinking vampire. I'm thinking this is worse than being a fugitive with a price on my head. Get the hell out of here. Somehow.*

Never having had someone kneel before me—other than, say, Donald, when he was half in the bag and singing to me in what he thought was French on our wedding night—I was completely at odds about what to do.

"Ah, I could use a Band-Aid," I repeated.

Nothing. So I went for the idiotic.

"Rise!" I declared, like Elizabeth to Essex. It was worth a try—right?

It worked. The two men got off their knees and stood before me.

"Do you have a Band-Aid?" I asked again, now sucking on my palm to stop the bleeding.

"A Band-Aid will never stanch the blood of *Christ,*" Father Paulo declared.

"I think it's just a cut, really."

Mr. Cesur brought me a cloth, which he wrapped around my hand as a tourniquet. When I unwrapped the thing two minutes later, the blood was stanched. "See? The blood of Christ has stopped," I said, as Jacobi and Cesur stared trancelike.

"Miss Russo, it is the stigmata—the *sign.* The unmistakable sign we have all been waiting for. You are the Chosen One we have waited for. The only one who can save the world."

"I'm just a reporter. I can't save the world. Seriously."

He didn't get the joke and looked at me somewhat bemused by my—what?—naïveté. He continued as though I hadn't just made this giant concession to my inability to save the world from destruction.

He picked up my hand again and said, "Look, there is no mark. It's as though it had never happened. You can't deny the truth of what happened to you."

*It was just a cut, for God's sake. But don't turn down an interview, now that the old coot's your willing servant! You may even get out of here without being killed.*

"Yes, I guess now that you mention it . . . okay, it was the stigmata," I said pulling out my notebook. "And please, Father Jacobi, sit down, for goodness' sake." He pretended to smile at my lame joke and showed a mouthful of yellowish teeth. I even hit the "record" button on

Sadowski's phone. For once, I really wanted a record of somebody's own words *in* their own words.

Cesur brought over a lit *nargile*—a water pipe, and Jacobi took a long hit and offered it to me.

"Is it hashish?"

He laughed—laughed! "No, just tobacco and fruit." I took a drag (what the hell) and was amazed that it tasted like I was smoking apples, but within minutes the buzz I got off it was not like anything I'd ever experienced after eating a Golden Delicious. (Turns out the water filters the tobacco in these pipes in a way that makes the nicotine hit quite sensational.)

"Miss Russo, as was foretold, fate brought you here."

*Not to mention running from the law after being accused of murder.*

"Only you will *know*—when the time is right—what to do to prevent worldwide catastrophe. I only have the honor of being your historian. The ignorant are damned to repeat history, as you know. I can't arm you with the weapons, but I can arm you with the truth."

"The truth of . . ."

"The true story of the birth thirty-three years ago of the Son of the Son. He who was born from the womb of a thirteen-year-old virgin."

*I'll be a son of a bitch!*

Again, as though reading my mind, Jacobi took a long hit of the pipe, handed it to me, and said, "No, we are not monsters, Miss Russo; we are warriors and servants."

"Of . . . ?"

"Why, of God, of course."

"God told you to impregnate a thirteen-year-old child?"

"She was twelve at the time of conception, actually. The cloning."

I felt bile rising in my throat. Was it the tobacco or was it the story? Both.

*My God. Jurassic Park for Jesus.*

Cesur brought out a tray of *mezzas*—Turkish appetizers—and laid them on the table and took the pipe from Jacobi. We were definitely in here for the long haul. And now, even disgusted as I was, I too was in all the way. Perhaps I could finally discover the whereabouts—if she was still alive, that is—of little Theotokos.

I swear that was *really* what I was thinking. I didn't even really absorb that crap about saving the world. I only wanted to save one now-grown woman from what I assumed was captivity. And clear my name. And win a Pulitzer.

And I was wrong.

## 21

"Okay, then, where do we begin?"

"First we eat," Jacobi said, blessing the tray of food and a carafe of delicious Turkish white wine. "We need to be nourished in our bodies, not just our souls."

*Is this what you said to the little girl you kidnapped for your disgusting purposes?*

We finished the rest of the meal more or less in silence. I realized that the old guy needed to get his strength back before embarking on his wild tale.

When we were finished, Cesur cleaned off the table, and laid down a pristine piece of exquisite white linen that looked like an altar cloth you see in a Catholic church. He then carefully put down a small wooden box. Jacobi opened it to reveal a test tube surrounded by satin. The tube was filled with blood that looked fresh.

He picked it up gingerly, made the double sign of the cross (that again), and handed it to me.

"Sorry, I'm a bit squeamish," I said, refusing to touch the thing.

He then held the tube aloft and sang in a rapturous,

strong voice: "Blessed is the blood of Demiel ben Yusef, Son of the Son of our Lord and Savior."

Then, with his eyes closed and beginning to drop tears, he proclaimed: "His blood is drink indeed. He who eats His flesh and drinks His blood abides in Him, and Him in You. As the living Father sent Him through *me,* we live because of the Father. So he who feeds on Him will live *because* of Him!"

Father Paulo then waved a hand, and Cesur brought a bottle of wine and what looked like two gold chalices and filled both. He helped Paulo to stand, and the old priest this time made a double sign of the cross over the wine goblets, handed me one, and said, "It's not poison, my dear, it's the blood of our Lord."

"Blood?"

He snickered, shaking his head. "No! We don't drink blood. Not literally. It's not what you think. Believe me," he said and took a swallow of the wine.

"This blood," he said indicating the test tube, "is the blood . . . different from all other blood on earth—except for the 'source blood'—the blood from which it came."

"Source blood. Right."

"Yes. This is the blood of Demiel ben Yusef. It is not human blood. It will match only to the blood of Jesus, the first Son of our Lord God!"

"And how do I know that—I mean for sure? That it matches Jesus' blood?"

"Find the source blood, find God. Have them both tested before it's too late. Only a laboratory in this golden age of science versus belief can prove to the enemies of God Himself that this is no human blood!"

"I'm sure they've given him blood tests—Demiel, I mean."

"I'm sure they have, too. That's why they want to kill Him!"

*Oh, crap. More Holy Grail nonsense.*

More than a bit annoyed, I challenged him: "Listen, I can't find the Holy Grail. I just want to find out who killed your friend Father Sadowski and get the cops off my back."

"Yes, tragic, that. He was a good soldier. Never wavered in his commitment. He could have confirmed it for you. But you need to find the proof."

"Listen, you supposedly cloned a baby from blood. Where did you get it?"

"Only Grethe knew. And, well, that's impossible."

*That name again.*

"Who is that exactly?"

"She was a nun. But she was also Headquarters' finest obstetrician. A painter of icons. All of those things. But most of all she was a geneticist, born to it, really, but to perfect her science she worked at it day and night. Could have won the Nobel, but Headquarters would never have let her submit, of course. She, *we,* had to remain above suspicion."

"Headquarters? You mean the Vatican?"

He sneered and spat.

"You're a Catholic priest, aren't you?" I asked.

He didn't answer.

"Well, if that's off-limits, then tell me where to find this Grethe."

"Oh, long dead. Such a shame, really."

"When did she die?"

"I don't know. We were all separated after the birth took place. Forbidden to contact one another. But I heard about her untimely passing some years later. Terrible loss to science."

"But you don't know for sure?"

"I can't believe she lived. She became a real problem. Headquarters, you see, felt it was imperative to re-create the first birth as closely as possible in modern times. That, you see, is the actual meaning of 'resurrection'—that Jesus could return one day. Literally, 'blood made flesh.' And so His blood has been kept hidden for over two thousand years. Some was taken for the Great Experiment, but that was all that was ever taken. As far as I know.

"She was fairly young at the time. In her early thirties. But you see, she refused to fully give up the child to its mother and appointed father. Always trying to find them, always trying to interfere. I would have loved to have been the one to school the boy, but Headquarters did not want us to continue once we completed the Experiment. So I didn't, but she kept at it. Too many renegades in this situation. I always felt it was Headquarters' only failing."

"Headquarters? What does that mean exactly?" I asked again.

He ignored me again. "No, I don't believe she died of natural causes," he chuckled. Chuckled! "I'm afraid she had to be eliminated."

*That word again! If nothing else, they are consistent.*

"Or," he continued, "she would have caused a world of trouble. Always trying to track the boy and his family. No, it wasn't acceptable behavior, even if she did make *Him* possible."

"So they killed her?" I asked, totally aghast.

"Don't play the innocent with me, please. It doesn't dignify your position."

"I don't have a position. . . ."

"I'm afraid that, yes, indeed you do. Whether you like it or not."

"Did any one of you think that perhaps the nun thought of him as *her* child? I mean, if she's the one who 'made' him from a hank of hair and a piece of bone, wouldn't she have been more his real mother than a twelve-year-old kid who was just chosen as a carrier?"

I had to get up and walk around the room, which was becoming more claustrophobic by the second.

He reached out and took my hand and asked me to sit with him again, which I did, but very reluctantly. "She was thirteen when she gave birth."

"Oh, brother."

"You will know what to do when the time comes—and Ms. Russo, or do you prefer Alessandra?"

"I prefer a vodka. Do you have one?"

"No, but I have some very, *very* fine wine," he said, pulling another hit from the pipe. He gestured to Cesur, who brought another bottle and a decanter to the table like one of those obsequious waiters in a tourist-gouging European restaurant.

Paulo poured the La Tâche—probably worth several thousand—very carefully into the decanter and let it sit a moment as he excused himself. I thought he might be going to use the lavatory, but instead he expertly wound his way to the back through the miles of piled-up carpets and slid aside a curtain to reveal a wall safe.

He asked to see my passport.

"No—I prefer not giving it over to someone standing in front of a safe, thank you very much."

He laughed gently and said, "O ye of little faith . . ."

*Not that again. Can't these guys come up with anything more original?*

"Okay," he said, "then read me your passport number."

"Well, I don't have my passport. I have this *other* one on me."

"Perfect," he shouted, practically jumping for joy.

I pulled it out and read the endless sequence of numbers and—voilà!—the whizzing sound of the safe electronically unlocking began.

I could see in the dim light Jacobi removing a diary-sized leather-bound book.

He walked back to the table, laid it on the altar cloth, opened it, and said, "This will not always be flattering to me, I'm sorry to say, but I was suffering then from the sin of vanity, I know. Please understand. I had been chosen for a great task, and I assumed, of course, that because I had been chosen from all other men, that I was different from all other men.

"I have since learned I was no better, only fated." *Sure.* He began reading:

> "Recorded December 25, 1990, 2:30 A.M.
>
> "We have returned to the place of His birth. It is time to once again see where it all happened and to fulfill my promise to finally record it all as I experienced it.
>
> "March 26, 1982, House of the Virgin, Selçuk, Turkey.
>
> "It was over, and I was crying.
>
> "As I lay in the bed in the tiny, ancient two-room stone house, surrounded by candlelight and machines, I kept repeating over and over almost like a mantra that could soothe me, 'Can I go home now? Please, may I go home now?'
>
> "But the mantra didn't soothe me, didn't help me. In fact, I was becoming more terrified and agitated by the second. The worst—the physical part, the dangerous part, the giving birth part—was over, but still the other three couldn't console me.
>
> "I was clutching the sheet and looking around wildly for my mother, who wasn't there. Who had never been there—not in this place.

"*They all knew that if they didn't do something, anything, to calm me down, I might hemorrhage— or even, God forbid, harm the baby somehow.*

"*They brought Him to me in an attempt to get me to breast-feed.*

"*I turned abruptly away from them and pressed myself against the wall, a shock for the others who'd planned it all out so well. I felt as though my baby was something monstrous and foreign to me.*

"*'Get away from me!' I cried. 'Stay away from me! He's not my baby, and you know it! He's not my baby!'*

"*My will was simply no match for my body, and I flopped back down, defeated. My long red-brown hair was matted to my head from having been through such an ordeal.*

"*As I drifted away in my mind, I could see the nun retreat, cuddling the Baby, but she was clearly confused and, I later learned, more than a little frightened herself.*

"*'Blessed One! Turn, look at your beautiful boy. . . .' the nun implored me.*

"*The older of the two men, the priest, a forty-year-old renegade American Roman Catholic cleric, moved in closer. He then gently pushed the nun aside.*

"*'Take the Baby to the trough. Try the bottle. Please,' he directed her. 'Try the bottle—it has the special formula,' he said in a way that wasn't so much a request as a command.*

"*The nun, a thirty-five-year-old woman, did as she was told, holding the Baby and retreating into the far corner of the cold room. He was her superior and therefore had to be obeyed.*

"My future husband, who was also in the room, moved to the other side and seemed oblivious to the commotion around him.

"The young man chosen to be my betrothed was an armed mercenary. His address was whatever it needed to be anywhere he needed to be in the world and was subject to change without notice, as I would later learn.

"He was almost forgettable in his looks, as he was bred to be and as he had worked hard to become. But he was a dangerous creature, and that always lay right beneath the surface. Sandy brown cropped hair, six feet tall, hazel eyes that saw everything but showed nothing. Mostly he didn't look like what he was: deadly.

"On the stone bench lay his stash of weapons—two semiautomatics, hundreds of rounds of ammo, and one rapid-fire machine gun.

"Not exactly 'Silent Night,' was it?

"The priest came to my bedside and tried to take my hand, which I yanked away as hard as I was capable of doing. I stiffened when he tried to touch my shoulder.

"'Get away! Get away from me!'

"He grabbed my hand and said in barely accented, upper-crust American accent, 'Please, Blessed One. You are doing God's work.'

"'No! I'm not going to do it. I want my mom. I want to go home! Please, when can I go home?'

"At that, my future husband looked up.

"'What is she on about?' he asked. 'You better give her the damned drugs before she brings the world to the door with all that whining.'

"Yes, this was the blessed event that had been in the making for almost two thousand years!

"The priest, almost always in command, was becoming somewhat alarmed himself. He'd exorcised demons, he'd presided at miracles, yes, but he'd never been charged with anything remotely like this. But then again, no one ever had.

"The priest stood up from my bedside, exhausted, somewhat beaten down and a bit resigned and removed a pill from his vestment pocket and handed it to me.

"I struggled to get out of bed, knocking the pill to the floor, and managed to roll away from the spot where I'd been lying, which was now sticky with blood from the strain.

"The priest motioned to the nun, who, though chastised, rushed into the other tiny room where the chapel was located. She was back in seconds with a hypodermic needle, and the priest held me down while the nun shoved the needle into my arm. It was methadone, which they swore was safe for nursing mothers.

"I became so drowsy I couldn't fight it any longer. I didn't even want to, actually. The nun wheeled the IV over and inserted the needle into a vein, looking terribly worried.

"She quickly removed the blood-covered white linen sheet with the skill and speed of a battlefield nurse and replaced it with a clean and starched one.

"I was just a child myself—kidnapped from New York City; a thirteen-year-old whom they'd said had been bred one day to bear the Second Coming."

The priest put down the book and then put his head down upon the table and wept, great heaving sobs that held a lifetime's worth of—I didn't know what—guilt, sorrow, loss?

When he composed himself—Cesur had brought him pristine white linen handkerchiefs with which to soak up his tears—he said, "Forgive me. I have not been permitted to read this before today."

"The author?"

"Why, the Blessed Mother herself! The Mother of Demiel ben Yusef," he said, wiping his eyes. "Not a story, but a report. Miss Russo, what we have been privy to *is* nothing short of the new gospel."

"Yes, I assumed it was the girl who gave birth, but who is she?" I thought I knew, but I wanted it confirmed.

It was another question that hung in the air unanswered.

"Let me ask you something else then. Where is the girl and this soldier now?"

"I don't know."

"What do you mean you don't know?"

"Perhaps they've gone back to where he lived as a young boy. In Carcassonne, France. But I doubt it. He was no good."

Then he waved me away. "I am very, very tired and need to pray on all of this.

"Mr. Cesur will see you to your hotel." Father Paulo stood up creakily, dismissing me with, "Until tomorrow, or should I say later today, then?"

I was thinking about the horror of their crimes: kidnapping a child and, worse, somehow impregnating her.

But I was too tired to concentrate, although I was glad I hadn't gone on the offensive. That's the last thing an interviewer should ever do, even though sometimes, like with a pedophile judge that I once interviewed and now this monster priest, you feel like there *is* only one side.

Cesur drew back the drapes that had surrounded us all night, opened the metal gates, and unlocked the door.

"There is a place you must see later," the priest said, getting up wearily and rubbing his bloodshot eyes. He again began to genuflect before me. This time I was definitely too tired to do the Elizabeth and Essex thing, and so I just said, "Okay, then. Sleep tight. *Domani.*"

He handed me the diary, albeit reluctantly. "This now belongs to you."

I took it, and stumbled out of the shop. Cesur took me out to an exit in the labyrinth of alleys that make up the massive Grand Bazaar. The market had not yet come back to life. Dawn was breaking over the city, and from the four corners of Istanbul I could hear the muezzins calling the faithful to prayer. The sound was so beautiful, it was hard to believe that anything that sounded so glorious could have triggered so much violence from all sides over so many years.

## 22

Cesur drove me back to the hotel without saying anything. I was emotionally and physically spent, and you didn't have to be a warrior/servant of God to have noticed.

He walked me up to my room and then went over the place like a detective, making sure no one was there. It was a tiny room, so it seemed more drama than necessity.

He asked me if I wanted to put the book in the room safe, but I indicated that I wanted to continue reading it.

"You are very tired, Miss Russo, and if anyone, *God forbid*, should want to break in, it becomes vulnerable."

*Forget* you, it *becomes vulnerable*.

I got his point and put the book into the room safe, put in a good combination, and told him I wouldn't open it until I was wide awake and on my guard.

With that he left and I double-bolted the door, rinsed off quickly in the shower, and fell on top of the bed in a heap.

The jangling of my room phone woke me. I reached for the clock—9:30!

I picked up the phone. "Miss Russo, Father Jacobi." I sat up scratching my head as though this would somehow clear it.

"How long will it take you to get ready? We haven't much time; the tribunal is winding down, and CNN reported that it should be done in a few days."

"What? Why? I've been covering trials forever, and the big ones always last for months, sometimes years."

"But not if there is no defense side, and our Lord refuses to defend Himself."

No, Jacobi was not being a wiseass when he said it. He actually meant it.

"What am I supposed to do about that? From Istanbul?"

"You must get busy. Unfortunately there is no time to lose. *Salvare il ragazzo, salvare il mondo,*" he finished up in Italian.

"'Save the boy, save the world'?"

He didn't bother with a response. I still hadn't made the connection about why he'd speak to me in Italian. Sorry, my brain was fried. Being a fugitive who hangs around with weirdo priests who claim to be present at the birth of Christ II can get to a girl.

"Let me turn on the TV. I'm still not comfortable using my tablet: I've had a few unnerving incidents since I arrived, and I don't know if I'm somehow being traced through my online connections. Anyway, lemme catch up on the court proceedings first."

"I'll fill you in during the ride. I need for you to see something. Right now. Time is not on our side."

*Our?* "Okay, okay. Give me twenty minutes."

"Bring the book. Put it in the plastic hotel laundry bag from your room. It will look like everyday junk. Don't let anyone in your room. Especially not the cleaning staff or room service. Don't mingle with guests down in the breakfast room, either. In fact, don't go to the breakfast room."

"I need coffee."

"You need God. Coffee can wait."

I packed up what few things I had and put the book in a laundry bag. Precisely twenty minutes later I walked down to the tiny lobby and saw that Cesur was already waiting for me. He escorted me to the car that was blocking the only lane on the tiny street. Father Jacobi was waiting inside, impatiently looking at his watch. I got a good glance at the breakfast room as I passed. *Now that's what you call a continental breakfast!* Fresh croissants, honey, jams, butter, Nutella—my favorite thing—hard-boiled eggs, breads of all sorts, sliced mystery meat with giant globs of white stuff (who *eats* that stuff?), Turkish coffee, cappuccino—and not *one* thing in a cellophane bag. Heavenly. But heaven would have to wait. I was about to enter a territory somewhere between heaven and hell.

"Where are we going?" I asked Mr. Cesur, who suddenly didn't understand English.

*Okay.*

We drove out of the city and seemed to be headed back toward the airport, but in fact we passed the national airport and drove onto a small private airfield.

"Huh?"

The priest led me into a sleek Gulfstream that had been waiting.

"So the exorcist thing pays well, then?" I said, hoping to catch him off guard with how much I already knew about him, but also wanting to check how much of Maureen's info was correct.

He didn't blink. "Yes, but I only do it for rich families. They can afford it and refuse to believe that their idiot children are simply drug addicts." Then he slipped out of character for once and made a comical face and waved spooky arms at me as a joke. *Weirdo.*

We boarded, strapped in, and took off. "Where are we going?"

"I prefer you see it for yourself without preamble."

*And I prefer not to be on a plane with a kidnapper slash child molester, but I am.*

Again I held my tongue. Too bad I'd never learned that art when dealing with my editors.

Blessedly, there was a small buffet laid out for us, so I gobbled down some fruit and yogurt and carried my espresso back to my seat.

"Did you read at all last night?"

"The book? No."

"Good." He indicated the plastic bag, and I dug it out again.

As I did so, he tapped his jacket to indicate that he had the test tube on him, and then he pointed to the book. He handed the tube to me. It was out of the box but still surrounded by satin. "It may trigger some memory."

"Of what?"

He didn't answer. Obviously, the discussion was over.

I opened the diary to the second entry, which was written on small sheets of lined paper from what must have been a field book, and carefully glued onto sheets of vellum.

"The book was assembled by a master bookbinder in London in 1990," he said. "These must have been the soldier's field notes exactly as he recorded them at the time."

I began to read aloud:

*"Day One, Year One. The Log of Yusef Pantera."*

The priest exchanged a look with Cesur, who got up and relocated himself at the back of the cabin. He was packing. Looked like a Glock. Great.

The priest let out a sigh that somehow made me know that he thought I couldn't have been more pedestrian.

"Continue, please."

"Yusef Pantera? That's the man who was named as Demiel ben Yusef's father at the tribunal—no?"

Jacobi just pointed to the book. And so I continued:

> "The Girl, who had spent most of the past eleven months in one long fit of fearful, mournful crying, this day spilled tears of fear, and also of sorrow and of pain. Today the nun and the priest had spilled tears, too—of joy, as they trembled before the Baby.
>
> "Even I, when faced with the wonder and power of the universe, was moved. But nonetheless I kept my own counsel, even as the successful completion of the experiment and the sight of the Child almost overcame me.
>
> "The recording equipment was of course operational inside and out. No sigh, word, accident, gesture, meal, or even bathroom visit could be overlooked. How would history, we often wondered, judge the teenage mother this time, now that there was recorded proof instead of oral history to rely upon?
>
> "Would She still be adored and glorified, or would She be scorned as a selfish, frightened, freakish, used-up kid?"

"He capitalizes 'She,' 'Baby,' and 'Girl.'"

Father Jacobi brought me up short. "Yes, yes, please do not interrupt the narrative with questions." Chastised, I continued:

> "As we gathered the equipment, we all silently wondered if 'it' would be there. The sign. But,

*there were things to do first before we would be able to step outside to look.*

*"Sister Grethe woke the Infant, washed Him again, making Him squall so loudly that even the arrogant priest quipped, 'He's got a set of lungs on him, all right. We can probably hear him all the way to Jerusalem!'*

*"'The cry heard 'round the world, eh, Father?' I added. Yes, I was happy that day.*

*"We'd had a rough time of it, the four of us, during the confinement. I knew the others thought I was the wrong man chosen for the great task, the task of eventually marrying the Girl and becoming human father to the Child.*

*"And while the other two accepted the decision, they wished it had been different.*

*"But who were they to question Headquarters? I was appalled that Headquarters had chosen them, quite frankly. I understood their qualifications: She was a master geneticist, and he had wormed his way into the heart of the Vatican without them ever suspecting he was shilling for the other side. Brilliant both—to that I will admit.*

*"Grethe's face revealed nothing—it never did—as the three of us admired the strange little light-skinned brown Baby boy with the giant black eyes, the strong little arms, the chubby little legs, and the patch of unruly black curls that sprouted on top of His head like a crown. The Girl was still asleep, which was a blessing in and of itself—even if a man-made one.*

*"I lifted the Baby's basket and put it firmly at the center of the wooden rectangular altar that had been placed inside the wide, ancient, brick, arched chapel section of the room. It was in this*

tiny chapel, in this small house where Mary, the Mother of Jesus Herself, had prayed, had lived, perhaps had died.

"It was the spot for which I and the others before me had been bred so that one day when He returned, we would be ready to serve and protect. It fell to me to fulfill that destiny.

"The altar had been laid with a long white cloth embroidered with a dove carrying an olive branch, the Occitan Cross, the Star of David, the crescent moon and star—a symbol of Islam—which had originally been the symbol of the goddess Diana, whose temple lay about four kilometers from the house.

"While Paulo and Grethe were silently praying, I knelt on my prayer mat, made the double and inverted sign of the cross.

"Sister Grethe picked up Demiel and held Him before me as I sat up. I cradled him and sang into His ear in Arabic, the Muslim call to prayer. It is the first sound a Muslim infant should hear.

"Next Paulo sprinkled the Baby's head with water and recited in English the traditional prayer of christening.

"He then dipped his fingers into a bowl of holy water on the altar and crossed the Baby on the forehead, on the lips, and on the heart with his wet fingers and recited the only prayer recognized by the Cathars: 'Pater noster qui es in celis, sanctificetur nomen tuum; adveniat regnum tuum. Fiat voluntas tua sicut in cello et in terra. Panem nostrum supersubstancialem da nobis hodie. . . .'"

I paused and thought, *That name again—Cathars— who the hell were they?* Fascinated with the narrative, er, gospel, as the freak priest called it, I put the book down a second and sipped the steaming espresso before continuing.

"Sister Grethe, still holding the Baby, then took over in Hebrew the Jewish prayer for the safety of travelers—to protect us on the coming journey.

"Paulo then rose and took the two chalices from the altar, handed them to me, and then painstakingly reached back for the bottle of exquisite, rare wine, the 1947 La Tâche, which he carried outside as delicately as if he'd been holding the Baby. Although it was the new moon, the sky was as bright as if it were a full moon on the clearest night.

"Then Sister Grethe and I, holding the Baby, followed him outside into the chilly night air. Father Paulo had already opened the bottle, and it was sitting atop the makeshift altar that I had built from rough-hewn planks

"We gazed into the night sky and saw that—yes!—it was there! A new star in the predawn sky that outshone all the others. It beamed down on us and lit up the whole outside of the house!

"And now here it was—undeniable proof. Frightening, glorious, undeniable proof.

"The priest then filled one chalice with water from one of the spigots on the front of the house, which flowed with the holy water of the Blessed Mother, and carried it back to the altar. Then with trembling hands he poured the exquisite wine into the second chalice, making sure not to stir up the sediment. It was exactly eight minutes since he'd opened it, and it had to have been drunk within ten.

"Exuberantly yet carefully I took the little

*brown nugget of a Baby and held Him up to the sky toward the star, whose light was nearly blinding if one looked at it directly. The Baby let out a cry whose sound was indefinable. It was not quite the cry of an infant—not quite that of a human, actually."*

I could see the old priest nod his head to Cesur from the corner of my eye.

*"With a steady grip on the Baby, I dipped my index finger into the holy water that the priest held in front of us.*

*"I placed a finger into the Baby's mouth and recited the traditional naming prayer of the Akan people of West Africa.*

*"Then, directly to the Baby, I cried exuberantly, 'You are Demiel!' At that the Baby seemed to look up—even, unimaginably, part His lips in a smile.*

*"I almost forgot myself, held the Baby higher again and again. 'Let's drink to Demiel!' I shouted. 'Son of the Son!'*

*"Then the two chalices were passed among us, and we all swallowed deeply and kissed one another on both cheeks.*

*"Paulo, that scum, however, scowled. He was pissed that the wine's peak moment had passed and he'd missed it. A taste he'd waited all his life to experience."*

I heard him sniff beside me.

*"Grethe headed back into the house, while I stayed outside with Paulo and uncovered the high-resolution telescope I'd designed. Gazing through*

the lens, I could see what the blinding star didn't yield to the naked eye.

"It was perfectly symmetrical. The sides of the star would, if folded in half, match up perfectly, something that could never occur naturally. But then again, was there anything about this night that had occurred naturally? I began taking photos through the lens. I had no idea whether the star was visible all over the world to any naked eye—or just to us, just in this little spot on Bülbül Mountain.

"I turned the telescope over to Paulo and walked back inside, assuming my role as bodyguard. I put on and then adjusted my shotgun and bandolier across my chest. To an outside observer it would have been difficult to tell who was in charge at any one time, as our roles seemed to change constantly. But to those on the deep inside, none of it was random. It was all, in fact, a perfectly coordinated dance, with no missed step, no toe stepped upon, no matter how many appearances to the contrary. Not so far.

"But that would be consistent with everything here—where nothing was as it appeared. I shut tight the second set of purple velvet blackout curtains.

"I then lit several other candles—still a strange sight in a room buzzing with the quiet white noise of high-tech medical equipment, three hungry laptops—created way before the time that such a thing was even possible to consumers—constantly being fed with information from the portable satellite dish, and, of course, the sleeping Girl and the newborn Infant.

"Sister Grethe went over to the Girl's bedside

*just as the priest—almost on cue—walked back inside and picked up the Infant with the expertise of a man who'd fathered legions of them. Which of course he had.*

*"As he held the Baby, the nun slipped on surgical gloves and then gently manipulated the Girl's engorged nipples until the first drops of breast milk—colostrum—the yellowy, thick, sticky first milk—appeared."*

Needless to say, unsettling for me to read these words about a little girl from a grown man to whom she had been "betrothed."

*"The Baby began sucking immediately, while the Girl continued to sleep, seemingly unaware that she was nursing the most extraordinary Child in nearly two thousand years.*

*"As calm settled over the house, and as Sister Grethe and Father Paulo were finally ready to get a few hours of sleep themselves, the alarm in my headset went off.*

*"We had been breached."*

## 23

I stopped reading and looked up at the priest. "My God! This reads like a sci-fi thriller!"

"I can assure you, Miss Russo, it involved a lot of *science*, but it is *not* fiction."

Just then our plane touched down so smoothly I hardly felt a thing. Or maybe it was because I had been so completely thrown back in time that my head was in a whole other place.

We deplaned at a small private airport and hurried across the tarmac and into a waiting car. The priest informed me that the car we were in was armored. "Secure against bullets and hopefully anything else they can throw at us."

"Who is 'they,' may I ask? And where the heck are we?"

"Need to know, Miss Russo, need to know . . ."

"*I* need to know. If I'm going to be shot at, trust me, I need to know."

"I can only say there are forces—black forces—who put Demiel into this position and who, frankly, need to take you out of the equation."

"Me? Why *me*?" I looked out the window and decided to come clean.

"And, ah, this is weird, okay? But I think I blew up a car and, along with it, the, ah, one of the 'black forces.' At a rest stop in upstate New York."

He laughed. "Do you think one explosion would eliminate an entire group thousands of years old?" He laughed again.

"Pardon? Sorry, but the joke escapes me right now."

"Shall *I* continue the readings?"

Not sure he'd not edit as he went along—taking out any unflattering references to himself—I picked up the book and continued, as he anxiously shifted in his seat, trying to read over my shoulder.

> "The inside of the house was instantly thrown into darkness. In seconds, the automatic lockdown gates slammed into place, and then the infrared emergency lights came on, casting a glow to the ancient walls of clay bricks and stones. It was all working perfectly.
>
> "We three assumed our positions as smoothly as if we'd been choreographed by Balanchine. Grethe remained at the bedside; I moved toward the chapel room; and Paulo headed toward the cache of weapons.
>
> "Theotokos stirred in her sleep, so Grethe kept Demiel steady at her breast."

I looked at the priest at that point. Damn! He was talking about the little New York City girl who'd been abducted in 1982. Somehow I kept reading without gagging. *Monsters!*

"I retrieved my thermo-controlled binoculars and Browning M2 .50.

"I carefully made my way into the other room—the chapel—and knelt at the small brick-arched window, slipped the binoculars between the panels of the velvet drapes, and pressed a code to release a tiny opening into the two-foot-thick stone wall and a corresponding hole in the outer metal lockdown gates. It was the modern equivalent of an ancient arrow slit.

"Sixteen satellite TVs built into the floor and flush with it had also already automatically flipped open and were lit up, feeding information into the laptops.

"'We've been breached! Hold your positions, and don't move. Die in your spots if you have to,' I ordered.

"I surveyed the mountainside from the window and from the monitors, looking closely and magnifying every inch of the area, around the Fountain of Health, the Fountain of Wealth, and the Fountain of Happiness. Nothing moved. My headset blared a warning signal into my ears again.

"Wait, was there motion on the far side of the old walnut tree?

"Nothing.

"I surveyed the ruins behind the house—what was left of the original monastery, a Templar stronghold during the fifteenth century.

"I looked down to the old cistern located between the house and the parking area. Nothing.

"That's when I heard the footsteps, at least three sets of them. The intruders were neither running nor creeping; the steps were the leisurely paced footsteps of men—definitely men—in leather-soled shoes hitting the stone walkway in front of the house. They were close enough to attempt an attack on the Infant.

"Yet the cats lazing in the tree, which were particularly skittish, surely would have scampered away at the first sound of human footsteps. They were still lazing in the early dawn. What the hell was going on?

"The footsteps were getting closer. Soft-soled, probably Italian leather shoes, I surmised. Very good shoes on one of the intruders. Possibly sandals on another.

"The sacred site had been closed to visitors for over a year now for 'renovations and refurbishing,' and so it was theoretically impossible to breach.

"Then the beeper in Paulo's vestment pocket began to vibrate.

"Sister whispered frantically, 'Yusef! Yusef! Headquarters!' Paulo slowly pulled it out—careful not to put the gun down nor inadvertently turn it toward Theo and the Infant.

"Only Headquarters had access to the beeper, which meant they were still, of course, watching us, guarding us, but nonetheless the possibility that we had been 'made'—and, more important, that the greatest experiment in two millennia may have been discovered—was terrifying to the other two. To me it was much more personal.

"'Who?' I whispered as loudly as the situation would allow. 'What do they advise?'

"'What does it say? I can't make it out. . . .' Paulo said, holding the beeper up.

"'Wake up, please, Theo. . . .' Grethe whispered, shaking the Girl. The methadone had done its job. In a former time Grethe would probably have been a monk or a nun working in the herbarium of a cloistered order, but today she was a defrocked Catholic nun and board-certified obstetrician/gynecologist with a vast knowledge of modern medicine.

"We all had worked too hard, the experiment was too perfect for Headquarters to have allowed a breach.

"Grethe stroked Theo's forehead, and the Girl opened her eyes halfway.

"After what seemed like a lifetime, Paulo called out, 'No breach! They say to proceed.' Then, 'Damn! I've lost it. . . .'

"'Tend to Demiel,' I ordered the nun. I was there to protect the Girl and the Infant, but these two suddenly seemed frozen in fear. If I could have, I would have put a bullet into each of them. Nothing was as important as the Experiment. Another transmission beeped in.

"'No breach! It says no breach,' he choked.

"'Are you sure?' I whispered back. 'Impossible. Bring it to me. . . .'

"I assumed the fool was so scared that he'd forgotten how to interpret the Phoenician lettering (which had been applied to an obscure form of Aramaic circa 600 BC).

"'Please, Yusef, don't do anything drastic. It says there was a power failure in Ephesus,' he said, bringing the device to me where I was crouched at the window. 'That's what caused the problem!'

"'Thank God. He's safe!' Grethe cried, carelessly raising her voice to a normal level again.

"'Keep your voice down! We are not safe! I am in command and I will kill you if you do not assume your station,' I threatened, now not com-

*pletely trusting Headquarters over my own instincts. Father Paulo made the double sign of the cross in thanksgiving. In many ways he was worse. She was a woman—and shouldn't have been given the assignment in the first place. This was a man's job.*

*"Then through my headset I heard the footsteps begin again. Distinct, sure, unhurried.*

*"The bitch, ignoring my orders, placed Demiel back in His sleeping Mother's arms, putting both the Baby and the Mother directly in harm's way.*

*"Just then we heard the unmistakable harsh metal-upon-metal sound of the steel lockdown gate lifting up. Next the bolted, titanium-backed, bulletproof front door opened easily and smoothly.*

*"'Dear God!' screamed the nun. She gasped with one hand over her mouth, the other hand pointing toward the front door.*

*"Three men stood in the doorway with their arms out. The blinding light glinted off something metal they each held in their hands."*

The car came to a stop, and he motioned for me to put the book down. When I didn't respond, he shut it for me and rested his bony hand on mine in some sort of fake beatific pose.

Cesur got out, punched in a code, and a locked gate swung open. The sign on the opposite side read MERYE-MANA. *This is the child Theo's middle name and the name of the supposed mother of ben Yusef!*

I looked at the priest quizzically, and he said, "It means, 'Mother Mary's House,' the last known dwelling place of the Virgin Mother."

"Oh, I see."

"It's the place where nineteen hundred and eighty-two years later Life Eternal was reborn."

"Oh. But I don't see. . . ."

As the big black car slowly made its way up the hill, I stretched my neck to see out the windows. What I saw, as we passed, though, was a little souvenir shop, locked up, but with the front still displaying wooden "icons," tchotchkes, rosary beads, snacks, and even cheap "religious" jewelry items.

*Hail Mary full of bracelets.*

We drove a bit farther and unexpectedly, a shiver ran up and down my spine and tears sprang to my eyes when the Meryemana came into view.

Here it was, the tiny abode made entirely of stone, looking just as it must have looked two thousand years earlier: solid, serene, and solitary. Not a soul was anywhere to be seen.

As we opened the car doors to get out, a white peacock scooted past the car, and for a second I honestly thought it was an apparition. The priest patted my hand. "Just our resident peacock, not the Ghost of Christmas Past," he joked.

*A laugh a minute this guy.*

We stepped out of the car, and fighting the crazy feelings that were beginning to overwhelm me, the reporter in me still managed to ask, "So how do you know this was *really* the place the Virgin Mary lived out her last days? I mean, no disrespect, but isn't this sort of like the Holy Grail of houses? And in Turkey of all places."

"O! Ye of little faith!"

"You've already tried that one on me. . . ."

Paulo looked at me, shook his head, and began walking toward the house.

"It must be very difficult to live without faith, to not believe in God."

"You are wrong, Father. I *do* believe in the *concept* of God—just not the execution."

*Damn. Had I just said "execution" to a man who had a cross around his neck?*

I sped ahead. "I mean, what I think is that there have been many great evolved beings—Moses, Jesus, the Prophet Mohammed, for example. They wanted everyone to know the truth, that one doesn't need riches or golden cathedrals or *any* cathedral in which to worship. They wanted us to know that life is what we ourselves create. I believe that we get not just what we want but also what we *fear.* We draw to us that which is most on our minds. You don't get what you deserve in life, you get what you *think* you deserve," I said, surprising myself that I'd unload my inner beliefs to this creepy stranger.

"But—"

I cut him off. "No, wait, did you ever have a friend who was a hypochondriac and feared getting cancer and then lo and behold, he *got* cancer? Or on the good side, there were always girls in high school who weren't the prettiest, the funniest, the whateverist, but they always had all the boys chasing them because they just *believed they deserved it.* Again, you call it upon yourself."

He looked at me. No doubt about it, you could only call his look "bemused."

"Your life plays out the way you expect it to, on some unconscious level."

"You think, then, that I always wanted to be the man who helped facilitate a world-changing event?"

I stopped, looked at him, and spread my hands out with a big smile on my face. "You're kidding, right? You aren't exactly a, er—how do I say this?—a modest guy?

"I think your subconscious put you exactly where you thought you deserved to be when you were there doing what you claim you did."

"Not claim, Ms. Russo—*did*."

I went on. "Anyway, I've thought this whole God thing out over my whole life. I'm not as ignorant as you think. It's just stuff I always knew, even as a kid. Anyway, I figure that when the evolved beings slash prophets died—"

He cut me off. "One *was* resurrected . . . twice."

I let that pass and continued, "Okay, but anyway, after the prophet was no longer among the living *humans,* the followers always ended up fighting among themselves to keep the truth that the prophet had taught them from the people. And as far as I know, the followers and/or the followers' followers, who then took over, generally always went on to build giant golden cathedrals in their honor. The exact opposite of what the prophets preached. No?"

He stopped short. "Why, Ms. Russo, you sound like a Cathar."

"I do? You know I never heard of them before a couple of days ago, and now I can't escape—"

"Neither could they," he cut in. We continued walking up to the house. "They were the fastest-growing, not religion exactly, but Christian belief system, shall we call it, in Europe in the twelfth through the thirteenth centuries. Those who identified as Cathars disavowed *all* material things—church buildings with their golden chalices and gilt ceilings, up to and including their own personal objects, other than what they needed to sustain a holy and Christian life. They tried to emulate the way Jesus had lived His life."

I shook my head, trying to absorb the information while feeling extremely cold in the warmth of the sun.

He looked directly at me as he continued, "The Catholic Church wanted two things from the Cathars: to secure the Cathar treasure and to wipe them off the face of the earth. It was a massive slaughter. Some accounts put the number at one million Cathars killed during the Crusades of hunt-and-destroy. A horrible holocaust perpetrated in the name of Jesus, who preached love."

"Why Father Paulo, now *you* sound like a Cathar," I teased back.

He laughed softly. He might have dressed as a Catholic priest, but this guy was a real rogue.

I continued: "Not that you seem to live like one! But tell me, why would people who eschewed all material things have a *treasure*?"

"That is your job to find out, I assume. . . ."

A horrid chill ran up my spine, and my teeth began to chatter uncontrollably—even though it had be seventy-something degrees that gorgeous day.

I unwrapped the terrible pink hoodie I'd tied around my waist and slipped into it, zipping it up tightly. The gesture did not go unnoticed. Jacobi gestured toward the house and made the double sign of the cross. And *his* gesture did not go unnoticed, either.

Wrapping my arms around myself, I changed the subject and asked instead, "So I heard the story about how John the Apostle supposedly brought Mary here to live after Jesus appointed him her caretaker as he was dying—"

"Not a story. A fact."

He sniffed and raised one eyebrow and began walking again, and I followed, chastised. Somewhat. "And this is the region where John the Apostle ended up? But please tell me how you know that this is that *particular* house or that John and the Blessed Mother were ever even *in* Ephesus."

The priest sat down on a small wooden bench and wiped his forehead. He was sweating—and I was freezing! I saw him take a small vial out of his black jacket and slip a pill in his mouth. He patted the seat for me to sit beside him, which I did.

"Are you all right, Father?"

"Yes, yes, old age is not, as they say, for sissies." He composed himself and continued: "Let us start with John the Apostle, who is also known as 'John the Evangelist'; although not everyone believes they are one and the same, they are. The Evangelist remained in Judea with the other apostles until the persecutions of Herod Agrippa I.

"At that point the disciples scattered throughout the various provinces of the Roman Empire—you can find that in Acts twelve, verses one to seventeen. It is our solemn belief that John then went to Asia Minor, where he began his mission."

"And you know—or believe this—why?"

"Well, because a Messianic Christian community was already in existence at Ephesus well before Saint Paul ever even began his work here! According to accounts from that time, John had been the leader of that community. In fact, it was here in this city that John wrote *three* epistles."

"But what does this have to do with the Blessed Mother?"

"John brought the Blessed Mother to live in Ephesus with him, as you said. . . ."

I still wasn't clear. "John was Jesus' favorite. He even called him 'the Beloved Disciple.' Our Lord instructed John to care for his Mother—and he gave him those instructions as he was hanging on the cross. 'Then saith he to the disciple, Behold thy mother! And from that hour that disciple took her unto his own *home*.'

"Yes," I said, remembering what Wright-Lewis had said. "Gospel of John. Right?"

"Exactly! I'm impressed, Miss Russo!"

I decided to come clean. "Don't be. I got that information just the other day from a woman—in fact it was the woman who urged me to come to Turkey in the first place."

"Who might that have been?"

"Maureen Wright-Lewis? She was with the CIA back in the day and then vanished after being accused of being a traitor . . . in the 1980s?" I asked more to judge his reaction than anything else.

The reward was quick. He looked aghast and shocked.

"Still has a huge price on her head, I think. She knew who *you* were, Father, back then even if you didn't know who she was."

The priest nearly jumped off the bench, unable to maintain his demeanor. Standing now in front of me, he shook his bony finger at me and exclaimed, "You met Wright-Lewis? She's alive?"

"Well, yes." I didn't react as he was expecting me to.

"Then trust me, she is not in hiding *or* wanted. She must still be on the company's payroll." His breathing started coming rapidly again, and again he popped a pill under his tongue. "And if she is alive," he seethed, "then she is still hunting."

"No, no, no, Father Paulo, *that* you've got wrong. I know that she *was* involved in the search for some kind of clone baby back in 1982. She confessed that much to me. But she thought until ben Yusef showed up that they had blown up the plane you all were supposed to be riding in—"

"Not some kind of 'clone baby,' as you call Him. The clone of Jesus Himself!"

"Oh, yes, ah, that's what I meant."

*Why is it so cold?*

"Your condescension is quite arrogant, you know," he said, and then continued, as though he assumed he'd just given me a huge blow. *Not.*

"They blew up *a* plane, not *the* plane," he said, not yet regaining his composure. "It was a decoy." He too was trembling now. I didn't think it was from fear or cold, since the sweat was pouring off his forehead in rivulets; more like blind rage.

"Wright-Lewis is the personification of pure evil!" he fumed, taking his starched handkerchief from his pocket and mopping his brow.

"I think she thinks the same about you! But anyway, whatever she was, she is not any longer. I believed her when she told me that she's spent her life in sorrow and regret about what they'd done. She is greatly relieved to even hold out the smallest bit of hope that she *didn't* kill him.

"She said that she now believes that ben Yusef *is* the reborn Christ, and that when he kissed me in front of the UN Building she realized that I was the one who was supposed to find the proof. She's now even a born-again, or something like it, and prays only for the proof that she didn't"—I felt foolish even saying it—"kill Baby Jesus in that plane."

He looked weary and wary at the same time. Standing before me, he leaned down and looked right into my face. His face was so close to mine that I could smell his breath, and it was clear he'd had something stronger than a communion host and a sip of religious wine that morning. He said, "You listen to me carefully. Very, *very* carefully. Trust no one, Ms. Russo, not even me, if you don't believe me. But I beg you *to* believe me. Maureen Wright-Lewis above all is not to be trusted. Maureen Wright-Lewis is a hunter!"

"A what?"

"An Inquisitor! Inquisitionist. *Inquīsītiō,*" he spat out disgustedly. I remained silent. I mean, seriously, how does one respond to such a statement in the twenty-first century?

"You think that they *don't* exist?" he asked, exasperated, as though he were addressing a complete naïf. "They, like *my* kind, Ms. Russo, *always* exist."

"I don't understand—your 'kind'? You mean an exorcist?" I asked, totally confused.

"Oh, God, no! Anyway, you don't need to understand. You just need to *believe*—even though I realize that idea goes contrary to your contrary nature."

Then he turned slightly away before turning back again. "Will you excuse me, please?" He walked toward the souvenir stand without waiting for my acknowledgment. I could see he was making a call on his cell phone, but try as I might I couldn't grasp what he was saying. Then it occurred to me: I had been straining to hear in English and he had been speaking in Italian. Before I could switch my brain, he'd hung up and was slowly walking back to the bench where I had been left shivering.

As though he hadn't just accused Wright-Lewis of being an Inquisitionist straight out of the twelfth century, he took my hand and gestured for me to walk with him again.

"Your hands are very cold. Why, my dear, you are shivering."

"Well, it's freezing here—especially in the shade."

"No—it's twenty-two degrees!" I made a face and he said, "Oh, that's about seventy-three degrees Fahrenheit. They still don't teach that regularly in the U.S.—ridiculous."

"Well, they do, but not when I went to school."

We slowly headed toward the house, and he said, "So you wanted to know how we know for certain that this was the actual home where the Blessed Mother lived out her days."

"Yes, I mean, there are nothing *but* old dwellings in this part of the world it seems."

"Well, this particular blessed house lay in total disrepair for nearly two millennia, until it was discovered in the early nineteenth century by Sister Anne Catherine Emmerich, a German nun, stigmatic, visionary, and prophet."

"She just happened to come upon it while traveling?"

"No, no; in fact, she'd never even *been* to Turkey. The vision of the house came to her in fevered dreams. The tomb of John the Apostle is in Ephesus, too. We just don't know where. She saw the house, knew *exactly* where it was. But the church never verified her vision. Rantings of a crazy woman."

"So . . ."

"So in 1881, fifty-seven years after her death, a French priest, Abbé Julien Gouyet, decided to follow Emmerich's visions and traveled to Turkey, where he searched for and then discovered the remnants of the house *just* as she had described it. The house, she had been told in her visions, had been built by John the Apostle for the Blessed Mother, on Bülbül Mountain near Ephesus.

"Parts of the foundation as well as coal found on the site date the house to the first century. Coal used by the Blessed Mother herself! The *abbé*'s discovery, however, was totally ignored in Rome. No surprise there."

"You mean to tell me that Rome would ignore the most important artifact in Christianity?"

"In fact, yes. For one thing the place where the Mother

of God died is in a *Muslim* country—a religion at constant war with Christianity. And religious differences aside, on the financial side—and the Vatican is nothing if not brilliant when it comes to managing their trillions—they would lose billions in tourist revenue if the holiest Christian place on earth were in a Muslim country." Then he sniffed disgustedly. "As if Jesus had ever traveled to *Italy*, where they have *their* headquarters!"

I stopped walking and looked at him. "*Their* headquarters? I thought you were part of '*their*.'"

He ignored me. "Anyway, we *know* what the Son of the Son thinks of all their gold!"

I ignored the "Son of the Son" reference and added, looking directly at the little stone house, "Not a hint of gold anywhere so far. I must say, Father, you sound as if you've gone off the reservation. . . ."

He let that pass, too, and took my arm as we approached the house. "At any rate, about ten years after Gouyet's discovery, a Lazarist priest organized a second research team and came to *this* site—and found the chapel in ruins. They also found an ancient statue of the Virgin with the hands broken off."

"But Rome doesn't officially recognize it as the House of the Blessed Mother, correct?" I asked.

"No—and yes. In 1896 Pope Leo XIII came to see it for *himself* . . . and he left believing that it was authentic. But it took another fifty-five years for another pope to come. That was in 1951. That's when Pope Pius XII came. He then bestowed upon Meryemana the status of 'Holy Place'; Pope John XXIII made that designation permanent, and then Pope Paul VI unofficially confirmed the little house's authenticity on July twenty-sixth, 1967.

"Did you know that even Pope John Paul II served

mass here in November 1979? As did Pope Benedict XVI in 2006?"

When I shook my head no, he finished: "Yes, Benedict came on November twenty-ninth, 2006."

"What? How come I never heard any of this?"

"Just another trip by another pope, that didn't mean much—to an outsider," he said sarcastically. "But we all know what this place means. I wonder what it will mean to you."

He then stepped up to the threshold, unlocked and lifted the grate, and then unlocked the front door. We stepped through an archway and into a room made of ancient brick and mortar.

Above us a skylight provided light, as did the small windows that were placed high up on the walls.

"Did the Blessed Mother play for the Knicks?" I asked inappropriately.

He took no offense. "People were very tiny back then, as you know. But this place? It was built as a fortress, basically, impenetrable—that's why the windows were so high, the walls so thick. Her protector knew that if they had killed her son, they would—if they could have found her—kill her as well. The Christian religion was spreading very quickly."

He placed his hands around the thickness of one arch. True, it looked at least two feet thick.

"For what other inconceivable reason would a house built in the first century have been created with such extraordinary security? Walls this thick were for castles, not peasants' homes."

I had to admit he was right. We stepped into the front room.

The floor was laid with an exquisite Turkish carpet that covered the entire surface, and to the left and right were long simple wooden shelves attached to the walls with benches tucked underneath. If there hadn't been votive candles covering the shelves, you might have thought you'd stepped into a Turkish tea shop. Except for the exceptionally old bricks and beautiful arches, that was it.

We walked through another open archway into the second room of the two-room house, where an ancient statue of the Virgin stood atop a white marble altar under an arched hearth. A very large, intricate silver crucifix on a metal stand stood to the right and slightly behind the altar, which was laid with a pristine white cloth embroidered with crimson. Two large candles were burning in metal candlesticks on either side of the statue, and a little bouquet of flowers stood in front.

The priest gestured for me to kneel down on the marble kneeler at the altar. I hesitated. I was already shivering uncontrollably, and kneeling on cold, hard marble was hardly what I wanted to do, but I knew that if I wanted to hear the rest of the story, I'd have to do the bossy old guy's bidding.

He gestured again, slightly annoyed that I hadn't jumped to his command immediately. Shaking as though I were dropping into some kind of hypothermia, I nonetheless managed to ease between him and the crucifix and knelt down.

I bowed my head and put my hands together on the freezing cold altar and waited for him to continue. Instead, a horrible pain—a blow?—to my head felled me. I felt a blanket go 'round my shoulders, heard the gate come down and the door lock, as the room went dark.

## 24

My brain felt as though it were swelling rapidly inside my head, squeezing the skull to bursting.

I heard the front grate opening, even though I didn't remember that we'd ever pulled it closed! Then the noise stopped, but a blinding light began pouring in under the door. It looked as though the sun itself had melted and was dripping liquid light that was crawling toward me.

The wooden door suddenly swung fully open, and the whole room filled with a light so unbearably bright that the air itself became one with the light.

Then I saw them. Standing at the threshold bathed in the frightening, glorious light were three men. And each was holding a box.

*It's a dream. It's just a dream. Calm down. You must have gone into hypothermia or shock. Doc said you had endometriosis back when you were trying to conceive. Did you get an early, heavy period? No—not due for at least two weeks. The priest will call an ambulance. Just a dream . . .*

It was almost harder to see in the blinding light than

it would have been in the pitch black, but I could make out the silhouette of a man standing over me. Not one of those from the doorway. This man was wearing fatigues with a bandolier of bullets strapped across his chest, a rifle and a semiautomatic pistol in his hands.

*Iraq 2005? No, that was long ago. But still, he's not an American soldier. I know that.*

I was shivering, I knew also, when the man spoke.

"Father—don't do anything foolish." I moved my eyes until they honed in on another man in the room, a young priest. It wasn't Father Paulo—I couldn't see him anywhere.

*Sadowski? No, Sadowski's dead. Dead. I think I killed him. No, no. Not me.*

The three figures in the doorway were still standing without moving a muscle. Like department store displays.

*Don't move; he thinks you're dead. He walks over and around you as though you're just an overturned piece of furniture.*

"Hand them over, Father. I don't want to kill you." His accent was undetectable. "But you know I will, and I'll take your pals here with me."

I could see that the priest was holding three boxes, one on top of another. "These are just gifts . . ." the priest said. "Gifts. They brought—"

"Hand them to me," the soldier said again, aiming the gun between the young priest's eyes.

"Your guns are useless here," the priest replied in a surprisingly haughty way, as though he weren't about to die. "Are you blind, man? Don't you see who our visitors are?" he said, gesturing toward the men in the doorway.

"Hand them to me or you may detonate or spread whatever is in the boxes. You *will* kill the Baby!"

*Oh, God. Has someone taken a baby into the house? I hear no baby!*

He turned to look aside. I could see the outline of a woman standing there. She seemed to be wearing a burqa and was standing stock-still.

Someone else was moving into my line of vision—but it/she/they were crawling on the floor. It was a young girl, blood seeping down her legs. Her tiny white nightgown was transparent with sweat—and occluded with *blood*. The poor little thing was whimpering but was so weak even her cries were barely audible.

*Please let me wake from this nightmare. Oh, God! The dying girl—what is she holding? Is it a baby? Yes. A tiny infant—can't be more than a few hours old!*

"Help me . . . please . . . help me," the girl tried calling to the strangers in the doorway. They immediately began to move forward toward her, arms extended.

I willed myself to open my eyes all the way.

*Move, dammit!* Nothing.

"Help me! Save me. Save my Baby," the girl implored. The men looked as helpless as she was.

*How could she have given birth? She is just a baby herself!*

"I'm a prisoner," she cried, her voice barely above a choked whisper. And then revealing what a child *she* still was, she implored with her last bit of strength, "Can you call my mother?" She looked to be twelve, or at the most fourteen.

The soldier stood between them. It was obvious that the rescuers were never going to get to the girl or the baby as long as *he* was alive.

*Am I dead? Is this hell? Why don't they do something?*

With the rifle still trained on the doorway, and the pistol on the priest, the soldier spat out, "Snap out of it!

*Gifts,* you fool? Biological weapons, chemicals. God-dammit."

The priest answered him by bursting into a high-pitched laugh—ridiculous, absurd, and uncontrolled. He then threw his head back and sniffed the air like a wild dog. "That's a good one," the young cleric snorted hysterically, while the soldier shot concerned glances at the terrified girl. She was still holding on to the baby, still whimpering. He then turned to the woman in the burqa. As soon as his eyes met hers, she threw her head back, too, but so far back that it was nearly perpendicular to her shoulders. She let out an equally high-pitched laugh and also began sniffing the air in quick, rapid snorts.

The woman jumped and clapped her hands together like a schoolgirl.

Meantime, the young cleric, taking the soldier's momentary pause for weakness or confusion, it seemed, tried to move forward. The soldier, in a movement so fast the priest didn't see it coming, aimed the laser directly between his eyes.

"Stop where you are."

He was squeezing the trigger and was probably a thousandth of a millimeter away from contact, when the priest said, "No, see? I'm putting them down," as he lowered the boxes and gestured toward the wooden shelf a few feet away.

The soldier let him put all three boxes on the altar, and with his gun, gestured for the priest to move away from the boxes as he moved toward them.

But as the soldier neared the table, the woman in the burqa literally leapt across the room and snapped up one of the boxes—the one made of silver. In a split second, before he could even shoot, she ripped off its lid, and, giggling again like a teenager, scattered the powder inside the box. It flew everywhere—toward me, toward the girl, and toward the poor, very, very still baby.

"What have you done?" the soldier bellowed. My own eyes burned terribly. I could still see the baby—it was in the girl's protective arms. It didn't seem possible that it was even still alive.

While he furiously rubbed his eyes with one hand and kept his his rifle pointed with the other, the three men in the doorway remained as still as the poor little baby.

With his gun still on the woman's temple, he pushed her to the floor and flattened her with the sole of his combat boot. With his free hand he whipped out a pair of handcuffs and cuffed her tightly behind her back. No one else moved.

"Against the wall!" he ordered the rest of them. "Move it!" The three men gingerly stepped in. I was shocked to see their clothing—it was all clerical, or at least religious, garb. One wore a hooded galabia, the next a Buddhist robe, and the third a huge fur hat and a white, fringed prayer shawl that extended to his knees over a black suit.

The solider commanded, "Hands up against the wall. Now!" They did as they were told, and with his rifle trained on them, he frisked each one in turn. Nothing.

"What was in that box?" Again, nothing. The lack of response so infuriated him that he struck the man standing closest to him, the Jew, with the butt of the pistol, drawing a gash from mouth to ear. Still, the man stood calmly, not even reaching to stem the blood gushing from his cheek.

The girl screamed, but still no sound came from the infant. Then in a coordinated move that looked rehearsed, each man turned his head to the left to stare at the newborn and its terrified child-mother, huddled, shaking, and soaking wet under the altar, where she had scampered.

The Jew opened his mouth to speak to her, but in a movement so quick it was almost unseen, the soldier put the pistol right up against the man's temple. "Who are you and what the hell are you doing here?"

"My name is Gaspar," the man said with an accent that sounded Israeli in a voice surprisingly deep for a man so young and so slight.

"You have exactly thirty seconds to tell me what you're doing here and how you got in."

*I'm not imagining this. These things are really happening.*

"You've used up fifteen of your thirty seconds. . . ."

Gaspar answered him in a voice that was quiet but firm. "We were guided here," he said, oblivious to the semiautomatic pressed to his temple. "To see it for ourselves, study it—"

"Study? What? The Baby?" snarled the soldier.

"The star. It guided us here. We are just astronomers."

He grabbed the Jew and put the pistol to his temple. "What is in the boxes? Anthrax? Botulism? You have five seconds . . ."

The Jew, unusually calm, simply whispered, "Myrrh. Just myrrh."

## 25

I vaguely heard someone yelling, "Grab the Baby! Get the Baby!" But it was far, far off as I again slipped into a blessed form of blackness.

Once more, I had no clue of time passing—or not passing.

I began to wake after a while and realized I was no longer shaking and my head was no longer screaming in pain. I felt for blood on the back of my head. Nothing. I crawled out from under the bench totally disoriented in the blackened room.

*Where the hell am I?* I smelled the thick scent of hashish mixed with some sort of incense.

I walked a few steps and heard a crunch under my feet. I reached down and felt the satin cloth and the shards of glass beneath it. The test tube! It had dropped out of my bag and onto the floor at some point.

*If ever there was evidence of Demiel's otherworldliness, it's gone now. Not your problem right now. Now your problem is getting the hell out of this place.*

I tried feeling my way around. I could see the glow of the hash pipe and the shadows cast by a candle through the arch in the other room. I got up. Father Paulo was sitting on the far side of the arch smoking the shisha with a bottle of wine before him.

"Where are they, Father?"

I felt around for my red satchel and found it lying on the floor—*had I left it there?*—and realized I may have been robbed.

Sadowski's phone, the new ID, passport, credit card, money—all were in there.

I checked the time and the phone's digital clock showed me that it was "17:24:53," that it was almost out of juice, and that there was zero signal in the house.

Nearly 5:30 P.M. An entire day had passed!

I started rooting around in my bag. As closely as I could remember, it seemed to be the same amount of euros as I'd had earlier. Passport? I opened it. There was my picture with the crazy moniker "Alazais Roussel." Even my old Gap scarf was still in there—although, really, I couldn't imagine who'd want that ratty thing. The answer I later learned was "everyone."

I felt the leather binding. *The book*.

No eReader, no iPad, no holographic tablet reader—nothing on earth—feels, smells, or gives comfort like the luxury of a well-bound book. Thank God, it was safe.

"You destroyed the blood," Paulo said, his voice choked with anger and with tears. He got off his stool and stood hovering over me, seething. "You destroyed the blood."

"What the hell just happened back there? What the *hell* is going on?"

"You were to see the holograph of the event. That was the plan. But then . . ." He started to drift again. "You began speaking in tongues before I could do that."

"I don't speak in tongues. Where is the girl? What have these people done with that child and her baby?"

"Headquarters had the technology way back then to produce it," he said, as though I hadn't asked him a question. "They needed to capture the magnificence of the moment, but you didn't need any of that, did you?"

"You mean it was a holograph? You showed me a holograph?"

"No. It's always the least deserving who see what others fail to see," he sneered at me jealously and pulled a deep toke.

*What the heck is he jealous of? I nearly had a heart attack.*

"I don't know why you were chosen," he went on contemptuously. "I don't even know why that animal was chosen to be the husband of the Girl. I only know that I was honored to be part of the Great Experiment. Then when you showed up . . . But you have ruined everything. Common people shouldn't be sent to do uncommon jobs.

"Astonishing, really." He took another deep drag; the smell of hashish filling the tiny walls was giving me a contact high. Or had I been drugged already?

*Holograph, my ass.*

I was still very shaky—no longer shivering, but just shaky—as I made my way to the door. I had to get the hell out of there. He didn't attempt to stop me.

"What now?" I asked, hoping he'd give me a clue about where the heck I was supposed to find this "source" blood.

"They will come to collect what they can of the blood you spilled, then I don't know," he said, slipping into a good ole Middle Eastern drug high, which I recognized from my days with the guys in Iraq. He began chanting in a low rumble that sounded terrifying in the close confines of that tiny stone house.

I tried the door.

*Damn! It's stuck! No, it's not. Breathe. Calm down. Breathe.*

The knob finally turned, but the gate was still locked down. I reached down and saw that the padlock was locked from the inside and the key was still attached. He wasn't apparently trying to keep me a prisoner here.

I unlocked it, lifted it, and took a huge gulp of the fresh spring air outside the confines of this sicko's hashish den.

As the heavy gate began to rise, I could hear chanting that matched the priest's coming from many, many voices. Fear—and a million more questions—ran through my brain.

*Sensory overload. Get out. Get straight. You've probably been drugged. Get out. Get straight.*

I lifted the gate all the way up and was astonished at the sight. Like a specter or a movie about the Middle Ages, coming up the path to the door where I stood were dozens of burning candles held by white-robed monks.

Their haunting chant—*"Pater noster qui es in caelis, sanctificetur nomen tuum; adveniat regnum tuum"*—reverberated like angel song in the crisp night air. The closer they came the more clearly I could see them. Embroidered on their robes were large yellow crosses that shimmered in the dusk. The shape of the cross was the same as that worn by Father Paulo.

## 26

I stepped aside as the line of hooded monks—male and female, young and old—walked solemnly past me while bowing their heads to me as though *I* were some sort of religious figure myself.

The first monk, a woman of eighty years or so, walked inside the house first, and the others filed in after her, chanting, "*Et ne nos inducas in tentationem, sed libera nos a malo*," as she walked toward Paulo.

I turned and headed back toward the parking lot.

I could see still Mr. Cesur standing there, waiting outside the car as though we'd been gone for only ten minutes instead of one whole day. He asked no questions, nor did he even inquire about Father Paulo. He opened the car door for me, and I flopped into the backseat exhausted.

*What now? Where the hell should I go?*

*Anywhere but here.* "The airport."

I grabbed a bottle of mineral water from the stash in the seat console as the nearly battery-depleted phone began to ring. The ringtone was not the usual one I'd heard on Sadowski's phone, but, bizarrely, the classic

*Dragnet* theme: *dum-da-dum-dum*. Caller ID: "Unknown."

"I swear every priest is insane!" I said out loud, although Mr. Cesur was in his own world at that point.

I immediately recognized the voice. "So the old SOB is still alive and kicking." Maureen!

"Ms. Wright-Lewis!"

"I think you have earned the right to use my first name."

"But how did you find me, and how the hell did you know about the priest?"

"You forget with whom you are dealing, dear. Old spies don't *really* fade away."

"You don't know how good it is to hear your voice."

*Stop gushing. You don't even know the woman. Just because she's alive and not looking to kill you . . .*

I continued, unashamed: "I was beginning to think I was trapped inside *Rosemary's Baby*," I joked. "Am I still a wanted woman?"

"More than you can imagine. It's imperative that you keep deep undercover. No one—not your friends nor your family—must know your whereabouts or be able to contact you. I've lived most of my life this way, and now you have to. Until your name is cleared, that is."

"But *you* found me. How hard would it be for everyone else? And I have two friends who are helping me."

"Again, trust no one. The more contact you make with the outside world, the easier it will be to find you. I can't stress that enough. Tell me, Alessandra . . ."

*My name has never sounded so, well, seductive.*

"Did you find any proof yet that the others survived?"

"I think so. The old priest had a book hidden away that has never been opened before. It is the supposed diaries of all the eyewitnesses to the event. The birth."

I heard a sharp intake of breath on the other end. She

may have been the greatest sleuth the world had ever known, but—damn!—if even *she* couldn't keep a natural reflex from surfacing once in a while . . .

"I was shown a holograph too—or I know this sounds crazy, it might have been a, ah, a vision."

"A vision or a holograph—which was it?"

"Does it matter right now?" *She has some bug up her rear. Dammit, lady.*

"Alessandra? You need to find Pantera. I believe he's still alive."

"The World Cou—"

The phone then made the ominous "you're out of time, lady" beep and went dead. How would I find this Yusef Pantera guy if the frigging World Court had declared him just—was it four days ago; who knew anymore?—dead in a plane crash. Talk about deep undercover.

"Excuse me, Mr. Cesur; do you have a cell I can borrow?"

He handed me his cell phone and told me I could charge my phone in the backseat lighter.

*Thank God it's Turkey, where everyone still smokes for a living!*

It immediately lit up. I tried calling her back but couldn't make a connection, and so I left it free, hoping Maureen would call back. Good luck with that.

I dialed up Sadowski's voice mail from Cesur's phone. Two calls. First one Donald. "I hope you are off the grid and don't get this, but in case you are foolish enough to check in, I got a bead on Wilson—the doorman you asked about? Well, I *had* a bead on him. But someone put a bullet in his brain. Last night. I went to the building where the old fella still worked—but I ended up photographing a crime scene. No witnesses, no suspects. Everybody loved him and all that crap." Click.

One from Dona: "Interpol is on your ass. My contact

at the Feds said they've traced you to Istanbul. Get out."
Click. The call had come in six hours earlier. Shit.

Airport it was then. "Mr. Cesur, take me to the commercial airport, please."

He just turned around and smiled.

What the hell did that mean?

The route was fairly well lit. We drove down the long gravel path, and fifty yards on the left there was a two-lane road, which we entered. We drove past a tiny mosque, then a long promenade of mulberry trees surrounding an excavation site at the Temple of Artemis.

Where could I possibly hope to find this Pantera guy?

I opened Sadowski's phone, still connected to the plug, hit a tab that disconnected the connection, and scrolled through his contacts.

*You never know—right?*

I typed every iteration and spelling that I could think of for "Yusef Pantera"—"Yusef," "Pantera," all the *P*s, all the *Y*s, and finally "YPanY" and found "Y, Pan, Y, Carcassonne + 33 4 68 88 98 71." Could that possibly be him? With Sadowski, who the hell knew?

I checked Cesur's map icon on his phone to put in "Carcassonne." It was a city located in the Midi-Pyrénées in France and was tagged "eleventh-century, walled city." The closest city with a large airport, however, seemed to be Barcelona, Spain. Air France seemed my best bet, after checking schedules.

"Air France, please, Mr. Cesur."

He didn't acknowledge what I'd said as I handed him back his phone, but I heard him call the airport, or so I hoped. He was speaking Turkish.

When we reached the airport junction, he turned the car left and headed toward the lower end of the Valley of the Ruins. *Boy, did I belong there!* I was surprised he didn't take the right. There was a sign pointing to the

TURKISH AVIATION CLUB, written in English and Turkish. I remember that sign when we drove out of the airport and passed the commercial airport. He was driving past it!

"Mr. Cesur, please. You passed the airport!"

He just kept driving—not acknowledging me at all. We came to road signs that pointed to Kusadasi to the left and the airports to the right.

He turned right and we passed what looked like the summer homes of the rich, visible through a forest of blackened pine trees.

"Miss, this forested area was destroyed by fire—the drought, you see."

He sped up as we passed small village after small village, with greenhouses blending into each other, then farmland, then the Tahtali Dam and a drought-dried lake bed.

"Please, sir, where are you taking me?"

He broke his silence on the subject just to say, "It's all good, miss, all good." He was going too fast for me to attempt to jump out.

After another ten minutes at a steady 45 mph we reached the big public airport, but Cesur continued driving straight on past the passenger terminals and toward the private area where thirty or so private planes—from antique biplanes to sleek Learjets—stood idly by.

"No check-in, miss, no check-in," he said as we pulled up to the same Gulfstream jet on which we'd come. Turkish police and security were swarming the field.

*Are they looking for me? Do they know I came in with Father Jacobi? Is this a setup?*

"Sir, I need to go to the Air France terminal—please!"

"This is the plane to take you where you need to go," Cesur said as the pilot opened the plane's door. He waved me aboard, and I rushed up the steps, trying not to look around, strapped in, and tried to make myself invisible. Two Turkish policemen approached, and the pilot calmly walked down the stairs to speak with them.

He showed them his papers, and he and the cops commenced walking around the aircraft, seemingly inspecting it for—what? I don't know. They came around to the side where I was sitting, and they all looked up—right at me. The pilot even pointed at me as I tried to sink down farther into the seat.

*Damn!*

The two policemen checked something on their handheld devices and looked up again. They said something to the pilot and then bowed slightly. He did the same.

As we began to taxi out, I saw the two cops make the double sign of the cross. *Extraordinary.*

## 27

The plane took off, and I poured myself half a tumbler of Jack Daniel's and gulped it down like one of those drunks on the TV rehab shows who get hammered the minute they get sprung.

Next I attacked the cheese, bread, and everything else that was in the cabin bar. I was wolfing down food like a death-row inmate—which I figured I was five minutes away from becoming anyway.

I had no idea whether what I'd seen and experienced in the House of the Virgin had been a holograph, or whether I'd been drugged, had a vision, or all of the above.

I turned on the seat-back TV to BBC International and got the latest on the trial. The British correspondent was going over yesterday's events prior to the start of the live courtroom feed. Mostly, the trial the day before, he explained, had been filled with delays while ben Yusef's lawyers tried to figure out what to do with a defendant who refused to cooperate in his own defense.

The trial was commencing later than usual this day, so I got to watch the overhead shots of the UN area of

Manhattan. (Would I ever be free to go back to my home?) The crowds seemed to have swelled from the first two days of the trial, if at all possible. The helicopter was shooting the FBI and police vans as they wended their way toward the UN.

When they finally arrived, the door to ben Yusef's armored vehicle opened, and the cops and Secret Service personnel hopped out first. Then, shackled, the tiny man who was considered the most dangerous human on the planet, ben Yusef himself, exited as well. He squinted as he stood waiting to be moved inside to the makeshift courtroom, as though the sunlight was disturbing to his eyes. He scanned the riotous crowds behind the gates and the rows of reporters in front of him.

*Turn away, don't look at him.*

I found it almost hard to watch the man. Not because of his alleged crimes, but because he had a sort of hypnotic way about him and I didn't want to be drawn in again. Ridiculous, I know.

*Terrorist, desert rat.*

But there was that something stirring in me again. Was it pity? God help me—love? Or was it a weird uneasiness that my reporter-self couldn't reconcile with my female-self? Something just seemed so wrong about the accusations and the man I was looking at.

*Stop it! You saw all those kids in the courtroom the other day. Spinal-cord injuries, blindness, burns from head to foot. He's a filthy murderer!*

At that exact moment, ben Yusef turned and looked directly into the camera as though he'd heard my thoughts—the same way I'd heard that soldier's thoughts in the house. I felt that he was looking directly at *me* through the screen—even though I was thousands of miles away, not to mention forty thousand feet in the air.

*OK, you are losing it. Turn off the TV. No, leave it on.
You must watch—it's your job. Not any longer. Now it's
your life. You need to know everything about his life to
save your own.*

I felt like his eyes were boring into me—yet his face
held the most loving expression I'd ever seen on a man.
Actually his expression transcended gender—hell, it even
transcended species. It wasn't *human*.

I could only compare his gaze to an expression on a
face I'd only seen once before. On Lefty One Eye, our
dog.

Lefty had shown it to me the night I picked up his
shivering little self on the steps of the brownstone we
lived in. I remember like it was yesterday how I carried
him up the three flights to our walk-up, covered him in
a blanket, and warmed up some milk for him. When
Donald came home he found me curled up with Lefty
on the bed, singing him to sleep. I explained his presence
to Donald by kissing Lefty's head and saying, "Lefty, this
is your new dad."

At that, Lefty gave me a doggy smile that was so filled
with love, it too transcended species. *That* was the look.
Peace, love, and, yes, an acknowledgment that I was the
only one who could save him.

*Even if you are innocent, I can't save you, mister. I am
too busy trying to save my own sorry ass.*

With that thought in mind, I drifted off to sleep (probably the Jack), and the next thing I knew the copilot was
shaking me gently awake. "Miss Roussel . . . we're preparing for landing. Miss Roussel, wake up."

I checked the time—four hours had passed—as we
landed at a private airfield adjacent to the huge Barcelona Airport.

*Now comes the hard part. Renting another car.*

But that was actually the easy part. I rented a Smart

car in no time using my bogus passport, license, and credit card.

The car was parked across the road in the huge—and very hot—rental car lot. It must have been eighty-five degrees, even though it was now nearing midnight.

If you've ever tried getting out of Barcelona Airport and onto a highway, you know that the whole roadway system there is designed to keep you from ever getting anywhere but back where you started.

After two solid hours of going around and around, I decided to call it a night and checked into one of those motel/hotel places near (I think!) the airport. I prepaid with cash.

I awoke at dawn, went down to the free continental breakfast, complete with horrible fatty ham hock that's as common a sight at every breakfast place in Europe as the Danish-in-a-bag is at our cheap brown motels.

Skipping the ham hock and going straight for the carbs and coffee, I studied a map that I'd gotten from Europa-car. I was not comfortable using the GPS ("It's imperative that you keep deep undercover"), so I kept it off.

It seemed like it would be a fairly easy ride into France through a highway cut into the Midi-Pyrénées—approximately three and a half hours. Three hours until I'd hopefully be on my way to Mr. Pantera.

Well, if the "Y, Pan, Y" in Sadowski's contact had really meant "Yusef Pantera," that is. And if "Y, Pan, Y" was the right guy *and* he was alive, that is. And of course, and worse, if "Y, Pan, Y" was alive, it also meant that he had to be at least as good an operative as Maureen Wright-Lewis, which meant I'd never find him—unless he wanted to be found.

I deliberately decided not to attempt to call that number beforehand—thinking somehow that I'd take him by surprise by showing up in the same village. I mean, it can't be that easy to run out of a walled city without being seen, right?

The "easy" three-and-a-half-hour ride somehow turned into over six. The map took me on every back road and through every idyllic (translation: speed limit zero) little Spanish town in the entire country.

After five hours on small (half dirt, half paved) roads and perilous one-lane, guardrail-free, endlessly curving slivers of road that hung on the edges of mountains shrouded in cloud, I slid down a mountain—clutching and downshifting the whole way—and finally hit flat land, and yet another unpaved street that looked like it was carved out of somebody's back forty. And then there it was—a hand-painted wooden sign nailed to a tree. It simply read: FRANCA.

*The border crossing between France and Spain looks like a driveway? What? This can't be right!*

But it was right. I'm sure I'm the only person who's ever gone that crazy, circuitous route, so I figured at least I wasn't being followed. I knew I'd entered France because the first little town I came to had signs only in French.

*I'll be damned!*

I stopped for lunch at a small inn, mostly because it had a parking lot.

The inside was typical of the region—beamed ceiling, plaster walls, and big comfy fireplace—and I ordered a steaming plate of duck stew with black currants, which, if I was home, would have taken a thousand hours on the elliptical machine to undo.

It was, however, worth it, because it was maybe the best thing I've ever tasted. Not that I had much choice. By the look of the menu, ducks in this part of the world had about a one-in-a-thousand chance of surviving past duck puberty.

I ordered a bottle of Perrier, deciding to be very un-French and forgo the wine. I still had a long drive ahead of me and didn't want to drive over the edge of one of these insane mountain roads.

As I was musing my lunch away, Sadowski's phone jangled me out of my respite. The other customers at two other tables glared at me, stage-whispering something like, *"Doit être un Américain à utiliser leurs téléphones pendant le déjeuner!"*

You only needed to be fluent in human to know that cell phones at a meal here were strictly for the uncivilized—or American—which to Europeans tend to be one and the same.

I made my *désolés* as I jumped up and ran toward the door while trying to find the damned phone, which had slipped to the bottom of my red bag.

I found it. "Caller unknown." Not good.

Risking it all for no real reason, I picked it up, hoping to God there was no one tracking me, despite what Sadowski had said.

"Alazais Roussel?"

*Where have I heard that voice before?*

"Who is asking?"

"My name is Pantera. I thought I'd make this easier and forgo the cat and mouse, yes?"

*Holy good God!*

"Well, okay, yes." I was desperately trying to "make" that voice.

"We need to meet."

I knew it would have been useless to ask him how he'd found me, so I just went with, "Okay, yes. Where and when? I'm heading toward Carcassonne now."

"Meet me in Montségur in Languedoc."

"I'm sorry?"

"The village of Montségur."

"The town where the Cathars . . ."

"*Précisément.*" His words actually sounded like they were made of honey.

*This is one slick operator. Watch this guy—if he is this Pantera guy, that is.*

"You should stay at the L'Oustal, a tiny little bed-and-breakfast run by a couple of friends of mine. You'll be safe there, I assure you."

"And who are you to assure me of anything, Mr. Pantera? Since I got caught up in this whole insane business with your *friends,* life, as you probably know, has been anything but safe for me—anywhere."

"You don't actually have a choice in the matter—if you want to meet me—which you do."

*That again.*

"Life on the run, *sans amis,* is a difficult life. I know."

"And you propose to be my *ami?* Teach me the ropes of living on the run . . ."

"I will arrange for a room for you. The address, although the town is literally no more than one small street, is—"

"Wait. I need to write this down." I dug out my reporter's notebook and wrote down precisely what he said, spelling out very carefully, "L'Oustal, 46 rue du Village, Montségur, phone number: 05-61-02-80-70."

"When you reach the end of the village—and really it is half a block long before you come to the mountain—cut a deep left and go up. On the right, you'll see a sort of grass driveway with a gate. Oh, and a lot of dogs—friendly, I assure you. Open the gate yourself; don't bother to honk; they won't come out.

"But they will be expecting you. Park next to the welding shed."

"Sounds charming."

"It is," he said, bringing me up short.

"Right."

"I will meet you at seven thirty this evening at the Hotel Restaurant Costes in the town."

"Shall I drive there?"

He laughed. "Only if you can't walk fifty yards. There's a restaurant and bar in the lobby. We have much to discuss." He sounded like the male Maureen.

*Well, he probably is the male Maureen—if Maureen had married a thirteen-year-old, that is.*

It took another hour and a half to get to Montségur, following the signs as carefully as I could. Then, finally popping out of the foggy mist, I saw it: Montségur's mountain, rising up like a vision.

I was so awestruck by its stark beauty that I stopped the car and took out the phone to take a picture. When I looked at the photo, I saw what wasn't visible to the naked eye—unless you know *what* it is you are looking for: A large castlelike structure sat on the very top of the very steep, seemingly impenetrable mountain. It must have been, I figured, at least four thousand feet high.

*How the hell did they ever build a castle on the top of that thing? In fact, how did they even get up that thing, let alone carry up building materials? Astonishing. Is that the very place where the Cathars had lived—and been burned alive? Plenty of time to find that out. Are you kidding? Live past the next couple of days and you'll be lucky.*

I got back in the car and drove on until I came to the village of Montségur. He was right; it was more like a street than a town. It didn't have so much as a grocery store, although it did have a handcraft/souvenir shop and a museum that looked like a tiny one-room stone house.

Following his directions, I easily found the L'Oustal, which was exactly where he'd said it would be.

I parked next to the welding shed, which I recognized because there was a guy inside welding and sparks were dangerously flying everywhere in the wooden shed. I headed toward the stone and plaster house, climbing what seemed like a bad attempt at steps, which were made of uneven rocks set into a steep slope. A jolly French lady who didn't speak a word of English came out of the old stone house, wiping her hands, I swear, on her apron. She somehow conveyed to me that *le coût de la chambre* (which was all of forty bucks) had been taken care of.

*Generous, that Pantera.*

We walked around the back of the house, up another ridiculously steep set of stairs, with cats sleeping on at least half of them, until we reached the top floor. She unhinged an old wooden door, and we walked past a beaded curtain and up another few interior steps. She opened the door to my room and, yes, it was charming. Complete with a sink across from the monk's bed. She was quite proud to show me the tiny attached bathroom, since this was one of the only rooms equipped with its own *toilettes et salle de bain*.

There was already fruit and wine laid out on the tiny cheesecloth-covered table in the center of the room. When she left, I immediately sat down on the wooden dining chair and turned on my iPad. I had been too long without information.

*No signal.*

It was only a few hours until I was to meet Pantera—or the alleged Pantera—so I decided to try to relax. I ran a scalding-hot bath in the chipped but clean oversized claw-foot tub and inched my way into the steaming water, yelping with every inch conquered. I sank down and dunked my head. The water turned an orangey color. The bad dye job was still running.

*Ahhhh. Forget for a minute that you are hunted. Just pretend you're back in college visiting France on the cheap.*

As I came up for air, suddenly great heaving sobs escaped from me like steam from a busted pipe. "Mom, help me!" I cried. I felt just like that poor little kid who wanted her mom to come save her from that house of horrors in Ephesus. I knew, however, that my wish was even more impossible than the kid's had been. My mother couldn't even know where I was—for her own safety, and mine.

*I am completely alone in the world. Like Blanche Du-Bois, I depend on the kindness of strangers. Well, the kindness of professional assassins, more specifically.*

## 28

I soaked and sobbed until the water was no longer painfully hot and the tears had subsided into gasps for air. I composed myself as best as I could, climbed out, and dried off with the towel. The operative word being *the*.

I realized that my wardrobe choices for dinner, or what I presumed would be dinner, were slim, none, and completely ridiculous. It wasn't like I had a party dress in my bag.

So I just rinsed out my undies, hung them on the windowsill in the hot sun to dry, and lay down on the monk's bed. I was afraid to nap for fear of not waking up, so I didn't close the wooden shutters.

At 6:45, I got up, put on my jeans, a T-shirt, my leather jacket (it cooled off at night up there in the mountains), and my Frye boots. I attempted to do something—anything—with my scary bright red killer clown hair, but it was impossible.

The attempt to hide the puffy eyes with under-eye concealer didn't work, either, since industrial-strength cover-up was needed at that point. I compensated by putting on too much black eyeliner, mascara, and red lipstick.

The light in the room was so bad I had no idea if I looked OK or like I'd wandered off from Cirque du Soleil.

*What are you trying to pull off here? You think the old coot with the honeyed voice will melt at the sight of you and give up all his secrets? You're lucky if he doesn't drop dead walking up the hill. If he was in his twenties back in '82, he'd be—what?—mid-to-late fifties? Or more.*

As I was leaving, I double-knotted the Gap scarf around my neck, hoping for a pulled-together look. It wouldn't pay to show up to meet an international man of mystery looking like a slob—despite my terrible dye job that was beginning to fade in places. One more check in the mirror.

*Crap. I look like a traffic light melted on my head— red, greenish, and yellow.*

I climbed down the rickety wooden stairs—it was chilly as could be—and tried to make my way down the rocky (need I mention unlit?) and unnecessarily steep path, past the welding shop. Three large dogs happily followed me, so I carefully secured the gate so they wouldn't wander off.

Pantera was right. It took all of a minute to walk to the Hotel Restaurant Costes. It was a lovely old plaster-and-stone building with quaintly chic shutters and a terrace overhung with vines, under which tables were aglow with candles, just waiting for customers. I had my doubts, however, about a big alfresco dinner crowd showing up in this chill.

I walked into a gorgeous (warm!) tiny lobby with an unmanned reception desk. There was a bar to my right and a minuscule library with books—all in French, of course—every one with a title that had the words *Pays Cathare* ("Cathar Country") in the title.

I walked a few steps to the ancient stone arch that led to the adjacent dining room. Lit by a few brass hanging lanterns and candles, it was one of those magnificently homey, beamed-ceilinged rooms with exposed stone where the plaster had worn away. There were only a dozen or so square wooden tables, each set with pristine beige-and-white tablecloths, linen napkins folded like lady's fans, candles, and tiny vases of local flowers. The walls were hung with swords and tapestries that looked equally old, depicting what I assumed were historical albeit pastoral scenes. Many of the figures in the tapestries were dressed as knights with those strange-shaped yellow crosses on their chests.

I could see that only one table was occupied—a middle-aged couple was mid-meal. The son of the landlady at the B and B told me that, unlike in other parts of Europe, the people in the Languedoc region dine early, so I assumed they weren't getting many more customers even indoors that night. I stood at the archway waiting to be seated, although there wasn't a staff person anywhere to be seen.

Eventually, a harried waiter / front desk / concierge / bartender came out of the kitchen door located behind the bar.

"*Madame? Avez-vous une réservation pour une personne?*"

*Is he kidding? It's empty.*

"Ah, no, sorry. Two for dinner, please."

He switched to English. *Damn those French!*

"This way . . ."

He led me across the red stone tile floor to a table in the center of the room.

My dad always taught me to keep my back to a wall so I could see who was coming in, while Donald always preferred sitting in the middle of a room so he could

shoot (photos!) while running out. I went with my father's advice, and asked if I could instead be seated at
the last table against the back wall, right next to the glow-
ing fireplace. I wanted to be able to see everyone who
walked in.

"Ah, our most romantic spot! *C'est romantique!*"

*Yeah, wait'll you get a load of "Gramps."*

I was a full ten minutes early, so I checked out the
wine list, which included Vin de pays d'Oc, Vin de pays
d'Aude, Vin de pays de l'Hérault, Vin de pays du Gard.
Not knowing one *vin de pays* from the next, I went with
the midrange red, hoped for the best, and waited nervously for Pantera to show up.

*7:25, 7:30, 7:35 . . . Where is he? Is he bagging on me?
Is he huffing and puffing up the hill?*

By 7:40, the couple had finished their meal and got up
to leave. I turned on Sadowski's phone—just to see if
there was a signal, and there was.

I couldn't help myself. I had a text message.

> I am regrettably running approximately 15 mins
> late. Y. I left you an e-mail as well.

I checked the new *untraceable* e-mail address. Same
message.

*How did he get that address? I've set myself up. I'm
screwed.*

The waiter brought the wine, and I sipped it shakily.
Something inside me was warning me against the whole
thing. *Get up and leave. But where do I go? He's got a
bead on me—whoever he is.*

I stood up to leave anyway—I'd get in the car and drive
the hell away from that town—when I heard the little bell
on the hotel's wooden front door jangle as the door
opened and shut. The long shadow of a man darkened the

wall against the archway as he made his way inside. Long and lean—even in shadow, that was clear.

The shadow took shape as the man reached the dimly lit archway. Leather jacket, jeans, and a bad attitude that was obvious even in that "romantic" French light. So was the bulge at his hip under that jacket.

*The sumnabitch is packing.*

Pantera entered the arch and turned full-face into the brighter light of the dining room.

Shock turned to panic and my heart started racing like I'd been shot up with adrenaline. Fight or flight kicked in. I tried to get up, but my knees buckled under me. I tried again but he'd already started walking toward me in the empty restaurant. He stopped, looked directly at me, fixing me in his stare, and then nodded his head in smirking acknowledgment.

*Oh, God! It's the German! And my back is to the wall.*

For the first time in my life—including my time in Iraq—I literally had nowhere to run.

## 29

Was Pantera my hunter, or was this not Pantera at all? Pantera should have looked older. This one, however, was sort of ageless—hard to peg—craggy face notwithstanding.

*It isn't him—it's my hunter.*

I stood and backed up against the wall as he came closer. I was smack against the fireplace wall now. He motioned for me to sit, and when I refused, he came around and grabbed my arm with incredible strength and forced me into a chair. With the other hand he pulled a chair out for himself and sat down next to me.

"No sense trying to run," he said, his in-person voice a combination of honey and poison. "Mind?" he asked as he picked up the bottle of wine and studied it. "We have some great wines here in Languedoc. This isn't one of them."

He nonetheless poured a bit, held it to the light, and said, "Nice color, though." He smelled it. "Even with a medium-grade wine, there is nothing like the bouquet of a local French." Then, holding it by the stem, he tasted it.

"Nicer than I would have expected." He filled his glass then and lifted it. "To you, Ms. Roussel. It has been a very good hunt."

I found my voice. "I'm not a deer—even if I look like I've been caught in the headlights."

"Yes, I know what you are."

*He hasn't unholstered the pistol, as far as I can tell. Turn the table over. Run for it.*

"Mind if I finish mine?" I asked sarcastically. I took a sip and then foolishly stood up and shoved the table at him as hard as I could and jumped to the opposite side. I leapt away from the table and attempted to run. The speed and strength of his grip as he grabbed my arm without even getting out of his chair was, I can only say, shocking.

Holding me with just one hand, he looked at me hard. "Sit down, Ms. Roussel. I think I invited you to dinner, and I never like my female guests to throw furniture. At least not before the entrée. It's not very French. Or very nice."

When I wouldn't budge, he forced me again into a chair—this time next to him on his right. He slipped his hand down my arm and forced it under the table, holding me with a death grip.

"Shall we begin again? I am Yusef Pantera. Nice to meet you, Ms. Alazais Roussel—aka Alessandra née 'Alexandra' Russo."

*No, the aka is the "Alazais Roussel," asshole!*

As if reading my thoughts, he smiled, "No, I do not have the order confused."

*Why do I know that voice?*

He signaled for the waiter.

*Is he kidding me?*

"Reni—what do you recommend this evening? And

please no *cassoulet au poulet*. Ms. Roussel had the dish earlier today."

I knew better than to ask how he knew, so I said, "I appreciate your speaking in English."

"Yes, one of us has manners."

"And that one of us is also packing."

He smiled and tightened his grip under the table as the waiter began reciting the evening's dishes. I distinctly heard "escargot."

"Listen, Mr. Pantera, I prefer that you kill me rather than force me to eat snails. I'd have a better chance with a bullet than a snail."

"You'd never make it as a Frenchman."

"That alone is worth living for. . . ."

"I can't imagine a sophisticated woman who doesn't love escargot."

"You just met one. I prefer my food without faces and fleshy horns, thank you very much."

"I see."

*That voice. Where?*

"Mr. Pantera. Why the hell are we making small talk when you have a grip on my arm and a gun in your holster?"

"No. In fact, I have a *hand* on you. Like a lover. Quite different from a 'grip.'"

"A lover? I don't think so. Look, you've chased me all over the world. I thought I killed you in that blast that *you* set to kill *me,* and now you think you will kill me up close and personal. How am I doing so far?"

"The chase part is correct."

"What about the killing part?"

"If I wanted you dead, you would be dead. As for me, you wanted me dead but didn't do a very good job of it, I'm afraid."

I took a big gulp of wine. "Excuse me? Are you a bounty hunter then? Were you trying to take me alive?"

He laughed. Almost out loud. I looked around for some way to get away. But the death grip had not loosened a bit. "Wanted dead or alive!" Then he laughed really hard.

*I hate this guy. Arrogant asshole.*

"What do you want with me? Why were you chasing me? Well, until I brought you right to me like a, a . . ."

"Not chasing, looking after."

"What does that mean?"

"Ms. Roussel . . ."

"Will you please stop calling me that?"

"All right, then, if you want to go on a first name basis. Alazais."

"That too."

"You are *very* difficult. I'm sure I'm not the first man to tell you that. Or woman. However, as you have been told *repeatedly,* none of this can be changed. It's your destiny—and mine. My job is to make sure you arrive at your destiny in one piece."

"Oh, brother. That's why you tried to kill me? That's why you followed me all over the world? To keep me alive to fulfill my *destiny*?"

*Nut-job psycho killer.*

"No. I am here to guard you—and keep you from getting killed. The world depends on it."

"Not that again. Such bullshit. You planted explosives in my car. You tried to kill me!"

"No. Well, I wouldn't have let you die, at any rate."

"Just maimed. What a guy."

"I wouldn't have let you get hurt."

"Yes, you would, but *I* detonated—"

"You beat me to the punch—yes—very clever."

"I saw you! You're a frigging liar!"

"You have quite a tongue for a woman who thinks she's being held by an assassin who has her name on his check-off list."

"Very funny. Who planted the car bomb, then?"

"I did. As well as a corpse in a suitcase."

"A corpse."

"They need to think you're dead."

"Who besides *you*? Perhaps you have me confused with a fool or, worse, an amateur."

"Yes, yes, I know all about it. Iraq. Car bomb. Your husband. 2005."

"Go on."

"You were set up in the murder of Father Sadowski. Fine, fearless warrior, that. Damned shame what they did to him. But he got sloppy, let it happen."

"Wow. Cold."

"*You*, on the other hand, had to be eliminated, at least as far as our enemies are concerned—and I had to take the heat off you."

"Why? Who am I in the scheme of things? I can't help it if I got kissed by a terrorist."

"You, dear girl, were born to it. In more ways than you can imagine. Anyway, I had to make it look like there was a third player in the game."

"Am I supposed to thank you now?"

"No. Being hunted has a way of taking one's mind off the mission."

"I'm still being hunted."

"Yes."

"So what are you saying?"

"Did I just say 'yes' or not? You were spotted in Turkey. That fool priest."

*Wait a minute! Now I know his voice! The soldier! Turkey!*

Just then the waiter brought some sort of fishy-smelling *amuse-bouche*. I was beginning to feel nauseated.

"No one associates you with that explosion in the parking lot. Well, not anymore," he said by way of ignoring me.

"Wrong. My friend in New York City connected me with it right away."

"Believe me. She hasn't a clue."

I let it pass. He let my arm go. "Excuse me, but I must release my hold on you. This looks delicious—no?"

*Freaking weirdo!*

"Were you just there—in the house in Turkey?"

"No."

"Not true. You *were* there. I heard your voice."

"Yes. I was there. But decades ago. I should have killed the pompous ass when I had the chance. He almost ruined the Experiment then, and now again, he's endangered the entire mission—bringing you to that house."

"So you *were* there!"

"Thirty-three years ago."

"With him? Explain how I saw you there just yesterday, for God's sake."

"How would I know?"

I told him some of what I'd seen and heard.

He studied my face without expression. I couldn't help but notice that through it all, he, unlike Donald and most of the reporters and prosecutors I'd dated, had impeccable table manners.

*For a professional assassin.*

"So? You're saying it wasn't you? I heard you and saw you—in shadow, yes—but I saw you!"

"The hologram."

"No—the priest said he didn't get to show it because I'd passed out."

He eyed me closely before saying, "I suspect then that

what you saw was a sort of vision: You were able to alter the time/space continuum."

"What are you, a physicist?"

"Yes. MIT."

"Oh, puleeze. You decided that being a professional killer paid better?"

"Let's get back to your vision. You realize that you relived exactly what happened in that house so many years ago?"

I gulped down another glass of wine.

"If this doesn't convince you of your place in the scheme of things—"

"I have no place in your—or their—scheme of things."

"You do. Just as it was mine to guard the Son of the Son, Demiel, and His Mother for all those years."

"You mean the child you molested and took as a, a wife? A little twelve-year-old child!" I was nearly spitting.

"She was thirteen, and I assure you there was no molestation involved. But there was a marriage much later on. Again, destiny fulfilled."

"You realize you are a monster?"

"I realize that I am a man with a destiny that can't be changed: I was born to fulfill this part of the Experiment. I have lived my destiny every day of my life—but you have just started to live yours."

"What happened to that girl? The judge said ben Yusef's mother was dead."

"No."

"Just no?"

"Yes. Just no."

I changed the subject. "The 'experiment.' What does that mean? I heard it from Father Jacobi."

Every time I mentioned the priest's name, his face would go blank with disgust.

"So you won't be inviting him to your next birthday party."

"Let's just say having lived with him during the girl's confinement, he's not my idea of a man—or, more importantly, a man of God."

"And you are—what?—a gunslinger for God?"

He raised his eyebrows slightly in that condescending way that the French have perfected into an art form.

I decided to get to the meat of it. "What do you all want from me? I don't kill people, and when you get right down to it, I don't even believe in God. Well, not your God. I'm not the person you want."

"Yes. You are. And what I want is for you to listen very carefully to what I have to say. You are going to be challenged in the coming days in ways you cannot now begin to imagine. The world is on the precipice. The Son of the Son is on trial, just as his biologically identical father was two thousand fifteen years ago."

"So you guys made a clone. But you can't really believe it is the clone of Jesus."

"Not believe. *Know. Know* as surely as I know who *you* are."

"Well, that proves it. You think my name is Alazais Roussel, which I've never even heard before I got those bogus credentials—which were made by friends of mine in New York."

He laughed lightly and took a sip of wine. "You are a very clever woman, but not as clever as I had hoped."

"Sorry to disappoint."

The waiter brought our dinner, and for the first time since this horrible odyssey began, I wasn't the least bit hungry.

"So tell me, how do you know this Demiel ben Yusef was actually cloned from the DNA of Jesus? Wasn't Jesus a man of peace, while this maniac is his exact opposite? That's what happened to that cow this farmer had cloned in the early 2000s. I saw it on *Discovery*. Bessie had been his favorite, so he had her cloned when she died. But it was reborn as the devil cow. Stomped the whole family to death. You must have read about it."

He looked annoyed; actually, it was more a look of disgust at my levity.

"No, I didn't read about it. And no, Demiel is not the exact opposite to the Son of God. He is exactly—and I mean that literally—the *same* being as the first Son. Jesus was called a seditionist. Demiel is called a terrorist. The only danger either of them ever posed was as a threat to the powerful. The truth—the truth of God—is a powerful thing. More powerful than all the men in Washington or Israel or the Arab states."

"Okay, suppose he *is* innocent—which I don't believe for a minute—what makes you think he's the real deal? Or the clone of the real deal at any rate?"

"Because a group that has been in existence since the beginning of the Christian era has protected the precious blood of Jesus—has held these drops for this long, knowing, *knowing* that it was the key to resurrection, the next coming. They didn't know how it would happen but only that it would. In the ancient times, they believed it would happen through some sort of godly miracle. And science is, in its way, a miracle of God."

"You mean these people kept a beaker of blood for thousands of years without it drying up?"

"No. Yes. But it's not what we should discuss right now."

"How do you know I'll have anything beyond 'now,' considering my status as a fugitive?"

"Because now you have me. To guard you."

"Not that I believe one word, but if I did, I'd have to

ask you why *you* of all people need to guard me. I still believe my life could come to a tragic end—if you have your way. Which you won't."

He picked his head up and looked right at me—yes, like a lover would—and said, "Alessandra, like you, I have no choice in the matter. I—we—*need* for you to live, even though you are an impossible rebel. Keeping you *alive* is the challenge."

"That explains nothing," I snapped, refusing to return his look. He then pointed directly to one of the embroidered tapestry wall hangings.

"Do you find it odd that such an ancient piece hangs in a restaurant in such an obscure village?"

"No. I'm not a scholar of embroidery, so I have no idea if it's ancient or just old." I decided that I needed at least a piece of bread. I had let the fish get cold.

"Doesn't it look familiar at all?"

I refused to admit that now that I looked at it, it did—in a sort of weird déjà vu kind of way. The tapestry depicted a woman from the Middle Ages standing in the foreground at the base of a mountain. Three companions were standing slightly behind her; one was definitely a man, the other, I couldn't make out. All had those crazy-shaped yellow crosses on red backgrounds on the front of their tunics.

In the forefront, the woman who was wearing trousers had a small sack around her neck and a knife tucked into her rope belt.

I pulled out my reporter's notebook. It was well past the time I should have started taking notes.

"Do you mind?" I began jotting before he began answering.

"It's 1244. The slaughter of the Cathars."

"Yes. I know about that."

"No, you really don't. I would appreciate it if you

would meditate on this tonight as you fall asleep," he said, gesturing toward the tapestry. "The answer may come to you."

"So then, let me ask you this: What does that odd-shaped yellow cross on red stand for?"

"Ahh, *la croix Occitane*—the Occitan Cross. Let's see how to best explain this. In the Middle Ages, the Cathar yellow cross was a distinguishing mark—essentially a badge of shame—ordered by the Roman Catholic Church. Like the way the Nazis forced Jews to wear a yellow Star of David so that they could be identified and scorned. In some instances these were on a red background."

"Weird that they would both use the same colors!"

"Not really. *Herr* Adolf was an occultist. He believed that Montségur was the site of the Holy Grail castle and sent archaeologist types to look for what he called the 'mysterious blood.'"

"What mysterious blood?"

"The Cathar blood. Many of the Cathars were nobles who had chosen to give it all up and live as Jesus had. But their blood—and the blood of several of the Knights Templar, who had come to the village as hired mercenaries and ended up converting to Catharism—symbolized for Hitler the purest blood on earth. White, noble, warrior."

"If Hitler didn't believe in Jesus, what did he care about Christian blood?"

"The term *Aryan* derives from the Sanskrit word *árya*." Yusef drew the word on a matchbook. "Meaning 'noble.' To Hitler's way of thinking, you couldn't get purer—or *whiter*—than that. He was looking for that blood, or at least that bloodline."

"I'm astounded. Hitler sent people here?"

"It was reported and I believe it—on March sixteenth,

1944, the seven hundredth anniversary of the fall of Montségur, he had Nazi planes fly over Montségur in formations of the Celtic cross and of swastikas. It was his way of fulfilling a thirteenth-century prophecy that after seven hundred years 'the laurel would be green once more.'

"We believe he thought the actual missing Cathar treasure was *their* bloodline. And he was almost right. It was blood all right—but it was the blood of Jesus."

"And you know this . . . how?"

"On the eve of the mass burnings right here in 1244, four Cathar knights—two were female—rappelled down the backside of the sheer cliff face of Montségur."

*That's what Maureen had been referring to!*

"This, after a siege by the pope's Crusaders and the king's forces, numbering possibly ten thousand, that lasted about eleven months. Their brethren the next day walked willingly—women, children, men, and Cathar and Templar Knights alike—into the giant pyre."

"Now I know why it's the Pyre-nees. . . ."

He looked surprised. "What's astounding is that these knights, under total cover of darkness, slipped away carrying that treasure. After the burnings, the troops sacked the village and found nothing much worth looting. For the soldiers, a very disappointing payday.

"The treasure, which they *thought* was the equivalent of Fort Knox, was nowhere to be found. Logic dictates that three or four people could not have rappelled four thousand feet down a sheer cliff in the middle of the night carrying chests of jewels and gold."

"Agreed."

"It had to have been small, unimportant-looking, and weightless—or nearly so."

"Again, that's true. So what could a group who divested themselves of all worldly things—"

"Even the Eucharist," he said, jumping in.

"So then what could they have had that was so valuable that the pope's and king's Crusaders killed and burned and died for?"

"Nothing less than the blood of Jesus. The blood of the man on trial right now."

"You mean, your son?"

"No, I mean the Son of the Son of God. I was only a guardian."

"He carries your name."

"But not my DNA."

"Well, you should know better than me about that."

"Yes. I do."

I looked askance but he ignored me. "So you think they carried a chalice?"

"I never said that. What I believe, what *we* believe, is that *something* held an actual drop of the blood of Christ, but what it is no one knows."

"Any idea if it's animal, vegetable, or mineral?"

"The Knights Templar venerated something called the 'Head,' or 'Baphomet.' There are stories that it was a skull, but I don't necessarily buy that. There are other tales claiming it to be a head or a face that was imprinted on a banner they carried into battle. It's a Templar belief."

"*Is* a belief? As in the present tense?"

"Of course."

"You mean they still exist?"

"Everywhere."

"But . . . ?"

"No buts.

"The Baphomet, my father believed, was not a skull but a banner imprinted with the face of Jesus."

"You mean like the Shroud of Turin?"

"Yes, like the Shroud but not the Shroud."

"How do you know?"

"Because the Shroud couldn't contain blood or DNA or any of it because it is a negative image—the way you'd see an image in an old negative of a photo. It was transferred from something else. This banner, if it were the Baphomet, would have to be like a photograph's print as opposed to the negative."

"I read something, or maybe it was on the History Channel, about the Shroud being a negative image and that it was impossible for anyone at that time to produce such a thing back then."

"True. But the image I'm referring to would have to be a positive image—something upon which the Shroud may have lain.

"A painting?"

"No. Perhaps an oxidation transfer or something of that nature. Have you heard of the 'Veil of Veronica'?"

"Yes. I remember something about a woman who wiped Jesus' face as he carried the cross and his imprint was left on her veil. Right?"

He took a long swallow of wine, looked over the rim, and said, "It's celebrated in Catholic churches as the Sixth Station of the Cross"

"Holy shit! Sorry. That's such an inappropriate expression right now."

He laughed. "I'm a soldier. I think I've heard worse."

A cloud began to lift. "Let me ask you something. Demiel said to me at the UN that day, 'Go forth for I am six.' Do you think that's what he could possibly have meant?"

He didn't respond.

"But coming from a long line of agnostics, I always heard that the story of the Veil was apocryphal."

"The story perhaps, but probably not the fabric. If it exists, *it* could hold the blood of Christ."

I remembered the test tube then. "If?"

"If."

"Now that you bring up 'blood,' there's something you should hear."

He leaned in closer.

"The priest gave me a test tube of blood. He said it had been taken from the clone baby."

Finally Yusef registered real excitement—or what would pass for real excitement on someone who never showed emotion.

"He, or somebody," I told him, "had it—you won't believe this—in a carpet shop in Istanbul."

"That sly old bastard! He kept it from them all that time."

"Who?"

"Headquarters, of course."

"Not that again."

"Tell me. Where in God's name is that shop? Could you find it again?"

I hesitated to tell him the rest, but did. "No. It's gone."

"What do you mean, *gone?*"

"The tube fell out of my bag and onto the floor and got crushed when it landed under, under, ah, my boot," I said sheepishly.

"Your boot? Where?"

"Inside the Meryemana in Turkey."

"That floor is made of stone. It could be washed up without a trace."

"A bunch of monks came in. They must have taken care of it."

A look passed over his face, and he seemed to understand something immediately.

"Forget it. It's gone now."

"How do you know? Wouldn't the monks have wanted it?"

"No. They didn't want it to exist in the first place. And the old damned fool shouldn't have been keeping it around like a trophy." He slammed his fist on the table. "Damn!"

"Well, that makes the search for Jesus' blood drops a little more difficult," I ventured sarcastically.

Either my sarcasm went right over his head or he was having none of it.

"A little?" he said.

"Maybe you should have been more on top of it, Mister Guardian."

*If looks could kill. Oh wait. He has a gun—he doesn't need a killer scowl.*

As though he hadn't just been furious, he calmed down and said, without affect, "The source still has to be found—to compare to Demiel's DNA. Before they kill him."

"You're sure they're going to execute him?"

He looked at me as though he were looking straight through some bonehead blonde. "Doesn't this Headquarters place have samples?"

"Probably. But even so, that wouldn't prove that it's *His,* you see. And they won't interfere. There was never to *be* any interference to change the divine plan. It was all to play out as it is destined to play out."

"No interference?" I was almost shouting. "These sons of bitches cloned a baby, for God's sake! Isn't that interfering on an extreme level?"

"No." He left it at that and continued: "But the source blood has to be found now and it has to be compared to Demiel's, and done in a way the world will believe."

"I thought there was to be no interference."

"This wouldn't have been interference—just proof."

"Jeez, I'm sorry I stepped on the blood after being

drugged—or whatever the hell that demon priest did to me."

"Don't be. It was wrong to begin with."

*But marrying a child of thirteen after abducting her and impregnating her with a clone is right? Lunatics.*

"I never worry about what I can't change," he said icily. "No?"

"I *guess* . . ." I said, even though I completely believe the opposite. "So even if I could find this head—which may not even exist—you're telling me two different stories. One is about Cathars and one is about Templars."

"The Templars, I believe, put the object into the possession of the Cathars, who were—are—the most trustworthy people on earth. The Templars used the Cathars *literally* as their safety-deposit box."

"But weren't the Templars the bankers for the nobility or something?"

"And in turn the Cathars were the Templars' bankers, so to speak. Yet, ironically enough, the Albigensian Crusade was begun by Pope Innocent the Third, who in 1208 exhorted all Christian knights to expunge the 'Provençal heretics' from all the lands of Count Toulouse." He made a sweeping motion with his hand around the room.

"It was all about wiping out the Christian sects that did not adhere to the wanton filth of the Vatican. He justified this because he declared he was 'below God but above man, who judges all things but who no one judges.' It almost worked, too."

"Almost?"

"Almost. Many of the Templar Knights ended up converting to Catharism and went to their deaths for it."

"Are you one of the 'almost' who remain?"

He ignored me. "Thus, the reason so many Templar Knights walked willingly into the fire *with* the Cathars:

Their mere presence and the chaos it created in the king's troops diverted attention from the four escapees. Those Knights Templar died as men of honor—at the end. Thus the mystery of the so-called Cathar treasure."

"The one that also may or may not exist."

"The one that does exist."

"How did I know you'd say that? What's *your* job, then?"

"To protect you on the trail."

"But you don't know what trail I'm supposed to even be on," I said, getting more exasperated by the second.

"Each of us who were part of the Great Experiment had been given only the information necessary to complete our jobs. Too much information in one person's hands was too dangerous, of course."

"Need to know?"

"Correct. But *that*, Ms. Roussel, I promise you, is where the blood from which my son, or the boy who came to be *as* a son to me, was created.

"Find it and match the DNA, and you'll save his life."

"Even if I were somehow to find it—impossible, by the way—before the end of the tribunal, how am I supposed to get Demiel's DNA to prove a match?"

"Too bad you washed your face," he said in all seriousness. "You are the one he chose to kiss."

"Sorry. I'm funny like that."

"But that is the very DNA that belongs to the Divine Being who is today on trial."

"You mean the DNA contained in the embryo that was put inside that child, your *wife*?" I said, my sarcasm beginning to overtake my reporter's cool.

*Don't forget the disgusting thing he did.*

As though he hadn't noticed, he simply stated the facts. "Contrary to what He's being falsely accused of, the boy grew up as the kindest, most loving person I've ever known. At six years of age, He began to have the ability to heal with his touch. *Never* would He be capable of an evil deed. But the point of the new resurrection would be to see if history would be forced to repeat itself, and of course, it has."

"So I heard from the priest. Nice way to play with a human life—and thousands of other human lives, I might add."

"No sense in trying to convince you of what the facts will show."

"Okay, so what about the, ah, *marriage*?" I winced even to think of it.

"She was Cathar Perfectae."

"Meaning—what?"

He answered me by waving his hand, as though that explained away whatever the heck he'd done to her.

"I think I'm going to be sick."

"The nun was her guardian. She was a child who became a woman, and we each had our roles to fulfill. But she of course has a higher purpose. When Demiel came of age, she took the veil, as was expected."

"The veil?"

At that he pushed his chair back, as though he hadn't just hit me with several weapons of mass destruction.

"What about the 'no interference' rule? Is that off the table now?"

"Not all of it, but some of it changed the minute he kissed you. Didn't it?"

Without waiting for an answer, he stood up. "It's getting late and we have to be up early in the morning. I'd like to get started no later than six A.M."

"Excuse me?"

"I'm afraid we really shouldn't leave any later than that. The bill is paid. I will see you back to your hotel."

"*This* is a hotel. *That* is a house. Since I managed to

get through dinner without being killed or getting sick to my stomach, I figure there's no sense in pushing my luck. I'll see myself home."

"No, you didn't get through it. Your dinner, I mean. You didn't eat."

When I didn't say anything further, he said, "A shame. It wasn't poisoned."

"A regular laugh riot, you are."

"And I won't kill you on the way up the hill, either. The locals are very picky about screaming and murder after nine P.M. You know how the French are. Anyway, there is something you must see in the morning, so you have to be alive."

"You, mister, are a freaking weirdo."

He took my arm again as I stood up—this time with just the half-nelson version of the death grip—and walked me back up to the house and up the rickety stairs. "I need to check your room."

"No."

"I need to check your room," he said as though he hadn't just said it and I hadn't just refused. He dug the key right out of my red satchel and opened the door and went in. He checked every inch of the tiny room, which took longer than necessary.

"You can come in," he said from inside *my* room. I walked in and we found ourselves standing very close to one another in the tiny space between the bed and the door. Suddenly I felt unexpectedly awkward—that way you feel after a first date has come to an end and neither person is sure what the vibe has been.

*Ridiculous. Am I supposed to kiss him because he didn't blow my brains out?*

Well, maybe it was just *I* who was feeling unaccustomedly awkward. Clearly he wasn't. He took my face in one hand and looked right at me. He leaned in and kissed me on both cheeks and then stayed almost pressed up against me—but not quite. It was close enough to feel his body heat but a millimeter shy of any part of him touching any part of me.

"I'll be nearby. No harm will come to you. *Bonne nuit.*"

"Oh, yes, good night."

*Stop it! Pantera is old enough to be your, ah, cousin.*

I realized that I was already upgrading him from old coot to hot, older male.

*Stop it! OK, but the fact that he didn't shoot you before the fish course—or even after—was kind of charming. Jesus Christ!*

## 30

I didn't exactly have a nightgown with me, so as usual, I washed up and stripped down to a T-shirt and my good white cotton panties that I'd bought in a bag in the drugstore, and lay down on the bed.

Everything seemed wrong. The pillow was lumpy, the bed was springy, the room was too hot, too cold, too quiet, too too. I was crazy restless, and couldn't sleep, so I decided to bore myself to sleep by perusing the pamphlets and books in the room. Yes, the L'Oustal did have tourist paraphernalia just like a regular hotel, except by the look of these they hadn't been updated since the Middle Ages. Or at least the information hadn't.

I read the pamphlets in French and quickly discovered there was basically nothing to do in Montségur except four things: Eat at the Hotel Restaurant Costes, which I had already done; have a family-style meal at L'Oustal, which I would do in the morning; go to the tiny museum, which was closed the next day; and/or climb Montségur, which I had no intention of doing. Ever.

Apparently you couldn't drive up there and there

was not even a towrope. If you wanted to get to the top, you hiked it—straight up. I couldn't wait to never do that.

I'd just have to hope that my newest new best friend Y, Pan, Y's "you must see in the morning" involved giving me the secret to the Cathar's lost treasure, clearing my name through his various connections, and getting me the hell back home with all charges dropped.

*Good luck with that, sister. Do not go getting your hopes up of Pantera coming up with any Hail Mary pass—literally—to save your sorry ass.*

I found one book of sorts on the shelf, which was written in English. It was a photocopied version of what looked like information collected from Web sites, but with a similar title to every other book in the town. They didn't seem to get much past the thirteenth century around there.

This one was titled *Cathar Country History.*

I opened and read with all grammatical and spelling errors intact:

> *Catharism was for many years the prevalent form of Christianity in large areas of France, Spain, and Italy. The Cathars called themselves the friends of God and condemned the Catholic Church as the Church of the Anti-Christ. Like the original Christians, the Cathars were vegetarians (Cathars interpreted the commandment "Thou shalt not kill" as referring to all animals), believed in reincarnation, and considered the Old Testament God Jehovah to be a tyrant. . . .*

Then there was a note typed separately and inserted into the text:

*Perfecti observed complete celibacy, while the Credentes—true believers—believed that sexual activity was to be enjoyed, but procreation was strongly discouraged. This resulted in the charge by their opponents of sexual perversion. (Wikipedia entry)*

Did Pantera mean that since little Theo was a Perfectae, they didn't have sex? Dear God, say it *is* so!

The regular text then continued:

*The Albigensian Crusade and subsequent Inquisition was launched by Pope Innocent III specifically to eradicate the Cathars, the largest and fastest growing Christina sect in Europe. The Crusaders undertook the task with ferocious enthusiasm, burning alive men, women and children. From 1139 onwards the pope declared that 'anyone who attempted to construe a personal view of God which conflicted with Church dogma must be burned without pity.'*

*Upwards of half a million people were maimed, dispossessed, slaughtered by the king's soldiers (French King Philippe Auguste who wanted to confiscate Cathar's lands joined the pope in this Crusade) or burned at the stake by the officials of the Catholic Church.*

*In 1208 he offered land to anyone killing Cathars, which launched a brutal 30-year pogrom, which decimated southern France killing at least 250,000 Cathars.*

Instead of being lulled to sleep, I was fully awake now. The Inquisition here in France was created just to eradicate the Cathars? Damn. They did such a good job, I never even heard of them.

> *Catharism disappeared from the northern Italian cities after the 1260s, under pressure from the Inquisition. The last known Cathar stronghold was at Montségur.*

I was dumbstruck to find out that there had been Italian Cathars. Who knew? The Russos, for sure, weren't among them. For one thing, we wouldn't belong to any group that preferred celibacy and vegetables to sex and meatballs. Agnostic over ascetic was definitely our motto!

And finally, there was this reprint from a guidebook:

> *The castle at Montségur was besieged in 1243 by Hughes des Arci, Seneschal of Carcassonne for the King of France, under the guidance of the Pope. For nine months a few hundred Cathars successfully resisted 10,000 Catholic forces until shortly before Christmas when a small group of Basque mercenaries scaled a seemingly impossible sheer cliff-face, and overran a forward position. They were defeated.*
>
> *The 225 or so remaining Cathars were given a choice: renounce Catharism or be burned alive at the stake.*
>
> *On March 2, 1244, Pierre-Roger de Mirepoix, the Cathar's military leader, negotiated a two-week truce with the king's forces for the defeated religious group. Fourteen days, he reasoned, would give the lay population among the Cathars time to leave the fortress, while granting those Cathars*

*who sought to become Perfecti time enough to take their vows and die in grace.*

*Sometime on the night before the mass execution, two males, most likely rogue Templars, and two female Perfecti rappelled down the impenetrable and nearly impossible sheer 4,000-foot cliff face on the northeastern slope of the mountain.*

*They carried with them Le trésor Cathare.*

*Theories vary widely about the nature of that treasure—ranging from gold to the Holy Grail itself.*

*The next morning, on March 16, between 200–225 Cathars willingly marched down the opposite, southern face to the meadow below where they climbed up ladders and positioned themselves onto the hundreds of huge stakes erected by the Catholic army. The pyres were lit and as the flames engulfed them the martyrs sang hymns of forgiveness.*

*Many people in Languedoc, France, still believe that when the wind is blowing in the right direction, a chosen few will always smell the stench of the burning flesh.*

I fell into a light sleep—I was more concerned about the assassin I knew than the assassins that I didn't know sneaking up on me. Nonetheless I began to dream—a nightmare.

In it, I, scary clown hairdo intact but looking like the lady in the tapestry, was standing on the sheer cliff face of a mountain. I was balancing on a rock with one hand, a rope around my waist, thousands of feet above the ground. From the belt of my tunic hung a small leather bag and a sword.

I looked down and saw a massive bonfire in the valley

below. My eyes, like binoculars, watched as hundreds of men, women, and children climbed ladders and found places for themselves on the massive woodpile, where they were tied to stakes.

Crusaders lit the wood, while they laughingly made obscene gestures and yelled obscenities to any Templar Knights who had joined the martyrs.

The flames caught immediately and the fire began to lick the soles of the feet of the doomed. They started singing and screaming as they writhed in the flames and their flesh burned off their bones.

I could see faces melting and babies at their mothers' breasts screaming in torment as their little bodies were consumed.

In a uniform gesture, all those melting faces then turned toward *me* high above them on the mountaintop. They were beseeching me to do—what? I didn't know! I could smell the horrible stench of burning flesh and hair. The screams, the screams! The near-dead on the flaming bier sang out words that seared into my brain the way the fires seared into their flesh.

I made a double sign of the cross, turned my back to the mountain, and fell backward into a giant abyss.

I sat straight up in bed—yet again—gasping for breath, covered in sweat, my heart pounding.

There was a horrible stench—and it was real—burning up my nostrils.

*Baghdad. God—no. It's burning flesh!*

I jumped out of bed, ran to the window, and threw open the wooden shutters. All seemed peaceful outside, but the smell was so overwhelming that I started to gag.

*We're on fire! I have to wake everyone up!*

I ripped the door open to warn the family in the house—and there *he* was, right outside my door. Calm as can be—Pantera, I mean—sitting on a chair that was propped up against the wall, still sporting that shit-eating smirk.

"You! Why are you sitting here? There's a fire!"

Without moving so much as a muscle, Pantera said, "No. That would be the smoke from the Prat des Cramats you smell."

"The Valley of the Burned?"

"Precisely."

"It's on fire again?"

"No."

"But—"

"But does your mother know you open the door to strange men in your underwear?"

I looked down and could feel my face getting red. No, it wasn't because I had ripped the door open in my panties, but because I had ripped the door open in giant white gramma drugstore panties.

His smirk almost widened into a smile. For the first time I noticed he had a gap in his front teeth.

*Shit. This isn't good.*

## 31

*Screw him. . . . I'm not going to try to cover up. Tough it out.*

He looked me up and down. "Don't worry, I have no desire to overwhelm you and make you mine."

"You should do stand-up. Ha. Ha. Ha. And frankly, I'd rather eat a pound of escargot. Two pounds."

I slammed the door, bolted it, and tried to go back to sleep, but the horrid, rancid-smoke smell kept me from falling into a deep sleep. Loath as I was to admit it, however, knowing that Pantera was outside my door, and clearly without malicious intent, did make me less anxious.

A rooster crowed at daybreak, then the church bells began pealing right outside the window, it seemed, and so I rolled around and finally got up.

*What are they all rushing to get up to do? There's nothing to do here.*

I took a brisk shower with the handheld faucet in the tub, wiped off with that same one towel, and got dressed.

Again, the choice was jeans, a T-shirt, the same jacket,

and boots. I ran my fingers through my tragic 'do and put on the red lipstick.

*Why did you do that?*

I opened the door. No Pantera.

*Huh?*

There were two ways downstairs, I discovered. One was via the outside staircase, and the other through a tiny door, which opened to an even tinier spiral staircase that was barely wide enough for my frame. It opened into the kitchen, where Pantera, I was astonished to see, was yucking it up with the family and taking the fresh croissants out of the ancient oven for the landlady, who was clearly smitten.

"Bonjour, Madame Roussel," Pantera said.

"Yes, good morning. I see you are up early."

"Early? Not really, it's five forty-five."

I had several cups of café au lait and one croissant (I was sort of embarrassed to eat like I had four stomachs in front of all these people), while Pantera took his sweet time about finishing off two cups of espresso and one croissant.

Finally, he said, "You should see this," and he handed me yesterday's edition of the *International Herald Tribune.*

Front-page story: by Dona Grimm; photos by Donald Zaluckyj.

Accompanying the story were photos of Donald and me at our makeshift Baghdad wedding. There were also photos of an older man identified as Dr. Mikaeel Hussein.

Tears sprung into my eyes.

"What?"

Pantera said nothing.

"Sorry if we were both of legal age and there are actual photos of our nuptials."

He pointed to the story. "You need to read this."

The article described a bomb scare outside the UN tribunal the day before and the details of the day's proceedings, which had begun hours late due to the scare.

The package turned out to be nothing other than a medical bag with a priest's stole and six empty transfusion bags marked "NYU Hospital: #4th, 6th."

There was also the testimony of Dr. Mikaeel Hussein, the astrophysicist who recanted the testimony I'd read in that old newspaper article wherein he first said it was a star, then a comet they discovered in 1982. Now he was saying that the heavenly body was in fact a star.

The article stated:

> Dr. Hussein, under examination by ben Yusef's counsel (and without the cooperation of the defendant) admitted that he had lied in 1982 about the sighting of a comet.
>
> Dr. Hussein had testified back then that the heavenly body in the skies over Turkey had been in fact a comet, after first claiming it had been a star. He testified, "Under intense pressure in 1982, I lied to the scientific community, and to the world.
>
> "My colleagues went along with me in the ruse," he said. "It was in fact the emergence of a new star, which disappeared as quickly as it had arisen over a small area of Ephesus, in Turkey."
>
> On redirect, lead attorney for the prosecution Lawrence Finegold pounded the timid scientist, demanding to know why he'd lied back in 1982. "If you had told the truth, and had actually discovered a star, wouldn't you have, A: recognized it as such, being an astrophysicist? . . ." His voice was dripping with sarcasm, causing the courtroom to break out in stifled laughter, as Chief

*Justice Fatoumata Bagayoko slammed down her gavel.*

*". . . and, B: hailed your discovery to the world? Instead, you expect this court to believe that you, an eminent astrophysicist, along with your colleagues Dr. Gaspar Bar-Cohen, of the University of Tel Aviv, and Dr. Balaaditya Pawar, now of U.C. Berkeley, went along with this lie of yours? Or was it—what did you call it?—ah, yes, a 'mistake'?"*

*"But it is the truth that now I speak."*

*"And who forced you to compromise your principles back in 1982, may I ask?"*

*To the astonishment of the court, Hussein stood up and pointed toward the front "distinguished spectators" row. "That man, the Reverend Bill Teddy Smythe," he said, his accent making it at first hard for anyone to understand.*

*When the reality sank in, Finegold spun around, approached Hussein, and said, "You say that this man of God asked you to lie? And, even if we were to believe you—an admitted liar—that you, a Muslim, along with your colleagues, an Orthodox Jew and a Buddhist, capitulated to the wishes of a Baptist minister?"*

*Since Finegold asked the question in a rhetorical manner, he was visibly shaken by the answer, which also shocked the courtroom, and by now the world.*

*"The minister told us that he came at the behest of the White House."*

*"What did you say?" Finegold said, stunned.*

*"I took that to mean the president of the United States as well as the prime ministers of many countries, perhaps as many as sixty. He said that*

*revealing this would have caused a worldwide panic, because the star signaled the birth of the 'soulless one,' a baby born in the House of the Blessed Mother in Turkey. A black mass ritual.*

"I told him we saw the boy, or as he called it, the 'creature' and the 'soulless one.' And that he was a beautiful little brown baby boy. The minister threatened our families and ourselves.

"He said they would not live to see the week out.

"So, yes, we lied to protect our families, and we lied because it was all the power in the world against three scientists who just wanted to be left to ponder together what we had seen and what we had experienced."

"And you believed these so-called threats?"

"Not until my colleague Dr. Gaspar Bar-Cohen's only daughter was found dead. 'Crib death,' they said."

"And you honestly believed that the most powerful people in the United States had a newborn baby killed?" He turned to the judges, who remained impassive.

Hussein continued: "So, yes, we lied, and we have lived to regret it, but we were frightened. I, for one, cannot allow it to continue. If you kill this man, the world will end!"

With that he nodded toward ben Yusef and began weeping, just as Reverend Bill Teddy Smythe rose up from his wheelchair, jabbing his finger toward the witness chair.

"You lie! You lied then and you lie now! God will smite you down. . . ." He began to shake his finger and move toward the witness.

The courtroom went wild, and at one point the

*minister had to be restrained by security. The spec-*
*tators and journalists, unable to remain silent,*
*broke out in shouts and murmurs. People rose*
*from their seats.*

*The chief justice slammed down her gavel as*
*security began hustling the world officials out.*
*Within minutes of the near melee, proceedings*
*were called to a halt for the day.*

I was flabbergasted.

Pantera stood up, helped bus the table, and then walked back into the dining room. "Hussein was, of course, scared in eighty-two, yes. But he lied not just because of the tragedy that befell Bar-Cohen. Regardless, this discovery would have won them the Nobel. He lied for us as well."

"But he said it was the coalition of world leaders who'd sent Smythe."

"He did. And they did. But it was us too—we also *asked* the three men to deny the whole thing. I asked them as a personal favor—once they were inside the house and had bypassed the greatest security in the world.

"It would have served no one's purpose for the truth to come out then. We wanted them to think the baby was dead and didn't want people looking for a risen Christ Child, obviously. We would have had every nut hunting us down.

"Hussein, Bar-Cohen, and Pawar have all, incidentally, come aboard since then. They are silent soldiers in the revolution of souls."

*He and the other men were the ones I "saw" in the house in Turkey.* Now *I'm beginning to figure out.*

"The 'revolution of souls,' right. I won't even begin to ask what the hell that means, but I will ask you this:

What did those objects and those numbers on the transfusion bags mean?"

"Blood, a priest's stole, fourth and sixth?"

Then it hit me: "Sadowski, the blood of Jesus, I get it. But Demiel had said to me 'six,' not 'four.'"

I hit my forehead with my hand so hard, it left a red mark. "Damn! Go forth—maybe it means 'fourth,' as in an ordinal number."

Even he looked impressed. "Now you have one more number to figure out."

"Aha. Damn! But who did it? Who left the transfusion bags?"

"Could be them. Could be us."

"I'm not part of *us* . . ."

"Yes. You are."

Then Pantera, his lanky frame towering over me, called a halt to the chitchat. "Ready?"

"For what?"

"A little hiking."

He checked out my boots. "Not good for trekking, but they'll do in a pinch. Now, let's get going."

"Where are we going?" I said, pulling on my jacket as we walked out the kitchen door, while he put on a backpack, into which he'd put several bottles of water.

"Up there," he said, pointing to Montségur, which was poking through the dense morning clouds.

"You're kidding me," I said, getting my first real good look at the mountain. I followed him into the welding shed, where the landlady's son was already hard at work, sparks flying everywhere. Amidst giant modern metal sculptures of Cathar crosses and robed figures were an assortment of hand-forged hammers, carabiners, and what looked like hiking and climbing equipment.

"*Tout est prêt pour vous,* Yusef," the man said.

"*Merci,* Pierre."

"*Petite hache, carabiners, corde . . .*"

"*Parfait, merci.*"

"*Bonne journée.*"

The two shook hands, and Pantera took from him a rope, which he hung on his shoulder, a small ax, some webbing harnesses, and two carabiners, which he hung on a belt. He was wearing a flak jacket, jeans, and sunglasses. And what looked like two pistols this time. He handed me a walking stick.

"Do I look older than you?"

"Take it. I'm taking one, too, don't worry."

As we walked back out and toward the trail at the foot of the mountain, I said, "This is a paved walk. Why all the drama with the rope, and all?"

"I'm a drama queen, all right?"

"Ha! I knew it. By the way, do you plan on killing any tourists today?" I snarked, looking directly at the bulges under his jacket.

"Only if they ask directions." He was lightening up. Oh, those crazy assassins!

We hiked for about twenty uphill minutes when we came to, of all things, a freaking parking lot at the base of the peak about a quarter of the way up.

"You're not serious! We could have driven up here?" I was already panting.

He wasn't.

"Have some water," he said, taking it out of his knapsack, handing it to me, and walking a few paces to a small stone monolith with a round circle on top that was shaped like a wheel with spokes carved into it. Under that was carved the Cathar cross and the words STELE D RESSEE PAR LA SOCITE DU SOUVIRIN ET D E STADES CATHARES PRINTEMPS 1960. IN THIS PLACE ON 16TH MARCH 1244 MORE THAN 200 PEOPLE WERE BURNED. THEY CHOSE NOT TO ABJURE THEIR FAITH.

He bowed his head, made the double sign of the cross, stood in contemplation a moment, turned, and said, "Are you ready, Ms. Roussel?"

"I told you not to call me that. And, yes, I'm ready."

*You may die trying to climb this thing. It's straight up!*

We began the trek for real this time. The "path" appeared to have been carved simply from the footsteps of the hearty pilgrims who had managed to climb this thing.

*Thank you, Jesus, for the walking stick!*

As we began climbing the mountain—it is the equivalent of climbing a more than three-hundred-story building—I quickly realized that if this was their idea of a French tourist attraction, it was no wonder there were no tourists.

It's a straight climb up a slippery slope of a so-called footpath worn into the rocky soil that was a foot wide at some points, and so muddy in most spots it was like maneuvering on ice. The tiny path had no side rails whatsoever to prevent hikers from falling straight down.

*And I was worried about that cliff in Rhinecliff?*

If one side of the "pathway" was a straight drop down, the other side offered no solace. It was just rock face (think a rock wall in a gym) but covered with sharp, thorny bushes. I could see that the higher we would climb the steeper the fall to *my* untimely death would be. There wasn't anyplace to go but straight down thousands of feet.

*If he pushes me off the edge, no one will ever be able to recover my body: There's no way to even get down there.*

He was hiking ahead of me and clearing what nettles were impenetrable. I was breathing hard and wanted to stop. The mountain air was getting thinner, and I was

more out of shape than I had ever dared to admit—
before this.

He kept climbing.

*What's with this guy? Jeez. He's killing me here. "In a
pinch" was right: Even my trusty old boots are starting
to cut notches into my ankles.*

As I was wheezing and climbing and leaning on that
walking stick like Old Mother Hubbard, my right foot
gave out and I began sliding backward on the tiny dirt
path. Within seconds I was on my face, my legs out from
under me. My body was twisted, and my legs ended up
hanging over the cliff.

I managed to grab onto a branch to keep from going
straight down. Only my torso and arms were touching
terra almost firma.

"Ayyyyy . . ."

Pantera turned then and stood there looking at me.
*Oh, fuck. He's going to push me.*

He put down his walking stick and walked back to
where I was half on, half off the cliff ledge.

"I can't take you anywhere. All right, now just move
your legs back away from the edge . . . slowly now,
slowly."

"I can't. I'm terrified. Grab onto me."

"No. If I do that, the ground could give way and for
sure you'll join the Cathars down there in the *Prat des
Cramats.*"

"I can't. I'm terrified."

"Son of the Son! Just do what I'm telling you."

"Okay, okay, ayyy . . ." I slowly turned my trunk
and maneuvered my legs away from the edge until I
was lying flat on the narrow path that was at that point
a forty-five-degree slope and not quite as wide as my
body.

I lifted my head and my torso up on my elbows and

looked up at him from this prone position imploringly. "Now what?"

"Now say 'Ommmm,'" he chanted.

"Very funny, you frigging . . . *desperado*!"

"Oh, for God's sake! Just get up on your knees and then stand up."

"What if I fall?"

"I will miss you deeply."

"So you won't help me?"

"There's no room for two of us on this slope, so just do what I said so we can get on with it."

Reaching out for a branch again, I held on and got up on my knees and then onto my feet. My jeans were ripped at the knee and I was bleeding. Palms too.

"Come on," he said, and walked a few hundred feet ahead, and I followed him. At this point, I was ready to turn back, but we were too high up for me to attempt a descent alone. He stopped at a large boulder and sat down, patting the side of the rock for me to sit beside him. I sat down, refusing to wince at my bleeding hands and knees.

He knelt in front of me, took his backpack off, and took out a tiny first aid kit. He opened the rips in my jeans and washed my knees off with water, swabbed them with a packet of disinfectant then with an iodine swab, and sealed each with big knee-sized Band-Aids.

"Always be prepared—right?" I said.

He didn't answer and took my palms in his hands and looked at them. He cleaned them with a new towelette and swabbed them with iodine—and, yes, it hurt like hell.

"What? No more Band-Aids?" I said, refusing to let him see me wince even once.

"They won't stay on since you're climbing. But this might help."

He took both of my hands in his, turned them over palm side up, and looked at them. Then he brought them to his mouth and kissed the left palm and then the right.

I nearly fell off the mountain again. No one had done that to me since my mom used to kiss my scrapes and scratches with her magic kisses.

"Let's go. Come on. Get up."

*Is this the guy who just made that tender—not to mention sexy—gesture? Manipulative horse's ass!*

I got up and we resumed climbing. After another half hour of straight up, we came to the thinnest part of the trail—just below the remains of the castle walls that I'd seen so clearly in the cell phone's camera the day before.

When we got to steadier ground, I pulled Sadowski's phone out of my inner jacket pocket, turned it on, and snapped a picture of the sunlight streaming through the turrets. At the sound of the camera's click, Pantera turned on his heels in front of me like a madman and grabbed it out of my hands angrily.

He turned it off. "Listen, monsieur, even I know that there's no signal up here. I tried it from the rooming house."

"Down there, no. Up here, yes."

He put the phone in his own backpack, and we proceeded up to the top and over the wall into the courtyard of what was once a great castle.

"This is where the Cathars lived?"

"Well, yes, but not in this castle. The village was destroyed. This was built afterward.[14] They lived on the pog here," he said, pointing out what looked to me like a crazy-steep, uninhabitable mountainside.

"Then why did you bring me up here?"

"To experience the walk our forebears took every day

that they lived in peace, and that same path, which they then took down to their deaths in the fire in the valley below."

"Our forebears? Are we related?" I joked. "Not for nuthin', but yours might have been French, but mine were Italian."

"Yes, they were. Well, beginning in May or June of 1244 they sure became Italian, at any rate."

"You're saying . . ." I remembered reading in the book last night about how the smuggled treasure had been allegedly brought to Italy.

*Stop with the "alleged." You sound like a police reporter—even to yourself.*

His answer was a crooked grin, and he said, "I want to trigger some memory for you. It's vital . . ."

"What the *hell* are you taking about? I promise you, I'd remember if I'd ever climbed this thing . . ."

Then I looked down over the ruined castle wall, as he pointed out the gorgeous valley four thousand feet down, already in bloom this early spring day, and at once a crazy sense of déjà vu followed immediately by the stench of burning human flesh hit me again.

"The stench is unbearable," I choked out, my eyes beginning to burn.

He smiled and simply said, "That, Alazais," pointing down to the valley, "is called a memory." He looked down. "That is where they were burned alive."

"But what is the smell now?"

"Legend has it that a chosen few can smell the fire even to this day. Guess that must mean you."

"No."

"Okay, fine. Let me show you something else. . . ."

"No more slippery slopes. Promise?"

"No," he said, and immediately walked me around to the most slippery slope of the unforgiving northeastern side of the pog, and I looked down. Straight down. It was indeed impenetrable. "Is this where—"

I heard a crack and at the same instant felt something whiz by my head so close that it literally spun me around. Pantera grabbed me, and we ran back around that steep outer edge and jumped into the courtyard of the castle remains maybe six feet below.

We squeezed into a five-by-three-foot opening cut out of the stone wall, which was hollow all the way around—a double-walled edifice with both an inner and an outer wall. The "doorways" opened into a passageway that went completely around the perimeter. *Must have been for defense,* I thought. We could hide inside, although we wouldn't be able to get out if they found us.

Following Pantera's lead, we crept around and positioned ourselves behind a slit cut into the outer wall. "For arrows," he whispered.

It was clear that that's how the inhabitants would have fought off invaders during the Middle Ages.

Pantera handed me a pistol. "Know how to use one of these things?"

"Maybe."

"Just point and shoot."

Three men armed with machine guns came stalking around the outer perimeter, heads low. Pantera stuck his Glock through the arrow slit and fired. Once. I heard the sound of impact and the sound of someone going down.

The two others, I could see from my tiny vantage point, flattened themselves against the outer wall and fired into the turrets near us, clearly not able to fire inside the tiny arrow slits.

One moved out and was heading toward the courtyard. Pantera maneuvered out of the wall and threw a rock up to the turret and then slid back in.

He handed me a cylinder. "Flash grenade. If it comes to that, go to the doorway, pull this, and throw."

The man who had remained on the outer wall came into view and fired into the turret above us, as Pantera picked him off.

The third must still have been moving around toward the courtyard and the southern slope. Pantera held me back.

"Use it if you need to," he said, referring to the grenade. "It will cause temporary blindness and deafness in the enemy and give you time to get away."

He then slipped out of the walls through the opening. When he reached the courtyard, I could hear him heft himself up to the courtyard wall with his arms. Then silence.

I took up his former position behind the arrow slit. The armed man started back; I could see his shadow. He looked up and pointed his gun. Did he see Pantera? I didn't wait to find out. I put my pistol into the arrow slit and squeezed the trigger. I saw him go down. But he wasn't dead. He was writhing and bleeding from his chest. I could hear him moaning like a wounded dog. He rolled over, got a bead on where the shot had come from, and aimed into the arrow slit.

The shots hit the rock wall millimeters from the slit. From on top, automatic fire blasted the stone wall, and then nothing.

Was he up? I couldn't look out, or he'd shoot me. I picked up the grenade and slowly crept back to the opening. If he made it into the courtyard somehow, I'd hurl it and then shoot.

*Oh, God.*

As I was feeling my way against the stone wall, a shot rang out from above. I heard a scream of agony, then silence. Someone had died.

*Is it Pantera? Is it the shooter? What do I do?*

Just then, Pantera called out as calmly as if he were calling Kmart shoppers to attention: "There were three. All dead."

"You sure they're dead? How do you know?"

He moaned back, "Do I tell you how to type?"

"Asshole!"

I could hear him walking and heard him jump back down into the courtyard. He called to me to come back out. Right. Nothing would make me willingly move out from the safety of the inner wall, and, in fact, I scrambled farther in and crouched.

"It's me, for God's sake. I told you they're dead. I'm coming in—it's fine," Pantera said. "We've got to go."

I made my way to the opening, gun pointed, and saw Pantera entering. "Who was that? Why did they shoot at us? It was my fault for turning on the phone!"

"Not unless they could climb a mountain in a single bound—they were here—although the signal probably gave them our exact location."

"I'm so sorry. But I may have killed someone."

"Don't get crazy."

"Who were they?"

"Sent by the same people who also convinced Hussein, Bar-Cohen, and Pawar to lie in 1982."

"What does that mean?"

"Like the wise man said, 'All the powers in the world.'"

It hit me then: Three astronomers showed up at the house when they saw a star and found an unwed mother and her baby. And that birth would threaten all the powers in the world. History repeating? This was too much.

"The rest of them—and probably the French authorities—will be up here soon," he said, taking binoculars from his backpack and surveying the area below. "Let's move. They're already here."

"What do you see?"

I grabbed the binoculars from him and could see dozens of police cars arriving at the bottom of the mountain.

"It will still take them forty-five minutes to get up here. But the choppers will be surveilling. They'll drop troopers."

I could hear them already approaching in the distance.

"What do we do? We're trapped. They'll get us on the way down!"

At that, Yusef unhooked the webbing harnesses and instructed me to put one on and lock it, which I did. He did the same. He went back inside the wall and came back out rolling a wooden wheel of rope.

"We've been preparing for this. . . ."

"Thanks for inviting me along. We killed three people."

"Will you cut it out? Next time you should let them kill you. Or I will."

He motioned for me to move, and I helped him maneuver the wheel up and over the courtyard wall and heft it back out onto the outer rim.

We pushed the wheel to the impenetrable, sheer cliff side, and he unraveled it—hundreds of feet of rope—and then cut it in half, looped each around a turret, secured them with knots, and attached them to our rappel devices on the harnesses. He anchored various other things, while I stood in shock, looking straight down into a four-thousand-foot drop.

He tested both the ropes and the devices, unclipped the daisy chain from the anchors, and said, "Get in position."

"What position? I can't!"

He took me by the shoulders, pushed me to the edge, and turned me around so I was facing the castle and standing with my back to the drop.

"Now, place your left hand around the rope. . . . Okay, good; move it down six inches above the rappel device. Move your left hand between the clip and the anchors."

I did as I was told, shaking every step of the way.

"Okay, good. Now grab the rope that hangs down out of the rappel device with your right hand—that's your break hand—and slide your hand on the rope back to your right hip and wrap the rope slightly around your right hip."

I was getting better at taking orders, and was doing fine following the next few directions—until he said, "Now step back off the edge."

"What? No!"

He locked himself in next to me on the next turret and came alongside of me. "Step off!"

I didn't budge. "Goddammit—step off, Alazais! You've done it before."

"I haven't done it ever before, so fuck you!"

*Yes, you have. Just not in this life. The dream . . . the dream.*

I rechecked the harness and then took the biggest step of my life. I turned my back to the mountain and fell backward—and put my future once again into the hands of the assassin.

Holding on for dear life and letting myself down slowly, I began to rappel downward. Or creep downward, is more like it.

"Let some of the rope in your right hand slide up through the rappel device," he ordered as he hung next to me. As I did this I felt myself sliding more easily down the rope.

When we got partway down, and we ran out of rope, he swung into me, grabbed me around the waist, and together we swung over to an overhang and stepped onto it, grabbing onto branches.

"Now what?" I said, shaking.

"Now we unhook ourselves and make our way down. We've gone through the worst of it."

He tied one end of a piece of the rope he'd taken from the welding shed to me and the other end to himself, and we began creeping, crawling on ledges that were no more than six inches wide at some points, until we finally got to level ground some one thousand feet up. The choppers were above us, but even I knew nobody in them would be looking on this side, and even if they were, they wouldn't see us in all the tangles of brambles and the jutting rocks.

"Toss your gun."

"No."

"Yes, leave the gun."

"And take the cannoli?"

With that he grabbed my gun and tossed it along with his into the brambles.

"Why did you *do* that?"

No answer.

It took an hour more of descending on hands and knees before we could see the valley clearly. In another half hour, we touched ground. Happy to be alive but in pain from the gashes on my knees, which had opened wide, I still kissed the ground.

He untied us and said, "Now let's go see what's going on."

"What?"

He took the water and disinfectant towelettes out of his backpack, redressed my knees and hands, cleaned my face and his, dusted us off, reached into his bag, and pulled out a terrible hat, which he pulled over my terrible hair, saying, "A bonnie boonie."

*Loony is more like it.*

He grabbed my hand and began walking me, or more accurately pulling me, around the perimeter. I could see dozens of flashing cherry lights atop cop cars, ambulances, armored vehicles, and even a tank assembled in the Valley of the Burned, where they'd set up a command center, as the cops prepared for all-out battle. With *us*.

Instead of sneaking back around the backside of the mountain, Pantera tightened his hand around mine in that death grip and, almost at a run, began dragging me toward them in the valley.

*Like the Cathars walking into the flames!*

"We're heading right back to the—" I tried saying, but he wasn't listening. I attempted to break free of his grasp, but it was useless. At a run now, dragging me with him, he began waving to the cops. In less than ten seconds I'd be in their hands—the hands of the authorities I'd been ducking for days, who were out for blood.

"You lying traitor," I screeched, as he rushed us into the fray, still holding my hand.

## 32

"*Ta gueule!* Seriously. Trust me." He actually said this as he was dragging me against my will into the hands of the authorities.

*Trust no one.*

He loosened his grip on my hand and then squeezed it—as opposed to crushing it—and put his other arm around my shoulder, draping it like a boyfriend would, as he forcibly "strolled" me quickly to the first cop we came up to.

Like a big buffoon, he said way too loud in the cop's face—or this is what I thought he said, but my French is worse than, well, anything:

"*Qu'est qui se passe? Pouvez-vous nous prendre en photo moi et ma femme? C'est comme dans un film!*"

The cop was having none of whatever it was, and threatened (or it sounded like a threat anyway): "*Mais c'est ridicule! Reculez! N'approchez pas. C'est une scène de crime, vous devez quitter immédiatement les lieux sinon nous allons ce faire arreter.*"

"*Juste une photo, s'il vous plait. Nous avons traversé tout le village dès que nous avons entendu les sirènes.*"

*"Sortez ces civils d'ici immédiatement."*

At that, two cops came over and forcibly escorted us out of the Valley of the Burned and then out of the area entirely.

*If you ever trust anyone, maybe this should be the guy.*

As we headed back down the paved part of the mountain road to the bottom, I turned to him.

"Damn! You are good."

"You have no idea."

"No, seriously. Really good."

"And seriously, I know that. Let's move," he urged, pushing me beyond my physical capacities right then. Or so I thought. I didn't realize I hadn't even been tested yet.

We hurried back to the boarding house at a jogging pace. I packed up my nearly nonexistent belongings, changed into my only other pair of jeans, and met him back downstairs.

"We'll take two cars. I don't want you to follow me, but I highlighted the route for you in yellow. We're going to Carcassonne. It's a fairly straight route, so don't get lost. We can't communicate by cell. Strictly off the grid, old-school.

"When you get to the city, there is parking at the foot of the village outside the walls."

"Walls?"

"It's a walled city. But tell them you are staying at Hôtel de la Cité, and you will be directed to a private area immediately outside the wall and they'll send a car or van to get you. I'll meet you there."

"What name should I use to check in, and should I use Sadowski's ATM card?"

"It's all taken care of. Just tell them you are Madame Roussel and that you would like your room key."

With that he got in his red Citroën and slowly pulled out of sight. I assumed by now everyone in the village of roughly one hundred citizens knew everything we'd done, hadn't done, and were about to do. Or maybe the French weren't like small-town folk everywhere else on the planet.

There wasn't a soul in sight, and I assumed that whoever was there had by now gone up to the mountain to see what all the excitement was about.

At the end of the village there was, as I should have expected, a police-manned roadblock. I showed my false passport, and they checked the car thoroughly. I told them in English, and then tried in Italian, that I had come to see the mountain, and then I made a big deal about trying to find out why all those cop cars and ambulances were there. Maybe it was the old-lady rocker hair that did it, but they just got annoyed and let me pass.

*If there ever was anyone who didn't look like a threat to anyone but herself, it's you right now!*

It is about fifty-seven kilometers (just over thirty-five miles) between the towns of Montségur and Carcassonne, but they may as well be on different planets. One is the kind of ancient rural village you can only find in France, and the other is the kind of ancient walled city you can only find in France. One has no commerce, while inside the other behind those ancient walls are high-end designer boutiques, hotels, and Michelin-starred restaurants doing business in stone buildings that were built in the twelfth and thirteenth centuries in a city that was founded by the Romans in the first century.

As I approached, the site nearly left me breathless. Rising above the walls was a city that looked like something out of a medieval tale, with an intact castle, dozens of turrets, drawbridges and, yes, miles of walls rising above the landscape.

After following about six thousand signs pointing this way and that and ending up back where I started, I realized that all signs for CITÉ meant the city itself and not the hotel.

After several misses, I finally figured out how to get to the hotel parking "lot," which was sort of a grassy knoll (I always wanted to use those words in a sentence that didn't relate to the assassination of JFK), and parked the car as Pantera had directed at the foot of the wall.

An attendant came by and asked the name of my hotel and then called it into a walkie-talkie thing. Within minutes, a car came by to pick me up. There were no cars inside the walls except for the one or two delivering guests to hotels. Visitors and residents of the city all parked outside the walls in designated areas and walked in through the ancient drawbridge entrance.

The Hôtel de la Cité looked like a palace with giant arched, leaded-glass windows on a cobblestone street.

There were hundreds of shops, restaurants, bars, several cathedrals, and a basilica, and, yes, a fortified castle within the city walls. Think real-life Disney World minus the annoying furry characters.

The interior did not disappoint. Disappoint? It was overwhelming. I walked into a lovely lobby with a cozy library bar and fancy restaurant on the lobby level.

I approached the front desk, gave the name Alazais Roussel, and suddenly the staff was all over me like a bad smell—but in a good way for once.

Astonished to see I just had that one measly carry-on bag, the bellman nonetheless made a big deal of carrying it to my room and attempting unsuccessfully to wrest from me my red satchel with my iPad, Sadowski's phone, and, oh, yeah, that same Gap scarf.

Did I say "room"? Think suite.

*Thank God this isn't on my tab.*

It was huge, with a beamed ceiling and a giant king-size bed (probably had belonged to an actual king) covered in luxurious fabrics, with a carved mahogany headboard that reached to the ceiling. The floor was tiled, and the white marble fireplace had already been lit. Beyond that, a desk and several comfy velvet easy chairs in gray with a matching loveseat were set around a leather steamer trunk. It had high-speed everything, from Internet to an even-higher-speed Jacuzzi tub roughly the size of an Olympic pool.

The bellman (Pierre, of course) opened the curtains to reveal a huge terrace complete with red padded lounges and a table and chairs.

*A little bit of heaven in the middle of my hellish life.*

I tipped Pierre, who seemed reluctant to leave, and I had to say about fourteen hundred *mercis* before he got the hint.

*What now? Wait and see what Pantera's got up his sleeve? Right. Like hell I will.*

I took out the tablet, sat down on the bed, and checked Sadowski's voice mail, despite Donald's plea to stay "off the grid." Message from Dona: "This crazy thing happened. Randy Mohammed pulled me aside as we were leaving court. . . ."

*If she's already calling him "Randy," God knows what she got out of him. The woman is irresistible to men.*

"He said, 'Tell Ms. Russo that Mr. ben Yusef says to "Go forth and trust the man who raised him."'"

That was it.

I checked the e-mail. Nothing. I sent one off to Donald. "Image of Yusef Pantera anywhere over the last, say, forty years in any archives anywhere?"

I logged off and turned the TV on to CNN International. The anchor, Seema Ving, said, "Coming up, our lead story. They are calling it the miracle of Demiel ben Yusef. But is it a hoax?"

As they broke for commercial, they ran footage of riots around the world, all in the name of ben Yusef. The final image was of Dag Hammarskjöld Plaza. My old neighborhood looked like a war zone. So much for peaceful and orderly.

After a bunch of ads for investment companies and medicines that seemed to make you ride a bike in slow motion while waving backward, Ving was back with the lead story. And I nearly fell off the bed.

"After court closed for the day," she reported, "an event occurred that many are calling a miracle. It involves the children who had been brought into court on the first day of the ben Yusef trial."

Filmed footage of the children as they'd been wheeled into court that first day splashed across the screen. Even though I'd seen it in person, I needed to turn my head away for a moment—it was that horrific and heartbreaking, even on video. There was the little angel without a mouth and hard plastic skin where once a beautiful little girl had been; and the little boy with the beautiful face whose eyes were rolling in his head as he lolled in a wheelchair, clearly brain-damaged; the blind kids being led by mothers; the miniature motorized wheelchair with the five-year-old girl strapped in to keep her upright.

"These children," Ving continued, "had been introduced on day one of the Demiel ben Yusef tribunal by the prosecution and identified as victims of the terror bombing of the Ingreja Matriz Church in Manaus, Brazil. The unforgettable sight of the children, whose injuries included third-degree burns, blindness, spinal-cord injuries, and massive brain damage, are, of course, now etched into the human consciousness around the world.

"But that all apparently changed yesterday after they were touched, so to speak, by Demiel ben Yusef. It began right after the courtroom disruption broke out, which caused Justice Bagayoko to unexpectedly call a halt to the day's proceedings. The children had been sitting outside the courtroom in anticipation of being called as witnesses. UN security had not had a chance to move them to a different location before they hustled the defendant, Demiel ben Yusef, out of the courtroom. As they moved him out, he passed directly in front of the children.

"We are told that despite being shackled hand and foot, the accused terrorist was able to stop short and shout a brief prayer in a language not understood—and not recorded, since reporters are forbidden in that area of the United Nations. Sources also told CNN that, inexplicably, security cameras were also not working.

"However, later in the afternoon, at approximately five P.M. Eastern Standard Time, as the children were sitting in the United Nations dining hall for their evening meal, unnamed eyewitnesses say that first a blind boy, name and age unknown at this point, jumped up from his seat, claiming that he could see.

"Then the quadriplegic girl in the motorized wheelchair started to wiggle her arms and legs, then the brain-damaged children, who no longer had speech, began calling for their mothers, as each child in turn seemingly was made whole again.

"One eyewitness told CNN off the record that even the horribly burned child was restored to a perfect, unblemished state.

"At seven P.M. Chief Judge Fatoumata Bagayoko came out to address reporters regarding the incident."

Footage of Bagayoko standing somewhere inside the United Nations, in a red wool suit and matching pillbox hat perched jauntily atop her braids, appeared on the screen as she addressed the reporters, who looked, if possible, even more rabid than they had on the first day. The judge was literally grinning from ear to ear.

"It is my great, great, *great* pleasure to confirm to you this day that I have indeed seen all of the smallest victims of the Ingreja Matriz Church bombings—yes, those very children who appeared before the court on the opening day of the trial.

"We all saw those children and the horrific damage inflicted upon each and every one. Well, I just saw those same children, and I am here, as God is my witness . . ."— she was openly fighting back tears now—"to tell you that the blind can see, the brain-damaged are now speaking at age-appropriate levels, the quadriplegic child, Laudenize Vasconcelos, is not just out of her wheelchair but joyously skipping about the room! And, yes, the burn victims are restored to perfection."

The reporters started screaming for footage, but the chief judge responded by saying that until United Nations security, along with the officials from Brazil, had made a determination of the facts, and also to protect the privacy of the children, no footage or photos would be released.

Then, in true media-hound fashion, Bagayoko said, "And now it is my supreme privilege to go back and visit with *my* children!" With that, she waved and was rushed back inside by her adoring minions.

Ving came back on-screen and reported, "While we have no official video or photographs, this grainy image *was* leaked onto YouTube earlier today, the authenticity of which, I must remind you, has not been verified."

The video showed a bunch of little children, wheelchairs in the background, running, laughing, jumping, yelling, and playing happily with each other.

"Calling the so-called miracle of Demiel ben Yusef a ruse, however, is the Reverend Bill Teddy Smythe of the worldwide Light of God Tabernacles."

The video feed showed Bill Teddy in a wheelchair giving a press conference outside the UN. Raising his fist to the heavens, white hair nearly lighting up the air around him, Bill Teddy attempted to rise up, but plopped back down.

*He must have forgotten how easily he rose up on opening day!*

"What is being perpetrated upon the unsuspecting world is a lie, a scam, and a sham regarding the so-called *miracle,*" he declared, his grimace truly frightening. "These children can no more rise from their wheelchairs than I can."

*What?*

"And if they could, it wouldn't be because of the miraculous healing powers of a filthy radical desert rat who is the spawn of the devil himself! Such a thing can only be performed by Jesus Christ Almighty—and this, this, this filthy *terrorist scum* is evil incarnate!

"Demiel ben Yusef must be destroyed before he casts the devil down upon all of humanity," he declared in a voice so booming, you'd never suspect, if you weren't seeing it for yourself, that it was coming out of the mouth of a wheelchair-bound octogenarian.

Ving came back on with a panel of windbags who were listed as "experts," including clerics, professors of divinity, and ACLU types. I turned it off and opened the bottle of French Bordeaux that was sitting in the large fruit-and-cheese basket in the room. I needed a big, *big* glass of wine.

It was then that I noticed the note on the basket: "*8:00 this evening in the bar downstairs. Y.*"

I had just taken my first giant gulp when there was a knock on the door. I peeked through the peephole and saw it was that same bellman. He was carrying what looked like gift boxes.

I opened the door, and he said in perfectly accented English, "Madame, you have an admirer!" as he brought in four boxes with a small bouquet of exquisite lilies of the valley tied up in ribbons and enclosed in clear cellophane wrapping.

When he left I opened the first box. In it was a classic little black dress that looked like it might actually fit my American body. I didn't need to look at the label to know it was vintage Chanel. The next box contained a pair of Prada spikes (in a size 37) and a Gucci evening bag.

The last box contained a red cashmere sweater, which was just about the right thing to go over these insanely expensive clothes. Tucked into the bottom of that box was a small gift bag containing a tiny, exquisite—did I mention tiny?—black lace La Perla thong.

*Pantera. Pantera? He bought me this stuff? Does he think he's going to get lucky because he shot our way out of Montségur? No. Sorry, buddy. I prefer my old-lady white cotton briefs, thank you very much.*

But I must say, after wearing the same dirty clothes and banged-up boots for—was it a week yet?— the haute-couture duds did look pretty damned good.

*You never wore an actual Chanel before. Shut up, idiot. Just stay in your room tonight. Yeah, but this is his town. He must know we're safe enough to go out without being shot, grenaded, or exploded—right? Don't*

*meet him all tarted up in his blood-money rags. Are you
insane? Order room service and eat like a pig—alone.
No, you will not meet him. That's settled. You're taking
a big, hot Jacuzzi.*

Never had water felt that hot or good on my very,
very sore muscles.

I dropped down and fell asleep on the wonderfully
luxurious bed and didn't wake until the fire had burned
down to embers. It was 7:00 P.M. I popped another
couple of logs onto the fire.

Then two things happened for which I have no explanation. The first is that my stomach began fluttering
around as though I was nervous or excited or something
equally inappropriate in my circumstances.

The second is that I found myself taking the Chanel
dress out of the box and slipping it on. Perfect fit. I didn't
mean to, but I couldn't help it, and yes, I stepped into
the very, *very* sheer black lace thong. *Why are you doing
this?* The Prada heels followed. Expensive shoes are, I
discovered, actually very comfortable. Or these were, at
any rate.

I looked in the wall mirror.

*Wow. Except for the ridiculous hair, you look pretty
good. Near death, real death, and being chased internationally wears well. Wait a minute here. Do I look—
please God!—thinner? Stop it and take the dress off.
Right now.*

I sat down at the dressing table, ran my fingers through
my hair, and loaded up on the makeup, including insane
Amy Winehouse eyeliner.

*You've lost your mind. He's old enough to be, ah, your
stepbrother? Yesterday it was cousin. Where's a straight-
jacket when you need one?*

Eight o'clock came and went. I sat on the bed paralyzed with indecision. At eight fifteen it was either call

room service and have Pierre think I was for sale looking like that, or go the hell down to the bar.

I picked up the phone, dialed room service, hung up, and put my tablet, wallet, passport, money, and the diary in the wall safe in the room. Then I walked out the door and into the bar, tottering on the ridiculously high heels.

## 33

Pantera was sitting at the bar nursing what was probably a very, very good Scotch. He was decked out in his leather jacket, a starched white open-neck shirt, and dark blue trousers. He actually had a cigarette dangling from his lips like Daniel Craig or Humphrey Bogart or someone.

He glanced up and saw me staring at him as I entered the impossibly sexy bar area.

*It's the atmosphere that's getting to you, not the man.*

Unlike what I had been expecting, Pantera simply said, "I'm so glad you decided to join me. You deserve a night off. You won't have one again for many, many days. Please, do sit down," indicating the stool next to him. "Or would you prefer to sit on one of the easy chairs inside?"

*He didn't even say how great you look. He is a giant horse's ass.*

"Oh, this is fine," I said, slipping onto the velvet bar stool next to him.

"Johnnie Walker Blue, I presume?"

"You presume wrong." I asked the bartender for a Belvedere martini, straight up, dry, lots of twists.

"Thanks for the duds. They fit."

*Stop looking for a compliment, big pathetic American! Fat-girl-without-a-date-for-the-prom syndrome strikes again!*

"I'm glad of that. There are quite fine shops in Carcassonne."

"I doubt that's why you call it home."

"Do I?"

We sipped our drinks in a strange, slightly uncomfortable silence. When I finished mine he said, "They are quite relaxed here in terms of *réservations pour le dîner,* but I'm sure you must be hungry."

"You made reservations? How did you know I'd show up?"

Immediately after saying it, I felt myself flushing with embarrassment. I mean, I had shown up looking like Anna Wintour meets Lady Gaga. Obviously this somewhat dubious look required effort and, worse, caring. Yusef was polite enough not to answer.

"So then, where are we going?" I asked, hoping to change the subject.

"Does it matter, and would you know even if I told you?"

"Wow. You really know how to charm a girl."

"I wasn't aware that I was attempting to do that."

*Son of a bitch!*

"Yes, you are. Okay? Is that settled?"

He laughed and put his arm lightly around my back as he led me out of the hotel's side entrance nearest the bar and into the cobblestone street. He grabbed an umbrella from the bin, and we walked out into the rainy night. He held the umbrella in one hand over us and put his arm around me with the other to keep me upright on the cobblestones in those giant heels.

He pointed to the beautifully lit city walls and said, "One of these towers housed the Catholic Inquisition in the thirteenth century. It is even now called the Inquisition Tower."

"Real knights and all that . . ."

"Actually, in 1142, an extraordinary thing occurred here. All the Christian tenants of the Jewish landowners donated their lands to the Templar Knights. Carcassonne became their stronghold."

"There were Jews here in the twelfth century?"

"Yes, in the whole Languedoc area, from Montségur to Carcassonne to Rennes-le-Château—all were populated with Jews. It's the source of the Magdalene chalice legend."

At that point, we ducked into a little place not one hundred and fifty feet from the hotel. It was an underground restaurant that probably hadn't changed since the Templars downed brews there.

We ducked our heads to get into the tiny front door. The fire was lit and music was playing on an antique stereo system complete with a turntable.

"I like the music here." He stopped, closed his eyes, and smiled. "Arturo Sandoval. Nobody ever did 'I Can't Get Started' like that man."

*Such a strange guy!*

"Old—*very* old school—all the way, huh?"

"Not necessarily. But sometimes I think I only got as far as Jovanotti and Paolo Nutini music-wise."

"Who?"

"Never mind."

*Touchy bastard, aren't you?*

He led me to a table in the back, and we sat down in the half-filled place. There was a banged-up piano in the corner, but no one was on board.

Immediately a bottle of Bordeaux was brought, along with *panier de crudités*, fresh vegetables, including a huge bulb of gorgeously fragrant anise, plus some bread, and a little bit of pâté.

He addressed the woman who brought the food, rising and kissing her warmly on both cheeks.

"*Chère Madame, je vous présente mon ami Alazais Roussel.*"

"*Non! Il ne peut pas être!*"

"*Oui!*"

With that I stood and Madame Cheri kissed me on both cheeks and then on my hand, tears springing to her eyes. She backed away, rubbing her hands together and mumbled what sounded like words of thanksgiving—in any language—and retreated into the other room.

"Don't bring the ladies around much? She's very grateful that you seem to have what looks like a date."

He grinned, and I saw the very cute gap in his front teeth. "Don't fill up too much on *crudités*. The food here is exquisite."

"But you come for the music."

"Definitely," he said, filling our glasses, clinking mine. "To a good hunt."

"Oh, jeez." Just as I was beginning to feel slightly ridiculous all done up in the black Chanel dress, the Prada spikes, the red sweater, and a face full of tarty makeup—as if on cue—a very sexy song started playing. Well, in fact it was exactly on cue. Clearly in this place, they knew what this guy liked. I slipped my sweater off. Suddenly I felt embarrassingly warm.

"Ahhh, a personal favorite. Gato Barbieri. 'Europa.' "

As I was about to take a sip of wine, Pantera stood up, grabbed my hand, and lifted me to my feet. He pulled me to him smoothly, and we began to dance—very, very slowly. I automatically put both of my arms around his neck, but he reached over and took my right hand, closed his around it, and brought our closed hands back in to our bodies.

*Holy crow.*

"Old—very old—school," he said in that honey voice, leaning away from me and looking directly at my face. Let me take a moment here to tell you that I am, in fact, quite a good dancer. Always have been. However, the "following the guy's lead" thing has never been my strong suit on a first dance. I tend to stiffen and have a hard time allowing anyone to lead me around anywhere, but that time, after an initial reserve, I was able to fall into his arms as comfortably as if we'd danced before. Many times.

As we were dancing, floating, actually, he exerted the slightest pressure with his hand on my back, and the silk of my dress felt exquisite as it touched my skin as we barely moved our feet to the delight of the other patrons. Madame Cheri walked in and almost split her face smiling.

When the music stopped, so did we, and he led me back to the table. I was slightly shaky. Hey—once a girl has held a grenade for a guy, a kind of camaraderie develops, OK?

"I feel like a Bond girl."

"Not a Bond girl, but a 'chosen woman' is more like it. One whose story has yet to be written. You will do well in finding the truth of Demiel, I'm sure."

*Did we just have that slow dance together, or am I mistaken here?*

I pretended that I was not feeling smeary-eyed and stupid, so I got back down to business.

*Screw you, mister—or better yet, don't screw you!*

Instead, in my best reporter voice, I said, "Speaking of Demiel, I had an extraordinary message from my reporter friend in New York. . . ."

"That would be Dona Grimm. . . ."

"And you know that—how?"

Of course he didn't answer. "All right then, at any rate, she was pulled aside very briefly, she told me, by Randall Mohammed, ben Yusef's lawyer? He said that she was to tell me to 'Go forth,' but also—and I quote—that I should 'trust the man who raised him.'"

"*C'est moi.*"

"Apparently so." Then switching the topic because I wasn't about to give him another leg up, I asked, "I guess you've seen the coverage? About the alleged healings of those kids who were victims of the Manaus bombings?"

He looked unfazed.

"What? You aren't saying anything."

"If you think it surprises me, it doesn't. The Son of the Son has healed since he was a little boy. I told you that."

"Yes, you did. Did you also see the reaction of that evangelical preacher slash TV personality Bill Teddy Smythe?"

"If Demiel is the Son of God, then Smythe is the son of Satan himself. He's part of the coalition that ordered the murder of Demiel and His Mother when the Girl was but thirteen and the boy just hours old. Smythe heads the Face of God Fellowship."

"The what?"

"It's also called the Black Robe. It operates as the opposite of Headquarters. But both are powerful shadow groups with international followers. Both have members in the highest realms of government, military, and justice. But Headquarters members choose to live more simply, more like the early Christians."

"What does this mean, 'Headquarters,' anyway?"

"It's been known by hundreds of names since the days of Jesus. Its goal has always been to bring about the Second Coming.

"The preacher's organization, on the other hand, has morphed into many different loosely connected groups since the end of the Inquisition to *stop* that from occurring."

"All right then, so that I understand your role here, tell me, why is all this intrigue and Holy Grail stuff concentrated in this rural area of Southern France?"

"Well, as everyone who's read contemporary thrillers knows, Mary Magdalene probably settled here and may even be buried here—or so the local legends have it. Remember I told you about the so-called 'head' that the Templars worshipped and used as a banner in war?"

"Yes, of course. How did it end up here, though?"

"That goes to the heart of the mystery itself. What I can tell you is that all the Templars in the Languedoc region, as I had mentioned, converted to Catharism. There were no finer or more loyal warriors—if they were on your side, at any rate."

"Let me guess," I broke in, "your ancestors?"

"The ancestors of many in this region."

I was beginning to get the picture.

"The blood may have been carried in something that Mary Magdalene brought here with her. Something that was placed into the hands of the Cathars."

"You aren't saying it was a skull with blood in it, are you?"

"Doubtful. The Baphomet might have not been a vial, but merely an imprint on a cloth—as in the tale of the Veil of Veronica."

"You believe this?"

"Yes. I do. But who knows where—or if—it exists

any longer. There are so many copies around the world, it's become a joke."

"But the real one—if it exists—is in the Vatican—right? I mean the most important relic in all of Christendom?"

"Have you not listened to anything I've said? It was the job of the Cathars and then the Templars to keep the thing *out* of the hands of the popes, who would do nothing but evil with it."

"Your people may have *cloned* with this blood!" I snapped. "That's not evil?"

"It was meant for good. Nothing from the actual DNA of Jesus, you must understand, could ever do evil. Trust me, I know evil."

"I'm sure you do."

"The Vatican claims to have a copy, which they bring out once a year. But it's a fake—or at least not the image of God."

"The Vatican has a fake? You sound crazy, if you don't mind my saying so."

Apparently not minding at all, he continued with the education of a Russo.

"What's interesting is that—and listen to this carefully—the Baphomet is only mentioned *once* in relation to the Templars, and it was right here—at the Templars' tribunal in Carcassonne. The Church held an Inquisition against the Templars to try to coerce the Templars to reveal what they'd done with the head.

"But even under unimaginable torture they refused."

"And what happened to them? I mean, they'd been Crusaders and had killed for the pope and his mission."

"Every one of them was convicted of worshipping the 'devil head' and was burned alive."

"Like the Cathars."

"But not all at once—and probably because they'd converted."

It was all coming together in my own *Baphomet.* I needed to find this "head," this cloth, this cup with a head on it, or whatever it was.

If I could find it, and the source blood, it would either prove the legitimacy of Demiel or unmask the hoax. Either way, I couldn't lose—if I lived long enough to find the story and tell it, that is.

"I'm sorry. You must be very hungry after I touted the cuisine here," Pantera interjected, allowing me time to let it all sink in. "May I order for you?"

"Sure, be my guest. No fleshy horns though." Back to reality.

He ordered *Carpe à la bière,* a local fish, for himself, and *Coq à la bière,* a kind of chicken stew, for me. Since the food arrived literally in five minutes, I assumed that he must have told them beforehand what we would be having. For once I kept my mouth shut.

It all smelled delicious, but I just wasn't hungry. Was it my reporter's zeal for a story, or was it the company that was making me forgo my previous ravenous appetite?

"You're not eating," Pantera said, gesturing with his fork at my steaming bowl.

"Oh, no, really I am." With that he put down his fork and picked mine up. He fed me a tiny bit of chicken, which I ate with deliberate slowness. Neither one of us misinterpreted what was going on.

"Sweet—no?"

"You sure you're not trying to impress a girl?"

"Positive."

Then a song I didn't recognize came on, and I gave him an inquisitive look.

"Like I said, Paolo Nutini."

Without saying another word, we got up again, and I fell into his arms. This time I completely relaxed into it, and as Paolo Nutini sang, "I just want you closer, is that alright? Baby let's get closer, tonight. Oh baby, baby, baby tell me how can, how can this be wrong?" Pantera pulled away, looked at me for a long time, and then tipped my head back, leaned in, and kissed me.

Just like that, Yusef Pantera, the only person in the world who was more vigorously hunted than I, had kissed me.

We came back together and continued dancing.

When the song was over, we went back to the table and I smiled at him and said, "Well, we've come a long way since I tried to blow you up five days ago."

He didn't answer.

*So what comes now? Do we fall into each other's arms and go on the lam together like* Natural Born Killers?

"Do you mind if I smoke?" he asked.

"No, I love the smell. Reformed but not a reformer."

He lit up a Gauloises and stared at me through the smoke, saying nothing for a long time. Somehow espresso and a chocolate soufflé were brought to the table.

*You ate seventy-five thousand bad Danishes in a bag, and now you've got the world's most exquisite-looking soufflé and can't eat a bite. Well, at least the eating spree seems to have abated.*

He took a few bites himself, but I said, "It looks wonderful, but really, I can't eat another bite."

He smiled, put some euros on the table, and we got up to leave. Outside it was still raining and the temperature seemed to have dropped quite a bit. The sweater didn't help at all.

I automatically reached for my scarf and realized that I had only the little evening bag and that the scarf was back in my room.

"Cold?" he asked, putting his arm around me and opening the umbrella.

"Yes. I forgot that I don't have my scarf with me." I stopped short, almost causing us both to tumble.

"My scarf!" I kicked off the Prada spikes and started running.

Pantera took off after me. I rushed into the hotel, not even holding the door for him. I went around the corner to the little lift and pressed the button over and over impatiently. "Hurry up, goddammit!"

I grabbed Pantera by the hand and ran up the stairs instead and sprinted back to my room. Fumbling with the key card, I swiped it. It kept coming up red. No access.

"Shit! If someone's broken in . . . I didn't put my scarf in the wall safe!"

"Stay calm. Why is the scarf suddenly so important?" he asked, trying repeatedly to get the key card to work. Red. Red. Red.

"Don't you understand? I wiped my mouth after the kiss! Demiel's kiss. The scarf's got his DNA on it!"

Pantera stepped back, stunned. *"Stercum!"*

"Is that some magic word?"

"Latin. You don't want to know. I'll stand here. You go back down and get them to issue you a new card. Hopefully it just demagnetized by itself, and the scarf will be here. Don't panic."

I ran down the stairs, refusing to wait for the lift, and rushed to the front desk.

"My key card," I practically screamed out at the two young women on duty. "It's not working!" I realized that they'd seen me come in with Pantera, and God knows what the hell they were thinking.

"Yes, madame," they managed to say without snarking. "It happens. Really, it is no problem."

*Whenever a foreigner says "no problem" it always means "huge problem." Goddammit!*

They handed me another key card, and I ran back up the stairs. I was shaking. Another break-in would mean there was no hope of getting the DNA. I'd already ruined one batch. This would be the end of it.

*That's why my apartment had been burglarized! The DNA!*

The scarf with Demiel's DNA was the only proof on earth that—what?—I didn't know. But I did know it was *only* up to me to find out. Rooting out a story was in *my* DNA. Especially when my life was on the line.

I took the stairs two at a time, and when I ran down the hall I could see Pantera standing there, gun drawn. "It's me," I called out, fearing he'd shoot me by mistake. "Put it away!"

"I see that it is you; I'm not blind. Never tell me to put my gun away."

"Jee-*sus*."

*Moron.*

I fumbled with the new card key but couldn't get it to work. Pantera took it from me and swiped it. His hands were not shaking as mine had been. Green!

We rushed into the suite, and I grabbed my red bag and started rummaging through it. The old scarf was still crushed up on the bottom, with bits of purse gunk, lint, and a few stray hairs on it, but otherwise intact.

"Banged up, but safe!"

He took it from me, handling it gently. "Do you have a cleaning bag in the room?"

I grabbed one from the closet, and he folded the scarf

carefully inside the plastic bag and pulled the draw-
string.

"You may have saved the world," he said, almost seriously.

"Well, I don't know about that. . . ."

"I do." He put the bag down on a table and walked
back toward me, stopping directly in front of me for a
few seconds. We looked at each other and smiled.

"That was close," I said as he put an arm around
me and pulled me in to him, pressing his body against
mine.

"Put your gun away," I teased, and he threw his head
back and laughed. "I hate it when a man tells me what I
can't say."

"Shhh . . . *Cala a boca,*" he said softly, in what sounded
like, well, I have no idea, and leaned back and placed
the gun on the nightstand with his free hand. "Good?"

"Good."

He then put brought his "gun" hand up to my chin,
tipped my face to his, and kissed me deeply.

"But, what about the . . ."

"*Damate, shizuka ni shite,*" he laughed, and kissed
me again as he pushed me back onto the bed. I didn't
resist but still couldn't help saying, "I don't know
about . . ."

"*Taci din gură,*" he whispered in my ear, kissing it,
rolling on top of me and opening my mouth with his
tongue. I responded by taking in his kiss and pulling
him even tighter into me.

He pulled back slightly and studied my face like he'd
never seen me, really seen me before, ran his hands
through my crazy hair, and said, "*Dormi mecum?*"

"Latin?"

"Latin," he grinned in a smile so wide I could see the
split between his front teeth.

"If that means what I think it means," I whispered back, "then most definitely."

"Oh baby . . ." was the only thing he whispered as he gently rolled me on top of him and unzipped my new-old Chanel dress, slid it off of me, and tossed it onto the floor.

*Oh, baby is right.*

## 34

I woke up at 7:30 and reached for him, but his side of the bed was empty. Not that he had a side, really, because last I remembered I had been falling asleep in his arms in the middle of the bed. We'd been so wrapped up in each other that there hadn't been enough space to slip a piece of paper between us.

*He must be in the bathroom.*

I got up, wrapped the sheet around myself, and walked toward the bathroom. "Pantera, you in there?" I knocked. No answer. I knocked again. Hard.

"Pantera!" Nothing. I checked the sitting-room area. Nothing. Then panicked, I looked for the plastic bag with my scarf. It was not on the table where we'd left it. I searched the entire suite. Nothing. The scarf was gone, and so was he.

*You've been had, lady!*

At first I fumed. Then I got very scared.

*The wall safe!*

I rushed to it and opened it with my combination. I rummaged around. Passport. Diary. Wallet. Tablet. Everything was still there—except the missing piece of the biggest puzzle the world had ever known: the scarf holding the DNA of the man they claimed was the son—more precisely the clone—of Jesus himself. Or perhaps he was, as Bill Teddy Smythe had claimed, the son of Satan. And if so, I had just slept with the devil himself.

How had I been duped this way? I had been careless on a grand scale.

*We didn't even use a condom! Idiot! Calm down. At least you can't get pregnant. Right. But what if he's carrying some terrible disease? What were you thinking? Oh, right, you weren't thinking!*

I plopped back down on the bed and tried taking deep breaths to calm myself down. My hands were shaking. Was it fear, rage, or hurt? Rage. Definitely rage.

*Jerk! You are smarter than this. Much smarter. Son. Of. A. Bitch! He will not outsmart you. He will not.*

Out of the corner of my eye I saw the message light on the room phone blinking. I hadn't heard it ring. Maybe Pantera had turned off the ringer? Why? I picked it up and hit the key for "voice mail." Him. Two hours earlier.

"This isn't what it seems."

*Yes it is.*

"In fact, I am—hell—I can't stop thinking about you. Really . . ." He hesitated.

*"Really"—what?*

"Don't worry. I have the scarf. I am taking it right now for testing. I cannot, and will not, put you in further danger; you are safer without me now."

Then: "Now I understand why it was necessary for them to implicate you in the murder. And why they had to assassinate Sadowski. He was, of course, well known to them—but they needed to get the FBI, CIA, Interpol, and whoever else they could get on board *officially* to hunt you using all their resources. Once they were involved, there wouldn't have been a border crossing in the world you would have made it through after a day or two.

"They want the scarf and they need you dead.

"The Son of the Son picked *you* out of all the women in the world for a reason. You were where you needed to be *when* you needed to be there. That proved that you are the one.

"And now you are the only one who can stop them—with the absolute evidence that Demiel is God, not human."

*Not human. Does he mean the DNA will show he's a clone? And?*

"That scarf will tie back to the source blood. But make no mistake: *Everyone*, and I do mean *everyone*, is on their payroll."

*Whose payroll? Trust no one.*

He continued—all business now: "I got a white scarf from a local shopkeeper who was kind enough to open up for me this morning. . . ."

*When—at dawn?*

"You'll find it among the towels in the bathroom. I took the liberty of removing those stray hairs from your scarf. At least I hope they were yours—they were brown. I put them back in the bottom of your bag. Please put the new scarf back in your red satchel, and be sure to get lint and other bits from the bag on it. It must look used. And of course stick those few brown stray hairs on it as well."

"Then, before you brush your teeth or have your coffee or anything, lick the scarf. Toss it under the bed, get your things, and leave. No need to check out. A friend will be waiting at the entrance—the one we used last night. He'll take you to the airport at Toulouse. He'll also have your ticket. Rome. Got it?"

*Huh?*

"Go to the restaurant Les Etoiles in the Atlante Garden Hotel on the Via Crescenzio. It's near Saint Peter's, and I'll meet you there. Trust me on that. I'm not done with you yet. I may never be done with you."

*Whoa. You sure I should trust no one?*

"My God, you are one helluva woman. Now, hit the number three on the keypad to erase this message."

I smiled and did as instructed, and then checked my e-mail. Nothing. I turned on Sadowski's phone. One text and one voice mail.

The text was from Donald. "Baby," he began.

*That's the second "Baby" in two days. One more of these bad boys and for sure I'll end up dead.*

"You owe me. Here it is—a photo of the deadbeat dad known as Yusef Pantera. It's a high school photo, or whatever they call it in Frog land. I can't believe how good I am."

I looked down at the attached photo. It was Pantera all right.

"It's from someplace called C-a-r-c-a-s-s-o-n-n-e in France. It's very old. The photo, I mean. Like forty years old or something, but it's him. Got it through a connection, a Fed who went rogue. Don't worry. He thinks I want to be the first shooter to break the photo of the man listed as ben Yusef's father.

"Have I told you lately that I love you? I do."

I stared at the photo circa 1975. Teens in France apparently didn't look as disco moronic or metalhead as teens in the USA back then. It was definitely Pantera, and I got that funny feeling inside again.

*How cute was he with that buzz cut? He must have looked like a freak compared to all the longhairs back then.*

This was great. At least I knew I could trust him.

*Trust no one.*

Okay, more specifically, I knew he was who he said he was.

"I love you back, Donald," I said out loud to no one. For the first time in a hell of a long time in what had been a hellishly long and overwrought relationship with my ex, I realized that I actually meant it. Truly, I did love Donald—but not in the way that I'd truly meant it before. Now I honestly felt that he was my friend, and I loved him for it.

*Sorry, Donald. How you gonna keep her down on the farm after she's been down in Carcassonne? I may never get over last night.*

I was desperate to dish with Dona about the whole escape-and-sexcapade thing, like I would have done in the old days. Of course the old days were just a few days ago. I hit the voice-mail button.

"Dahling." It was Dona, but she didn't sound like she was ready to dish. In fact, she sounded frantic, and music was playing very loud in the background. Not good. An old Mafia trick to keep the Feds from hearing you on bugs.

"Things are really heating up. I was taken to Federal Plaza quite by force. The Feds, the CIA, Interpol—it was a reporter's dream—except I was the prey this time. They grilled me for three hours. Thank God I know nothing. I pointed out that there were more pressing issues right now, like stopping the rioting and figuring out who was inciting it, which, by the way, they seem to think is you, or your *operatives*.

"I know they're tailing me. Please. Stay deep under. *Please*. If any of my online postings have the words *Little Big Man* in them, it means I found out that they've got a bead on you again. I'm calling in some big favors here. I love you. This is a pay-and-toss phone, and I'm about to toss. Stay safe."

*Too late.*

I took a quick shower and packed up the few things that would fit into my red bag. It was either the Chanel dress or the Prada shoes, which I just noticed Pantera had been cool enough to pick up from where I'd dropped them outside last night, and which I had been ready to blow off. I knew the shoes meant extra baggage, but damn! That was a killer right there.

*No. Leave them. If you've only one life to live, you should live it as a redhead in a Chanel dress.*

I walked down the stairs to the side entrance, where a man was waiting. "Ms. Russo, I am a friend of Yusef's," he said, with just a hint of a French accent. "I shall drive you to the airport." Somehow I hadn't expected a motorcycle. I hopped on the back of his Ducati and we took off. In minutes we were through the drawbridge and out of the magical city and on to the airport.

The airport was fifty miles away, but we sped like crazy. I was able to make the morning EasyJet Rome flight without any of the usual airline fuss. The flight was smooth, and more important, it was quick.

Fiumicino Airport is not my favorite place in Italy—or anywhere, actually. But thanks to the European Union, however, I didn't have to go through the dreaded customs, which was more of a blessing than getting blessed by the pope himself.

*Now what? Wait for Pantera?*

I took a cab to the Atlante Garden Hotel, which was located right near the Vatican. The restaurant overlooked the Vatican and was literally a stone's throw away. I ordered a cappuccino and turned on Sadowski's cell. There was a voice-mail message.

"My dear, did I not warn you to trust no one?"

*Maureen!*

"Naive? I'm very surprised. How can you not know

that Pantera—who clearly is not dead—is more dangerous than you seem to comprehend? He is an assassin—a
paid killer for one of the most radical groups on the
planet. Worse, he's a true believer. Nothing more dangerous.

"Do not ever forget that he was part of the team responsible for the monstrous cloning of a child. Really, I
thought you had more grit and more wisdom."

*You thought wrong.*

"He *will* use you to find the source blood, and then
you, my innocent girl, will be history. I hope you did not
give him anything that you may have uncovered, because
if you did, he'll take off and you'll never see him again.
You will probably think he's dead. They are very, *very*
good at that, as I know all too well. Get away from him
any way you can."

*Too late for that.*

"I just hope you get this message and that you have
escaped with your life. Believe me, if you never believe
another thing, believe this: He is your sworn enemy.
He will charm and disarm you, and then he will disappear again. It's seduce and abandon on a global scale.
Just hold on to every bit of evidence you have amassed
and let nothing out of your sight or you are doomed.

"He *will* find you when he needs to. I just hope you
see him first."

*Oh, shit. The scarf! She can't be right. You're not some
babe in the woods who can't tell the truth from a lie.
You're a reporter, for God's sake! But seriously, the fact
that he's not here is not good.*

I began sweating.

I downed the cappuccino and ordered a cold double
espresso. The TV at the bar was tuned to the local
news. After the weather—clear and sunny—came the
news. A reporter was standing outside a tunnel and was

reporting on a horrible smashup. The burned-out wreckage of a car being towed away on the *autostrade* made my blood run cold. The reporter said that the driver of the car, a man, driving alone, had died on impact, after his car had crashed into the wall and flipped over in one of the tunnels dotting the roads in, around, and outside of Rome.

I could see it was a Citroën. But it was so charred I couldn't make out the color.

*Don't panic. Every other car in Europe looks like that.*

The announcer then said in Italian, "The man's car was caught on surveillance video when it crossed the border from France into Italy earlier today. It was registered to one Edward Gibbon of Carcassonne, France."

*Oh, God. They got him. Or did he get me?*

## 35

I watched the rest of the newscast with my hand stuffed into my mouth to keep from screaming. The body bag was placed on the stretcher, and the ambulance drove off with all the bells and whistles blaring.

*"I'll meet you there. Trust me on that. I'm not done with you yet. I may never be done with you."*

I was torn between anger and tears, hope and fear. Had he simply arranged an accident in order to disappear with my DNA-loaded scarf? Was he really dead? Or possibly had he directed me to a restaurant because he somehow knew they'd have the news on? He was, after all, very good at arranging accidents. That I knew from firsthand experience. But last night had not been arranged; it had been from some deeper place. *Sure.*

*Can any man fake it like that? Answer: You're kidding—right?*

And so I just sat there not comprehending what the hell had just happened. I was playing a rough game in a playground not of my own making, against a team of bullies who all had bats, while I was alone and armed with just a keyboard.

The word may be mightier than the sword, but except for the *s* they are pretty much the same. Both are used to kill—and to save.

And both were out of my reach right now. Use the word and get nailed on my location. Use the sword and be outgunned.

*If Pantera was really dead, the other side wouldn't have made it such a spectacular event,* I thought. Then I remembered Princess Diana and all those death-by-tunnel conspiracies.

If he *wasn't* dead, then he'd just screwed me over—literally and figuratively. I was back where I started, almost. I had more information, but I didn't know what to do with it or where to go next. Tears, nausea, disgust, hope, and misery hit me all at once.

*Do what you do. You're a reporter. Do what you do. Don't stay here.*

I paid the bill and asked the waiter if they had a computer terminal available, and he directed me to the business office. For ten euros I got an hour of Internet service.

In Google, I entered the key words "Cathar treasure" (904,000 results), "Baphomet" (5,230,000 results), and "Veil of Veronica" (1,750,000 results).

Overwhelming when on a short leash, for sure.

I refined the search and added the keyword "Vatican" to each of the above. "Baphomet & Vatican" (12,200,000), "Cathar treasure & Vatican" (989,000), and "Veil & Vatican" (3,650,000).

The top hits in the first two categories seemed like too many amateur sleuths, wackos, and conspiracy theorists with equally nutty videos—mostly overweight men sitting in Barcalounger chairs in their dens spouting hidden wisdom. But none of any of the top hits connected the Veil with the Cathar treasure.

The third category, "Veil & Vatican," however, seemed to be filled with researchers and fewer kooks.

I scanned the results, and the second one on the hit list was for a book called *The Face of God* by a journalist named Paul Badde, whose credits included Vatican correspondent for the German newspaper *Die Welt*.

I looked up his book, and he was apparently the foremost researcher of the Veil of Veronica. One review particularly caught my attention when it stated that his book unmasked the popular and accepted account that a woman called Veronica wiped the face of Jesus as he carried the cloth. The actual cloth that came to bear the image of Jesus was kept in a monastery in a town called Manoppello. It was known there as the Holy Face.

It also said that there was a so-called Holy Face or Veil of Veronica in the Vatican—but that it wasn't the authentic one. I was getting more confused by the minute. Whether it was a woman named Veronica or Maryanne, for all I cared, and whether the Vatican had the fake or the genuine article—I needed to see it for myself.

I Googled up Badde's Italian book publicist and placed a call. I introduced myself as Alazais Roussel, a producer for the History Channel. I explained that I was doing the preliminary research for a two-part special we'd be doing and would very much like to speak with Paul Badde about his research on the Veil.

You would have thought it was the pope himself calling. Of course I knew why: A hit on History would translate into a big bump in book sales. She put me on hold while she made a conference call to Badde himself.

"Mr. Badde, thank you for taking my call," I said when he was connected.

"Yes, it is my pleasure. History Channel is one of my favorites," he said in a very refined German accent.

"The feature I'm working on is about the great treasures of the Vatican," I lied, praying he wouldn't look up my bio.

"Oh, wonderful," he said, but I could tell he was disappointed that it wasn't a whole show about the particular Veil in Manoppello that he'd written about.

"I understand that you are an expert on the greatest relic in the Vatican, the Veil of Veronica, and I was wondering if we could meet."

"Yes, of course." Now he sounded downright disappointed. "When would you like to meet, Ms. Roussel? I have some time tomorrow afternoon."

*Not good.*

"I'm, ah, leaving for, ah, Perugia, tonight," I said, paranoia rising.

*Don't overdo it. You'll sound like a liar.*

Instead of listening to myself, the pushy reporter took over.

"Are you free today?"

"Well, not really. I have an appointment."

"What about right now?"

"Ms. Roussel, I am at work on a book now. It's not a good time."

His publicist cut in. "Is there another time you could meet, Ms. Roussel?"

"Not really. Like I said, flying to Perugia later."

"May we call you back, Ms. Roussel, with a more convenient time for Mr. Badde?"

"I'm sorry, but I'm on a time constraint. There's a relic in Perugia that takes precedent, I'm afraid."

*You sound like a nasty American bitch.*

It worked.

He told me to meet him at one of the private gates of the Vatican—which he explained was around on the side of Saint Peter's on one of the myriad streets that encircle the complex. "Ask any guard and he will direct you to the proper gate."

I met him on a side street after asking directions. He was standing alone. Middle-aged, handsome in tweed jacket and brown slacks—very old-world gentlemanly and elegant. Not like my crowd. If you're a print or on-line reporter in NYC, and you wear clean jeans to work, everyone thinks you hit the lotto the night before.

Two Swiss Guards who were standing watch saluted us and parted the gates like Moses at the Red Sea. Inside those gates was a spectacular garden complete with helicopter pad and shiny Pope-a-copter sitting idle but ever ready for Christ's representative of the earth's poor and downtrodden to hop aboard. The garden was blooming, despite how early in spring it was, with roses and every imaginable flower God ever dreamed of and more. There were mini-mazes, contemplation benches, and little chapels for private prayer.

We sat on a bench—and I was surprised that we were totally alone in this magnificent place in the center of the Vatican grounds. I took out my notebook.

"This is the pope's private garden. He loves to sit here and read, pray, and contemplate."

"Well, if ever there were a place for contemplation, this is definitely it."

"Yes, I love it here. But tell me, what do you want to know of the Holy Face?"

I was relieved to see that he didn't connect the crazy redheaded rocker chick named Roussel with the brunette reporter in NYC named Russo—the one who was kissed by ben Yusef and had become a worldwide sensation/disgrace.

I continued lying: "I was told that you are the foremost expert in the Veil of Veronica, which I understand is kept right here in the Vatican."

I was baiting him. He knew it, I'm sure.

"I guess you have not read the book then?"

"Not fully." He looked annoyed, as well he might be considering I got him in the middle of work and hadn't even bothered to read the book.

"We didn't actually know about it, and when I discovered *The Face of God* this morning on the Internet, I thought I'd better meet the author slash expert before I left Rome."

"Where would you like to start, and what time is your flight?"

"Ah, in three hours."

"I see."

"Can you show me the Veil?"

"Can I show you the Volto Santo?" he repeated incredulously. With that he rose and said, "It took me one year—using every bit of influence I had—to get permission to see it *once*.

"But I can show you the location of the Vatican's relics. Yes, there is a relic of the Holy Face here, but . . ."

"But?"

"But there are at least six images purported to be the *real* relic. The real Veil."

We began walking toward the same gate from which we had entered. The day was warm and clear, and we moved at a good pace, walking toward Saint Peter's Square.

"Six images. I'm astounded to hear this. But the one that's here is the *actual* Veil of Veronica—correct?"

Again, he laughed. "Real? Yes, perhaps if you believe the legend. Which I don't."

"What?" We were walking along the back cobblestone streets, which I'd never seen before despite having been to the Vatican many times as a tourist and also when I covered the election of Pope Benedict. Ancient residences lined the streets and were still occupied and hauntingly beautiful.

"I thought you were an expert on the Veil, and yet you call it a 'legend'? You are not a true believer?"

He stopped and looked at me. He was not just startled but almost aghast. "True believer? There is no truer believer!"

"Oh. I'm sorry if I've offended you. But frankly, I'm confused."

We turned a corner, and Saint Peter's came into full view. It still had the ability to take my breath away.

"As I said, there are at least six 'true' Veronicas or at least 'authentic' copies of the true image. But there is only one authentic Volto Santo. I believe they are not one and the same, nor do I believe in the legend associated with it."

"Are you saying there was no Saint Veronica?"

"No, but I am saying that even her name, Veronica, is a myth. The very name means 'true image' or 'true icon,' in reference to religious works."

"Of course!" *Bingo.*

As we walked around the cathedral, he continued: "In the Acts of Pilate there appears a report allegedly made by Pontius Pilate to Claudius. It is an anti-Semitic description of the Crucifixion, and an account of the resurrection of Jesus; both are presented as if they are official reports.

"A series of Latin manuscripts, *Cura Sanitatis Tiberii* or 'The Cure of Tiberius,' is the first time that the Veronica legend is mentioned anywhere. It states that the Veil cured Emperor Tiberius of some sort of malady. The interesting thing here is that the real Veil is made of a fabric called 'byssus,' made from the *hair,* if you will, of mollusks, those long filaments that protrude from mussels."

"And that's important because . . . ?"

"The most famous weaver of byssus back then in all of Jerusalem was . . ." he said, pausing to gauge my reaction, ". . . Princess Berenike, the daughter of King Herod."

"The king who ordered the slaughter of all infant boys when he heard about the birth of a new king of the Jews? Wow. That *is* hard to believe!"

"Faith is hard to sustain without belief, Ms. Roussel."

"Yes. I know. But the possibility that the Veil that Veronica allegedly used to wipe the face of Jesus *could* have been made by Princess Berenike, the daughter of the man who tried to kill Jesus as an infant, is, well, incredible."

He didn't answer.

"Whew. So where are all these Veils and 'authentic copies' now?"

"One is in Vienna, there are two in Spain, one in Genoa, and one in the Matilda chapel in Saint Peter's Basilica."

"Surely that must be the real one?"

"Not unless this so-called woman Veronica wore a veil made of wood," he sniffed. "It's a painted image on wood, you see."

I smiled. "I see."

"Not yet do you see, not yet." He continued, "I am one of the only people who *have* been granted permission to see the *cloth* imprinted with the image of Jesus that is kept in the Vatican since 1907. This image is stored in the chapel behind the balcony in the southwest pier— one of the supports of the dome."

We entered Saint Peter's from a side door, again blocked by two members of the Swiss Guard. Badde showed his credentials, and they opened the doors without hesitation. He began describing to me the significance of Veronica's Veil within the Catholic Church.

"The four pillars of the church, and the statues that adorn each in the niches below, support the dome," he explained as we walked around the magnificent basilica, pointing up. "They celebrate the greatest relics kept by the Vatican—which were all kept in one place."

"Which is?"

"The Veronica pier."

"The saint represented in the Sixth Station of the Cross?"

"Yes, exactly. It is the fourth pillar," he said, pointing to the four pillars.

*The fourth pillar represents the Sixth Station—"Go forth for I am six!"*

"Is the Veil of Veronica kept here?"

"Yes, and no. I will get to it in a minute."

A minute? My heart was coming out of my chest wondering how I would manage to steal the precious relic out of the cathedral with the highest security in the world. I mean, they have their own army!

As I was overcome with the vastness, he kept up his guided tour of the reliquary.

"The pillars that support the Church—literally—are named for Saint Veronica, Saint Helena, Saint Longinus, and Saint Andrew."

As we walked around, he picked up a guidebook to show me what we were seeing in person. "Each pier has a huge statue of a saint in each pillar's niche representing each of the basilica's *Reliquae Maggiori,* or four 'major relics,'" he said, pointing to the northwest pier and its statue of Saint Helena.

"In this statue, created by Andrea Bolgi, Helena, Constantine's mother, is holding a large cross, which represents the one 'true cross,' which she said she found in Jerusalem."

We took the long walk to other side. "Here on the

northeast pier is the statue of Saint Longinus, by Bernini. Longinus was the Roman soldier who thrust a spear into Jesus' side at the Crucifixion, from which poured water and blood. Longinus converted and was later martyred. The relic is the spear."

We headed south in the cathedral, pushing past literally thousands of tourists.

"Here at the southeast pier is the Saint Andrew pillar. The statue is by François Duquesnoy," he said, shaking his head at the enormous crowds. "It's much more crowded lately, if possible. The line outside must stretch to the Capitoline Hill!"

"Folks suddenly getting religion?"

"I think it has to do with that terrorist on trial who claims to be descended, or whatever he's saying, from Jesus himself. It has brought out all the conspiracy theorists and fanatics, I'm afraid!"

I let it slip by without comment as we reached the next pillar.

The Saint Andrew statue was against the diagonal cross upon which he was martyred.

"Is the relic then a piece of that cross?"

"Hardly. It is Andrew's head."

"They keep his head?" I tried not to look too disgusted and instead asked, "Do you think that's the Baphomet?"

"Have you been reading the conspiracy Web sites, Ms. Roussel?"

"Ahh. Yes," I said, looking appropriately sheepish.

"Well, this relic head of Saint Andrew? It's no longer here. It was returned to the Greek Orthodox Church in 1964."

"So the Vatican has a Saint Andrew pillar but not the relic?"

"Correct," he said, walking to the southwestern side

of the basilica, where the gigantic pillar with the colossal statue of Saint Veronica stood.

It was a highly dramatic statue of a woman swirling a large cloth against what appeared to be a great wind that whips both the cloth and her clothing. It's almost erotic. "Bernini as well?"

"Noooo. It was Francesco Mochi who sculpted this."

He interpreted the Latin inscription: "The splendor of the church might keep in proper fashion and in safety the image of the Redeemer on Veronica's *sudarium,* 1625."

"So it's been here since at least that time?"

"Well, that is what is so interesting. The Veronica icon kept *here* is a hoax."

"What? You can't be serious!"

"More than serious. The True Face of Jesus still exists, yes, unharmed, in all its glory, but not at the Vatican. It is in Manoppello, a small mountain town.

"Another cloth identified as the Veil used to be in Rome—or *some* version of it.

"That version was saved, stolen, heisted—call it what you will—from the plundering German and Spanish soldiers by an unknown person during the sacking of Rome in the sixteenth century.

"The pope ordered that it be substituted with a copy— until the original could be found and brought back. That never happened.

"Now a version of the Veronica, which is quite rotted—I saw it for myself in 2005—is the one they *still* display in the Vatican once a year from high above."

"How do they get away with it then?"

"Ahhh, an interesting conundrum, no? Whatever it is, we know that to this day this mysterious cloth is celebrated as the most important of the four *Reliquae Maggiori*."

"It's the most important—and it's a fake? Is the whole story a fake, then?"

"If you mean, 'Does the Veronica story appear in the New Testament or anywhere in the biblical writings?' then the answer is no.

"Yet it *is* nonetheless venerated as the most important pillar of the church," he said, as we stood before the magnificent, sensual statue of Saint Veronica. "That is why I saved this fourth pillar for last.

"This is where all of the other relics are kept—right within the pillar. There is an entrance at the base.

"*That* is the level of importance given to a woman who is more legend than we may have been led to believe."

"So there *was* no real Saint Veronica. What about the Sixth Station of the Cross?"

"The Veronica of the medieval Veil legend has never existed. There was no woman who wiped his face as he carried the cross, that we actually know of."

"What? But they showed you the Veil imprinted with the face of Jesus, did they not?"

"No, they allowed me to see *their* 'Veronica's Veil,' which is up in the pillar," he said, pointing up. "It's only brought out once a year, two weeks before Easter. They display it very swiftly from high above from that column.

"Only God knows why I was allowed to see it. But I saw with my very eyes that what it is, is a nearly rotted cloth showing exactly nothing. It has to be a fake, according to this 'nothingness.'"

"So there is no *real* Veil?"

"I didn't say that. In fact, three days after the election of Pope Benedict XVI, I *was* granted permission to see their *earliest* copy of the original Veil, which they keep hidden away in the Sacrestia della Cappella Sistina. It is a tremendously precious icon from the third century.

"It's kept in a cardboard box, covered in layers of tissue paper. Their icon in a cardboard box! The relic has gilding around the outline of the face and has nails holding down the edges. We were even allowed, my wife and I, to shine a light on it. The face covers almost the entire linen cloth. But it had turned black, nearly completely.

"Here's what's even more interesting: When I gazed upon it I realized, Ms. Roussel, that I *had* seen a similar image before—but on the *authentic* Face of God, the one that is truly the most important relic in all of Christendom.

"The Volto Santo—what many call the Veil of Veronica. It was stolen from the Vatican during the sacking of Rome and brought in 1527 to Manoppello, although residents there claim that it was in 1506 . . . which I think is impossible.

"It has been kept in a small church monastery in that mountain town—about 106 miles from here—ever since. The church of the Capuchin friars on the Tarigni hill outside Manoppello. What is clear is that about 100 years after its arrival, the church was built. In 1638."

"Astonishing. And the Vatican gets away with it—showing a fake, I mean?"

"For nearly five hundred years so far, yes. They obviously must have thought they would get the original back in the beginning, and that it might be better and wiser to keep quiet about the robbery until it was returned. But it never came back to Rome or to Saint Peter's."

"So I should not even try to see the Veil that is kept here?"

"No, I'm sorry, but the Veronica at the Vatican is not the Face you are looking for."

"But it makes no sense! I mean, how could the most

important relic in all of Christendom be hiding in a town no one's ever heard of?"

"Well, many *have* heard of it, for one thing, and for another, it's actually hiding in plain sight. It's on display at the altar of the church there. In fact, in September of 2006 Pope Benedict himself went there and knelt down and prayed before it!"

"What?" I couldn't believe what he was saying. "But you said the Veronica was just a legend. . . ."

"It is. But the actual cloth with Jesus' true face—created without a drop of paint or dye or *any* coloration made by man—does exist. The cloth of Manoppello. Manoppello, by the way, ironically enough, means 'napkin,' even though the village name was in place well before the Veil arrived.

"In fact the Veil, wrapped in a package, was left by an angel, as the legend goes, on a bench in Manoppello right after the sacking of Rome. A doctor, Giacomo Antonio Leonelli, found it, opened it up, and found the cloth imprinted with the face of Jesus."

"Jeez," I piped in, "it's like finding the original Gutenberg Bible in a cab!"

"That is correct. Leonelli's family kept it until 1608, when, after a series of events, it was donated to the Capuchin friars, who have kept it until this day."

"So it's been there all this time?"

"Yes. But the real Veil, the one I've described and that is kept there, is *not* Veronica's Veil."

"Now I'm really confused."

"Rather it is, I believe, the face cloth, or *napkin,* that was placed over Jesus' face in the *tomb.*"

"By whom?"

"By the last person who laid our Lord to rest in his grave. However, in order to explain the image on the cloths, over the years a tale was created that a woman wiped the face of Jesus on His way to Calvary and His image mysteriously appeared. Nowhere does this tale appear in the Bible, however."

"Let me ask you something else," I said. "Why was a napkin laid over the face of Jesus? I don't understand."

"I remember reading that it had been common practice back in the time of Jesus to lay a napkin or cloth upon the face of the deceased in the tomb. When Jesus arose from the dead, I believe this cloth was left with His imprint!"

"But who took his cloth from the tomb, do you think?"

He looked at me, studying me to see, perhaps, if I could absorb what he was about to say or if I would dismiss him as a kook.

"Mary Magdalene! She was among the last who saw Him in His grave and the first person to whom He appeared after His resurrection—in front of that same tomb. The veil or napkin was then discovered by Peter and John—*in* the tomb. As John reports in his gospel, 'at a particular place.'"

*So that's why the Magdalene Chalice legend persists in the Languedoc area around Montségur. She brought it* with *her when she settled there with the other Jewish émigrés!*

"The Holy Face of Manoppello is the proof—almost a photo—of the face of Jesus at the exact instant of His resurrection from the dead.

"And it matches up exactly with the image on the Shroud, which very few people know." He then took out his wallet and gave me two transparencies roughly the size of funeral cards—the ones that are given out at wakes and such. He held up the first one.

The Shroud of Turin. I recognized the image. He held up the second, a nearly transparent card on which a face was faintly visible.

"This one, the Shroud of Turin, is an unchanging opaque negative—while the image on the Holy Face is a positive, transparent image with a million different expressions. The Shroud is like a faded negative of a photo."

I had to ponder for a moment what that meant. *Negative and positive? Same image?*

Then he put the Veil transparency on top of the Shroud opaque image. "They match up precisely." I took his word for it because it was so hard to see in the light of the cathedral.

"Who took these photos?" I knew that no one had photographed the Turin Shroud out of its glass—at least not in modern times.

"A nun who has devoted her life to the study of the images."

"In Rome?"

"No, Manoppello. Up the mountain above the Monastery of the Volto Santo. But she must have gone back to Germany. No one has seen her in a few years. I understand another nun lives there now."

He handed me a copy of his book and got up to leave. "It's something you must see for yourself. Read the book, learn the history. You may even learn enough for your *documentary* for the History Channel," he teased.

With that he got up to leave. "You may want these," he said, handing me the cards. "You're not with the History Channel, are you?"

I shook my head. "Good luck with whatever you're doing. Next time try telling the truth."

"How did you know?"

"For one thing, a researcher would have figured out that it's much easier to go by rail than air to Perugia."

"Then why did you show up?"

"Curiosity," he said, clearly expecting, and rightly so, a payoff for time wasted.

"You don't want to know," I said. "Trust me, Mr. Badde, you *really* don't want to know."

He looked at me, saw that I was telling the truth this time, shook my hand, and quickly disappeared into the impossible crowds in the vastness of the basilica.

I looked at his thick book, with an image of the Manoppello Holy Face on the cover. The subtitle of the book? *The Rediscovery of the True Face of Jesus*. It was sort of the task I'd been assigned—rediscovering the real face—and, I was beginning to believe, the real meaning of God as well.

I walked to a spot where the light was better and held the cards with the images on them up to the light. One—the same image as the face on the book—was barely visible, nearly transparent, while the other, the Shroud, was totally opaque. I put the opaque image behind the transparency, and what I saw floored me.

When the positive transparent Manoppello image was laid on top of the negative opaque Turin Shroud image, they not only matched up perfectly but also formed an almost 3-D image. Every line of each face aligned exactly to the other. These were the completion of one another. How could two separate ancient images residing probably four hundred or five hundred miles apart, neither allegedly containing paint or dye, match up?

Only one explanation: At some time, these two pieces of cloth lay one upon the other and recorded the image of the man they lay upon. The napkin over the face and the Shroud then wrapped around the head and body. Astounding!

The image was that of a young man with a wisp of a beard, wounds on his nose and forehead. His mouth was open, and his teeth were bared in a scream. I put the cards down to catch my breath and held them up again. This time the young man who stared back at me had his mouth closed in a slight smile, and he bore what I can only say was a look of perfect peace. How could that be? These weren't silly trick hologram cards with faces that change when you move them around. These were two simple transparencies made by a cloistered nun who lived alone in a house in the mountains of Manoppello.

I couldn't tear my eyes away. I realized that the image had a hauntingly familiar face. Was it Jesus? It certainly didn't look remotely like the face of any Jesus I'd ever seen. But I *did* know this man from *somewhere*. But where?

His calm yet imploring brown eyes took hold of me.

*What do you want?*

I suddenly felt so hopeless—as though I were back in that dream I'd had back at the beginning of my nightmare, in which I was the only one who could figure out the coded message on that wall.

Being so moved by these twin images was surprising, sure, but more surprising still were the tears that began to run down my face. I immediately wiped them away with my hand. They felt sticky. I looked down to see that my fingertips were streaked with blood. I touched my face. No scrapes, no wounds—nothing. I took out Sadowski's phone and did the unthinkable: turned on the camera so I could see my face. Tears of blood were streaming down my face! Then I did the second unthinkable: I snapped the shutter icon.

Was it *His* blood? My blood? I didn't know, but I knew that I knew the man in those images. "Who are you? Why do I *know* you?" I cried aloud to the mysterious image in the crowded basilica.

The answer that came to me was as swift and as terrifying as the blood streaming from my eyes. Yes, I did know the man in the Veil.

I had stared into those eyes before. He'd kissed me.

*This man is Demiel ben Yusef.*

## 36

*If I wasn't being played, then Jesus was going to be executed. Again.*

But was *I*, for whatever reason, the butt of some elaborate hoax? That seemed more far-fetched than the idea that Jesus had been cloned thirty-three years earlier—a time when the technology shouldn't even have existed. Right? Right.

What I *did* know for sure was that I had to see that cloth in Manoppello for myself. Could it really be an ancient image somehow created without paint or dye? If so, I would have my hands around the biggest story in two centuries—but first I'd have to live to tell it.

Somehow the scent of blood—literally—hanging on this story was stronger than my need to protect myself.

I had to start by finding this cloistered nun whose name I didn't even get. But how many nuns can live alone in a shack above a monastery on a mountain in a tiny town? My guess was one. If I was lucky. But then again, this was Italy—a land where the unusual is usual, especially when it comes to the secrets of Christianity and the literal veil of secrecy about most things connected to the Vatican.

I searched around my bag and found the mini hand sanitizer from the plane and an old tissue to wipe my face. I was relieved to see the blood had stopped, so I cleaned up as best I could and hurried out of Saint Peter's.

How, I wondered, had such a thing happened to me in a place where I felt so devoid of actual spirituality? Jewels and treasures, yes; God, no.

I was raised to believe that the Vatican is a temple in honor of the spoils of war, of human wealth, greed, and power—rather than the titular home of the prophet who preached poverty and nonviolence. Demiel ben Yusef wasn't wrong about all of that.

I sat down at a *pasticceria* to gather my thoughts and get a cappuccino, despite the fact that it was well past breakfast and something no self-respecting Italian would ever drink after 10:00 A.M.

The cappuccino came with a heart elaborately "drawn" on top of the foamy milk with espresso. I smiled up at the waiter, grateful for a tiny bit of civilized normalcy, but the heart made me think of Pantera again, and I fought back the tears. I could only imagine what would happen if I started weeping blood tears outside the Vatican.

It occurred to me that the nun living up in those mountains now might, in fact, be Grethe! It *was* possible that the geneticist/cloner/rogue Catholic nun was not just alive but alive and working behind the scenes.

If so, it meant that so far, of the original people in the Great Experiment, only Pantera had been killed.

The sound on the little TV over the bar was turned up suddenly, and I couldn't help but look up. It was tuned to the news, and I immediately turned away to avoid again seeing the charred body of Pantera being carried out of his flaming car. But a familiar voice made me look back up after a few minutes.

It was Dona. She was doing a stand-up outside the UN.

"Today was perhaps the most explosive day in the extraordinary tribunal of accused terrorist Demiel ben Yusef," she said, her perfect blend of Cockney / rich girl carrying easily over the din of the café. She looked more gorgeous than usual, if possible, in a black coat with her knee-high black boots gleaming in the misting NYC rain.

She continued: "The defendant, ben Yusef, sat once more silent and serene as the most damning witness *yet* for the prosecution, former follower and top adviser Yehuda Kerioth, was called to the stand.

"To get ahead of any of today's testimony, however, last night the veiled woman known only as il Vettore took to the Internet to allege that any testimony we'd hear today from Kerioth would be false.

"She accused ben Yusef's close friend and follower, Kerioth, of a massive betrayal—the result of his having accepted a plea deal."

Dona then cut to last night's video of il Vettore. It was a well-lit, beautifully filmed close-up of a woman's face—or what you could see of her face—the veil of her light blue cotton burqa covering almost everything but her magnificent bright blue eyes, which were heavily rimmed in black kohl.

Il Vettore claimed, in unaccented, almost-American-sounding English, that Kerioth had cut a deal with the international "powers-that-be" (unnamed), in exchange, as Dona had reported, for turning in ben Yusef and testifying against him. She claimed that in doing so he had received a deal that offered both freedom from prosecution and some thirty *million* dollars in gold and silver bullion.

Il Vettore then alleged, "Who is it that paid so exorbitant a price for the head of the Son of the Son?

"This blood-soaked bargain was brokered by a consortium of world leaders, who this day stand in judgment of Him as they will one day be judged *by* Him!"

*Son of the Son? Pantera's terminology!*

Dona came back onscreen. "Neither il Vettore nor any of ben Yusef's followers have ever named even one leader in the alleged plot against ben Yusef. The prosecution has vehemently denied these claims.

"However, the mysterious il Vettore has become a massively popular figure in her own right. The veiled woman has captured the imagination of people around the world, many of whom have taken to the Internet to even speculate that she is ben Yusef's wife, calling her 'the modern Mary Magdalene.' TV pundits have taken to calling her 'Mary ben Magdalene.'

"How popular is the blue-eyed woman behind the veil? As of ten A.M. this morning, before the start of to-day's proceedings, il Vettore's video had clocked in over nine hundred *million* views!

"As for the trial itself, Kerioth took the stand for the prosecution and called his former leader Demiel ben Yusef, quote, 'Hitler, Milosevic, Idi Amin, and bin Laden rolled into one.'

"Defense attorney Randall Mohammed grilled Kerioth on the consortium-for-testimony theory, accusing Kerioth of being a turncoat for profit, a man who is now in the pocket of several world organizations, including a DC-based secret right-wing Christian organization called the Face of God Fellowship or Black Robe, a radical breakaway branch of the Fellowship, whose members include senators and many recent U.S. presidents.

"Since this is a World Court slash United Nations

tribunal and *not* a trial as we know it, he asked Kerioth if he was familiar with a news story in which Fellowship leader Doug Coe had indicated that a personal commitment to Jesus Christ is comparable to the blind devotion that Adolf Hitler, Joseph Stalin, Chairman Mao, and Pol Pot demanded from their followers.

"Kerioth denied ever hearing that claim or having ever met any leader of the Fellowship, its radical arm, the Face of God Fellowship, otherwise known as the Black Robes. Mr. Mohammed then asked the most explosive question of the day—an accusation seemingly without basis: If Kerioth had been contacted or *contracted* by any group anywhere in the world, including the Light of God Tabernacle, headed by the Reverend Bill Teddy Smythe, in exchange for revealing the location of ben Yusef's camp or for testifying against him. Again, Kerioth denied the allegations.

"Finegold then asked him if it was not true that he had knowledge that a so-called consortium of world leaders and secret organizations was in fact actually responsible for the bombings that brought on the quote 'wanton injustices, executions without trial, and ceaseless and grievous cruelty, which have brought an innocent man to this point.'

"'No!' Kerioth countered, jumping from his seat and declaring, 'I do not know any of those groups. It is Demiel ben Yusef's Al Okhowa Al Hamima that is responsible.'

"He further claimed that he witnessed a mass execution of ben Yusef's inner circle, eleven men who *had* tried to escape. He had been the twelfth member.

"'They were, each and every one, carried out by the soldiers of ben Yusef, in the extreme southern portion of Israel, a desert area,' he declared. However, he provided no photographic proof that ben Yusef or the 'Little Big

Man,' as some have started calling him, committed a massacre in the desert or that one had even taken place.

"Judge Bagayoko immediately requested an investigative team of United Nations specialists be dispatched to search the area. This is Dona Grimm reporting from outside the United Nations building in Manhattan."

*Dona said "Little Big Man!" They've got a bead on you. Get the hell out.*

I walked around the winding streets of the Vatican area until I found a car-rental place, and using the bogus credit card, I managed to secure the last rental car they had—another tiny Smart car.

I was grateful for whatever I could get, *but* would it be powerful enough to get me over the mountains and into Manoppello if I had to move faster than the—who?—the CIA, Interpol, this Black Robe God Squad, and everybody else on my ass? Not that I would ever have the DNA so-called proof I needed, now that the white Gap scarf had been incinerated along with Pantera.

*The tears of blood just now? Maybe the tissue has something of value on it.*

I opened it up and, when unfolded, it formed as perfect a heart as the one on my cappuccino.

I tucked it into my bra to keep it close to my heart, got into the car, old-fashioned paper map in hand, refusing to even turn *on* the GPS tracking system. The traffic of Rome was as bad as I'd ever seen it, and negotiating my way out could have earned me a spot on a NASCAR team.

Once I got on the mountain highway heading toward the Abruzzo region, I was able to turn on the radio to the BBC news station. It would be a straight run pretty much from here, and that meant I wouldn't have to check the map every second.

If Dona's testimony report had been a tossed grenade,

the next report was a nuclear attack. I had to hold tight to the wheel and shift into a lower gear to keep from careening right off the slim mountain road.

"Interpol is reporting," said a male voice, "that internationally wanted terrorist Michael Forsythe was killed in a motor vehicle accident in a tunnel at La Turbie, France, this morning.

"The victim, originally identified as Edward Gibbon of Carcassonne, France—one of the many aliases the terror suspect had used in his thirty years on the lam—was involved in a high-speed car chase at the time of the crash."

*Pantera's not dead.*

Then he continued: "International law-enforcement sources have confirmed to the BBC that it was Forsythe who had escaped yesterday after the shootout that left three Interpol agents dead at the castle keep atop Montségur in France."

*He is dead.*

"Michael Forsythe was wanted for multiple counts of murder, forgery, impersonating an officer of the French armed services, aiding and abetting a terrorist group, gun running, kidnapping, and bank fraud. He is credited with funneling nearly one billion pounds sterling into the terrorist group Fratele Meu Iubit, which has ties to Al Okhowa Al Hamima."

*Trust no one.*

"It is also reported that yesterday's shootout may have involved Alessandra Russo, a former *New York Standard* reporter who was traveling with Forsythe after escaping a warrant for the murder of a Catholic priest, Father Eugene Sadowski, in New York City. Russo's identification was obtained from fingerprints on a gun recovered at the scene."

*Toss the gun. Damn, what a sucker! The son of a bitch*

*set me up! But why? Never trust a man who gives you a gun. Why didn't my mother ever teach me that lesson?*

"Witnesses say Russo, a petite brunette in her late thirties or early forties, now has short, very bright red hair. It is believed that she is traveling in France or Italy and is considered armed and very dangerous. Her photo is available at BBC.com. This is Andrew Jennings reporting."

I caught my breath and pulled off the next exit. It was a typical small Italian town, and I was lucky to find a *farmacia* just opening up after the noonday siesta. I slipped on the terrible pink sweatshirt I'd bought back on the New York Thruway and put the hood up.

I searched through the store's very limited selection of hair coloring and found one that looked to be an ash-blond shade. Good enough.

I found an outdoor kiosk and bought a black baseball cap with ROMA scrawled on the front in gray. I then drove through the back streets until I found a motel-type inn a few towns away, and checked in with the cap on my head.

I took the tiny two-person rickety lift to the fourth floor, opened the door of the room, locked it behind me with the giant skeleton key, and walked into the mini room. I opened the shutters a bit and looked down. No cars.

*Calm down. You were practically alone on the highway. Any other cars passed you at 140 km because you couldn't go faster than 85 km. No one exited off the highway behind you, and no one parked near you at the* farmacia. *OK, you're safe for the minute. Concentrate on the task at hand.*

I began to attempt to strip the red color out of my hair. When I rinsed the peroxide out, however, what remained was a mess of dull yellow strings. Worse—it was even more of a bull's-eye than the red hair had been. I applied the second part, the ash-blond color mixture, and prayed I'd look something like Madonna circa 1987. I waited a half hour, stood under the shower, stepped out, and dried my hair with a towel. I was now prematurely gray. Perfect.

*Ladies and gentlemen, put your hands together for international terrorist and legendary actress Jamie Lee Curtis!*

I plopped down on the bed and put my head in my hands.

I looked out the window again by opening the shutter slats. My car was still sitting alone in the little parking lot. I closed the window and the shutters tightly, throwing the room into darkness, and turned on the small table lamp.

*You're no good if you're a wreck. You're safe for the minute, safe for the minute, safe for the minute. . . .*

The old-fashioned room phone blasted me out of my momentary sense of safety.

## 37

*Who the hell found you? Don't pick it up. No, pick it up. The jig is up. No. Do not pick it up!*

After four attempts, the ringing stopped. My heart was racing. I opened the slats of the shutters and tried to look down again. I could only see that there was no way out other than to jump straight down into the parking lot.

*Take a shot and call the front desk. If you're trapped, it can't get worse.* The desk clerk picked right up.

"*Pronto.*"

"*Buon pomeriggio, signore. Ci sono dei messaggi per me? Numero venti?*" I hoped I was making sense, but the man at the desk seemed to understand.

"*Sì, signora.*"

"*Chi?*"

"*La suora. Mow-reena.*"

"*Mi scusi?*"

"How you say? Yes, *la sister* . . ." He pulled the phone away and to his chest to ask a question of someone there.

"*Sì, signora. Suora.* She is the non."

"A nun?"

"*Sì! Sì.* A non."

*Is it the nun from the Manoppello? A trick? What?*

"Did she leave a phone number?" My Italian was completely gone from me now.

Again, the desk clerk put the phone down, and I heard him talking to someone before he handed it over to his "translator."

*Hopefully his colleague speaks English.*

"Hello, Alessandra."

I froze and said nothing.

"It's Maureen. I'm downstairs. May I come up?"

"Downstairs? But how did you—"

"Room twenty—correct? Fourth floor?"

*Black Robe? Headquarters? Rogue agent? Friend? Foe?*

My options were up. I said nothing.

"Good then. I'll be right there."

Five minutes and one slow lift ride later, I heard a light rapping on the door. I looked through the peephole. It was Maureen, all right, but she was dressed as a nun—one of those modern-day nuns complete with the plain dress and giant crucifix dangling over the bodice. Over her dress she wore an equally drab coat, sensible shoes, and a short gray veil, which covered her hair. She was even carrying one of those nondescript black old-lady purses. In her other hand, she was holding a plastic bag from a grocery store.

I would never have recognized her out of her habitat and into this habit. (If that house in Rhinecliff *was* her real habitat, I mean.) Gone was the upright, strong posture and sure presence. In its place stood a little old lady nun. *Sorella Mow-reena.*

I opened the door and she walked in and shook my hand. The power shake more than told me she was still the same lady.

"How did you find me?"

"How did I *not* find you, is the real question," she answered without answering. "I can't believe you turned that phone on in the Vatican! The camera automatically turns on the GPS if you don't change the camera setting. You would never make it as a spy, my dear."

"I will take that as a compliment. Okay then. *Why* did you find me?"

"Because *they* will very soon, and then you'll be dead. For a reporter you leave a very sloppy trail. And spending the night with a—what shall I call him—a source? What an amateurish breach."

I felt myself getting red in the face—partially from embarrassment, as though an actual nun were scolding me, and partially from anger. Who the *hell* was this washed-up old spy to go all moral on me anyway?

"First of all, how the hell do you know *what* I did or didn't do? And secondly, you were a goddamned spy, *Sister* Maureen. For all I know *you* slept with everyone from Idi Amin to Papa Doc. Or would have if it would've helped you infiltrate," I seethed.

*Am I pissed at her for nailing me, or am I ashamed that Pantera screwed me—literally? Calm down. She's old enough to be your mother. Nasty bitch that she is.*

She approached me and stood less than a foot away, a deliberate violation of personal space, and said, "Understand one thing: I never, *never* slept with Duvalier. He was before my time." Then she burst out laughing.

I was totally disarmed. *She made a joke? Can't be. Trust no one. Of course she's disarming—and charming. She had been a damned master spy.*

"My dear, the real difference here is that whatever I did or didn't do, I had the United States of America watching my back. You have, well, only me to watch your back. Other than that, you are completely alone."

"You had the United States watching your back—until they didn't watch it anymore and accused you of being a double agent."

"But they trained me so well, I could even outsmart *them*. While you? You can't even outsmart one pedophile."

"He wasn't a pedophile."

"And you know that—how?"

"He told me. "

*Did he actually say that? No. Worse, did I actually say that? Yes.*

"And, and . . ."

While her expression never changed, it somehow still spelled: *You've been had nine ways 'til next Christmas.*

As quickly as she'd become a wit, she changed back to the dour woman who was all business. "Nonetheless, you trusted a man who committed sins against God and crimes against man. I *know* he must have gotten what he needed, or he wouldn't have left."

I *had* behaved like a fat girl without a date for the prom, sleeping with a man I thought—what?—had fallen in love with me?

*Jerk. Pathetic jerk.*

I averted my eyes and admitted, "Yes. He took my white scarf."

She tilted her head, puzzled. "Your scarf? The one you were wearing at my home?"

"Yes."

She waited for an explanation. "When ben Yusef kissed me?" She nodded. "His kiss was . . . it left my mouth, you know, wet. So I wiped it with the scarf."

"Dear Jesus in heaven! DNA. Pantera wanted to compare it to the source blood."

"But now he's dead."

"But now he's dead," she repeated.

"You don't think he faked it this time, do you? His death?"

"Is that hope or dread I read in your face?"

"Both. Pantera's got the scarf, so that's hope—*if* he's alive. But if he's not, both the scarf and the man are incinerated and wiped out forever." I somehow couldn't bring myself to say "dead" and his name in the same sentence. *Fool.*

She switched the subject. "We have to leave here. Now. The world is about to be rocked off its foundations"— she checked her watch—"in about ten minutes. But regardless of that, this place isn't safe for you—*now.*"

"Why, what's happening?" I demanded.

"Ben Yusef. He's going to make an announcement. From prison."

"Are you sure?"

She gave me that look again.

"Okay . . . and?"

"I think it will not just alter the course of his tribunal but the course of the world—one whose end, it seems, has already begun."

"Excuse me?"

"Tsunamis, earthquakes, routine class-five hurricanes, tornadoes, and volcanic eruptions, for starters, have already become commonplace—no? Anyone who thinks the end hasn't begun is a fool. What he says today may hasten it—that's all. Unless you can *prove* before they kill him that he is indeed the cloned Son of the Son of God! Perhaps you can rally those who believe in Jesus to rise up."

"Do you believe he is the Son of the Son?"

"I saw the children from the UN," she answered. "I saw them."

"How? I thought they were now hidden away and only Judge Bagayoko has seen them."

She just looked at me. *Right.*

The subject was changed. "I assume you have a lead on the source blood or you wouldn't be heading north. The mountains?" she asked.

"Yes. I think it may be in Manoppello—a small town in Abruzzo. In a monastery there."

"And how do you know this?"

"Reporters investigate," I said, playing her game her way. She let it go and opened the plastic bag she'd brought with her. Inside was a nun's veil, a gray dress, some sensible shoes, and a bottle. She held it up. Instant tanning lotion. "You really *will* be a 'sister' now."

*How many times in one lifetime—or make that one week—am I going to dress up like a nun? I'm like a fetish hooker.*

I went into the little bathroom and applied the tanning liquid by the dim light of the bathroom fixture. In Italy the ceilings and the light fixtures are all too high to cast any decent light for you to actually see anything very well in a mirror. But from what I could make out, I didn't look tan, I looked African-American.

"You forgot your hands," she said, sticking her head into the bathroom. "Black women do not have white hands." She took the bottle and rubbed the tops of my hands and handed me the clothes. "Now put these on," she said, before washing the tanning lotion off her own palms.

As I slipped the dress on, Maureen took her gun out of her little-old-lady purse, walked to the window, and opened the shutter slats a hair to survey the area below. "Hurry now."

I slipped into the clothes, and she helped me attach the veil and hung a crucifix around my neck. "I'll divert the clerk. You take the next lift."

When I came back down to the lobby, the clerk was

nowhere to be seen and Maureen directed me to a non-descript black car parked across the street, and we got in. "It has an Alfa engine; don't worry," she said.

"My rental car . . ."

She just looked exasperated at my idiotic compulsive-ness as she started her car.

## 38

The minute we got back on the highway, I heard a loud explosion in the area of the motel.

"The car?" She said nothing.

We could also hear gunfire from towns around us and small fires blazing in the trees on the mountainsides. She pushed the pedal to the floor and accelerated to a dangerous speed.

"It's begun," she said, and turned on the radio.

She switched to BBC.

"Ben Yusef. He's about to do it."

From his jail cell, the voice of Demiel ben Yusef was clear and strong, even though he'd been fasting for what must have been at least forty days by then.

"Now that I am about to give up the shell in which I have been entombed in this lifetime," he said, "neither do I refute nor admit to the charges against me. Only God, my parent, can judge me.

"Do not mourn me, nor exalt me, and do not kill in my name. You cannot mourn me, for I will never die. As you will never die—no matter what you fear in the coming days.

"Death is just an altered state of being. Life after life is the normal state. Everyone who is alive is already dead and also now alive. Understand this and fear death no more.

"If you believe in the concept of life—the undeniable fact that humans are born from the love of two people, and from that coming together you were made flesh, each with hands and eyes and organs and blood and minds and hearts, then you do believe in the concept of life.

"The very idea of life itself is so complex that anything and *everything* that comes after the creation of life is simple. And ongoing.

"If you know life, you already know the unending wheel of life and death. You already know God. The spirit that is *you* continues with you and around you after you give up the shell of the human body.

"So I too will be with you and all around you. Just look and you will find me. I am everywhere. In the trees, the air, the sun. I return to the home of my parent, yet I will remain with you.

"I beg you not to fear what is coming in the next days.

"The gift of the earth, like all life itself, has a cycle of life and death. Has it been hastened by the hand of humans who corrupted it, polluted it, sickened it?

"Meditate on this: You took the great oceans and made them filthy and then claimed they were clean. You took the fertile fields and made them give up barren fruit. Instead of following the natural and perfect order, the fields were not allowed to lie fallow in rotation—even though by divine design, all things must be allowed to rest to renew—each on its own Sabbath.

"You developed chemicals and killed the mother that fed you. You have reaped the harvest of that death by growing obese while wasting away in mind and body.

"You took God's very spark of life—the atom—and split it. It is as though you split your own child in half. Then when it became the monster that is destroying its own mother, the earth, by spewing Her with its toxic breath—radiation—you react with surprise and shock.

"You are still shocked at every nuclear reactor that melts down. Why? For everything there is a season.

"You refuse to believe that when you take you must give back or you lose it all. That is the law of all things in nature.

"Know this: My blood—the blood of Christ—can*not* die. I shall, like my parent before me, rise again. And again and again—for the blood that made me lives as surely as does the blood that runs in your veins. So do not lose faith in the Lord, our God.

"The blood of my parent that runs in my veins and remains here on earth is the only measure against the end of days. It is all that remains to restore the earth to its former grandeur.

"So I implore you: Do not mourn me in the coming days. Nor mourn your loved ones who will pass. Instead contemplate the words of the Creator, our parent, and only then can you truly love God. Only then can you be saved.

"*For I am the first and the last.*
*I am the honored one and the scorned one.*
*I am the whore and the holy one.*
*I am the wife and the virgin. . . .*
*I am the barren one*
  *and many are her sons. . . .*
*I am she whose wedding is great,*
  *and I have not taken a husband.*

*I am the midwife and she who does not bear.*
*I am the solace of my labor pains.*
*I am the bride and the bridegroom,*
*    and it is my husband who begot me.*
*I am the mother of my father*
*    and the sister of my husband,*
*    and he is my offspring.*
*I am the slave of him who prepared me.*
*I am the ruler of my offspring.*
*    But he is the one who [begot me] before the time*
*        on a birthday.*
*    And he is my offspring [in] (due) time,*
*        and my power is from him.*
*I am the staff of his power in his youth,*
*    [and] he is the rod of my old age.*
*    And whatever he wills happens to me.*
*I am the silence that is incomprehensible*
*    and the idea whose remembrance is frequent.*
*I am the voice whose sound is manifold*
*    and the word whose appearance is multiple.*
*I am the utterance of my name.*

"In love I came to you, and in love I leave you."

The voice of the BBC announcer came on. "Those were the first and, by the sound of it, the last words that will be spoken by the thus-far-silent Demiel ben Yusef, the man on trial for terrorism and crimes against humanity.

"We have with us a panel of religious and political experts here to interpret the words of the suspected terrorist. Nut job or prophet?"

Maureen turned off the radio. "I'm amazed that he chose to recite that passage from the Nag Hammadi library. It's called, 'The Thunder, Perfect Mind.' He knows how to manipulate the people enough to have used just some parts and not others."

"Nag Hammadi—that's where the Gnostic gospels were found in the 1940s in Egypt, right?"

"In 1945 to be exact. Fifty-two tractates about Jesus Christ that were uncovered by Arab peasant farmers, including one named 'Alī al-Sammān, at the base of the Jabal al-Tarif, a cliff near the town of Hamrah Dawm in Egypt. While digging for fertilizer near a giant boulder, they hit an earthen jug. They dug it out. Huge. Six feet high.

"Inside of this enormous jug was a stack of books produced sometime in the fourth century AD. None of the fifty-two tractates in the thirteen leather-bound books they found are included in the New Testament. He was digging for fertilizer, thought he'd found gold—and was disappointed it turned out to be just leather-bound papyrus."

"But worth its weight in gold, though."

"More than that. They are considered to be the most important find of the modern age, in fact. You see, these are allegedly the words of the private Jesus—mystical teachings he imparted to his closest disciples. They are not the sermons he gave for the multitudes."

"So was 'Alī al-Sammān the Chosen One of his day?"

"Perhaps—if you believe the words in the books are the words of Jesus. I, for one do not. And 'Alī al-Sammān? Hardly what you'd call a visionary. In fact, after bringing these extraordinary lost books home, his mother used some pages as kindling for the home fires. Shortly after that, according to 'Alī al-Sammān himself, he and his brothers set forth to avenge the death of their father by another local."

"And?"

"He said they found him, hacked off his limbs, ripped his heart out, and proceeded to eat it. Then, fearing they'd be caught and needing money, they sold what was left of the books on the black market."

"Wow."

"So while you are a Chosen One yourself, it's not necessarily because of your specialness."

"Thanks, I appreciate it. Anyway, I don't think I'm special as much as cursed at this point. Unless I get a great story out of it . . ."

"Well, hurry up with that. I think ben Yusef just announced the end of the world."

"Or maybe the beginning."

"You mean his reference to 'again and again'?"

"Yes. I think he meant, if I'm not mistaken, that the source blood, if we find it, will be his resurrection."

"So you believe that he *is* indeed the clone of Jesus?"

"I've come to believe that he's not evil, if that means anything. I believe that he wasn't responsible for those atrocities. Is he the Son of the Son? Hell, I don't know. But I know I need to find out for myself."

As we came over the next rise, the traffic, which had been nonexistent a moment earlier, was now at a dead stop. Up ahead red lights were flashing, sirens were blaring, and a lot of angry Italians were standing outside their cars and cursing.

"Roadblock. That would be for you, my dear."

"Oh, crap—as they *don't* say in the Nag Hammadi."

We inched our way up car by car until we were five or six from the roadblock itself and the inspection of our vehicle.

"I have this fake passport and license. . . ."

"I just need to show my license and you can show yours if asked. We are just a couple of nuns traveling to see the various churches in the area. You don't even need to show your passport—no reason you'd be carrying it around for a car ride. Got it?"

"Got it."

As we approached the roadblock, a news flash came on the radio and every Italian standing outside his or her car, previously cursing and yelling, grew silent to listen. Even the cops stopped checking IDs momentarily.

"Another message? You mean he didn't finish?" I ventured.

Instead, a reporter from the BBC came on breathlessly to announce, "Chief Judge Fatoumata Bagayoko, president of the United Nation's Special International Criminal Court, has entered the General Assembly room, temporary home of the ben Yusef tribunal, to make a special announcement."

Even Maureen's eyes widened. If we hadn't already been at a standstill, I think she would have slammed on the brakes.

The voice of Bagayoko came on clear but not strong. She sounded—what?—defeated.

"Good day, ladies and gentlemen. First let me thank you all for attending the tribunal these past days and reporting the facts as accurately as humanly possible. It is, however, my sad duty to inform you that due to a gross and unforgivable breach on my part, I will not be able to continue in my role as chief judge of the most important tribunal in modern history."

*What the—?*

"Because I was moved to visit the children who were victims of the terrorist bombings allegedly masterminded by Demiel ben Yusef—children you all saw for yourselves in court on the first day of the tribunal—and then to make a public declaration about it, I tainted the process. I went so far as to declare that they had been healed after being prayed for by ben Yusef.

"I therefore can no longer serve as a fair and impartial overseer of these proceedings. For as God is my witness, I *am* no longer impartial.

"These actions, along with my deep conviction, after witnessing the healings of the children, that Demiel ben Yusef is not an ordinary human being, have been deemed by those who sit with me in this tribunal to be a breach of ethics and protocol. And they are correct.

"I therefore bow to their wisdom and remove myself from the position of chief judge of this tribunal and beg the pardon of everyone who has worked so tirelessly to see that justice is done in this case. I wash my hands of these proceedings and retire to contemplate my misconduct in solitude."

"Wow," I said, turning to Maureen. "She didn't just say she washes her hands of the whole thing, did she?"

"Yes, she most certainly did."

Just then the world came back to order—or make that chaos—and the stuck motorists, instead of returning to their vehicles, ran to hug and confer with one another outside of their cars. We heard another explosion in the distance.

The cops were trying without success to get the traffic moving again when the BBC announcer brought on the usual suspect talking heads.

"Do you believe that the extraordinary removal of Judge Fatoumata Bagayoko from the United Nations Special International Criminal Court proceedings could potentially lead to a mistrial?" the reporter asked.

A jurist from some country or other answered, "Yes, Carter, I do believe that we are looking at exactly such a possibility. The chief judge just said in no uncertain terms that after seeing the children she was no longer impartial. She even said that the defendant is 'no ordinary human being'! Shocking, really."

Said another panelist, "It's practically a guarantee that this is going to be declared a mistrial. . . ."

"Or a mis*tribunal*, in this case," someone else quipped.

At that point Maureen got out of the car herself and decided to be proactive. A real Yusef move, I thought.

She was speaking in Italian to one of the frustrated cops, and I could see her pointing and gesturing like mad, as I sat there in my new role as a black Catholic nun. The cop came with her to the car and looked in. He asked for my credentials in Italian, and I just sat there paralyzed as to what the right thing to do was.

"She's from Guatemala," Maureen said in Italian. And then she said something to me in some language or other, which I assumed meant, "Pretend to reach for your documentation." I opened her black purse and fished around until the cop grew impatient, what with hundreds of cars backed up behind us. Instead, he mumbled something, Maureen got back in the car, and he let us and the five cars ahead of us go through the roadblock, stopping the car immediately behind us for an inspection.

"Nice work," I said, trying to high-five her but immediately realizing this wasn't exactly what two nuns would do. My hand stayed in the air and I pretended to adjust the veil.

We drove up the mountains, glued to the news on BBC. Dona came on to report that the Reverend Smythe had taken the platform in Dag Hammarskjöld Plaza to address the crowds, which, if possible, had only grown bigger and more unruly than they had been on day one.

"I wonder what the old bastard has to say," I said aloud.

*Is that a look of disgust that passed over Maureen's face? Wow. She must really hate the guy.*

"Now we take you directly to Dag Hammarskjöld Plaza and Reverend Smythe," Dona reported.

To the roar of what sounded like hundreds of thousands of people, the reverend began: "Today, the devil himself rose from the depths of hell and began the process of destroying the living Christ within you.

"When Judge Bagayoko declared that Demiel ben Yusef, who is the personification of evil on earth, was a healer and *not* a destroyer, she revealed herself to be the devil's own concubine.

"Do not rest believing that the devil failed because the other fair-minded jurists saw fit to throw this whore of Babylon off the throne. They too are just as likely to become possessed by the human Satan, Demiel ben Yusef.

"Do you believe those children—his legless, blind, and burned victims—were really healed? No! Those were media tricks by the infidels. No one believing in the Christ Almighty was fooled by their chicanery. No one in their right mind would believe those fools, magicians, liars, and murderers.

"Those poor children were whisked away and killed by Demiel ben Yusef's minions who do his bidding. The mainstream media is playing a vicious game with you— one in which other children were flown in to replace them. I know this. Do not, I repeat, *do not* let Demiel ben Yusef, the devil incarnate, walk away free to destroy the world. Because, my fellow believers in Christ, that is what ben Yusef, Bagayoko, and all those who hate Jesus are doing.

"Those who trespass are but the evidence, the mirror that shows us that men and women who live without Christ are lost, eternally lost, condemned, damned to follow the serpent! Do not be swayed by the words of sinners.

"'You shall not yield to him or listen to him, nor shall your eye pity him, nor shall you spare him, nor shall you conceal him; but you shall kill him; your hand shall be first against him to put him to death, and afterwards the hand of all the people. You shall stone him to death with stones.'

"All people must rise up against this false god and his followers. Demiel ben Yusef—I repeat, and I beg you to understand and take action—is none other than the devil incarnate!"

Dona returned to the air amid thunderous applause and what sounded like mad rioting.

"The Reverend Bill Teddy Smythe's supporters have begun to clash wildly with ben Yusef's supporters, and the whole of Dag Hammarskjöld Plaza up as far as I can see to the United Nations is in a riot situation! It is total bedlam," she screamed into the microphone above the roar.

Just then gunfire broke out, and Dona screamed, "The riot police on horseback have entered the park! Horses are trampling the—"

Then nothing—the station went dead. "Oh, my God! Dona! What happened to Dona?" I screamed in the car, burying my hands in my face. Maureen leaned over and patted my hand.

"These are terrible times, and the police are on the scene. . . ."

Instead the radio made all kinds of old-fashioned crackling noises before we heard the voice of il Vettore, whose group had pirated the station and, I later learned, all the radio frequencies in the world.

"Stop in the name of Demiel ben Yusef," she declared. "The rioting, the killing, the torchings, the bombings that have already begun must stop immediately. Stop in the name of the Son of the Son, I beg you!

"Everything you are doing is against everything, *everything* that Demiel has preached. He just implored you to not die in his name, nor to kill in His name—nor in the name of any person, church, or religious institution.

"The tribunal will continue regardless of the inhumanity of man against man. This is not a process you—or any human—can stop. If Demiel must die, as He said He would, then please let Him die a man of peace. Let Him die in the peace of our Lord, knowing that He left the earth better for His being here than worse than before He came to us.

"Do not, I beg you, listen to false prophets like the Reverend Bill Teddy Smythe," she continued, choking back tears. "He proclaims war against all who do not believe in Jesus. He is wrong. Do not take up arms in the name of Jesus or His Son. Do not take up arms against one another. In the name of the Son of the Son of God, I beg you, do not allow killing, profiteering, power mongering, or hatred to sully His name and destroy everything He worked for."

The radio went silent again, and so did Maureen and I as we each contemplated what we'd just heard as we drove the next two and a half hours through the mountains, with hillsides ablaze on either side, overturned cars, and burned-out towns and beautiful vacation homes being torched in the distance.

"Armageddon doesn't happen in a day," I finally said to Maureen as we drove off the Alanno-Scafa exit.

As we passed through the unmanned tollbooth, we narrowly avoided running over the corpses of two *carabinieri* lying directly in front of the booths.

Maureen sped up and we pulled off the highway, tires

squealing, onto the local road. People were running amok through the first small town we came to, some smashing windows, others holding torches like some old *Frankenstein* movie, setting fire to the local police station.

Because of the congestion of people in the road, we slowed down to a crawl.

"Get ready . . ." Maureen said as she accelerated slightly. Instead of people being mowed down and climbing onto our car in fury, as I thought they would, the crowds instead parted, and on either side of the car people knelt down and made the double sign of the cross as we passed.

*"Salvatore del Salvatori! Dio vi benedica! Filius Salvatori! Dio vi benedica,"* they called as they bowed before us. Maureen just looked at me calmly.

"You really *are* the one picked by fate to save the Savior's Son! Even these people who have never laid eyes on you before stopped the chaos for a moment to pay homage. Extraordinary, really."

"This is so weird and so creepy I can't stand it."

"Why?"

"This business of crowds bowing and crossing— happened to me once before. After I left your house in Rhinecliff."

She didn't answer, so I continued: "This crossing twice, do you think that's what the term *double-cross* means?"

"Perhaps."

"The Cathars—those folks who were burned in the thirteenth century?—they double-crossed the Crusaders by sneaking away in the middle of the night under the very noses of their occupiers."

She just looked at me briefly without answering and then went back to concentrating on driving through the crowd without running anyone down.

I pushed. "No, I mean, are you sure it isn't *you* who they are bowing before? It only happens when I'm near or around *you*, Maureen."

She just looked at me and kept on slowly and very, very carefully driving out of the burning village.

## 39

The drive from the Alanno-Scafa exit to the town of Manoppello took another forty minutes, given the narrowness of the road and the fires burning randomly but fiercely in the wooded areas as well in many towns along the route.

We followed the signs leading to the sanctuary, and drove into a village square dominated by a strange-looking monastery church. Yes. Finally, the church of the Capuchin friars on the Tarigni hill outside Manoppello. From the front at least, it looked like a kid's drawing of a church—except the entire façade was inset with a repeating pattern of dark stone crosses, broken only by a giant rose window and a steeple on the side of the building.

Think classic medieval church gone Pop Art—even though it was built two hundred years after the Middle Ages and three hundred before pop anything.

*What the heck is this thing?*

The tiny town was quiet. Too quiet. While rioting and burnings were going on in the surrounding towns and villages, this one was so still it was as though the apocalypse had already come and gone and no one had been left standing.

Maureen stopped the car in front of the church, and I got out. "Coming in?"

"No, I'd better stay with the car—just in case."

"I wouldn't worry about it. It looks like everyone's skipped town."

"Trust no one. Remember?"

"Right." I turned back. "I assume that includes you?"

"That includes me."

I walked up the seven or eight wide stone steps leading to the entrance and tried to open the church doors, but they were all locked.

I turned back to look at the town. Nothing. Just Maureen in her nondescript, now that I think about it, cop-looking car.

*Maybe everybody fled to escape the rioters—or to join them.*

There was a tiny hotel right next to the monastery, so I walked back down and looked in the windows. I tried the door despite the fact that there was a sign in the window reading CHIUSO!!! ("Closed!!!")

From the lower vantage point, looking up, I noticed that the monastery church had a tiny gift shop attached on the hotel side and that a window was slightly open.

*Is that a monk peeking out the window? Definitely. That's definitely a monk.*

A brown hood obscured the monk's face. It almost looked as though he didn't have a face. Nonetheless, I waved and walked back toward him and, taking my chances, used the nun's name. *"Dove posso trovare la suora che si chiama Grethe?"*

He opened the leaded window slightly and gestured

with his hand to the mountain. Then: "*La suora vive nella piccola casa sulla montagna,*" meaning that—yes!—Sister Grethe did live up on the mountain!

He abruptly closed the small window, and I saw a tiny point of red light on my chest. A laser site.

*Get your ass in gear, lady.*

I made a quick, if deliberately measured walk back to the car and opened the door and got in.

"Damn! There's a monk in the window and he's packing heat," I barked at Maureen, trying to catch my breath. "I don't know whether we can trust him, but he said to go up that mountain road. The nun supposedly lives up there. By the looks of some of those big houses, it must be the smallest house on the mountain—easy to find. If not, and we knock on the wrong door, we get our heads shot off by some very rightfully paranoid Italians."

We made our way up the dusty mountain road, and there wasn't a soul to be seen either in any of the upscale vacation homes or even in smaller year-round houses dotting the mountainside. All shut up tight. It was impossible to see if anyone was there, because all the window gates were closed tight and even some of the front doors had giant bars and homemade devices across the front to keep out marauders.

We drove farther and farther up, the road getting more and more winding, until suddenly amid the ghost hill of houses, a tiny stucco cottage came into view—its front door ajar, the windows wide open.

Pristine white linen curtains were flapping slightly in the balmy spring breeze. I could hear singing and the sound of an organ coming from inside.

"Stop the car! Stop the car!"

Maureen slowed then stopped the car and put on the emergency brake to prevent us from rolling backward.

The singing stopped, although the organ music continued. As we were looking up at the house, a nun in full habit stepped out onto the tiny porch and looked at us. She was in her late sixties and squinted against the sun to get a better look.

"That's her!" Maureen cried. "Grethe. The mad scientist. Literally! She's still wearing the Carmelite habit despite being defrocked decades ago."

If ever anyone didn't look like a mad scientist or defrocked nun, it was that lady standing on the porch. She looked, if anything, like a little old lady who'd given her life to Jesus.

Or maybe like a nonkilling version of Maureen. I opened the car door and again Maureen declined to join me as I walked up the path to her house. In fact, she ducked down in the seat.

*Will the nun buy this cheesy nun outfit?*

She looked me over carefully, not giving an inch, studying my face as I studied hers in turn.

*I've seen that look before. Right. In every subway car in New York. A genuine nut job.*

She leaned on the railing and simply said, in a *very* thick German accent, "The end has begun. Don't you see? Oh, yes."

Then she touched my face the way a blind person would—to "see" me with her fingers.

"Soon they'll be here, *cara* Alazais. They'll come for me. *Sie werden mein Junge bald töten!*"

"How do you know my name?"

*It's not your name—remember? Not your name.*

The nun began to weep then. "They will kill my boy soon." She looked down uncomprehendingly at the rosary hanging down the front of her habit and mumbled, "*Sie werden unser Gott bald töten . . .* They will kill our Lord."

She squinted at the car, but Maureen was down enough so that she wasn't visible. She moved to the threshold of her front door and gestured for me to enter.

The cottage was a tiny two-room affair. The front room was unfurnished save for a small cot, an easel with a painting-in-progress of Armageddon, and a table with a microscope on it. There were many large and small icons on the walls, floor, and on every available inch of space. They all had one theme: the Holy Face of Manoppello. It smelled of oil paint and turpentine.

She ushered me into the back room, which had a Pullman kitchen, a state-of-the-art computer, an electron microscope, and what looked like right-this-second medical testing equipment.

The back wall was made up of skinny metal drawers—the kind that hold medical slides or photos. Each was marked in symbols I'd never seen before.

Off the back of the house was an enclosed porch with candles and incense burning on a small altar.

"Did he give you the sample?" Grethe implored, still searching my face for—what?

"Who do you mean?"

"Jacobi. The priest. Did he give you anything?"

"You mean Father Paulo?"

"Ha. Lying scum," she spit out, her German accent getting thicker by the second. "Almost ruined the entire Experiment. Him and that filthy soldier. Two badt ones—yes, very, very badt!"

*How did this group ever spend time together without killing one another?*

"Well, I had a test tube with blood. . . ."

"Yes! Yes! Give it now to me," she sang almost like a little ditty, as she clapped her hands and began a little jig.

*So nuts.*

"I don't have it. It broke."

"What does this mean?" she wailed, and began keening in that "ululu" way the Iraqi women did over their dead during the war.

"It got crushed under, ah, a boot."

She grabbed me by the sleeve and tugged violently. "Why were you so careless? Why did you let him have it?" Tears were pouring down her face, and she began rending the fabric of her habit.

"I didn't. The test tube was in the safekeeping of a friend of his, in, ah, in a carpet shop. In Istanbul."

The nun stopped dead and turned on her heel and stared at me.

"Headquarters entrusted that, that, drug-addict *pig* to hold on to the precious cord blood? Noooooo. Impossible. Quite impossible." She ripped the top portion of her habit, and it hung down over her bodice while she rocked back and forth, crying and keening.

As quickly as it started, the hysteria stopped. Grethe wiped her eyes and stood up as though none of that had just happened.

"So you have other proof?" she asked crisply. "Didn't Paulo give you anything else? Did he?" she asked hopefully.

"No, but see, I met Yusef Pantera and—"

She cut me off midsentence and menaced me with her balled-up fist, causing me to take a few steps back. Good thing, because the little old nun spat a big one right on the floor between us.

"Filthy! Filthy fornicator. Filthy."

*I don't know about the filthy, but, yes, he was a helluva fornicator.*

Grethe then took my hand and led me out to her little altar, knelt down, and began a fevered, fervent prayer.

She got up again and said, "You took the veil? When?"

I told her the truth, that no, I wasn't a nun, and that a friend had given me the habit to help us slip through roadblocks.

Grethe ignored me and bade me to continue my story. When I told her that Pantera had taken the scarf with Demiel's DNA on it, she calmed down.

"He is scum. But he loves the boy."

"But he died. In a car accident this morning."

She seemed to shrink before my eyes with sadness. Then, regaining her calm demeanor once again, she simply said, "Sit," and pushed me down onto the chair at her computer. "Write."

"Write what?"

"The greatest story ever told in modern times. It will remain somewhere in cyberspace after the end of days."

"And you *are* convinced the world will end?"

"Yes, yes, maybe when they kill the Boy. The Boy will be executed in the next day."

"I don't understand. Haven't you been listening to the news? It looks like a mistrial. He's safe—at least for the moment."

She leaned down and put her face an inch from mine at the computer. "No, no, *no!* He *will* die! But he will rise again. I will *make* him rise again. That is the next resurrection. Now you write it down, Alazais Roussel."

"Can I ask you something? Why does everyone call me that?"

"Because that's who you were and that's who you are. A Cathar. Like the first Alazais Roussel. Saved the Veil. Escaped—bless her—with the Veil, the treasure, to Italy. Yah. That is you. You come from her—carry her DNA. Descended from her. She fled with the others to Italy. You remember?"

*The dream. It was a* recollection, *not a dream.*

She pushed me from the keyboard, keyed in something, and a JPEG of the tapestry I'd seen in the Restaurant Costes popped up.

"Yah. You—no?" she said, pointing out the woman in the foreground with the sack at her waist and the knife in her belt.

*That's why I had déjà vu when I looked at it. Looks like me.*

She leaned back down over my shoulder and began *her* version of the story of the birth of Demiel ben Yusef. Her version was at once similar and yet very different from the book that was still sitting in my red satchel.

*I wonder if Maureen is taking this opportunity to go snooping. Of course she is. What the hell, we're all in this together. I guess.*

"Theotokos Meryemana Bienheureux, Mother of the new Jesus, Demiel ben Yusef, had been groomed for this honor from the time of her own birth, as had all girls born into the line of Mary of Magdala since the beginning," she began.

"The Girl, Theotokos, was the right age; she had already had her first bleeding and at twelve years old was small in stature but able to bring a pregnancy to full term."

I could feel the bile rising in my throat at what this crazy nun was saying.

*Twelve? Jee-sus Christ.*

"I implanted the embryonic clone of Jesus into the Girl, and when it was determined to be a success, the filthy priest, and Pantera, Theotokos, and I all moved into the Virgin's house in Selçuk. We stayed there during her confinement." She made the double sign of the cross and looked to heaven.

I felt a fool even asking the next question but did anyway. "Where did the DNA of Jesus come from?"

"*Das Heiligen Gesicht, natürlich.* The Holy Face."

It came from the so-called Veil of Veronica!

I didn't ask *which* one of the existing Veils just yet, but since she was living up the mountain from the monastery where one was kept, I didn't need to.

"But the Girl, Theotokos. Oh, what a stubborn girl. Wild and unruly. I felt—God and Headquarters, forgive me—I thought they might have made a mistake. But I never said this aloud of course. No, no, no, no . . ."

She looked to me for confirmation, so I nodded my head. "Of course not, no."

"When the blessed day came," she continued, breathing down my neck now as I typed, "the Girl, after much hysterical crying and unnecessary carryings-on, delivered our Lord!

"It was all gloriously planned—until three intruders came during the blackout—and then soon the whole world was hunting us like we were wild beasts or monsters."

*You are.*

"What about the plane you were supposed to have escaped in?"

"Oh, no, that was a drone. Yusef took the girl to live with him. I was assigned to be her guardian, but he threw me to the curb when she was but seventeen years old."

*Bastard.*

I kept writing and trying to look down at the keyboard. But as crazy as Grethe was, she spotted the look of disgust on my face and said, "I have nothing to apologize to the likes of you for—you are merely the worker. The worker!

"You are simpleminded, poor thing, simpleminded. Don't you understand?"

*No, not really. And you, lady, are a big nut job!*

"We had to have everything *exactly* as it was the first time. To see if it was all destined to be the same again. Don't you see? The Virgin Mother was most probably only thirteen when she delivered the Infant Jesus—and so was Theotokos. It was good, don't you see?"

"Oh, of course," I lied. "Please continue. I have one question, though. Why Yusef Pantera? He seems an unlikely Joseph in this scenario."

"Oh, oh, oh. It *had* to be Pantera. Had to. Had to. You see, Pantera is from the line of Tiberius Iulius Abdes Pantera. But not like his ancestor at all. No, no, no."

"Who?"

"Tiberius Iulius Abdes Pantera, a mercenary soldier that many of his kind still believe had been the one who impregnated the Virgin. But noooo, no, no, no, no, no, no. That's wrong. He was her protector, not an impregnator, *not* a fornicator!"

*She's so insane, I can't believe it.*

Grethe then shoved me aside hard and punched in a code on her computer. Photos from a locked archive popped up. First up was a JPEG of a little girl, nearly dead, nursing a sweet little brown baby.

*Demiel?*

Then came a photo of a young Paulo and Grethe looking rapturous as they leaned down and gazed upon the Baby. Other JPEGs showed Pantera, with flak jacket and guns, standing next to the Girl and the Baby, looking angry. Or at least distracted.

Much to my amazement, the next set of photos showed the three young astronomers who had made their way to the house: Gaspar, Mikaeel, and Balaaditya. I recognized them from those old photos in that faxed article Dona had sent.

They stood there stiffly in their religious garments inside the little house holding their boxes. There was a final photo: Theotokos, Yusef, and Demiel, twelve years later. The caption read: "Jerusalem, 1994." Somehow they almost looked like a real family. Pantera looked almost the same, and the child had grown into a twenty-four-year-old woman—or so it seemed: She was in a burqa with everything but her bright blue eyes covered.

*What is this? The second-greatest story ever told? For sure, it's definitely the weirdest.*

"The Veil," I said. "Does it still exist?"

She looked at me as though I were the one who was crazy as a loon. "Of course it does. You must think me a fool!"

"Well, no, of course not. It's just—"

"Tomorrow. I will take you tomorrow." She looked at her watch and giggled in that crazy way again. "It already is tomorrow. But I will take you after seven o'clock mass."

"I will see you at the church, then."

She turned on me like I'd just cursed her and her entire family.

"It's not just a church!" she seethed.

"I ah, I—"

"No, no, no, no. It is *Basilica* del Volto Santo. Pope Benedict XVI came and prayed before the Holy Face of our Lord Jesus and then two weeks later he elevated the little *santuario* to a papal basilica."

"When was that?" I asked, surprised. I knew he'd visited, but to elevate this obscure church to a basilica? I mean, Saint Peter's is a basilica.

"In 2006. Only the pope has the right to do that, you know. You know that—yah?"

When I looked perplexed, she narrowed her eyes at me and said, "How could you come here and know nothing?"

When she turned away, anger boiling over, I discreetly placed the cursor on the "send" tab of her computer, and sent the document to my Hotmail account.

I tried to change the subject. "The hotel is closed. Do you know where I can sleep?"

"Our Lord likes to sleep in his car."

"Right."

I heard another explosion in the distance. *The world is coming undone, and my last night is going to be spent with an ex-spy sleeping in a car in front of a crazy nun's house in the mountains next to a monastery holding the greatest relic in all of Christendom.*

*OK. I can live with that. A reporter's dream, really.*

## 40

I made my way back down the dirt path to the car. Maureen, I wasn't surprised to see, was sitting upright in the car, not even close to being asleep at the wheel. She had taken out her mobile device and was reading something or other.

I saw the light of the device go out as I approached the car. She unlocked the door and I got back in.

"Looks like we'll be spending the night in the car," I said.

She patted my hand. "No—I've managed to get them to open up a room at the hotel."

"How . . . ?"

"Not to worry. It's only one room but it's better than sleeping in the car."

"You bet. I feel like I haven't showered in three years."

As she turned the car around she began peppering me with questions about what Sister Grethe had to say. I had the impression that it was a mere formality on her part and that she already knew everything we'd said.

"You were listening in somehow, weren't you?"

"Of course. She's quite insane. And violent. I couldn't let you be alone with her. God only knows what she's capable of. Well, I take that back. We know what she's capable of. Dr. Frankenstein in Carmelite clothing."

"But I thought you now believed that ben Yusef—"

She cut me off as we rounded a particularly sharp curve on the mountain road. "I believe it, yes, but that doesn't mean she had the right to create a human clone—no matter whose DNA it was. What they did was monstrous. But what *I* did on orders from the CIA—and I know this to be true now—was monstrous as well. Now I have no choice but to try to help you save the life of the Son of the Son—do I?"

"You do, yes, but it seems that I don't. Have a choice in the matter, I mean. So, if I haven't said it before, I want you to know that I appreciate that you are here for me. For Him. For whoever."

As we made the next severe curve on the one-lane mountain road in the dark, we barely escaped a brush fire that was starting up on the hill right next to the road.

"I hope Sister Grethe is all right," I said, getting my breath back. "I think we should turn around and force her to come with us."

"She'll be fine. She knows these hills and woods better than a tracking dog. If she senses danger, I'm sure she's fully prepared."

"Why would you think such a thing? I mean, she's an old lady."

"Because I'm an old lady, too. We were both soldiers on different sides of the same war, and she's about the toughest lady I've ever come across."

"I thought you never met—"

"We never have. But when you're on opposite sides of a conflict, you had better know not only exactly how your enemy thinks, feels, and moves, you had better for damned sure know exactly what she looks like—no matter what disguises she puts on."

Truly, I was still an infant in this grown-up game that had been going on for at least two thousand years. Who was my enemy? And what disguises were they wearing? Oh, right, no disguise. Just a naked muscular body on a man at least fifteen years my senior.

*Moron!*

"I wonder how Grethe would feel if she knew you were on her side now."

"She'd never believe it. And that's why I don't want her to know I'm here. If she saw me, I'm afraid her delicate mental state would tip over into a full psychotic episode. You'd never get your hands on the source blood."

As we pulled into the parking lot of the hotel, she turned off the car. We could hear explosions and gunfire in the distant hills.

"I appreciate your putting your life in danger like this."

"This isn't an entirely selfless act on my part," she responded. "As I indicated back in Rhinecliff, I truly do not want to die with this horrible sin on my soul. I'd forever be remembered as a modern-day equivalent of one of the execution squad that killed Jesus. There were four soldiers at Jesus' Crucifixion, just like on the modern executive committee, but ultimately? I was the one in charge of the Infant's elimination."

*The word* elimination *again. Why doesn't she just say* assassination, *for God's sake?*

We took our few belongings and walked to the aluminum front doors, which were locked. The light of the vending machine was all that illuminated the tiny lobby.

We rang the bell, and eventually a beleaguered-looking woman in a maid's uniform unlocked the door, opened it just enough for us to enter, and closed and locked it right behind us.

She said nothing, asked for no identification nor even payment, and led us to a room on the same floor.

The accommodations consisted of a small room with only two narrow beds fit for monks, a dresser, and a small bathroom. I was so achingly tired, however, that it felt like the Plaza Athénée in Paris. Maureen let me use the bathroom first, and I climbed under the shower and was done in two minutes. I had to make it quick—the whole country was blowing up and shutting down around us—and the water had only been lukewarm. I knew there wouldn't have been enough water for two if I hadn't made it quick.

I pulled on a T-shirt and clean underpants, and fell into one of the beds as Maureen took her turn in the bathroom. When I heard her turn on the shower, I sunk into the pillow.

Without warning, great gushing sobs escaped from my throat. I was crying for myself. I was crying, dammit, for Pantera as well.

*This is too much for me. I can't do this—I can't even save one man, let alone the frigging world. Hell, my mere presence has caused the death of two men I care deeply about.*

That was immediately followed by my rational side taking over from the emotional mess side of me.

*Right. One got you into this mess, and one SOB took horrible advantage of you and stole the only proof there is on earth from you.*

I didn't want Maureen to hear me crying, so as soon as the water shut off in the bathroom, I forced my own personal waterworks to shut down as well. I fell into a deep and, for once, dreamless sleep. In fact, I was so deeply asleep that I didn't even stir until I felt Maureen gently shaking me awake.

She was already done up in her fake nun's habit. Damn

if she didn't look like she'd sent it out to be cleaned and pressed overnight.

"What time is it?"

"It's nearly six thirty. I believe you are to meet the sister at church this morning?"

"Yes. Oh, right. You were listening in." She made no indication that she'd even heard me, which I know she did.

"Are you coming to church with me?"

"Yes, but I will sit in the back. Just another anonymous nun."

"I hope Grethe is all right. I'm really worried. I can smell the fires." With that, I got up and opened the shutters a bit and could see wildfires all over the hills.

"As I said, she's fine. She entered the church at five. Before sunrise."

I didn't bother to ask her how she knew this, because it would have been a waste of my breath and of her time.

"You'd better hurry, my dear."

I kept the same white T-shirt on, scrambled back into my jeans, threw on my leather jacket and boots, and grabbed my red bag.

"Coming?"

"I'll follow in a few minutes. Please be careful not to look around the church for me, or they might suspect you've brought along a cohort."

"They?"

"Well, whoever. *She.* I don't want to tip your delicate balance with her."

I opened the door to leave, and turned back. "I don't know what I'll find out, aside from the fact that I've seen a relic, but if the nun can somehow prove what she says is true, I will make sure the whole world knows the truth, and knows it ten minutes after I do."

"Eleven. I come first."

I walked out into the beautiful spring day and heard the sound of gunfire and explosions around the area surrounding Manoppello. They sounded much closer than they had the night before. The hills were not just ablaze; they had become a war zone.

*The whole world is coming undone. Has everyone gone crazy because ben Yusef might get a pass?*

I climbed the steps to the church and tried a door. I was shocked to see that it was not just open, but that the church was fairly full and that the 7:00 A.M. mass had already begun. I was also more than shocked to see such a beautiful lush interior. The inside structure totally belied the façade.

Rows of plain, wooden pews sat upon a decorative marble floor leading up to an altar with three marble steps. On the first tier of the altar was the same white altar cloth covering it as I'd seen in the House of the Virgin. Behind the altar in the apse, however, was something I'd never seen in a church. Two rows of steps with banisters—almost like a bridge—converged at the center around an elaborate marble-pillared tower. It was topped by a cross not dissimilar to the Occitan Cross that I'd seen all over the Languedoc area in France. The tower reached nearly to the ceiling.

An arch was carved out of the center of the tower and topped with marble rococo angels. Inside of that arch sat an elaborate gold frame with a crown and a cross on its top. But with the sunlight hitting the frame, it looked like it held nothing but blank gauze.

*Has the Veil been moved?*

I refocused my eyes to the parishioners themselves—townsfolk, nuns, and monks. I saw Grethe's brown habit from the back.

*This whole town was deserted last night. Where the heck did all these people come from?*

Even from the back, I knew it was Grethe because she was praying at the top of her lungs, letting out screeches and "ululu" sounds every so often. Apparently the locals were used to her, because no one even turned around to see who was making such a fuss.

But she wasn't the only one who was visibly upset. In fact, many of the congregants were crying, albeit in a more controlled manner.

As soon as mass ended and the church began emptying out, Grethe turned around, and I thought that she must have had a vision, because her expression turned to pure terror. She pointed her finger toward the back of the church and began screaming, "They will kill Him. Save the Lord!" Then on a dime, she turned back around and ran up to the altar, screaming in German.

As she ran toward the altar, a rotund brown-robed monk bounded up the altar's staircase and grabbed the heavy gilded frame off its pedestal. Holding it tightly to his chest, he ran down the stairs and disappeared through a door in an archway. The metallic sound of the lock resonated loudly within the perfect acoustics of the church.

*The old lady was going to steal the frame!*

I followed Grethe as she frantically ran after him, yelling over and over, *"Jesus! Retten Sie Ihre Sohn! Jesus! Retten Sie Ihre Sohn!"*

When she finally reached the locked door, instead of pounding on it, as I had fully expected, she turned around and spied me through the edge of her veil.

"Come, come. Hurry now, we must keep out the devil!"

She reached into her habit and pulled out a big ring of keys and quickly unlocked the door and slammed it behind us. I could hear footsteps on the other side of the door frantically running this way and that.

"It is Satan," she said now calmly, as though this were an everyday visitor, and began humming some hymn or other.

I followed her as she scurried up a long metal staircase to the second floor. A door at the top opened onto what looked like a reliquary museum. Along the walls were letters, photos, military medals, and many, many old braids of human hair behind glass showcases.

I followed her to the end of the long corridor, and we stopped before a wooden door. She unlocked the door, and we entered a room entirely lit by candles except for one old metal, dimly lit small chandelier way up on the ceiling.

This small room was again adorned with what looked like bizarre relics—more human hair braids, a human femur behind a glass case, a shelf with human skulls, and many worn, ancient-looking books and bits of papyrus.

At the front of the room six monks were lying prostrate on prayer rugs on the floor before a tiny altar. A door at the back of the room opened, and the rotund monk entered carrying the very elaborate gold frame. Now I could see, without the sunlight hitting it, that there was indeed something inside it. That gauzy fabric I'd seen did have an image imprinted upon it after all. The face, though quite transparent, was that of the same bearded man I'd seen in the transparency, but now he appeared, oddly enough, to be smiling.

*This looks like a joke. A cosmic joke.*

It measured maybe seven or so inches by ten, and was stretched between two framed panes of glass.

As I looked at it, I could see the wavy horizontal threads, but otherwise, the fabric was so thin and transparent that I could see the monk's hand holding the image right through the other side.

The effigy itself was the same long-haired man with a broken nose, a bloodstained or bruised forehead, and swollen cheek. Upon closer inspection, he looked uncannily like the photos of the torture victims in the current wars.

The contrasting shades of brown on the man's face in this dim candlelight made the bruises look almost fresh. But again, it was his eyes that captured me. They seemed to be looking directly at me—almost as though they were content despite his injuries.

*What the hell?*

I had to photograph this image. But I couldn't imagine that they'd let me. So I gingerly took out Sadowski's phone and gestured for permission. Not only did the monk allow it, he seemed to encourage me to take many photos, which of course I did. But this time, I made sure to check that the global tracking was off.

As swiftly as he'd granted permission, the monk grabbed the phone from my hand and started scrolling through the pictures I'd shot. As he did, tears started running down his face, and he passed the phone around to the other monks, who also began to weep.

He handed me back the phone and told me to scroll, which I did. I didn't start crying myself, but I knew why they had. What I saw couldn't be—could it?

Every single photo of that same image held a totally different expression. In one, the image was slightly smiling, with his lips closed and his eyes heavily hooded. In the next, he appeared to be screaming, with his mouth wide open, his teeth bared, his eyes open in terror. In yet another, he bore a calm demeanor, as though he were a man at total peace. This last one was almost expressionless—yet the face was the same face as in the transparency I'd gotten from Badde.

But how could these photos all be so very different?

They were taken in rapid succession without any difference in lighting or angle. It was triple what I'd seen changing in the transparencies.

As I was turning the phone this way and that, I noticed all the monks rise and head toward me.

"*Ecce electus! Ecce electus!*" ("Behold the Chosen One!") they chanted, coming closer. "*Pater noster qui es in caelis, tuum; adveniat regnum tuum . . .*" It was the same chant I'd heard those monks in Turkey sing as they entered the House of the Virgin.

*Oh, shit. Who the hell are these people? Time to get outta Dodge, baby. But how?*

I moved back toward the door, but in a flash the monks and Grethe completely surrounded me, chanting.

"What do you want from me? Who are you?" I shouted, still trying to back out, but clearly without a shot—at least of getting out alive.

Then it hit me: *They* were Headquarters.

*This is like a scene out of* Rosemary's Baby! *Again.*

I backed up once more and could feel the arms of someone in back of me grab me around the waist.

I got up my best New York tough act and spat out, "I'm going to move back, and I am going to leave. You all should leave, too. There's a war raging. . . ."

"No, no, no! You must not leave." It was Grethe. "You can never leave us now. No, never. Your destiny is fulfilled."

I moved back an inch and while someone else kept the grip around my middle, she grabbed my arms and shoved and held them behind my back with the strength of a twenty-year-old wrestler. "Tell her, *Fratello Antonio.*"

It was the man I'd seen behind the window who had turned the gun sight on me yesterday. "You have nowhere to go," the friar reasoned.

*He's trying to reason? They're are all insane. I have to get out!*

The circle tightened and the robed monks surrounded me, suffocating me with their breath and their chants. Louder and louder. The more I struggled the tighter the circle became.

"*Ecce electa! Ecce electa! Ecce electa! Ecce electa! Ecce electa! Ecce electa!*" The sound was piercing my brain.

"Stop! Stop!" I shouted above the din, but the chanting was growing more frantic. Others made the double sign of the cross as they sang.

Antonio, who was standing outside the circle, lifted the frame and held the Volto Santo aloft. "Behold the lord!"

I struggled to break free, but was helpless against their combined strength.

"Help!"

*Help me somebody.*

A shot rang out, blasting the monks out of their reverie. They jumped back in horror as Brother Antonio dropped to the ground in the middle of them, blood gushing from a giant hole in his chest. I spun around to duck, but before I or the monks could take cover, the robed brothers began falling around me like bloody dominoes with each new, precisely aimed gunshot.

*Who the hell is shooting?* I was too tired to run for it, but I stopped dead. *That can't be the shooter!*

Standing at the back of the room was Maureen, two hands around a Glock in the shooter position. The only other person left standing was Grethe, who, shocked, turned to look at Maureen, recognition and disgust registering on her face at once.

"*Daemonium, Antitheus, Diabulus,*" Grethe cried out rapid-fire. She reached into the pocket of her habit—it looked like she was reaching for a gun—but as she did so, Maureen turned her pistol on Grethe and fired. The old nun fell wounded but not fatally, bleeding from her shoulder, a bloodstain spreading down the right side of her habit.

"They were going to sacrifice you," Maureen cried out to me. "A pagan ritual! I saw a pyre already prepared down on the hill; they would burn you to get rid of the last of the Cathars."

"But I thought they were the last of the Cathars . . ."

Grethe, weakened and gasping, managed to croak out, "We *are. You* are!" She pulled herself up by holding on to the altar, and she and Maureen faced one another.

"Once before but never again," Maureen said, shoving the barrel right between the old nun's eyes tauntingly. Grethe didn't back down.

"Murderer! Paid assassin. Whore of Babylon!" Grethe spat back before *literally* spitting in Maureen's face. Maureen wiped the sputum off her face with her sleeve as gracefully as she could. Her gun never wavered a centimeter from its spot between Grethe's eyes.

"You can kill me, but you can't kill the spirit of ben Yusef, Son of the Son!" Grethe taunted.

At that, the light from the old chandelier flickered and died, and except for the candles, the room was thrown into semidarkness.

I felt as though I'd suddenly gotten vertigo and could no longer keep my balance. But it wasn't me—it was the earth beneath our feet that had started to shake. I could hear buildings collapsing and the roar of what sounded like the earth literally being torn asunder.

Despite this, Maureen never moved her gun from between Grethe's eyes. "We have to get under a doorway— it's the only place that's safe in an earthquake," I yelled out, like some demented Girl Scout.

The two women were seemingly oblivious to the danger, locked as they were in their deadly hatred of one another.

"You think you've won?" Grethe shouted at Maureen. "You will never win!"

Maureen just kept steady.

*What the hell?*

"Please, we've got to get out of here before it's too late," I begged.

Instead, Grethe started keening. "It's done! They've killed the Son of the Son!"

The room was shaking more and more violently, and I ducked and held on tightly under a doorway, as objects flew off the walls. Relic bones and a blond braid of some long-dead person flew at me like missiles.

*"Mortuus!"* Grethe cried out amid the noise and chaos. *"Mortuus!* The Son of the Son will rise again!" As the women stood in that deadly standoff, the giant chandelier broke free and knocked Grethe to the ground, missing Maureen by inches. As she lay in a heap at Maureen's feet, Grethe mouthed the words to me, "She is Black Robe."

Then Maureen, calmly and as though the world literally weren't falling around our heads, said, "You are insane," and put a bullet clean between Grethe's eyes.

To this day, I swear—even though the crumbling room was too filled with plaster dust to see clearly—that Maureen then spat on Grethe's corpse.

## 41

Maureen squatted down to Grethe's body and fished around in the pocket of the dead nun's habit. "What the hell are you doing?" I called out over the din.

She came back up with Grethe's ring of keys. As I stood in the doorway, Maureen crawled through the rubble of the shaking room and picked up the frame holding the Volto Santo.

She fumbled with the keys and found a small gold one and inserted it into the crown at the top of the frame. The glass easily slid out—and she removed the image of Christ after it had for untold decades been encased in an airless environment. I briefly thought about the damage that the fresh air would cause and then realized that I had more important concerns at the moment—like somehow getting out of this collapsing church alive.

"What the *hell* are you doing?" I called out again, leaving the alleged safety of the doorway to climb over rubble and dead bodies to get to Maureen's side.

"At least we can save the image if not the man," Maureen yelled over the din, and pointed to a stained-glass window, from which we might be able crawl out. She ordered me to climb up and push it open, which I did, and immediately the darkened sky shed at least some light into the room.

"Go! Go!" Maureen yelled behind me as I began to shimmy out of the small space of the open window. I was halfway out when I smelled smoke behind me. I called for Maureen, but when she didn't answer I shimmied back in to help her.

*She's caught in a blaze!*

But in fact, she didn't need help, and what I saw her doing instead turned my blood cold. Maureen was holding a large blazing wooden cross above the altar, where she'd laid out the Volto Santo, the Sixth Station of the Cross—the very cloth that had been laid over Jesus's face before he rose from the tomb. It was the last and only vestige left of Jesus on this earth.

"Maureen! Stop! Stop! What are you doing?" I screeched and lunged for her.

"I am destroying the evil thing! The evil dies only when that Face of their god is destroyed! Now he can *never* come back!"

She easily sidestepped my lunge, and as she did so, my head hit the marble of the altar and I fell backward. Nonetheless, I got back up and lunged for the tattered Veil, but Maureen grabbed it up as the earth continued to split. The small rug under the altar caught fire when sparks from the flaming cross blew onto it.

I stomped on the flames with the soles of my boots. When I looked up, Maureen, who was still holding the flaming wooden cross, turned the Glock on me without so much as a change of expression.

"What are you doing?" I asked, not sure what to make of what was happening.

"The Son died and now *you*, you who think you are

the savior of the Savior, you proud, stupid, foolish woman."

"Why? I thought—"

"You thought wrong. You and those despicable heretic Cathar ancestors of yours. They preserved your line, like you could save their treasure *again*," she said, lifting the Veil with the fingers of the hand that was still holding the gun. She took the Veil and rested it on the end of the gun barrel.

"I can shoot you through the Veil. Perfect justice. You can die with His DNA all over you. Would you like that?"

She squeezed the trigger and a shot crackled through the air. I felt nothing. Where was the blood? I hadn't been hit!

*Is she toying with me?*

Maureen looked down at her chest. A large red stain spread over the front of her habit. "Son of a bitch" is what she said as she fell on top of me, knocking us both to the floor. The blazing cross and the Veil dropped in front of the cloth-draped altar, and the altar cloth went up immediately.

I rolled Maureen off of me, and grabbed the Veil literally a second before it too caught fire.

I could feel myself splattered in her blood, which was all mixed up with the plaster, bone fragments, and pieces of burned wood, and without thinking about what had just happened, I tried to get back up.

That's when I saw Pantera standing in the light that was pouring through the stained-glass window. He was in the open doorway, long, lean, and as calm as he had been that night in the Restaurant Costes. In one hand he held his gun, and in the other, he held out an envelope.

I reached out for him as more and more of the room caught fire. "Pantera!" He handed me the envelope, and then two more shots rang out, sending him flying backward against a pillar.

He'd been clipped in the right leg and shoulder; blood was pouring from the wounds. He yelled out, "Watch it! Watch it."

I spun around. Maureen. The old snake was still alive, though paralyzed from the waist down. She turned the gun on me. I leaped across the space between us and kicked her hard in the head with the toe of my still-burning-hot boot in a blind fury. I kicked her Glock out of her hand, picked it up, loomed over her, and pointed it directly at her face. She locked me in her gaze. I pulled the trigger and shot *her* clean between the eyes.

"Trust no one, you fucking bitch."

## 42

The draperies had by this time caught fire, and the stained-glass windows began blowing out all over the room. The pillars supporting the room and others supporting the building shook, and I turned back to Pantera, who was sprawled against one of them. I had to get to him before it gave way. I shoved the envelope into my jacket pocket and turned back to him. We were about seven feet apart.

The crack of the breaking pillar was louder than the gunshots had been. The one Pantera had been propped against gave way and crashed to the ground, followed by the ceiling above him. The whole room was shaking, and the dust was so thick that I couldn't see anything and began coughing and choking. The rubble had sealed off that portion of the room where Pantera lay.

"Pantera! Talk to me," I called, trying to claw my way through the ten-foot-high pile of plaster and dust. "Pantera! Pantera! Can you hear me?"

Finally, I heard a faint voice on the other side. "Go. Save yourself. Save the Veil. Get out!"

"Not without you. Pantera!"

Silence. The pillars supporting my side of the room started to crack and shake, and the blazing draperies were threatening to engulf the entire space.

I grabbed the Veil, whose edges had started to singe, and shoved it into my other pocket.

"Get out. Now!"

"I can't."

Nothing. "Pantera. Pantera!" Nothing.

The room was collapsing around me, and I had to get out. "Pantera!" I yelled. Again, nothing.

The fire was rushing toward me, so I turned away and crawled on my hands and knees as best as I could in the smoke and rubble to the window. Dodging the flames that were licking at me, I climbed to the blown-out window frame. I looked back one last time and could see Grethe's body being consumed by the flames, just as the Cathars' bodies had been in 1244. And for the same reason: to keep alive the blood of Christ.

Like my distant ancestor, I knew for certain that I was the one who had been assigned this time to save the Cathar treasure—the Veil holding the DNA of Jesus— the treasure that was now stuffed into the pocket of my old leather jacket.

And yes, I too had been assisted along the way by a rogue Crusader.

*Did Alazais Roussel fall for her rogue Templar, like I fell for mine?*

The acrid, terrible smell of burning flesh assaulted me once again. But this time it wasn't the stuff of nightmares. This time it was very real.

## 43

When I had fully shimmied out of the window and my feet touched the tiles of a roof, I realized that I was on the second floor of the swaying building. The church began to collapse, and I crawled along the edge until I reached the front of the church and jumped onto a ledge below and from there onto the ground.

As suddenly as it started, the earthquake stopped, although the morning sky was dark as night. The town was deserted—many bodies lay scattered around the parking lot in front of the church. Some had been crushed by boulders that had flown off the mountainside, while others, I could see, had been shot dead.

It was a scene out of Armageddon, and I still had no idea of what really had happened outside of this earthquake-ravaged town. A massive downpour began, complete with lightning and deafening thunder rolling off the mountain, which literally looked as if it were cracking apart.

I took out Sadowski's phone just for the light and began climbing up toward Grethe's house, using the phone as a flashlight. I still don't know why I went up. The rain, the brambles, the fallen rocks, and the mudslides made climbing nearly impossible, but somehow I was forced onward.

*Alazais climbed down. And you're impelled to climb up. Why? Go back down—not up!*

I began to hear cries from somewhere on the mountain, but I had no idea from where exactly, and still I climbed upward. I could barely see in front of me, let alone see anything in my peripheral vision.

The cuts I'd sustained climbing through the broken window—which hadn't even registered at the time—were now bleeding quite heavily. Still, I kept climbing, crawling, climbing up. To what, I had no idea.

When I was perhaps one-quarter of the way up, I heard a woman's voice. *"Sorella, vieni, vieni con noi. Qui è la sicurezza che cercate."*

I saw nothing but felt a wet hand reach out and pull me in. I instinctively jumped back but was stopped by someone immediately behind me on the muddy trail.

Another hand reached out and handed me a cup of water. *"Sorella, vieni, vieni con noi. Qui è la sicurezza che cercate,"* the woman said once again.

I was led inside a small cave on the mountainside, in which perhaps fifty survivors sat huddled around a fire. Torches and flashlights lit up the interior, and I was taken aback at how odd it was to see fashionably dressed Italians huddled around a campfire in a cave. Jaded New Yorker to the end, I guess.

When I'd finished my water and had been given a blanket to wrap around myself, a woman in a veiled burqa approached. She took both of my hands in hers as she knelt down beside me, weeping softly. I could see her bright blue eyes blazing in the firelight.

The woman unhooked her veil and I saw the face. Il

Vettore! And hers was the middle-aged face of little Theotokos Bienheureux. Clearly she had been expecting me.

"They killed my boy today," she groaned, waving her hands around to indicate the destruction. "Did they think it wouldn't happen? Did they think they could kill the seed of Jesus with no consequences?"

She put her head in my lap and I stroked her. "But what happened? I thought he was going to go free or at least be retried because of the testimony of Judge Bagayoko."

"Yes. That was supposed to be, but it never came to be. I knew at His *birth* that I would witness His death."

"How did he die? I know nothing about it."

"They brought Him shackled into the General Assembly room. Again," she said, disgust filling her voice. "When the new chief judge, Alberto Sant'Angelo, brought the court to order, Reverend Bill Teddy Smythe rose from his wheelchair in the front row, rushed my son, and shot Him dead!"

She too began softly keening that "ululu" sound. "I knew He would die, but I watched Him die; it was broadcast all over the world. My son. My little brown baby. The kindest, gentlest, finest man I have ever known."

I was astounded. "He managed to sneak a gun through the tightest security in the world?"

She looked at me. Even though we were only a few years apart, she seemed so much older—even with her Ralph Lauren WASP-ish freckled face.

"How is that possible?"

"Because they wanted it to happen. All the power in the world was frightened of one small man who preached goodness."

"And Bill Teddy? Is he in prison?"

"Rioters outside the United Nations gates somehow—

mysteriously, they want us to believe—were able to break through all barricades, all the heavily armed security forces, all of it. These so-called rioters rushed the chamber and whisked the reverend away. Just before the earthquake, we saw it on a laptop—the son of Satan, killing the Son of the Son of God. He was uplifted on the shoulders of his liberators. 'The slayer of Satan,' these ignoramuses cried out. He is being saluted as the hero."

"I am so sorry."

"So am I. I somehow, even though I knew He would end as His Father ended—executed—I naively always thought somewhere in my heart that my love could save Him. And then when you surfaced, when He kissed you, I thought you would be the one."

"I'm sorry I couldn't save your son," I answered and pulled the tattered Veil from my pocket, handing it back to its rightful owner.

She stared at it. A nearly two-thousand-year-old portrait of her Son. She cradled the cloth to her chest as if it were a living thing.

Then: "Thank you for this."

"I know it's not much. . . ."

"Today you were in a war against evil. Nobody won. But this," she said, lifting the cloth and kissing it, "means we can continue to bring the light—"

"You mean, the proof?"

"No, that I'm afraid even you couldn't bring us. You see, what we needed was my son's DNA in order to prove that He was indeed the Son of the Son."

I had failed. There *was* no proof.

She got up and came back with a blanket, and we could hear boulders falling around the cave and down the mountainside, but she didn't appear to be frightened.

"God will show us the way," she said, reading my thoughts.

When I laid down on the wet floor of the cave, I felt the puffy envelope that was still in my jeans pocket. I sat back up and pulled it out and opened it up. It was a standard-sized sheet of paper and a square cut from my tattered old Gap scarf sealed in a tiny plastic envelope. It was roughly the same size as the Veil.

In some idiotic fantasy, I'd somehow thought that Pantera had written me a love letter or something equally ridiculous. But it just looked like some kind of mathematical formulas. I called to il Vettore in the dark. "Madam. I just remembered, Yusef gave me this paper," I said, embarrassed about having loved the same man as she had.

She came over, and although she didn't have to, she said, "He was a kind and understanding husband to me. But I always wanted to give my life to the Father of my Son."

"I'm sorry?"

"God," she said. "*I* was born to serve God. And you, my lovely friend, were born to save the Son of the Son of God."

"I'm afraid I wasn't up to the task."

"You know, thirty-four years ago I was plucked out of my regular American teenage life. I was scared and angry and lonely. But I didn't have a choice because I was chosen. Now it's your turn."

"Huh?"

"*You've* been called by God," she said.

I remembered telling Sadowski, *Next time God chooses up sides, can I be the one left on the bench?* Now I felt awed by what had happened to me, to the world.

I handed her the paper Pantera had given me. She held a flashlight up to the pages and tried to make out the equations in the half-light. She called over an old man, who held the flashlight, read it, then took his glasses off, cleaned them, and read it again.

They looked at one another, he whispered something to her, and I could see shock mixed with something akin to joy spread over her face.

"What is it?"

"It's the laboratory test results from your scarf," she said, her blue eyes finally dancing with joy in the fire-light.

I didn't ask how she knew it had been from my scarf—but nothing surprised me any longer.

"The DNA, which I am more than sure will match the DNA on the Veil, holds the imprint of the life of *Jesus*—and of my son."

She handed me the paper as though I'd understand what the *hell* she was showing me.

"I'm sorry, but what do these numbers mean?"

"Ms. Russo," the old man said, waving the paper and holding the envelope with the small bit of scarf, "this proves that Demiel ben Yusef is the Son of the Son of God."

"I'm sorry? How can you know this? I mean, it doesn't say, 'This is God's DNA' on the laboratory results, I'm sure."

"Hardly!" He laughed and spun me around. If he were younger I swear he would have lifted me off my feet. "The DNA sample from your scarf? It contains only *twenty-four* chromosomes per cell."

"And that means—what?"

"It means Demiel and Jesus only had one parent—God."

"Again, I have no idea what you're saying . . ."

"Every *human* being, you see, has forty-six chromosomes per cell," he answered. I could see the tears once more springing into Theo's eyes, but this time they were tears of joy.

She took up the explanation then, excitement overcoming her reserve. "What Dr. Litano is saying is that my son, as I know and now the world will know, was *not* conceived from man—but from *God*. He has only *one set* of chromosomes per cell. A human *being*—even a human *clone*—is made up of twenty-three *pairs* of chromosomes, or forty-six chromosomes per cell. Demiel's cells only had twenty-four chromosomes, total."

"But half would be twenty-three, not twenty-four—no?"

"Ahhh, even the Son of God needs a gender-determinant chromosome," the old man answered. "The extra chromosome is what made—makes—her son a male. The Son of God has but one parent."

With that she lifted the piece of white Gap scarf, held it up, and kissed it.

"The second execution yields the second veil of miracles," she declared.

With that she pounded her chest softly and once more began the "ululu" lamentation, which reverberated around the walls of the cave.

And it was as beautiful a sound as I'd ever heard: It was as beautiful as the muezzins calling the faithful to prayer in Istanbul; the Mormon Tabernacle Choir singing in Salt Lake City; carolers outside my parents' Long Island house on Christmas Eve; the voice of the cantor on the Friday night that Donald and I attended services at the temple in Rome. They were all the glorious sounds of eternity—when the sweet sound of God is the only sound you hear.

*Yes, that* was *me, the jaded agnostic, speaking.*

I didn't try to go to sleep and instead turned on my tablet and began to write. I included it all—the written and spoken testimony of everyone involved—as you have just read. When I was done, three days later, I turned the old leather "Selçuk diary" back to il Vettore to keep. It rightfully belonged to her as the only surviving member of the Great Experiment.

I wrote a much-abbreviated news story. The earthquake had ravaged everything on the mountain, but I was able to make my way back down to the shattered village after I'd finished.

First thing I did was check the roll of the dead that the Red Cross had compiled. "We think everyone has been accounted for," the man in charge told me.

I read and reread every name. There was no Yusef Pantera, or Michael Forsythe, Edward, Edouard, or Ed or even Eddie Gibbon—yes, I had finally made the connection that he'd been the one who had probably sent me those Italian e-mails.

"Are you sure about that?" I asked.

"We think so. But there's a tent set up to treat the injured," he said, pointing to the Red Cross tent that had been erected in the town square.

I rushed over and walked the long aisles of the tent. He wasn't there.

*What the hell? I saw him die.*

The Red Cross mobile truck had a wireless signal, so I logged in, attached my story, and sent it to Dona, whom I prayed was still alive in the war zone that had become the United Nations Plaza. Then I sent photos and the laboratory results to Donald, who was, I knew, too slick to die.

Within an hour, both the story and the proof were blasted around the world.

God bless the news media. Even when the world is

collapsing, it still seems to figure out how to exist, *and* to report on the end of the world.

*The Standard* online edition gave my story the front "page."

Me, who had been fired. Me, the accused killer.

This time *The Standard* ran my story intact, with a headline that screamed: THE *NEWEST* TESTAMENT, with this byline: By Alessandra Russo (aka Alazais Roussel).

The subhead was tabloid baby, all the way: PROPHET OR NUT JOB?

But you know all that already.

# Epilogue

## Manoppello, Italy

Immediately after the assassination of Demiel ben Yusef, the epidemic of plagues, superviruses, and natural disasters that had been sweeping the planet escalated, as did the warring.

There is too much misery and too many real killers roaming the planet looting and carpetbagging for the authorities to worry about one reporter; a few dead, probably fake Interpol assassins; and one beloved but very sly priest.

Still I have to clear my name. More important, I want to be with my family. It's time to make my way back to the states any way that I can. It won't be easy. Not much is working in these mountains these days.

I'm really concerned that I haven't been able to contact my parents. Donald went out to their house in Hicksville, Long Island, for me, but found that it had been boarded up. The upper dormer (my old bedroom seven thousand years ago) was caved in. Hicksville, and a few other towns on the North Shore of Long Island, had been hit by a tornado. My hope (belief) is that they fled to safety.

My brother and his family are totally off the radar, too. I hope to God that they are all safe together, but I'm wracked with worry. I can only pray that they haven't, God forbid, been targeted because of me.

But I've got to find out.

I figure that if I was able to find a few drops of almost two-thousand-year-old blood on a tiny bit of sea silk in a monastery in the mountains of Italy, then finding my family should be, well, not as tough as finding that haystack needle.

As hard as it is to stay here, it also won't be easy to leave, knowing—or more precisely *not* knowing—whether or not Pantera's body is in the rubble.

Each day when we dug through the debris, I somehow half expected to hear his voice coming from under a pile of bricks or stones. It never happened. Still, why hasn't his body ever been accounted for? I kind of refuse to believe that he won't show up someday when I find myself in yet another insane situation. Foolish, I know.

So I've said my good-byes and am ready to go from here and all that I found here. If I have to walk back to Rome, I will.

I've put off leaving for too long already. It's just that with everything that's happened, I've been so light-headed and nauseated lately. At first I was terrified that I'd caught one of the superviruses, but now I think—because my period is so late from weeks of unrelieved stress—that all I've actually "caught" is a raging case of PMS.

But, seriously, it feels like the mother of *all* PMS.

# Hard to Fathom Facts

**Fact:** The Volto Santo, aka the Veil of Veronica in Manoppello, and the Shroud of Turin match up exactly.

**Fact:** Father Heinrich Pfeiffer, official advisor for the Pontifical Commission for the Cultural Heritage, declared the Volto Santo in Manoppello to be the true image of Jesus.

**Fact:** Ultraviolet examinations of the Volto Santo, carried out by Professor Donato Vittore of the University of Bari, confirm there is no paint on the cloth bearing the face of Jesus. Several small reddish-brown flecks may be blood.

**Fact:** The image is identical on both sides, a feat impossible to achieve by human hands in ancient times.

**Fact:** Orthodox Catholic tradition maintains that John brought the Blessed Mother to live in Ephesus with him and it was there that three epistles attributed to him were written.

**Fact:** About two weeks after Pope Benedict XVI made a personal pilgrimage in 2006 to pray before the Volto Santo at the little church in Manoppello, Italy, he elevated the little church from *santuario* to a papal basilica.

**Fact:** Most modern popes have visited Mary's House.

- 1896: Pope Leo XIII visits and leaves believing its authenticity.
- 1951: Pius XII comes and bestows upon it the status of "Holy Place."
- 1961: Pope John XXIII makes the designation permanent.
- After that designation, the Catholic Church removes plenary (absolute) indulgences from the Church of the Dormition in Jerusalem (figurative death) and bestows them for all time to pilgrims to Mary's House in Ephesus.
- July 26, 1967: Pope Paul VI unofficially confirms the authenticity of the House.
- November 30, 1979: Pope John Paul II serves mass there.
- November 29, 2006: Pope Benedict XVI visits and declares, "Muslims have more veneration of Mary—those who are believing Muslims—than most Christians today."

# REFERENCES AND
# RECOMMENDED READING

*The Face of God,* Paul Badde, Ignatius Press, 2010

*The Monks of War,* Desmond Seward, Penguin Books, 1995

*Mary Magdalene,* Lynn Picknett, Basic Books, 2003

*Montségur and the Mystery of the Cathars,* Jean Markale, Inner Traditions, 1986

*The Templars,* Piers Paul Read, Phoenix Press, 2001

*A Most Holy War,* Mark Gregory Pegg, Oxford University Press, 2008

*The Yellow Cross,* Réne Weis, Alfred A. Knopf, 2001

*When Religion Becomes Evil,* Charles Kimball, HarperOne, 2008

*The Gnostic Gospels,* Elaine Pagels, Vintage Books, 1979

*The Double Helix: A Personal Account of the Discovery of the Structure of DNA,* James D. Watson, Touchstone, 2007

*Living Buddha, Living Christ,* Thich Nhat Hanh, Elane Pagels, David Steindl-Rast, Riverhead Books, 1995

*And That's the Way It Really Is,* Jack Boland, David E. Caldwell, Master Mind Publishing, 1997

*Turin Shroud,* Lynn Picknett, Clive Prince, HarperCollins, 1994

*Esoteric Christianity,* Ricky Alan Mayotte, Steerforth Press, 1971

*Existential Jesus,* John Carroll, Counterpoint/Berkeley, 2007